Blademaster of Norda

Blademaster of Norda

Jacamo Peterson

iUniverse, Inc.
New York   Bloomington

This is a work of fiction. All of the characters, names, incidents, organizations, and dialogue in this novel are either the products of the author's imagination or are used fictitiously.

iUniverse books may be ordered through booksellers or by contacting:

iUniverse
1663 Liberty Drive
Bloomington, IN 47403
www.iuniverse.com
1-800-Authors (1-800-288-4677)

Because of the dynamic nature of the Internet, any Web addresses or links contained in this book may have changed since publication and may no longer be valid. The views expressed in this work are solely those of the author and do not necessarily reflect the views of the publisher, and the publisher hereby disclaims any responsibility for them.

ISBN: 978-1-4401-3585-9 (sc)
ISBN: 978-1-4401-3587-3 (dj)
ISBN: 978-1-4401-3586-6 (ebook)

Printed in the United States of America

iUniverse rev. date: 6/18/2009

PROLOGUE

His Majesty Killian III, King of Keltan, was sitting at his desk, in the small study next to his bed chamber. He was relaxing after a full day at court, the hour was approaching midnight. When suddenly, the doors from the outer hall flew open without a sound, heralded only by an inrush of cool air. The King looked up from the scroll he was reading, to find his younger brother Danell standing there smiling.

"Well! Danell? What means this intrusion? Just what brings you here this late in the evening?"

"Why, I only bring Death! Dear Brother, Your Death!" Replied Danell! He stood just inside the doorway with his hands on his hips smirking. Behind him there appeared a shadowy figure, a Wizard by the look of him, he was incanting a spell. The King leapt to his feet, dropping the goblet of wine from which he had been drinking, while grabbing for the sword which lay unsheathed upon his desk

At that very instant the Wizard cast his spell from extended hands and dark red, crackling, lightning bolts flew from his fingers, striking the King full in the chest, quite literally burning him to death from within. While he silently screamed in agony, his brother stood there smiling.

"Oh Yes, I will be a far better King than you have been, my dear Killian," Danell stated, "and your lovely wife will become my favorite concubine. Oh, and by the way dear brother, know you this! Your sons also shall all die this night!" As the King, Killian III, collapsed to the floor dead, his body was jerking and smoking slightly.

Meanwhile, in another part of the Royal Quarters, two young boys died instantly from being stabbed through their hearts as they lay sleeping. At the same time, in their chambers, their sisters were pounced upon by others. They were bound and gagged. Then they were moved to the top chamber in the tallest castle tower, and there imprisoned. Aurelia the Queen, the children's mother, was far away at that moment in time. She was visiting with her kin in the country of Danfinia, located to the north of Keltan. She knew almost instantly, through a vision had by her seer, exactly what had transpired.

Danell, a Prince of the Realm himself, along with those Dark forces who aided him, including a powerful Dark Priest named Rigorda, had all failed to note that the eldest of the Kings sons Prince Killian had in fact left the King's City two days before. They were hunting boar out in the great forests located to the east. Rigorda was enraged by this news. He managed to control himself enough to contact others of his order. He arrange for a mercenary force to be sent to find the Prince and kill him and all who were with him.

Now the Dark Lord's plan for the conquest of the vile "Humans" can once again go forward. First he must take over the Kingdom to establish his rule on the surface of the Earth.

Chapter One

Crown Prince Killian, along with Captain Grayhawk the Knight Commander of the Household Guard, with ten Knights of the Realm, and their retainers, had ridden out from the King's City. They were on a boar hunt headed to the eastern forests of Keltan, at the foot of the Auserlian Mountains, near the head waters of the river Saar. There the forest is almost as thick as the Great Forests of Norda.

On the fourth day of their six-day journey eastward, Grayhawk sensed some sort of danger, coming from behind them, and informed the Prince that they were being followed. Prince Killian surmised that they must be Gaulan bandits raiding north of the Keltani border, as they sometimes do, looking for caravans or travelers to rob. However, Grayhawk knew that bandits would not risk attacking a party of armed Knights of Keltan, though a large enough group of the Drulgar (evil servants of the Dark Lord) would. Whoever they were they were closing the distance as the day wore on and that most likely meant an attack on their camp during the night. This was a common Drulgar tactic.

"What do you recommend then Captain Grayhawk?" asked the young Prince, "For I freely admit to having no experience with this sort of thing."

Grayhawk thought for a moment, and then answered, "Your Highness, I suggest that we should prepare an ambush of our own, and beat them at their own game."

"Now that definitely sounds good to me," replied the Prince. "I will follow your lead in this matter Captain. How shall we do it?"

"First, Your Highness, let us up the pace for an hour or so, to a canter, that we may have a goodly amount of time to prepare when we stop. If they are any good at all in tracking, they will see that we are moving at a canter, and think that we are just trying to make good time before stopping for the night."

"Then let it be so" said the Prince. The group moved into a canter and in the next hour covered about six miles. They came to a good hilltop, covered with large rocks and trees.

"Let us stop here and prepare a normal camp in the center of these large rocks, in this open area" said Grayhawk. "Everything must look as though normal, the same as our camps have been thus far." They pitched their tents in an almost complete oblong with the opening towards the road. They then prepared a large fire ring in the center of the camp. They chopped and collected a good size pile of firewood, set out all of the campstools and other camp supplies as normal. They even placed the Prince's pennant in the ground in front of the largest tent. Four smaller cook fire rings, with iron tripods and stew pots were set up, two at each end of the inner circle. All members of the party were horse mounted, thirty five men in all, counting the Prince and Grayhawk. There were ten Knights, twelve Squires, eight Yeomen, a Cook and two Wranglers, and sixty total horses. The result was a fair sized camp.

A hearty dinner of stew and trail bread was prepared. All members of the party ate well in preparation for what might turn out to be a very long night.

"What do we do now Captain," asked the Prince, "Sit here and wait to be attacked?"

"Not here, Highness. We will shortly move across the road and into the trees. All but a few men who will remain and make the camp seem normal. Our enemies, whoever they may be, will likely not attack without first having a scouting report about the layout. It is the scouts who we must fool so that they will go and report just how relaxed and vulnerable we are."

"While we hide, back from the camp in the trees, waiting for the main body of them to commit themselves. For only then shall we come to know who, and how many are our enemies and then we shall deal them an unsuspecting blow."

"I see," said the Prince. "Surprise them at their own game hey!"

"Well Highness, we are sure to be out numbered, and must hold on to whatever small advantage we may. The outcome of this is not set in stone for either side."

"Think you then that we are at some considerable risk to our lives in this?"

"Aye! Your Highness. We are surely in some danger. Whenever steel is drawn, life is at risk for someone. From there comes the primal question that all men face in these circumstances."

"And that question is exactly what? Captain Grayhawk"

"Why, fight or flight my Prince! What else?"

"Run! Why Captain, surely you jest?" asked the Prince.

"That I do, my Prince. That I do." And everyone around them was laughing. For Grayhawk's love of fighting was well known.

The camp was laid out east-west off to the north side of the road, with the entrance facing the road or to the South. The horses were picketed on the north side, behind the camp in front of a large rock formation. The east end of the camp was also rocks and trees. The west side of the camp was more open. The layout was such that an attack could only be effectively mounted from the west either up the road and through the front entrance or through the trees to the west on foot.

They will do both, Grayhawk surmised, splitting their force to achieve maximum effort, in an attempt to catch the camp asleep and take it with minimum effort.

After full dark Grayhawk detailed, three Knights and three Yeomen with bows, to be placed in the rocks at the east end of camp. Everyone else then moved across the road and into the trees, well back from the road, so as not to be seen, except for a group of five Squires and Yeomen who were left in camp as though they were sentries and servants still moving about.

Two hours after full dark, three scouts came, moving quietly and efficiently up the road from the west. A number of people could be seen moving around in the camps interior. The fires had burned low. The smell of the evening meal was still in the air. Horses could be occasionally heard blowing and stamping and jingling their bridles.

Two of the tents had the soft glow of candles burning inside. The sentry at the front entrance was sitting on a rock sharpening a knife.

Their scouts spread out below the camp, and only stayed to observe for quarter of an hour or so. Apparently then satisfied, they pulled back as one, and moved back down the road out of sight.

As soon as the scouts had gone, Grayhawk had stacks of firewood placed over the coals of the big fire and two of the cook fires. One at either end of the camps interior, stacked so that the wood was not touching the coals, but close enough to begin heating up. Then he had the two wranglers and the cook hiding behind the tents with prepared flasks of lamp oil, to throw on the stacks of wood when the attack started.

Everyone in the party was armed almost the same. All carried boar lances, most had recurve bows, a sword and a dirk, all except the wranglers and the cook. They each had a short sword and a dagger.

The Knights of Keltan do not wear heavy plate armor, even on horseback. Their swords are heavy sabers, and they wear hip length chain mail with hoods and round steel helmets with chin straps. Their shields are of the round buckler type, and their battle lances are similar to the boar lance only lighter and longer. They can and do effectively use their recurve bows from horseback even at a full gallop. Their Squires are trained exactly the same. Yeomen are trained primarily with the bow and the straight sword, and fight on foot in war, as light infantry.

This night, the fight would begin with bows. Grayhawk instructed each man, after the scouts had departed with their report. Take out five arrows, and stick them in the ground on the right side of the archer in a line. He figured if each man got off, three to five shots, then dropped the bow, and picked up his boar lance. That even in a ragged line, they should be able to take down many of their foe. He told them bluntly, only the winning side could call a night ambush "honorable" and that their opponents intended to give no quarter, and take no prisoners, or they would not be attacking at night.

The night grew quiet and still, as they stood waiting behind trees, a good ten to fifteen paces back from the road. They were all grown men here, and most were veterans. Half an hour passed, then another. Everyone was becoming tired of standing still for so long.

Finally, they were there, several hundred yards down the road, dark figures in the moon light. There were many of them in a dark mass, moving slowly. Then they stopped, about a hundred yards west of the camp. Part of the dark mass broke off and began moving into the trees on the other side of the road. Three or four long minutes passed and then almost as one they mounted up, military style.

"These are not bandits, nor are they Drulgar" thought Grayhawk. But before he could ruminate on it further, a sword flashed up in the moonlight and the riders surged forward, first at a trot, to a canter and then at a full gallop. Thundering up the road and turning into the opening before the camp, directly in front of Grayhawk and the hunting party, shouting war cries, waving swords and spears they turned to their right, into what they thought was a sleeping camp.

There were then three almost simultaneous whooshes, coupled with bright yellow flashes, as flasks of lamp oil shattered on piles of hot, dry firewood set over coal beds. As arrows then began buzzing out from the darkness and striking with meaty thunks, into the mass of mounted horsemen, even as dismounted figures, came out of the darkness and leapt onto tents stabbing and slashing with swords and spears. All were shouting and screaming blood curdling yells and battle cries. Now even more arrows came out of the dark, striking horse, rider, and dismounted alike. As the last of the horsemen rode into the camp area, the scene was chaos. Burning oil had been blown onto several horses and riders who were swerving into other mounts and shrieking in fear, and pain. Both riders and horses were going down, only to be trod under the hooves of others. Two of the tents were now burning, adding to the melee of noise and confusion.

Grayhawk loosed his fifth arrow at the figure closest to him, then dropped his bow, caught up his boar lance, as others to the left and right of him were doing the same and ran forward into the red mist, behind the veil of the bezerker.

He took the first rider off his horse with an impact that lifted the man free of his saddle and pushed him over his horse. The man grabbed the shaft of the boar lance and pulled it with him as he went over. Grayhawk now drew his great sword, taking a two-hand hold, he stabbed the riders horse, which was trying to bite him, through the neck and ripped out to the side. The horse went down in a heap and he jumped on top of it to get at the next rider who was trying to impale him with a lance. A hard downward stoke severed the lance and a follow up roundhouse cut took off the riders head. He slipped in blood and gore and went down between the dead horse and the live one. He very nearly got his head stomped flat but managed to roll over the dead horse and get back to his feet. Laughing now, a true bezerker, he charged into the thickest part of the fray and engaged enemy after enemy, stabbing, slashing, spinning and chopping.

The fight lasted for over two hours, until at last, Grayhawk rallied together a group of knights and squires around the Prince, and the enemy finally realized they could not get to him. For it was now obvious to all that their intent had been to kill the Prince.

They broke off the fight and fled running, back into the darkness, those of them who could. They left behind over a hundred and twenty dead and dying. Two full companies of mercenary soldiers had begun the attack. The Princes party lost six Knights, four Squires, five Yeomen and one Wrangler, which made for a total of sixteen dead. The bards would sing for the next two centuries about this battle. But what would be most remembered is that the Crown Prince had killed ten men in personal combat. Though he was but eighteen years old! This fact was later documented by eyewitness accounts.

When the daylight at last arrived it was a far different Prince Killian who greeted the sun that spring morn. The aftermath of that battle was not a pleasant sight to gaze upon even for a battle hardened Blademaster. There were also some thirty horses down.

The young Prince rose to the occasion. He had funeral pyres constructed for his own dead. Then he spoke for them as they were consumed, sending their spirits on with a royal blessing. Their personal items were packed up for their families.

All the stray mounts left by the enemy were rounded up, stripped of their gear and tack and turned loose to become wild horses.

He left the entire enemy force lying where they fell. The place became known as Killian's Hill and is covered in bones and ghosts to this day.

He did, however, have all of their bodies searched for clues as to who had sent them. Many newly minted Keltani gold marks were found on them, along with many unusual knives and pieces of jewelry.

Some were very rare and expensive. At the end of the day, the Prince called Grayhawk over and said "Captain, I will not stay in this place another night, with all that has happened here. Let us pack up what we can and move back towards home. I fear there is more involved here than an attempt to kill me. I have dire feelings, and fear for the safety of my family."

So, pack and move they did. They rode until midnight before they stopped to sleep in a cold camp. Arising at dawn, they rode again. Thirty five had ridden forth from the King's city, only nineteen rode back.

On the morning of the second day, they were intercepted by dispatch riders who informed the Prince of the death of his father the King and of his two younger brothers by unknown assassins, killed in their beds in the middle of the night. Further, that his Uncle Danell had named himself Prince Regent, because he believed the assassins had also killed Prince Killian somewhere in the wilds of the East. Old Cedric the King's Seneschal, had in the hopes of finding Killian alive, sent the dispatch riders.

They stopped beside a small lake for a few hours rest, while the Prince went around the shore to the other side by himself, to come to grips with all this life changing news. Grayhawk meanwhile ordered a hot meal prepared and all the men were fed, including the five dispatch riders, who were all from an Army unit stationed some miles outside of the King's city. All were glad to have hot food and as they sat eating, one of the young soldiers who had arrived with the news, said around a mouthful of food,

"Do you not fear for the Prince, all alone out there by the lake? What if we are attacked?" One of the older squires said,

"Son, then I would fear for whoever attacked him. Your Prince is no dandy milksop."

"How so?" asked the soldier.

"Why a couple of nights ago, when we were attacked by about a battalion of hard core mercenaries, the Prince killed over a dozen of them by himself!"

"Thou art jesting," said the soldier.

"No soldier, he's not." said one of the young knights. "He speaks the truth."

"And so the legends begin" though Grayhawk to himself.

After a time Killian returned to the fire and motioned to Grayhawk, he said,

"Walk with me a bit Captain Grayhawk." Together they walked back down to the lake.

No one knows what was said in that conversation, but for over an hour they stood on the shore of the lake talking earnestly and often gesturing or shaking their heads, not as if arguing but very serious. When they returned, as they approached the men, all conversation ceased, and they were mostly just standing there looking. The Prince started to say "Men" when Grayhawk put his hand up.

"Forgive me Sire, let me say this. Men of Keltan, your King, Killian III is dead, long live the King." They all answered,

"Long live the King!"

"Now it is required that you swear loyalty to your new King, Killian the Fourth, by right of succession. May the Gods bless, our King!"

"May the Gods Bless our King," they all answered. Then all came forward, Knights first, took a knee and sword loyalty oaths. Grayhawk was the last in line to do so.

Killian looked at his not so large retinue and said

"I thank each of thee for thy pledge of loyalty, but I fear we must be about acquiring a somewhat larger Army or we may all find ourselves without heads." Everyone laughed nervously. "For I know there is at least one other person who would claim my father's crown, my Uncle Danell."

"Well Majesty" said Grayhawk mounting his horse, "Let us be about doing just that."

"Aye" said the King mounting his own horse. "Though I must admit Captain, I don't think I look very majestic today," looking down at his bloodstained tunic. "Perhaps if they don't get downwind of us we may fool some."

"Highness, er Your Majesty! I mean" said one of the younger Knights. "We could stop long enough to bathe in yon lake."

"What!" exclaimed Killian, "And ruin the fishing here for years! Nay! Sir Knight. Better that my people see me returned covered in blood and grime as further evidence of this foul business we are all involved in. For having cast thy lots with me, you are all now in mortal danger. My father's enemies will seek to destroy the entire line including all friends and supporters. We, therefore, best ride like the wind and see what further support we can garner."

"Sage words, Majesty," said Grayhawk. "We will truly need all of the support we can muster. I am thinking that perhaps I know where such support might be found."

"And where prey tell might that be?" asked the King.

"Why at the Knights and Officers Academy, of course."

"Yes indeed, excellent thinking Sir Grayhawk. There must be over two hundred loyal cadets and knight instructors there. We need only deviate a few hours north to get there. Ride hard men!! Time is precious. Truly!!

Two full mercenary companies of seventy five men each, had launched an attack against thirty five men in a royal hunting party, and lost! A tale to be retold that was!

Chapter Two

Many years before the Battle of Killian's Hill, in the far north, below the Arctic Circle, in the great forests and mountains of Norda, a boy was born unto the Stone Clan of the Rungar, a people of myth and legend about whom many sagas have been written. They were a large people, as Norsemen tend to be. They were feared for their great courage, skill, and power in battle. Every Rungar is a war party unto himself. Like every other race of warriors they favor steel, edged weapons, but are proficient in the use of spears and the heavy laminated recurve bows they make from the horns of the Auroch or Norda bull, a very large forest animal, with a very bad temper and forward curving pointed horns. Many a warrior has lost his life to an Auroch.

In order to be named a man, a Rungar youth must kill either a full-grown panther or a great wolf. To be called a warrior he must be blooded in battle against an armed enemy. To become a master warrior he must kill an Auroch, anyway he can. From the Aurochs horns he must fashion the great Rungar laminate recurve bow and the handles or "scales" for his great sword, short sword, dirk, dagger and boot knife.

The meat from the Auroch he will trade to the weapon smiths, the legendary Rungar steel makers, who will forge the blades of his weapons, which will then be rune marked with the Master Warriors new name. A name he must choose, usually that of his animal totem a custom dating back to the beginning. No other warrior may bear or use these weapons while the owner lives.

Twenty years ago a young warrior of the Pietre, or stone clan, had slain an Auroch, a huge one, with a boar spear in a bloody battle deep in the forest of the northland. He then took the name of his animal totem. The great gray Hawk. His blades were made and duly inscribed for him by the weapon smiths. Once properly named and armed, he then entered into the two-year program of learning to become a Rungar Blademaster. The training is conducted by the sect of holy warriors known as Odranna's Chosen. Odranna is the Great Spirit of the Rungar, Chief of their Gods. Who is also called the "All Father" by many. This young warrior was named Grayhawk.

The Chosen live and work in a dark, immense set of caverns in the Kraggen or mountains of the North. Grayhawk had been blessed with both vision and hearing above that of most men. He possessed a "sense" of danger. He was a quick learner with a keen mind. These things he would need.

The Blademaster training consists of twelve levels of proficiency. Each level is two months long. Each is conducted in a different area within the caverns. The last is in almost complete darkness in a deep cavern. A few drop out of the training. A few do not survive it. Sometimes one is chosen by the Odranna to remain as one of them. No one ever speaks of what transpires in the caverns but it is rumored to be the twelve levels of hell.

When a warrior emerges from the caverns, he has a dagger and winding rose tattooed on his upper right arm. He is given a new set of leathers and boots, five gold coins and his choice of mounts, from the Great Chief's herd. His clan must also provide him with a packhorse, sleeping roll, a hip length shearling vest with three-inch wide Auroch hide belt and a shearling hat, the panniers of the packhorse must contain enough supplies for a month.

All of this because he is banished from Norda, for a period of five years, during which he is to journey to foreign lands, works as a mercenary soldier learning different ways and customs. He must learn at least two different languages. When he returns he must pay back ten times the gold he was given, or fifty gold pieces, to show that he was successful on his journey.

He is made to do all of this because, when he emerged from the caverns and was tattooed as a Blademaster he was then eligible to become chief of his clan, or even Great Chief of the Rungar. The old chiefs do not want the competition from a young eligible, and since not all of them survive the journey for five years, there are not many contenders who return.

Grayhawk conceded that this was a good custom. It had been done for over two hundred years that he was aware of and perhaps much longer. When a man returned successful and moved into the clan hierarchy, he was a seasoned, well traveled, veteran who even spoke other languages. If a man was unsuccessful, he did not return and was forgotten.

When Grayhawk departed the people of steel and horses, and left the main Kraal of the Great Chief, it was in the first month of winter, and this one had all the signs of being a very bad one. He was warm enough now but he did not have a winter cloak. He knew he could not make it out of the cold lands before the onset of real winter.

His clansmen and women kin had been very proud of him and the two leather panniers on his packhorse were totally stuffed with supplies. In addition, his clan chief Targen had given him an extra purse with twenty five silver marks, the big ones. Two of which are equal to a gold mark. This, and the five gold marks, is a goodly sum for a Blademaster to start out in the world with.

At the first Kraal he came to on the second day of his journey he stopped and bought himself a boar lance, with an oaken shaft as tall as he was, a foot long leaf shaped blade with cross quillions to stop it from going all the way through. He purchased a third leather pannier, designed to go across the top of the other two, which could be opened on either side of the horse, two good wool horse blankets for the animals, an extra fire making kit, a candle lantern with a dozen extra candles, extra food and tea, plenty of tabac and a pair of good blackthorn briar pipes, four bottles of brandy, extra wool leggings with the feet in them, and a fine hooded leather cape lined with wool blanket material (the type of cape used by Norda foresters who often spend the winters in the wild), lastly a pair of heavy shearling mittens.

This Kraal or Stetting was the home of the Earth Clan and sat in the middle of a mile and a half long, mile wide meadow. Here are grown the three types of grasses that Norda horses are fed on. In good years, they harvest twice a year. Two hundred years ago, this meadow was one-fourth the size it is now. As the clan grew more and more trees were cleared for fodder planting, and now other clans send wagons and trade goods from as far away as his own clan, the Pietre or stone clan, who live in the mountains far to the northwest in a high valley. There the wolves are half the size of a horse, the panthers there are not as big as the wolf, but are twice as mean, and of course in the great forest below the valley dwell the Auroch. And everyone knows they invented meanness!!

The weather was gray and still and very cold when Grayhawk left the relative comfort of the horse barn where he had been staying and headed south across a half mile of open ground to the edge of the great forest, which here is only another forty miles deep to the south. There begins the open steppe country down to the south. He knew full well that winter was about to close in, but to remain longer in the Kraal meant the possibility of being snowed in for a week, a month or the whole winter.

By pushing hard all the day through the dark quiet, eerie forest, he managed to make it to a known travelers cave twenty miles to the south, about half way through the forest. When he arrived, the cave was empty but showed signs of recent use. There was firewood cut and stacked inside, and a good spring just down from the entrance.

It is a natural cave, about nine feet tall, fifteen feet wide and thirty feet deep with a sand floor.

Over the years, travelers have improved upon it. The back half is fenced off as a corral. There is a three-foot wide fire pit of stone in the center of the floor, a wood sleeping platform, and half of the entrance is walled off with stone and mortar. No doubt, the foresters have maintained this cave for a long time.

On the road in to the cave area, a huge tree had been felled by lightening. Someone had started cutting it up for the firewood pile. He had no axe, so he returned to the tree with his horse and dragged a pair of the larger cut portions of the tree back to use as fire logs. By building a good fire and then placing one end of the great logs into the fire, he had only to push the log further into the fire every few hours, and the cave was quickly heated to a level that was livable. The log would last through the night.

There were also hand tied bales of fodder for the horses. Rungar warhorses are trained to be unafraid of fire and the mare packhorse was content to follow the big stallions lead into the back of the cave.

Grayhawk did not know loneliness the way other men do. He was quite content with only horse companions as he made his evening meal. Afterwards he enjoyed tea with brandy and a good smoke. Before long, he gave in to the tiredness of a long day in the cold. He moved the log further into the fire, shook out his sleeping roll of waxed tarp and wool blankets, and lay down on the sleeping platform. He leaned his great sword up against the side, short sword and dirk across the head end and his cape rolled up for a pillow. After first casting out with his senses for danger, there being nothing amiss, he went to sleep.

He awoke to the dim grayness of first light showing at the cave entrance. The log had burned down and there were but few embers still showing red. He placed a double handful of kindling on the embers. After blowing on them to get a small blaze started, he put on several lager pieces of wood. He set the teapot close to begin heating.

Taking up his heavy vest and belt, arming himself with short sword and dirk, then his shearling hat, he ventured out into the morning light and cold to relieve himself and check out his surroundings. Very cold, light snow was falling. The ground not even covered yet. He returned to the cave and brought out the horses to drink from the stream, after he broke the ice with a large piece of wood from the pile.

A breakfast of boar sausage, seasoned with sage and red pepper, chewy dark trail bread and tea. He packed the horses, cleaned all traces of his visit from the cave. Then he headed south on the forest road in the falling snow, caped and hooded. He was hoping to make the edge of the steppes by nightfall.

By mid morning, the snow had turned to large wet flakes. The temperature had actually raised some. Before noon the snow was two inches deep and the forest was so quiet it made your ears hurt. Grayhawk then halted under a giant umbrella oak, with a canopy so thick the ground underneath was bare of snow.

He prepared himself a soup of dried compressed vegetables and smoked, shredded Auroch meat, thickened with crushed acorns, and a sliced end of trail bread. All prepared within a very short time over a small fire. He made weak tea from the leaves in the tea ball still left from breakfast.

He had already given the horses a bit of fodder and a sugar lump each. He thought, "Ah, still enough time for a bowl of tabac." Then the warhorse's ears went flat, his gaze went hard and mean and all his muscles tensed. Now, all know who have ever been to war, that a fourteen hundred-pound Norda warhorse is the most intelligent, and the meanest of all possible war mounts. They are loyal and protective of the rider, even unto death. Their sense of smell and hearing are augmented by an all most magical ability to sense danger.

Grayhawk immediately dropped his cape and drew his great sword, actually a two handed saber with a four foot slightly curved blade, so sharp that in the hands of a Blademaster they have been known to take off the head of a real bear in one cut.

Blademasters fight normally on horseback in war, or when afoot on open ground with the great sword. In a close quarter battle they fight with short sword and dirk. In tunnels, buildings or dark alleys they fight with dirk and dagger. They are immensely strong with unbelievable stamina. Grayhawk was stronger than most of his peers and lighting fast.

For now, he was standing very still, sniffing the wind the same way a great wolf does when on the hunt. The heavy wet snowfall was dampening his senses.

The warhorse now pawed the ground. The danger was close. Then, as if materializing out of the snow, they came. They were a party of ten Drulgar, which are foul creatures from the underworld, a combination of man and reptile. They have mottled green and black leathery skin, extended snouts with flat nostril slits and dark, deep set glittering eyes. They are as tall as a man. They are cunning but not smart. They have no mercy and they crave human flesh. It is very odd for them to be this far north as they hate the cold.

They came forward without slowing, in a line, clacking their jaws in their guttural speech, no doubt thinking they had found easy prey. A lone man and two horses is meat for a week. They were mistaken. They had failed to recognize a Blademaster. It was a fatal mistake. Black was their visage, intent upon a quick kill and feasting.

Grayhawk did not wait for them to close the fifty-foot gap. He began running towards the Drulgar as they came forward. His thoughts turning blood red as he moved. As he began the spinning move, known as "A Passing Wind" in which he pivoted once to the left for momentum, bringing the great sword around at shoulder height with tremendous force. Upon impact, he clove the middle Drulgar's head completely off and then continued the stroke. Turning the blade slightly downward, cleaving the next Drulgar to the right from its neck downward to under the right arm, bringing the blade completely around and up. Then with a downward stroke, turning the blade slightly, cleaving the one on the left of center front from the neck downward to under the left arm. He dropped three of his opponents almost as if saying one, two, and three. Diving forward over the headless one, and rolling into a standing position with his back to the enemy, his sword held up in a two handed vertical position, while the remaining Drulgar turned about to come at him again. They were armed with long knives and clubs, but in the open they are no match for a skilled swordsman. Howling now, like wraiths of the mist, they all crouched low and began coming towards him. By doing so, they forgot about the warhorse. Two of them were suddenly crushed under the front hooves of a snarling, stomping, wild eyed, enraged monster horse, who grabbed a third Drulgar by the right shoulder with his teeth and shook him like a dog shakes a bone or a rabbit. Norda warhorses do not like foul folk.

The remaining four all came at Grayhawk with their long knives. Two of which had upturned hook bills on the end, meant to grab a foe with, and pull him down. In an instant, they had him surrounded on all four sides. They were not especially fast, but he was hard pressed to engage four blades at the same time. One of the hook bills came at his throat from the side, while the other went for his groin from the front. Spinning to avoid both he felt the point of a third blade skid across his lower back, while the fourth passed right in front of his eyes. It was at this point for the first time in his life, that the red veil fell before his eyes. Now roaring and laughing as though possessed, he spun completely outside the circle of four Drulgar and as he did, with an upward stroke of the great sword, he disemboweled the one whose knife had been in his face, and who was now emitting a high-pitched shriek, grabbing for his entrails. Continuing his spin, bringing the sword up and then down again, he split the skull diagonally of the one stabbing at his back. While grabbing him by his chest harness and throwing him back against the other two with hook bills. As the body collided with them, the one on the left opened his mouth to roar but no sound came out because there was over a foot of steel sticking out of the back of his head and his tongue was clove in two lengthwise. Jerking his sword free as the last Drulgar turned to flee; he had made only three strides, when he was felled from the rear with a downward stroke of Grayhawk's great sword.

Then, standing spread eagle, face turned up, sword raised high, in his right hand, eyes glazed over, heart thumping, breathing huge lungs full of air, Grayhawk then screamed the ancient blood rage roar of the true Berserker. While the horse reared on its hind legs echoing the same scream.

Long minutes passed while the blood rage subsided, the heart rate slowed and the vision cleared of both man and beast. The glory of the blood rage fades slowly from the system, like a strong narcotic wearing off. It leaves one with the sure knowledge that you will seek to feel such a glorious wonder again.

When he finally, completely returned to reality he looked around at the carnage. The warhorse had stomped three of them into ugliness on the ground and was standing still about twenty feet away. He gazed at the animal for a few seconds and the horse looked steadily back at him. He raised his sword in salute and said, "Well done war brother. We have won this day!" The horse threw its head up and snorted in answer. The mare was still standing by the tree seemingly unaffected.

That battle happened more than fifteen years ago. The warhorse had died under him five years later in a battle with mountain trolls, when Grayhawk was Captain of Cavalry, in the employ of the Duke of Malvoria. At that time he was then eligible to return to Norda and take his place in the political hierarchy of his people. Instead, he had sent the fifty gold marks by messenger, with a note that read,

"I still have not found what I seek."

Since that time, he had been in a number of armies, fought in many battles and traveled in many lands. He had seen all of the great wonders of the world, sailed on oceans and seas, once or twice even as a pirate, never staying in one place for more than a season or two. He has known many women, drank many kinds of wine and brandies, and even smoked the dream herbs a time or two.

He has been sorely wounded a number of times and has suffered numerous lesser wounds. He has proven himself time and again against all manner of foes, human, fell, mythical, and magical. Now he is considered a Warrior of great renown

Chapter Three

And that is how, now "Captain" Grayhawk, Knight Commander of the Household Guard, came to be on a forest road, two days after the infamous battle for Killian's Hill. That evening they camped a mile off the road, back into the deep woods, where their camp could neither be seen, nor easily found. Cold camp rations for supper, but small fires were allowed for tea and some warmth. All but the young King and his Captain got a full night sleep, for they were up long into the night talking, they spoke of many things.

By noon the following day, they crossed the main river at the shallows, just after the convergence of the Masul and Saar rivers, avoiding the main road crossing several miles further on. They arrived at the Academy before eventide. Warmly were they received, after Grayhawk rode in first to prepare them for the fact that Killian yet lived.

The Preceptor of Knights, a member of the Consistory and 33rd Degree Temple Knight, Lord Gregory, turned out the entire contingent to welcome Killian IV, the new King of Keltan, who was speechless and teary eyed. Not long before, Killian, as a Knight Cadet, had lived in fear of displeasing Lord Gregory. The same as all cadets had, for over forty years including the late Killian III. Now Lord Gregory knelt down before him and pledged his allegiance, as did his staff of thirty Instructor Knights and two hundred twenty five Cadets.

A formal and somber table lodge had already been scheduled and prepared, as the Royal Academy was conducted under the direction and tutelage of The Military Order of Temple Knights an ancient, military brotherhood known throughout the world.

The ceremonies for toasting and eulogizing the passing of the King, who was also a brother Knight took several hours and concluded with toasting the new King and then the Preceptor informing the cadet corps that on the morrow all but the twenty five youngest cadets, and the five oldest instructor Knights would ride with the King on the one day march to the King's city. There they would take the Royal Palace, by force if necessary and install Killian IV on his throne and further deal with any usurpers and traitors as might be found to be conspiring against the lawful right of succession

The next morning there rode forth from the Academy Fortress a force of over two hundred, led by a Knight Commander and twenty five Knights of the Realm, escorting the Heir Presumptive and the Preceptor of the Royal Academy. Over half of the cadets who rode were upper classmen, and had undergone three to four years of military training and were due to receive their own spurs within the year.

Many were also blooded warriors, having grown up in the border regions where their families had to deal with bandits and brigands. All were well trained and eager for battle to prove themselves as Knights. They were well armed and well mounted. All wore chain mail over their green cadet leathers.

They rode past farmsteads and through villages. Many people came out to watch as such a large force was rarely seen in these parts. The King rode with a white tabard over his chain mail, on which both front and back were embroidered in gold thread the Royal Double Headed Eagle of the House Penthanius of the Kings of Keltan. Two Yeomen were riding in front, one carrying the banner of the Household Guard, the other carried the Preceptors Banner of "Order of Templars" with its blood cross emblem, four red spear points coming together in the center with a gold circle surrounding, over crossed swords indicating the Preceptors rank,

They rode fast in order to best the speed of the common word. Which, like rumors, travel on a fast wind even to the far reaches of the land. They stopped for an hour in the early afternoon to eat and to rest the horses.

By the fifth hour past noon, they were approaching the North gate of the city, with the King well hidden in the middle of the force. Now the Preceptor moved to the front of the formation. The Household Guard banner was cased and everyone hoped that, as normal, the Preceptor would not be challenged by the Gate Watch. He usually arrived via the North gate. The King was cloaked and hooded in a dark cape. It was hoped to get him onto the Palace grounds in the center of the city before anyone recognized him.

With the tension running very high, they rode up to the gate, which stood open. The guards on either side came to attention as normal and bowed slightly as the Preceptor passed. Down the crowded avenue towards the Palace Gate, they clattered with people, horses and carts moving to make way as usual. No one yet had made anything of the Preceptors escort being three times its usual size.

Right up to the Palace and through the north salle port they rode, right into the rear courtyard of the Palace proper. Pages were now appearing to take the horses of the Nobles and Knights. The Cadets formed up in two lines as though on parade, then dismounted in unison on command, very smart and proper looking.

The now dismounted Knights gathered in a group around a hooded, caped figure, which they kept in the center of the group. The Preceptor in his formal white tunic, with gold trim, black trousers and boots and ceremonial dress sword and dirk, announced with an uplifted hand

"If you will, please, attend me Gentlemen, this way." He then turned and entered the Portico to the main hallway. The group of Knights, all talking casually, turned to follow, and then came all of the Cadets in four files.

Once inside the main hallway the King dropped his cape and moved to the front, between the Preceptor and Grayhawk. Amazingly, no alarm was raised. They walked down the main hall. As they approached the front corner ready to make the right turn into the front of the Palace. Two Knights rounded the corner and stopped, on the points of the Preceptor and Grayhawk's swords. Their hands flew to their sword hilts until they saw whom they faced. At that point, both paled and swallowed very hard and almost in unison exclaimed "But, you're dead!"

"Not, hardly" said the King. Then, gritting his teeth, "Where, pray tell Gentlemen, is your illustrious Prince Regent, as I believe he is currently calling himself. Quickly now, if you value your lives!"

"In the throne room, your Highness er Your Majesty. He is still holding court."

"Really!" said the King. "Well, do let us all go pay our respects, shall we!" Several Knights then came forward and disarmed the pair who stood rather speechless.

Around the corner they strode, down the front formal hallway to the big double doors of the throne room. There were two guards at attention with lances, in their formal uniforms of the Household Guards. Neither moved a muscle as the party approached. As the King came into view, their eyes grew very large.

Grayhawk stepped up to the one on the right and said "Niall, may I borrow your lance?"

"Of course, Captain" he replied as he handed it to him. With a slight smile, Grayhawk said, "Sire, with your permission, I will announce you?"

"If you would be so kind, Captain" he replied. Grayhawk nodded at the Preceptor and said, "Shall we?"

"By all means" said Sir Gregory as he drew his sword. Grayhawk looked at the two guards.

"Gentlemen, open the doors if you please."

The two then stepped forward, grasped the handles and pulled the great doors open. Grayhawk and the Preceptor, swords drawn, Grayhawk carrying a lance in his left hand, they walked straight into the throne room, which was filled with people, many of whom were scurrying to get out of the way of the two armed men. All talk ceased, and the room went silent. All present were now turning to see what was happening.

At this point Grayhawk reached the area just inside the main hall itself. He and the Preceptor both stopped. One on either side, they turned and faced each other. Then Grayhawk who was carrying the lance in his left hand, lifted it straight up about a foot and brought the metal cap on the end of it down on the marble floor, hard, three times. The sound reverberated around the hall. Then in his best deep voice and very loudly he intoned "His Imperial Majesty by the Grace of God, and Royal Right of Succession Killian IV the King of Keltan!"

Dead silence fell over the throne room, and Killian walked through the doors followed by twenty-five Knights of the Realm, swords drawn, in rows of five. Beyond them were two hundred Royal Knight Cadets, also with swords drawn and also in rows of five. The rhythmic cadence of their footfall, echoed through the entire keep, and vibrated the floor and walls of the throne room.

Ladies and Nobles, Courtiers and Courtesans, Ambassadors, Knights and Soldiers of the realm all were scrambling and stumbling to move out of the path of the grim looking group coming down the aisle, straight across the center floor and up to the dais, where sat the dual throne chairs of Keltan. One of which was now occupied by a dour looking, gray haired man of medium build, dressed in yellow silk pantaloons, white stockings, a purple waistcoat over a cream colored ruffled shirt, wearing the ceremonial sword of the King.

After handing the lance off to one of the incoming knights, Grayhawk and the Preceptor fell in behind Killian, one on either side of him. As Killian and company reached the bottom of the 12 steps up to the dais of the throne, the silence was broken by loud chanting of an incantation from a dark cloaked figure beside the throne where Killian's Uncle, Danell was seated. A blue crackling field appeared in front of the throne. From within, it sprang a creature from some nightmare, dark red, somewhere between a man and a crocodile. With roaring jaws spread wide, it sprang into the air towards Killian, who did not have his sword drawn.

Grayhawk, who was to Killian's left and slightly behind him, moved forward and shouldered Killian to his right, while bringing up his great sword to defend the young King. Lord Gregory grabbed Killian pulling him to the right further out of harm's way. Pandemonium exploded in the throne room. Danell's supporters were drawing swords and trying to move towards the throne while encumbered by women and civilians trying to flee.

The Knights and Cadets moved forward as a group to engage. As this was happening, the creature landed at the bottom stair roaring and moving forward to get at Killian. Seeing this Grayhawk stabbed at the creature's side and over a foot of blade penetrated it. Shrieking in pain and rage, it turned on Grayhawk, biting air where a second before Grayhawk's head had been. Its left claw raking him from shoulder to elbow on his sword arm, pulling the sword still stuck in its side out of the hands of Grayhawk whence it fell to the floor with a clang. Grayhawk, moving to the creature's right turning it further away from the King, reached across with his left hand and drew his short sword from his own right hip. His right arm was now going numb and falling to his side. Turning his body to the right, his left shoulder dipping down, bringing up the point of his short sword, as the shrieking monster, jaws open, clawed arms spread wide, came at him again. He drove the short sword up with his left hand under the creature's lower jaw, through the throat and out the back of its head. The jaws clacked shut an inch in front of Grayhawk's face as the creature wrapped its clawed arms around him and they both went down to the floor,

Killian and Lord Gregory had meanwhile bounded up the stairs of the dais and at the top; Killian lunged forward with his sword and ran the wizard through just as he had drawn back both arms to cast another spell. Danell, mean while, had drawn the ceremonial sword which was of rapier design, a long thin blade, very fast to handle and very sharp. He made a head cut at Lord Gregory, which missed. He quickly recovered and they engaged sword to sword. The wizard threw both arms downward and grasped Killian's blade with both hands. His eyes like glowing coals, mouth open but no sound came out. Killian ripped his blade out and back and most of the wizards fingers fell to the floor as he collapsed to his knees and fell to the side.

Killian turned now towards his uncle, who made the fatal mistake of looking at his nephew. At that moment, Lord Gregory ran him through the heart. The blade was penetrating out of his back. He died without uttering a sound.

At that moment, the air crackled blue again around the throne and dais. Both the wizard and the creature now, lying dead on top of Grayhawk, blinked out of existence as though they had never been there.

Less than a minute later, all fighting in the hall ceased, Most of Danell's supporters had been killed in the battle. They had been outnumbered three to one. It was now quiet again except for some moaning here and there.

Then Grayhawk rolled over to his side and tried to get to his feet. His entire right side was bloody. He only made it to his knees when the world went black. The King was down the steps in a couple of bounds. He rolled Grayhawk on to his back. Killian looked around the room. There were a number of prominent physicians and healers present. He pointed to several different ones. "Come here, NOW." He commanded and they all came scurrying to tend to Captain Grayhawk. "Know you this if he dies you die, as well!"

While the healers started working on Grayhawk, the King went back up the stairs to the throne. He turned and looked out over the carnage. Not as bad as it could have been. If he had returned other than in the manner he had, there probably would have been a pitched battle for the castle, and a lot more dead people than the twenty or so scattered about the throne room. The bad part was that now he would have to deal with the traitors. Well over twenty more of them were in the custody of the Cadets.

The rest of the Court, which had scattered like a flock of pigeons when the fighting started, they were now being rounded up all over the Palace grounds. Killian had ordered the guards to close off the Palace grounds while he and the others had gone inside. After they had assured him that almost all of the Household Guard still remained loyal to the King and his family.

In very short order, Killian had restored order to the Palace and the Royal grounds. He sent Heralds into the city, to relay the news of the return of the rightful Heir. He then appointed Lord Gregory as his High Counselor Pro Tem until such time as he selected his own permanent candidate. He had his two young sisters freed from the north tower, where Danell had kept them imprisoned. Their reunion was joyful and tearful. Danell had already made plans to give both girls as gifts to Gauli Bandit Chiefs, as a token of friendship with the new King of Keltan. Himself of course! He had summoned Queen Aurelia to return from Danfinia, in order to become one of his concubines, and prevent her from remarrying as a queen and potential enemy.

The healers and physicians worked around the clock for two full days to save Grayhawk's life and his right arm. The physicians fought the poison and infection from the monsters claws. Grayhawk's fever and delirium were intense. He hovered close to death for a long time.

The healers at the same time used their magical skills to cause new flesh to grow where the poisoned and infected flesh had died. The wound had been bone deep, claw cuts, running from the top of his shoulder down to his elbow. The two groups alternately force fed Grayhawk drugged wine and soup made from pulverized, dried Auroch meat. He was given drugs for the infection, protein for the healing and wine for the spirit. The end result worked better than anyone had hoped.

Chapter Four

Grayhawk came around on the third morning. He opened his eyes to the sight of Killian's mother, the Queen, rubbing a pleasant smelling save onto the wounded arm, on which now were three wide, purple scars running down to his elbow.

Aurelia Elania Pentharious was a strikingly beautiful woman of thirty five years. She was auburn haired, green eyed, with fair creamy skin. She was tall for a woman. Her eyes were large, heavy lidded; she had long lashes, a long aquiline nose over an almost pouty set of full lips, white even teeth. Her hair was very full, thick and wavy. She did not look like a woman who had been married for twenty years and who also had borne five children. The first when she was but fifteen years old.

Grayhawk had been quite taken with her from the very first time he saw her. It was in one of the palace gardens where she was playing in a wading pool with her two daughters. He had come to bring her a message from the King. She had come out of the pool and sat down on a bench, with her gown hiked up to her knees. She had sat drying her legs and feet with a towel before taking the message from him. He remembered his first thoughts of her at the time. "Ye Gods, The woman has beautiful feet!" She had smiled as though she heard his thoughts. She read the message and said, "You may tell my Husband I will attend him at the time and place requested. Captain?"

"Grayhawk, Majesty, Captain Grayhawk."

"Ah yes" she said looking straight into his eyes. "I have heard that you are a Blademaster of Norda, Captain, is that true?"

"Yes Majesty that is true" he had replied.

"Is it also true that you train for two years inside some dark mountain to become a Blademaster?" she asked.

"Yes Majesty, that is correct."

"And that you have killed an Auroch with your hands?"

"No Majesty, for that I used a boar lance."

"But never the less, you did kill an Auroch?" she asked, "and used the horns to make your weapons?"

"Your Majesty is well informed about the Norda. Yes Majesty, that is our custom, it is required of a warrior, before he can become a Blademaster."

"Then" she replied, "You must be a very formidable warrior indeed, Captain Grayhawk, to have survived thus far."

He had studied her face for a long moment before replying. Then he had answered in the formal.

"I am so taken, and accepted amongst the Brethren and Friends, Your Majesty."

"My words were not intended to insult, Captain." She replied, "Nor to offend.

"No insult or offense was taken, your Majesty."

"So very proper, and formal, Captain. Very well then! Thank you for bringing me the message." He bowed and backed away, before turning to leave.

Now she was sitting beside him, with his hand tucked under her left arm and rubbing salve onto his wounds. He had been swimming in a sea of pain, fighting monsters who were trying to drag him under. Now his head cleared somewhat, and he knew he was alive and awake.

"Where am I?" he croaked. His voice sounded awful even to him.

"You are in the Royal Palace, in the King's city," she said, now wiping his face with a cool wet cloth. As she leaned over him, he could smell her, like lilacs and roses combined with myrrh. Even in his current state it made his heart pound, "My Lady, I"

"Shush!" she said, placing her fingers over his mouth. "Lay quiet and rest Grayhawk. Everything is as it should be. The crisis is ended, our side was victorious. I returned from Danfinia last night by fast ship."

"I thought I would surely die myself, when word came, that my beloved husband and all of my sons were dead at the hands of assassins and that I was commanded to return immediately to be concubine to that bastard Danell. He had sent a ship for me even before he committed the murder, so confident was he of the success of his scheme. That night on board ship my witch-seer Jumolda cast for the truth and told me that my oldest son still lived. I was most relieved to hear that."

Grayhawk tried to speak, but could not get the words to come out. Aurelia picked up a cup, placed a hand behind his neck, and helped him rise up enough to take a drink. It was sweet wine with a bitter after taste, but he drank several swallows of it and then lay back on the pillow.

"How long have I been out? He said in a gravelly voice.

"Today is the fourth day," she answered. "You were sorely wounded by that creature you slew." Aah! Now he remembered. Ugly damn thing, half human, and half crocodile.

"What happened?" he asked.

"Well, as I understand it, you killed the beast, Killian killed the wizard, and Lord Gregory killed Danell. There was a brief fight in the Throne Room in which a score of Danell's traitorous friends were also killed. Another score were taken prisoner. Two of our young Cadets were killed and one Knight was wounded."

"And what about you My Lady, how are you?" He asked.

"I have made peace with the situation as beat I can" she replied. "I spent most of the night in the catacombs with my husband and my sons, but I realized that I could do nothing more for them. I will honor their memories and cherish the times we had together. I will grieve for a time, but life must go on." "After I left the catacombs last night, or rather early this morning, I had a long talk with Killian. He told me exactly what all has happened and how you saved his life both in the forest and in the throne room. How it was really your leadership that got all of you safely back to the Academy. And, again it was your leadership in taking back the throne."

"My Lady, I only suggested some choices. Killian was the leader," he said.

"Oh phooey!" she replied. "Your false modestly is belied by all those scars you bear."

"Scars my Lady?"

"Yes, the ones all over your body." At this point Grayhawk looked under the covers and found that he was quite naked.

"Who, Did you? My clothes"

"Yes, I did. My ladies and I undressed you and bathed you early this morning."

"MY LADY, I MUST PROTEST THIS!" he was roaring now.

"It's a bit late for that Captain Grayhawk," she stated flatly. "You were extremely dirty and covered with blood and grime. The stench was over powering. So, I summoned my ladies in waiting, and we cleaned you up." She folded her arms and gave him a big smile.

"Ladies in waiting" he stammered. "How many, ladies"

"Why all of them of course. I couldn't very well lift you into the bath by myself' she replied.

"And they all saw me?" he asked in a squeaky voice.

"Ah yes" she replied. "After we got you cleaned up, we thoroughly examined thy scars" The last spoken as she went out of the door.

"WHAT!!" came the roar. "YOU DID WHAT? ALL OF YOU??"

Queen Aurelia looked back through the door, and saw that Grayhawk has passed out with that last exclamation. She went back into the room where she tucked him in like he was a child. With her fingers, she gently brushed the hair out of his face and eyes.

"Oh yes, my dear Blademaster" she whispered "and we all agreed that you are a fine specimen of a man, scars and all."

With the help of more drugged wine, Grayhawk did not awaken until the following morning. When he tried to sit up he almost blacked out again. His right arm felt very weak, but the pain was minimal. The hangover and headache from the wine and drugs was what bothered him the most. After half an hour of slowly maneuvering his legs around and sitting on the side of the bed, he got to his feet, using the post at the foot of the bed for support.

He had just gotten to a straight standing position when the door opened, and there stood Queen Aurelia and two of her ladies.

"By all the beards of all the Gods!" was all she could say before the blackness claimed him again and he fell to the floor.

When he awoke, again he was lying on his back in his own chambers. He was fully clothed in riding boots of black, black leather breeches, a black leather hip length vest with a wide belt, over a cream colored, puff sleeved, linen shirt that laced up the front. His dagger was in his right boot, and his dirk was belted on his left side.

"Oh Great! Now I have women, dressing me as though I were a toddler" he thought, as he rose up on his elbow and looked around the room. There seated by the window reading a book was the King of Keltan.

"Well, well." said the King. "My Captain and the talk of the Ladies in the King's City, has finally awoken. Here I thought you were sorely wounded and bed ridden, and yet I hear rumors of you chasing Ladies in Waiting through the castle, while wearing nothing but a smile. Really! Captain Grayhawk!!"

"Ye Gods!" groaned Grayhawk. "Does the entire Kingdom know?"

"Why yes, I believe, by now they do!" said Killian laughing heartily and slapping his knee.

"I will never be able to live this down. Now even the King is laughing," said Grayhawk. "That does it! I will resign my post and leave for Kushia in the morning, early - "He made it to a standing position, holding on to a bedpost. While the room spun slowly around, speaking slowly now, he said, "Majesty, I feel as if I've been on a four day drunk."

"You have my dear fellow, you have indeed" said the King. "That's how they kept you alive, drugged wine and some soup. Quite a lot of it too! Or so I hear."

"Well Sire, that would explain the roaring headache and the hunger pangs. I am afraid I do not remember much after that thing fell on me. So I'm assuming that since we are both sitting here that we won the day!"

"Oh right handily Sir!" replied the King. "It was over in a few minutes. Some of the conspirators and their agents are still being rounded up, but we caught them before they got fully organized and they were not able to establish full control of everything."

There came a knock on the door at that point and the King said "Enter." Six young pages came in bearing trays of food and stands for them along with a large pitcher of dark brown beer and two stone mugs. "Aah! Good show," said the king. "Stag and stout, that's what was needed! The perfect combination to restore health and spirit"

"I couldn't agree with you more, Sire." said Grayhawk, stomach rumbling and mouth watering.

The pages had finished setting everything up, Killian stood before them and said

"Gentlemen, whom do you, serve?"

"We serve you, your Majesty" one of them piped, "none other."

"Good!" said Killian, giving them each a silver quarter mark. "Go now to the fair in town, and make no mention of where I am to anyone. Agreed!" they all bowed with big smiles and scrambled out of the door. He grinned, pulling his chair over to the makeshift table. "My Palace spies" he said. "Anything I want to know, I just ask them."

"For certain" replied Grayhawk, "Anything happening in this Palace, and they will know about it."

Grayhawk, sitting on the end of his bed, the King seated across from him. Both pulled out their daggers and dug into the repast, which consisted of thin sliced brisket of stag in dark brown hunter sauce, thick slices of dark bread smeared with butter, fresh onion slices, honey mustard chutney, a bowl of red potatoes in butter, a couple of beautifully roasted partridges stuffed with mushrooms and green onions, and a golden brown, crusted plum pudding, and of course a gallon of stout.

Not much was said for about fifteen minutes, while both men ate their fill. When both of them had pushed back from the table, cleaned and sheathed their daggers. The King asked "How now Grayhawk? Wilt thee survive?"

"Aye Sire, I believe now there is hope. An excellent meal, every part was just right."

"Agreed" said Killian. "What say we place chairs by the fire and break out your pipes? I know you keep some."

"Aye Sire that I do. If you will but look in that chest there by your right side, you will find pipes and tabac. The two white meerschaums smoke the smoothest." In the top of the chest was a tray with twenty different pipes of various woods and styles. Killian brought out two carved white bowl, long stemmed pipes and a packet of fine shredded, smoke cured black tabac. Handed them to Grayhawk and said

"Here, if you will do the honors I will move the furniture closer to the fire."After a bit the two men, King and Captain, were seated in comfortable stuffed horsehide chairs in front of a crackling fire, smoking fine tabac in meerschaum pipes, drinking stout ale and enjoying each other's company.

Grayhawk was feeling very revived and, in spite of being stiff and sore, quite comfortable. Killian was at least relaxed and taken to staring into the fire for long moments, looking sometimes very far away. Finally, he said, "I wanted to kill that bastard myself you know. Better all around that Lord Gregory did it. But still."

"Indeed Sire, it is far better that you did not kill your uncle. And for Killian the King, it is the stuff of legends, that you have killed a wizard in a magical duel."

"Magical duel, I stuck a foot of cold steel into him. There was no magic in that."

"But that is not how the bards and storytellers will see it" said Grayhawk. "To them it was a great magical battle between a young King and an ancient wizard."

"Ancient?" Killian replied. "Hell's bells man. He couldn't have been more than thirty or so."

"That was before you stuck a sword in him, Sire. At that instant, he became ancient and evil. The most powerful and ancient wizard of them all sort of a bardic transformation, if you will."

"I see" said Killian. "So now I will become "Killian the Wizard Slayer" in song."

"Most likely" said Grayhawk grinning. "A true hero, King Killian of Keltan"

"Oh brother!" said Killian, "Just what I need."

"Actually Sire it is just what you need to begin your reign, a heroic deed or two. Now, if we could just find a few more wizards for you to slay, or perhaps a dragon or two" said Grayhawk, grinning.

"You just continue that line of thought, Grayhawk, and I will personally write the ballad of the Naked Blademaster, Slayer of Demons, and Feared by Ladies in Waiting."

Both were laughing now, loud and hard, when the door opened and Queen

Aurelia walked in. "Ah, Captain Grayhawk, I see you finally have your clothes on!" Grayhawk was choking on pipe smoke.

Killian said "OOPS" and laughed even harder.

"What was that I overheard about a naked Blademaster?" asked the Queen, without cracking a smile. Grayhawk's eyes bugged out and King Killian IV of Keltan fell on the floor howling with laughter."Well I just stopped by to see if you were mending properly, Captain Grayhawk" said the Queen. "I can see that you are. So, I will take my leave now and leave you gentlemen to whatever you were talking about before I came in. Killian, please get off the floor dear. It doesn't look well for the King to be on the floor. With a soft rustling of her skirts she was out of the room, closing the door softly behind her.

Killian picked up his pipe where it had fallen and sat back down in his chair. He picked up a mug of stout and handed it to Grayhawk. "Here Sir, I think you had best drink some of this. You are looking decidedly peaked." Grayhawk complied taking several drinks, in fact.

"Well!" said the king. "It would seem Master Grayhawk that my mother likes you. Or do you suppose the Queen goes personally to check on all the wounded?"

"Me? The Queen! Uh, I'

"And why not"

"Sire, she is a very beautiful and gracious Lady - and uh, well"

"Oh, come on Grayhawk, I am her son, and I think I can tell, she likes you."

"Yes Sire, but she is still the Queen" said Grayhawk, obviously embarrassed.

"That she is" replied Killian "but she is also a woman, and a good looking one at that. Wouldn't you agree?"

"Of course I agree Killian, but frankly speaking, if I may?"

"Of course old boy, speak frankly."

"Well, given all that has happened, the death of your father and brothers so recent, all the changes in the Kingdom and in both of your lives and all."

"Grayhawk, listen to me. I am fully aware of everything that has happened, as is my mother, and I know full well that any other woman in the land would be a total wreck after all of these events. Both I and my mother, the Queen, were aware that political assassination was always a possibility. Another of the fine "privileges" of Royalty. My father always made us all aware of the dangers and that if, and when something did happen to him, we were to pick up our lives immediately and continue with ruling the country. We the living, do not have the luxury of falling apart, or even getting drunk for a month. Because, on the day an old King is buried, someone has to be the new King. That is the way of it."

"Yes, of course it is, I understand that fully" replied Grayhawk.

"So what is your problem, my Lord?" said the King.

"Well that in and of itself is the problem Sire. I'm not a Lord, only a Captain of the Household Guard."

"Oh, is that all?" said the King. "Why I have already rectified that. Sorry old boy, I forgot to tell you. The reason I was waiting for you to wake up earlier. I have already appointed you as the Lord High Counselor to the King and Warlord of Keltan. Here is your symbol, and badge of office." He took from his coat a large gold medallion of the double headed eagle of Keltan over crossed sabers, on a heavy link gold chain. "I have also ceded to you a large estate along the southern border, and I have vested you with the title of Duke of Surlandia." He hung the medallion around his neck, patted him on the shoulder and said "There! Now you are a Royal and wealthy! All in one flourish of my pen. You will have copies of your appointments and charters presented to you in the morning. What have you to say to that Lord Grayhawk?"

"I am not sure that there is anything adequate which could be said, your Majesty. A thank you is certainly not response enough, but, I thank you. Maybe somewhere in here I will figure out exactly what to say."

"Oh, that look on your face is worth it all right now, Lord Grayhawk, and you are welcome. It was not a difficult decision. You have proven yourself worthy, both as an officer and a friend." They clasped forearms in the Rungar style.

"I pledge you my blood oath, you are my Liege, and King" said Grayhawk. "I will defend you as Blademaster, and friend from this day forth, until the time of my death."

"I accept your blood oath Blademaster, and I give you mine in return, until the time of my death."

The following morning in the throne room, before the duly assembled full court of the King, Killian IV made his proclamation official. Appointment and charter documents were signed and sealed. Many other appointments and changes were made. The traitors were made to forfeit titles, lands and wealth. Several were sentenced to death; more were banished from the kingdom for life. Loyalists were rewarded, some with titles and land, some with promotions in rank and some with coin of the Realm. All decisions were ratified by the reigning Queen, Aurelia Elania who then abdicated her throne in favor of her son Killian who then was formally crowned, Killian IV. Queen Aurelia then announced the beginning of her thirty day mourning period in seclusion, as prescribed by custom. She departed the throne room with her ladies in waiting for a castle owned by her family, in the east between the rivers.

It was a very long day, all in all. At the end of which Lord Grayhawk retired to his new, spacious, apartments in the North wing of the palace, next to the Kings. The King also retired for some privacy and rest. There was great feasting in the Palace as well as in the King's City, as the people of all levels celebrated the crowning of their new King.

There was as well, a great deal of lamenting and tears of sorrow amongst the families of the conspirators. Many of whom took what they could carry, and disappeared into the night. Some went by horseback or carriage, some aboard ships from the harbor. None even realized that the King had allowed them to do so. He preferred having them long departed, rather than skulking and scheming causing problems in the realm.

Chapter Five

Later that night, when both the city and the palace were dark and most of the people were abed, well almost all of the people, except for two separate and very different locations, one in the North tower of the Palace, another in a squalid part of the waterfront area, known as the Holding Stead. Well over two hundred years before had been a camp for roving raider bands of the Norda. The Holding Stead was still the area within the old wooden stockade, now a part of the King's City where an underworld of vice and crime ruled. Every King so far had made himself a promise to clean out the area, but the politics of money, have always ruled otherwise.

In the north tower of the castle, Lord Gregory, Templar Preceptor and Soldier of the Light, was conducting magical rights to call upon the Servants of Light. Who are beings from another plane of the Cosmos. Who, from time to time take a hand in the affairs of man to prevent evil from ruling the world. The servants provide guidance and information about coming events and threats to the existence of mankind. For the Lord of Darkness, truly had been a God before his casting out by the All Father, and now was intent upon the enslavement and final subjugation of all mankind.

Meanwhile, in a chamber beneath a large house in the center of the Stead, as it is commonly called, there a Dark Priest, a servant of the Dark Lord and an adept in the dark arts of Hell, the place on another plane of existence. He also conducted magical rites, though of a very different sort, involving the use of black blood candles, pentagrams of salt and ashes, drawn upon the floor and summoning spells for Demons. The Dark Priests name is Rigorta, a Kushian by Birth, a sorcerer by trade and powerfully versed in the dark arts, was furious. All his hard work and monies spent to gain control over Danell and his closest followers had been for naught. His plans now ruined by that bastard from Norda, Grayhawk and that idiot, Prince Killian.

Rigorta seethed in his anger. He had intended those fools to be sacrificed to the Dark Lord along with a number of others including Danell and that fool sorcerer. While the Queen, Aurelia and her two young daughters were to have become his personal body slaves. Years of pleasure for him, and pain for them he had fantasized. Absolutely none of his plans had gone right. He had been forced to sacrifice ten pairs of human children to appease the Dark Lord. Fortunately the orphans of the King's City were plenty and easy to acquire from certain corrupt "caregivers."

Tonight's sacrifice was a female sailor off a trading ship that had sailed already, so she would never be missed, even on Sardos where she was from. She was a large girl, tall and muscular, not very good looking, but the Lord wanted her soul not her looks, and her body would go to feed the messengers. She screamed and pleaded pitifully when he sliced her open to remove her beating heart. For long moments he savored her screaming and agony before he released her soul, and ended the spell. Carefully washing his hands before performing the incantation which allowed the messengers to penetrate the veil into the light of the room long enough to take her body, even though he knew they were ravenous tonight and watching his every move. When the red/orange glow faded from the room, he knew it was safe to move about. Sometimes, if a human Dark Priest is not careful, a major Demon may enter through the veil and the Dark Priest becomes lunch.

Being careful to sweep up the tainted salt and ash which formed one point of the pentagram on the floor, he scooped it up with a copper scoop and placed it in a bag made from the scrotum of a pig. Now the symbol could not be redrawn without the contents of the bag. No portal could be spun. The tainted salt and ash compound takes a long time to prepare and can also be used as a deadly poison, with no known antidote.

Rigorta knew that now he must begin again to find a way to conquer or usurp one of the kingdoms of earth, so that he could commence building an army of the Dark Lord as he had been commanded to do. And while he had allowed him this one failure, he would not be allowed a second. Rigorta did not wish to be eaten alive by Demons.

At the same time, across the city in the North Tower of the Palace, distance wise only about a mile, but in the realities of time and space they were light years of distance apart. Lord Gregory felt the rush through time and space as he returned to his body from the hall of the Servants. He knew the essence of the All Father was in the pillar of pure light from whence came the voice known to the Knights as the "Source" that spoke to him whenever he was brought to the temple made without hands, across time and space, flying through the astral plane.

Everyone, more or less, believes that the Temple the Knights serve is one of the ancient structures somewhere down in Canah. That is exactly what is wanted. The Knights spread rumors to that effect everywhere they go. It would not do for the world to know that the Temple Knights have existed as an organization for thousands of years, even going back before the last Ice Age. To a time before the last great civilization was destroyed in a war with the Dark Lord.

Before the end of that age, the Dark Lord had walked the earth as a living being. He had started a second war to control all of the earth and all of mankind which almost destroyed both. Once again, the All Father had intervened and stopped him. This time he was banished from the light completely and imprisoned in Hell, a plane of darkness and misery, inhabited by demons and vile creatures of every kind. It is a place where man flesh is thought to be a delicacy and human souls exist in perpetual agony. It is their suffering that sustains the Dark Lord. The more souls he acquires the stronger he becomes. So, he has decided to have them all.

In this most recent visit to the Temple, Lord Gregory had been informed of the Dark Priest Rigorta. He had been warned of his intention to gain control of one of the Kingdoms through the use of dark magic and evil until he became strong enough to begin taking by force. His goal is to control the entire world.

Lord Gregory was also directed to arrange for Grayhawk to become a Templar and a member of the Consistory. In order to do this he would have to perform the initiation ceremony himself and then give Grayhawk a word and a token. This would then allow him to enter Mount Solace, the secret stronghold of the order. Anyone trying to enter without the word and the token would never find the entrance, high upon the mountain.

Mount Solace was more than a fortress inside a living mountain or a temple. It also guards the entrance to the Reliquary of the Gods. It is a vault containing objects of great power, which were left by the Gods. Things not meant to be in the hands of men and especially not Dark Priests like Rigorta. The Dark Lord only suspects that such things are still on the earth. If he knew for sure they were, or where to find them, well, it would not be pretty.

Mount Solace has been a well kept secret for millennia. It has been in the care of the Templar for sixty thousand years or more. The fortress is located in the southern part of the Auserlian Mountains, an autonomous region controlled by the Order and not a part of any Kingdom or government. The mountains are a wilderness inhabited by mountain trolls and giants. In the north reportedly there live a tribe of dwarves not seen by humans for thousands of years now. They are said to live in a mountain hold or keep that goes miles deep into the rock.

The only way into Solace is up an ancient glacier track from the north shore of Lake Gani. There is a steading or town occupied by people from all over the world whom the order has saved from sacrifice by the Dark Priest. These people are all still marked for death, so the Templars send them to the steading, which is also named Solace. They have all experienced the horrors of the Dark Lord first hand. Now they are fiercely loyal to the word and token.

While Lord Gregory ate a late supper and had his bath, Rigorta completely removed the pentagram of ash and salt, packed all his magical accoutrements and removed the protective wards from around the house.

Lord Gregory prayed in the small chapel prior to retiring to his chambers for the night. The Dark Priest Rigorta left the house in the holding stead for the last time and made the short carriage ride to the wharves, where he boarded a black Kushian galley. The long narrow ship immediately cast off and within a turn of an hourglass was out of the harbor. Setting all sail for the voyage to Merkesha where Rigorta would hatch his next plan to control a country.

At daylight the following morning, the King's Sorcerers had discovered the evil taints left behind in the old stead, as they were no longer shielded. Within an hour troops were dispatched and the house was raided, yielding only the fact that a Dark Priest had been in residence and that sacrifices had been preformed. The soldiers rounded up everyone that they could find that was involved with the house but gained very little information for their efforts. The King ordered the house burned to the ground; the hole filled in and then left as a vacant lot.

Grayhawk had only just begun to assume any of the duties associated with his new position. He received a summons from the King to meet in private council. When he arrived at the King's official "Office (actually a drawing room off of the King's chambers) he found Killian and Lord Gregory waiting for him, enjoying a glass of brandy. Upon entering the room, the King hailed him "Behold, the Warlord of Keltan doth approach. All bow."

"Well" he said "I am glad somebody knows who I am around here. I sure don't."

"Feeling a little lost, my Lord?" asked the King, as Lord Gregory handed him a glass of Brandy.

"Just exactly what does a Warlord do?" Grayhawk asked "Start wars?"

"No, of course not" answered Killian. "You have to run the wars after I start them. Isn't that the correct procedure Lord Gregory?"

"I believe that is the way of it, your Majesty" answered Gregory.

"And have you started any yet today Sire?" asked Grayhawk.

"No but it's early yet. I'll see if I can put together something by this afternoon" answered the King. All three men were laughing now. "If it's any comfort Grayhawk, I still haven't figured out what the King is supposed to do either. My Father always seemed to be busy. I guess I wasn't paying attention to what it was he was busy doing. Now I wish I had. I always knew that someday I would be King. I just thought I would be a lot older when it happened. To tell you the truth my Lords,

I do not feel like a King. I feel like an actor playing a role, and I do not even know my lines."

"Good for you Sire!" said Gregory "that makes you a man first and a King second."

"I agree Sire" said Grayhawk "Walk like a man, talk like a King when you must, but always be true to yourself. Keep steel always at your side, keep your friends close but hold your enemies even closer. Never take your eyes or your mind off of them. And, when the time comes for your journey to end, you will have been counted a great King. I feel it."

"Here here!" said Gregory, and they raised their glasses in toast.

"Sage words indeed" said the King, turning to the scribe seated at a table across the room. "Take down those words as spoken and have Lord Grayhawk sign the parchment. Have it placed in a frame on the wall here in my office that I might read them again from time to time." "Now" began Killian, "as to why I sent for you, My Lord" looking at Grayhawk. "It seems that you have been chosen by authority higher than me, to receive additional honors and offices."

"What is this?" said Grayhawk. "Sire, I am up to my ears in honors and offices as it is and the only authority higher than you is the Gods themselves!"

"Precisely Lord Gregory informs me that you have been chosen for initiation into the Order of Temple Knights, and for a further office beyond that. But, I'm sure that will all be explained to you fully, in due time. Is that not the way of it Lord Gregory?"

"So it is, your Majesty" said Gregory, stepping forward and extending Grayhawk his hand. "Allow me to be the first to welcome you to the order soon to be Brother Knight Grayhawk." Grayhawk clasped his forearm, in the style of warriors greeting one another.

"A Templar Me why on earth would you select me?" he asked looking very puzzled.

"Not on earth at all" replied Gregory. "Your selection was made on a higher plane, as all of the Brothers are."

"Now I am really lost" said Grayhawk.

"Be not confused Grayhawk" said Gregory. "Soon you will know the truth of it. For now all you have to do is state "Of my own free will

I do accept" and I will give you my personal word-bond you will never regret it." Grayhawk looked at Killian, who then said,

"As your Liege, I give you my leave to do this" and placed his hand on their clasped forearms. "And as your friend I urge you to accept this honor."

"Then I guess I should do this Lord Gregory of my own free will I accept." And at that moment inside of his mind a bell tolled and a bright light flashed, and his training and memory told him, that the bell and light are also seen and heard by Odranna's chosen when they are selected to serve. Then the full realization came that the All Father and Odranna are one in the same just called by different names. In addition he knew that some doors in his mind had opened while others had closed. All of this occurred within a blink of an eye.

'Thus has your initiation begun my Brother" said Lord Gregory. "Over the next several days many things shall you come to learn and know. Much will be made clear to you. We leave in the morning for the Academy where the actual initiation will be performed. I have sent word to all members of the Keltanish Lodge to attend. Some fifty Brothers in all will be in attendance."

"Why the Academy?" asked Grayhawk. "Why not do it here in the city?"

"Because" replied Gregory, "Only the King and I, and now you, know how many Knights of the Order there are in Keltan. Since I am Preceptor of the Order here in this land I must be a public figure as are certain others, who are here as my assistants. All others are held in secret except to the Ruler of the Land. Almost all of our work and study is done in secret to prevent the Servants of the Dark One and his Priests from knowing what we are about. For they do know, that our prime directive is to seek out and destroy them. While we are known throughout the world as the Soldiers of the Light, most of our work is done in the shadows where the forces of Evil and the Dark Lord lurk."

"Will the Evil ones not just watch the Academy?" asked the King "And identify everyone who comes."

"They would if they could" said Gregory "But the Servants of Light confound their minds if they come within miles of the place and we ward the premises and the approaches from scrying even from a distance."

"Ah" said the King "So you are in fact wizards, just as everyone suspects."

"Some of us are, Majesty. If a wizard is chosen to become a Knight, he is still a wizard. In fact, his magical powers are increased greatly. As you will come to know, when, your initiation comes about."

"I know, I know. When, I am fully grown. When I reach my majority" replied Killian. "Isn't that something to ponder Grayhawk? I am old enough to be crowned King but not old enough to become a Knight!"

"Well Majesty, I will convey your complaint to the All Father directly if you wish it" said Lord Gregory with a smile.

"Now now, Your Lordship. Let's not be too hasty there. I don't mind waiting. A rule is a rule, you know" said the King waving his hands. "No need to involve the Gods unnecessarily!"

"The point here is this" said Gregory looking at Grayhawk's unspoken question on his face. "Killian was chosen at his coronation, but cannot accept or be initiated until his twenty first birthday which by ancient rule is when all men reach what is called their majority, or full grown manhood."

"Are all Kings chosen thusly" asked Grayhawk. "No, they are not." replied Gregory. "Most are never chosen. Killian's father was chosen, but his Grandfather was not. The choices are never explained. It is said, I believe in the ancient runes of Norda, that the skein of our lives was woven long ago by Odranna, whom we know as the All Father."

"That is true" said Grayhawk, "Every Rungar child is taught that from the time they can walk."

"So we are bound to do, that which we are born to do?" asked the King.

"Well, to a certain degree, Majesty. There are choices and decisions which affect the outcome of our lives. At some point in life, right up to the moment of our death, each must choose whether to accept the Light or go into the Darkness. Each side promises great rewards both spiritual and material. Both the Light and the Dark offer and promise eternal life, but on different planes. Exactly just what sort of "eternal life" is not fully explained but left up to the imagination? Choose carefully! For the choice is irrevocable and forever is a long, long time." Lord Gregory drained his glass at that point and placed it upon the table.

They all stood in silent thought for a few moments, until Gregory cleared his throat. "And with that your Majesty, if I have your permission, I will take my leave. I have much correspondence to prepare in order to arrange Lord Grayhawk's ceremony and then the trip to Solace."

"You have my permission to leave us Lord Gregory" said the King. At that Gregory turned and went out of the door, closing it behind him.

"Solace, Majesty, Lord Gregory is going to Solace?" asked Grayhawk.

"No My Lord you will be going to Solace to receive some high office within the Order. You will be leaving soon after your initiation and the trip there and back will be several months long. Lord Gregory will be staying here with me, as my primary counsel until your return."

"I see!" said Grayhawk. "Looks like I am going to be a very busy fellow for a while. And I still don't know what I'm supposed to do around here."

"Well" said the King "I promise that while you are gone I will compile a list of your duties for you to go by."

"Excellent! Sire, just don't start any wars without me."

"Agreed" said the King. "I won't."

The King then called for a meal to be brought and the two of them ate and discussed the affairs of state which were currently being reviewed. Killian made a number of decisions and with input from Grayhawk, did issue several edicts of change to old policies and added a few new ones, until late afternoon was upon them. The King began yawning and said "Enough of this! I fear I will go blind reading these parchments. Little wonder that scholars and scribes are such irritable people."

As so they adjourned to the exercise yard for an hour's work with swords to relieve tension as much as to keep in practice. The King was already a fine swordsman, trained since childhood. Now he was learning to fight with two blades in the Rungar style.

The evening was spent preparing for the trip. Lord Gregory had told him earlier that he would be gone for a month or more and that he should pack for cold mountain weather in Auserlia. Fortunately he had ordered three complete sets of leathers and two new pairs of boots for winter wear, much more expensive ones, commensurate with his new position as warlord. They were somewhat fancier, with a new cape, and new under garments, including a thick lamb's wool gambeson for wear under chain mail. So he had everything needed for such a journey already. Almost as though he had known that he would be going on a trip. Makes you wonder, doesn't it?

At any rate, he was glad. He sharpened his blades, cleaned and oiled all of his leather gear. He even uncased and strung his great bow. He made a quick trip down to the postern yard and fired a few arrows to check his arm and his aim. Both proved to be good. Grayhawk was satisfied that he was ready.

Chapter Six

The morning dawned clear and bright. Grayhawk and Lord Gregory joined the King in the military mess where he had breakfast every morning with his soldiers, the same as his father before him. A leisurely meal and all ate heartily. Afterward in the hallway they took leave of the King and went directly to the stables, where their bags were waiting, mounted and rode out of a small sally port instead of the main gate. So as not to be seen by anyone, who might be watching the main gates. They rode quickly on a little known trail that brought them back to the main road a good four miles outside the gates to the city. They had no escorts and both were wearing plain cavalry courier uniforms.

Riding as hard as possible with pack animals and stopping for a break, every two hours, for a half an hour. To give the horses a break, some water to drink, and a handful of grain. They made excellent time and arrived at the Academy gate just at dark. In time enough to still have a hot meat and a hot bath, followed by a game of darts and a couple mugs of ale.

In spite of his protests, Grayhawk was received as Royalty, according to his rank, and billeted in the King's chamber. Much to his chagrin he was waited on "hand and foot" as the saying goes. At bed time there was a fire in the grate, big enough to roast a pig. The bed was huge, way too soft, the pillows were the size of grain sacks and there were more comforters than he had ever seen before. Quite a playground, he thought. Too bad this is an all male institution. A couple of wenches in here and a man could really enjoy himself. Anyway, with a short sword and a dirk under his huge pillow, he slept like a King.

Up at first light, he breakfasted in the Great Hall with the Cadets. A good hot porridge of oats with butter and honey, sausage, and small beer warmed in crockery mugs. Then two full hours on the weapons ground with the cadets both in drill and sparring. Grayhawk sweated more than he had in a very long time. He kept pace with sixteen and eighteen year olds. By his presence and participation, he made many a friend this day.

After bathing and dressing in one of his new leather sets, a dark green, banded collar, hip length tunic, with a Rungar style embossed hawk device on the left breast that buttoned across the right breast and down the side, a broad brown leather belt with dirk at the cross draw position over tight fitting, dark green leather breeches tucked into the tops of knee high, brown leather, cavalry style boots with his dagger in the right one.

As Warlord, Grayhawk, was entitled to go armed at all times, even to ceremonial functions, where arms are forbidden. Though he wore the gold medallion, which was the symbol of his office, this day he carried no sword.

As the noon hour approached, so began the arrival of the Temple Knights, in ones and twos, on horseback. Most were dressed as though on a hunting trip. Some were carrying cased bows, while others carried boar spears or throwing javelins. All wore swords and dirks and a hooded cape. All had the military bearing and presence of a Knight.

Since Lord Gregory was busy with preparation, Grayhawk took it upon himself to greet each Knight as he arrived. Though he had seen most of them prior to today, he only knew a few by name. All of them greeted him as Brother and were genuinely pleased to be greeted by him. Several of the older Brothers had retainers with them, but most had come alone with only a packhorse.

All of whom, so it would seem belong to various hunting clubs and lodges and whenever they need to meet, a hunting trip is arranged. Some had left home three days ago, some of the closer ones this morning. All would arrive back home over the next few days with fresh game, hides and trophies, provided by the foresters who are closely allied to the Order.

By early afternoon all fifty of the Brothers had arrived and have been quartered and unpacked their gear. For the most part they were gathered in the Great Hall, visiting with one another, partaking of some refreshments and talking about the upcoming ceremony.

The afternoon seemed to have lasted a long time. However, it finally ended at the 6th hour and all were called to the collation repast. The traditional dinner meal before a lodge meeting, even though at this meal, most present were not members of the lodge. They, the cadets and cadre, were certainly aware of the event about to take place even though they were not a party to it.

The meal and fellowship afterward lasted for nigh on to two hours. It was a long time to be at mess in a military school environment. Finally at a few minutes before the eighth hour Lord Gregory rang the bell on the head table signaling an end to the gathering. The Cadets and their Cadre filed out to their evening tasks and studies.

Lord Gregory and about half of the Knights assembled took their leave and repaired to an identical, Great Hall below this one. Not many people knew of the second Great Hall's existence. There was only one entrance and that was a stair way in the Preceptor's study, hidden well behind a sliding bookcase.

This other Hall has been the home of the Keltani Lodge of Temple Knights for over two hundred years now. It is a large room some fifteen paces wide by thirty paces long with a small alter in the center of the floor. Which sits on top of, an inlaid mosaic Templar Blood Cross, which consists of four red spear points going towards the middle, and their V shaped bases pointing out to the four cardinal points of the compass. Each point a full two pace's long. Between each point at equal distance from the center an engraved candle base the thickness of a man's thigh reaching to chest height. Each holding a thick candle, as long as a man's forearm. These candles represent the four cardinal elements, Earth, Water, Wind and Fire.

The room is laid out lengthwise from west to east. The entrance is in the west end. In the east end there sits a throne chair on a dais where sits the preceptor during the meetings as commander of Knights. Above the chair, hung from the ceiling on a gold chain, there is a five sided lamp with crystal panes. It is about the size of a man's head. It glows constantly with a bright blue light that cannot be extinguished. It will turn a blood red if a lie is ever told in Lodge. The Lamp is imbued with a magical power given by the Servants of the Light. This one has never yet turned red in over two hundred years of meetings. Should it ever happen, the person telling the lie will be summarily executed by the four sentry Knights, one standing in each corner of the Lodge during meetings, each holding a razor sharp halberd at his side.

It is said, but not known for sure, that no servant of the dark can live in the glow of the blue lamp which is known as the Pentameter of Truth.

The ceiling and the north wall of the Hall are painted a dark blue and inlaid with faceted glass and crystals to resemble the night sky. The other walls are painted light blue to show the light of day. Along the north wall are two rows of chairs for the member Knights to sit during the meeting.

On the west wall in front of the entrance is the station of the Adjutant Major. He is the second in command of the Knights. On the South wall is the station of the Captain of Horse and beside him to his right the Secretary/Chief Squire. All are seated at writing tables facing the center of lodge. Behind the Adjutant Major at the entry doors are the two Knight Sentinels armed with short half shaft, pike point, battle axes, to guard against unlawful entry. They are razor sharp highly tempered steel.

It must be mentioned that Squires (Sergeants at Arms) of each of the Knights are also fully fledged members of the Lodge and share equal voting and speaking rights in Formal Lodge procedures. Because of the recent assassination of the King and the attempts to overthrow the Royal Line, all but the Chief Squire have remained at the homes of the Knights for security reasons. But have, if they so desire, given their proxy vote to their Chief Knight to vote in their stead. This may be done, under Temple Law, by either side. In most cases the squire, is also Major Domo, of the Knights home or keep.

This fact is also a well kept secret of the Lodge. "The Lodge" being the way the Order is most commonly spoken of by its members. Squire/Sergeant at Arms/Major Domo positions are held in high esteem and honor. In most cases they are permanent family positions handed down from father to son. In some case the family ties are very close, going back many generations.

Grayhawk was trying to absorb all of this new information as fast as it was being given to him. But he knew if given a test on all of it, he would be lucky to remember half. He was also absolutely mystified as to just how and why he had been chosen to become one of them. Though admittedly he was both pleased and honored by all of it.

He sat waiting now in the Great Hall with three Knights who were detailed as his handlers and guides. At a few minutes before the ninth hour, they rose and bid him to accompany them into the Preceptors study. There they informed him that for reasons of custom and lodge rule going back to antiquity, the ancient form of Keltani is spoken in ceremonies. Through the hidden entry way, down a full flight of stairs to a small candle lit room, in which there were six chairs. Three stood against each wall. On the far wall there were two iron bound, thick wooden doors, which were closed.

The two doors were embossed, the left with the Templar Blood Cross and the right with crossed Sabers. Both doors were done in heavy polished pewter. Above the door across the curve of the arch engraved into the stone was "Let no evil pass these portals." Seated before the doors was a brother Knight in full chain mail and hood, holding a short sword in each hand, lying flat on his knees in a crossed pattern.

As the party stepped off of the stairs onto the chamber floor the brother Knight rose from his seated position. He assumed a left foot forward fighting stance both short swords at the ready and stated in a loud voice "Hold! Who approaches? Identify thy selves, and know ye this. Be ye Hell Spawn or spies of the dark ye shall not pass whilst I live!" His voice reverberated in the stone chamber. No doubt this was a signal to those within. The escort party halted. One brother Knight stood in front of Grayhawk and two behind him forming a triangle or pyramid.

The brother in front spoke up in reply, also in a loud voice. "Hail! Brother Warden of the Portals, we are seekers of the light, and knowledge, desirous of gaining entrance from the darkness into light."

The brother warden responded with "I see before me three who are garbed as brother Knights and one stranger. By what right dost thou demand entry into this hall of light?"

The brother again responded "By right of the sign and the word, and upon my honor as a Knight in the service of God."

"Show then this sign" said the Warden "In such a manner as only I may see it."

With his back to Grayhawk, the brother Knight raised both of his hands to the middle of his chest with his elbows out to the side and made a sign that could only be seen from the front.

"I recognize this sign, advance thee then to the point of my right sword and give me a word in a low voice that only I might hear."

While Grayhawk and the other two brother Knights remained still, the brother walked forward about five paces until the point of the Wardens right hand short sword was touching the center of his chest. He then leaned forward and spoke a word in a low voice and then took two steps backward.

The Warden lowered his swords, stepped back into a feet together position and with a master swordsman's move, spun and sheathed both swords in one fluid movement.

"I am satisfied" he stated "Thou art, who thee claim to be. What of this stranger in thy company? Do thee vouch safe his presence here?"

"Verily" said the brother, "He is in our charge as a brother candidate under escort to this place for examination and acceptance as a brother of the Order."

"Then let him approach the portal for my examination" said the Warden. The brother stepped aside and motioned to Grayhawk. "Come forward Brother Candidate."

Grayhawk and the two brother Knights behind him took five paces forward until they were in front of the Warden.

"I welcome thee Brother Candidate on behalf of this Lodge of Brother Knights. Do not tell me yet, thy name, in the event that I must refuse thee entrance. But instead answer me truthfully, on thy honor, the following. I pray thee answer simply Aye! Or Nay! Such, as the case may be." "Is this application for acceptance an act of thine own free will?"

"Aye it is" Grayhawk responded.

"Did anyone promise thee payment or recompense for thy attendance here?

"Nay"

"Art thou of legal age, sound of mind, body and spirit?"

"Aye"

"That being the case, I am required to make one further inquiry of thee, before I can grant admittance. Think carefully upon thy answer. From what source or power dost thy Faith and Beliefs derive?"

"From the All Father" replied Grayhawk.

"Thou art found worthy and entrance is granted. Wait while I inform the Preceptor and those assembled within of thy presence. Now, give me thy name and that of thy people."

"I am Grayhawk of the Rungar."

"Well met Grayhawk of the Rungar, Blademaster of Norda, and be assured thy name is known amongst us. I am Owen of Dan, Blademaster of Danfinia."

"Well met" replied Grayhawk with a slight bow. Among Blademasters a slight bow is considered proper and polite.

At that point the Warden turned and picked up his chair, moving it from in front of the doors to the right side of the portal. There also stood a waist height table, about four feet long with a pair of red silk cords of the same length lying upon it.

The Warden then stepped up to the double doors and banged his mailed fist loudly three times. Then after a few seconds wait, he knocked twice more, and then once. The right door then opened partially and a voice from within demanded

"Who comes here signing upon the portal door?"

"Owen, Warden of the Portal, to announce the arrival of a candidate, whom I have examined and found worthy of entrance for examination."

"His name and people" said the voice from within.

"He is Grayhawk of the Rungar, a Blademaster of Norda" said Owen.

"Have the candidate prepared and in waiting while the Preceptor is informed. Has he proper escort?"

"Aye!" replied Owen "He is accompanied by three Brother Knights of the Order."

"All is well!" said the voice. "You will be informed in due course" and the door closed with a dull boom.

Owen turned back to face Grayhawk and the others saying "Now brother candidate I must call upon thee to trust me as a brother. For no candidate may enter the Lodge in possession of weapons, or any metallic object. I must ask thee to place thy weapons, thy purse, jewelry, buckles and any other metal as thee may possess upon yon table. I give thee my word bond as a brother Knight that all will be here just as thee has left it, when thee doth return. Upon my life's blood! Wilt thou trust me?"

"I will" said Grayhawk, knowing that if anyone tried to take his belongings they would first have to kill Sir Owen. That would be no easy task. The two Knights clasped forearms in the "Lion's Paw" grip of formal agreement.

Grayhawk then removed his sword, short sword and dagger, even the small thin one from his boot. He removed his seal and chain of office from around his neck. Then his purse, and lastly the wide leather belt around his waist which held a large silver buckle. "That is all of the metal on my person" he stated, holding out his arms.

"My brother, thy word will suffice" said Sir Owen. "If needed the silken cords on the table may be used as a belt" pointing to them.

"Ah, yes" said Grayhawk, taking one and placing it around his waist and tying it. "I can see where it would be embarrassing to have ones trousers fall down upon entering."

"Most assuredly" replied Sir Owen "And it has happened, and trust me, those brothers are never allowed to forget that moment."

"Ah! I can well imagine" said Grayhawk, smiling.

"Now" said Sir Owen "Let us stand in front of the Portal and await permission to enter. Now brother Grayhawk, as candidate thee shall stand here in the middle, with one of your escorts on either side and one behind thee. I must remain without to guard the Portal against evil cowans and eavesdroppers who might wish to spy upon these proceedings. Lastly I am to inform thee, that as a brother, thou hast no enemies in this place, though thee are unarmed, thy person is protected by three. These proceedings are ceremonial and allegorical. Learn from them. Wait here at the portal until thee are bid enter." With that the Warden moved away to where he had previously sat his chair, picked it up and placed it behind Grayhawk and his escorts. He drew his swords and sat down, facing back towards the staircase. During all of this his escorts had said nothing, merely standing off to one side looking slightly bemused, as though all of this was normal and familiar to them.

A long moment passed, with the four of them standing facing the double doors in silence. Then both doors suddenly opened wide inwardly without a sound. Grayhawk stood looking into a long, cavernous looking hall, lit by large candles in sconces of polished bronze along each wall, six to a side, each candle over a foot tall encased in a glass chimney so they burned bright and steady. Along the left side or north wall, a row of heavy wood chairs with arms and high backs. Grayhawk could see forty or so brother Knights seated in those chairs.

In the middle of the room was a low alter stone with a kneeling bench in front of it, of a size for one person, there were four large candle holders, each about four foot tall. Upon each a single candle the thickness of a man's forearm and two feet tall. The holders were situated one on either side of the altar, at the four points of the compass, at about 4 feet distance. The altar was facing the East or far end of the hail.

At the far end of the Hall, a good thirty paces from the door, was a large throne like chair with a writing table. In that chair sat the Preceptor of Keltan, Lord Gregory, clad in chain mail with a white tabard on which were crossed swords under a blood cross. Across the front of the table lay a sheathed sword. Above his head a lantern was suspended by a chain from the roof of the hall. The lantern was brass (or perhaps gold) five sided, with blue glass panes and a candle within. The blue light symbolic of the presence of the Supreme Being. On the wall behind the Preceptor hung a large plaque representation of the all seeing eye of the Supreme Being. On either side of the plaque a wall sconce with candle. All of which were situated in the East from where the sun rises.

To his right along the south there were three writing tables and chairs, each with a Knight seated at them facing the alter or center of the Hall. They also were clad in chain mail with white tabards. Upon each tabard a symbol, the farthest from him had a short sword and a key crossed. The Seneschal or second in command, the next had crossed feather quills over a horizontal short sword, the Secretary or Runes keeper, in front of him on the writing table a large book lay open with ink pot and quills. The closest to him has the all Seeing Eye with crossed arrows behind, the Chaplain, also apparently an archer. All were well set up, middle aged men with beards.

To his left and right he noticed as they took their first steps into the room, in the corners, in shadow were four Knights in black mail, and with black tabards edged in silver with crossed battle axe symbols. Each was armed with a short halberd, sort of a half sword, half spear with a pointed spike for a butt cap. A deadly close quarter weapon, when wielded by an expert. The black mailed Knights are all experts. Only the deadliest fighters are allowed to wear the black. It is said that even the Darkness fears them.

Guided by his escort, Grayhawk walked forward into the hall, until they were behind the altar. There they stopped as a soft dull boom echoed off the walls indicating the closing of the doors behind them. "Well!" thought Grayhawk, smiling slightly to himself "I would not like to fight this bunch to get out of here."

After a long moment of total silence, Lord Gregory's baritone voice spoke out. "Who comes here? And for what purpose?" The escort on Grayhawk's right spoke up.

"We are three Brother Knights of the Order, escorting a candidate for admission into the Light and Rights of membership of this Holy Order. Having been tested and tried, in life and in battle. He has been found worthy and well qualified, and comes well recommended."

"It is then an act of his own free will and accord?" asked Lord Gregory.

"He has so stated" answered the escort.

"No promise of gain of either personal fame or fortune has been made to him?"

"None has been made" came the answer.

"It is well then" said Lord Gregory. "Let the candidate stand alone at the altar and henceforth answer for himself in these proceedings."

At this point the escorts moved to a position some five paces behind Grayhawk All of the other Knights in the room came forward and formed a half circle on either side of the alter going from the three escort Brothers, left and right to a point in front of the alter. Lord Gregory came down from the dais to a position directly in front which closed the circle.

Lord Gregory then drew from his sash a gold and silver Ankh, an ancient symbol, meaning many different things to many different peoples. This particular one had a blue teardrop shaped stone in the top or loop. The stone was glowing faintly. He began to intone a prayer or chant in a language Grayhawk had not before here heard. The stone began to glow brighter and blue/white rays began to emanate from it, playing about the chamber like reflected beams from a glitter ball only more intense and warm on the skin.

"Approach then, and kneel before the altar" intoned Lord Gregory. Grayhawk stepped forward to the altar and knelt, placing his hands on the cool marble surface.

Again Lord Gregory spoke in the deep voice. "Grayhawk of Norda, in whom dost thou place thy trust? Wherein lays thy faith?" Grayhawk answered "My trust and my faith lie with the All Father, Lord of the Universe." Somewhere far away, a clear bell rang out.

"What sayest thou then of the Dark Lord?" came Gregory's deep voice. "I do reject him utterly" stated Grayhawk "In all his many guises." Again the clear tone of a bell rang out.

"Art thou then prepared to dedicate thy life to the ultimate defeat of the Dark Lord and his minions?"

"I am"

"Art thou prepared to shed thy life blood in defense of a worthy brother or his family?

"I am" "Art thou prepared to vouch safe, on penalty of death, the works and secrets of this Holy Order?"

"I Am" For a third time came the sound of a bell being rung once, as though far off.

"Arise Templari" Lord Gregory said to Grayhawk. "Thou art now accepted and consecrated as a Temple Knight."

As Grayhawk stood the radiating blue/white light from the ankh went out and Lord Gregory returned it to his sash. "Allow me be the first to welcome thee as a Brother Knight and to say how pleased I am to have thee join the order. This ceremony tonight was brief of necessity. If thou were but a young and inexperienced warrior, it would have been much longer. But, know this, within the light thy heart and soul were searched and tested. Had thee been found false or wanting the bell would not have rung and thy life would have ended here in this room. It has happened only twice in the history of the Order. Both were adepts of the Dark Lord sent to infiltrate."

"Know then that our Order is at least fifteen thousand years old. Possibly as much as sixty thousand years. It was begun in an age long gone when magic was far stronger in the world than it is now. The Knights were imbued with powers greater than those of today's sorcerers. There was a war of such proportion and power, that the face of the world was virtually destroyed or changed, and a five thousand year period of cold and ice prevailed. So bad was it that it almost wiped out mankind, and did in fact wipe out some other races of beings. But the All Father did not want humans to perish so he allowed some groups here and there to survive. Amongst those groups were the Templari, carefully hidden from the Dark Lord, disguised as warring nomad tribes barely surviving the elements. While during the cold times, the surviving servants of the Dark Lord were driven underground into the earth and only survived in a few places. And the rest of mankind was reduced to uncivilized tribes, of hunter-gatherers living in patches here and there. This condition lasted for millennia"

"Since the great warming trend began again, these groups have begun to emerge as civilizations again began to form and to build. The Dark Lords servants have also emerged from under the earth and once again mix with the human race in order to subvert all and convert those they can to the service of the Dark Lord."

"During this period the Dark Lord has become aware of our continued existence and has once again set his minions to the task of destroying the Order and everyone connected to it in any way. We are his strongest enemy. He believes that once we are totally destroyed the conquest of the entire world will be within his reach."

"For this reason we seek to make our order stronger. We do this by seeking out certain warriors who we believe possess the mind and abilities to fight the darkness and the shadows. When they have been examined under the true light of heaven as thee have just been, as all of we gathered with you have been. They are then introduced to the arts and powers of the ancient magic, which are based in Truth and Enlightenment of both the mind and the spirit."

"Each warrior's strengths and abilities are different. Each serves in a different capacity. We are all equal when standing on the floor of a lodge or temple. This is called "on the level." Here every man's voice and vote has equal value and weight, whether he is commoner or King."

"Your own people, Grayhawk, are one of the nomad tribes. The Rungar were chosen because of the strength of their belief in Odranna, which is one of the names of the All Father. Long ago your people were nomads, wandering the high plans of Mondola and Indusa. When the cold and ice came they were pushed as far south as Jarudi and Saladan. When the ice retreated, the Rungar came north, once again to occupy their ancient homeland of Norda."

"Odranna's Chosen, the warrior-priests who trained thee, are a branch of the Templari Dark knights. They live and train in the underworld in order to enable them to fight against the demons and their spawn, who are the true people of the Dark Lord. It is for this reason so many Blademasters like thee are chosen to become Templari. While others remain in the caverns of Norda to become Odranna's Chosen. Not all become one or the other. Some Blademasters are content to remain as mercenaries in one country or the other. Some return to Norda after exile, to lead ordinary lives. Some, very few in number, become servants of the Dark Lord. They are the only humans the demons will allow in their domain, except, of course, the ones who are brought as food."

"Those warriors who turn to the service of the Dark Lord become members of the Blades of Shai-Tan, the equivalent of our Dark Knights. Shai-Tan is one of the Dark Lords ancient names, carried over from the olden times. They are trained as adepts of the Black Arts. It is said that when one of them is killed, he instantly is reborn as a Demon, in a cauldron of pure evil, but they are seldom seen by anyone"

"Tonight, Grayhawk, you have begun the journey on the road to becoming an adept of the Light. I congratulate thee on thy selection. This ceremony and lecture is concluded. My brothers let us adjourn to the dining hall above and sit in collation and fellowship with our newest member."

Where upon, all of the brothers trooped out of the chamber, and up the stairs to the dining hall of the Academy, there a great feast had been laid out. The toasting, drinking and eating went on until the cock crowed, and a good time was had by one and all.

Chapter Seven

Grayhawk awoke late in the morning, after what seemed like a long night of strange dreams and the feeling that someone or something was watching him, something evil.

Not to mention the hangover from all of the brandy consumed during the night while toasting everything and everyone. After an hour in the famed Academy hot baths, and a good meal of kippered herring, black bread, plum pudding and tea, He felt good. Ready for the journey back to the city and to getting back to his duties as the King's Prime Advisor. He dressed for travel in his black leathers. He packed his kit and checked his room to see that he had forgotten nothing. He hoisted his own bags rather than calling for one of the cadets and headed down to the main hall.

Though it was late morning, almost the midday hour, Grayhawk felt good. Entering the great hail he immediately noticed a goodly number of Brother Knights present. Most in full mail with tabards showing the blood cross emblem. As he walked into the hall he was acknowledged by all. Both friendly and cordial greetings were exchanged and the level of conversation seemed to increase with his entry.

He scanned the room looking for Lord Gregory. He was not present. Owen of Dan came forward from a group of Knights on the far side of the Hall.

"Good Morrow! Brother Grayhawk" he smiled, extending his hand.

"Good Morrow Brother Owen" he replied as they clasped forearms. "What tidings bring all of these Brother Knights in mail together? No ill occurrences have transpired while I slept I hope."

"Nay, my Brother" said Owen. "These Brothers are gathered here to act as your escort."

"Escort? Brother Owen I need no escort to return to the King's City!" he replied.

"I doubt that not!" said Owen grinning, "If that was where you are going. But you do need an escort to Solace. Which is by the order of both Lord Gregory and the King is where you will be going."

"What! So soon?" said Grayhawk. "Well, if that is the case my steel is sharp, my bags are packed and I am bathed and fed. Though I must admit a little embarrassed!"

"Why so?" asked Owen, looking puzzled. "Well it would seem that I have kept all of you Brothers standing around in steel underwear whilst I lounged the morning away in scented bathwater, sipping tea and stuffing my face!" Now all the Brothers who had been gathering around the two were laughing.

"I'm quite sure; my Lord that all who will ride behind you this day will appreciate the fresh scented air." There followed more laughter at this.

Looking around at all of the mail clad Knights Grayhawk asked "Brother Owen would not a smaller group draw less attention? Why then, are there so many Knights and Sergeants?"

"We have already drawn the attention of the Dark Forces, my Lord. When you heard the peal of the bell last night, they heard it also, across the astral plane. Even as we speak they search for our location. Here we are shielded from view, so to speak. But sometime over the next few days they will sense our movement and begin to move forces against us, both real and magical."

"They will make every attempt to capture or to kill us. Especially you! The Dark Lord needs information, since thus far he has not been able to infiltrate the Order. He relies on torturing captives, even innocent ones, looking for some way to plan a cohesive attack. An attack could change the balance of power. So we do **everything** that we can, to mislead and confused his minions, whenever and however possible."

After a quick lunch for all the Brothers, Grayhawk was still full from his late breakfast, fifty one Knights and Sergeants, along with twenty pack horses, mounted up and rode out of the Academy. They headed southeast towards the crossing at the river forks. They crossed the river in late afternoon with no incidents. They turned due east and headed into the deep forest on a little known and seldom traveled trail. After a few miles they let the trail and headed more south-easterly.

Grayhawk had always had a feeling that the fabled Keep of Solace was in Auserlia. He kept his thoughts to himself as he rode. Long through the afternoon they rode. Often they were moving slowly through the deep forest, at other times moving at a canter for several leagues. Stopping only twice for rest breaks and to give the horses a bit of grain and some water. An hour before sunset, scouts were sent ahead to find a camp site for the night

When the main body caught up, the scouts guided them a good mile north of the direction of travel through some very thick woods. Exiting the woods they found themselves in a large meadow. In the center was a ring of Oak Trees, very old and large Oak trees. "Some sort of Holy Place" said Grayhawk, to no one in particular.

"Yes" said Sir Owen from his right. "Holy and Ancient! Can you not feel the power?"

"Aye" said Grayhawk, "I can. Whose place is - or was this?"

"No one knows for sure" answered Owen "these trees are at least six hundred years old."

"I believe it" said Grayhawk as they rode up to the circle and dismounted. "Why, look at the size of their trunks it would take five men holding hands to go around them. How many are they?" Grayhawk asked.

"There are thirty six my Lord. Each about three paces apart."

"Thirty six, hmm, I wonder, does that represent one tree for each ten points on a compass."

"Sounds reasonable to me" said Sir Owen, "but, anyway, here is where we camp as we have oft in the past, because while within the circle we are invisible to the Dark Lord."

By full dark camp was set up within the trees. Supper was being prepared, boiled white beans with salt pork, trail bread and wild green onions. Ah! Life on the trail, what a wonder! If you poured the beans over the trail bread to soften it, and added a few green onions. The meal wasn't bad, and after an apple for dessert, a couple of pipes of good tabac and some brandy. A pleasant night under the stars passed with no incident.

Awake at the first sounds of stirring in the camp, at about an hour before first light. Within half an hour everything was packed. They were mounted and moving south east. By full light they were over a mile from the campsite and back on the track, just south of the one that they had been on the day before.

On this day they traveled hard and far. A long ten hours in the saddle, with few breaks and a fifteen minute lunch stop. At about two hours before sunset they came upon the remains of a steading. What was a small village, inside of a log and earthen berm. This one had been sacked and burned long ago, and judging from the growth weed and bushes, no one had been here since, at least that is how it looked.

The place actually was a well camouflaged way station, and supply cache. Hidden under sections of the floor of each of the ruined buildings was a storage area, stable or quarters area. Within ten minutes of their arrival the place was just as deserted as before, at least that is how it looked.

There were sentry boxes in hollow spaces in some of the standing walls. At full dark all ramp ways and passages to the surface were closed, except for the drop chutes under each of the six sentry positions. They were left open, both as escape routes for sentries and to help with the ventilation.

It was at mid night guard change that the first ill foreboding came. That gradually increasing feeling that something is going bad wrong. Or that you are being watched by an enemy. Within the span of ten long minutes, everyone was awake. Two minutes after that, everyone was up, weapons in hand, looking about the dimly lit chamber for the source of this apprehension.

Less than a minute later, the first wave of fear hit. It stuck all at once like a wall of pressure. Mind numbing, eye bulging, cold sweat, with the metallic taste of fear in the mouth! Fear! Many went to their knees. A few lost consciousness and fell to the floor. A few began praying out loud.

Grayhawk stood rigid, still, at first unable to move for what seemed an eternity. It was actually only a few seconds. Then a single thought burst through in his mind, this is DRAGONFEAR!! He had heard of it, of course, all warriors had. But all Dragon kind had been killed a thousand years ago, or so they said. Well "they" were wrong!

Now a second wave hit and it was even more intense than the first. It was almost palpable, like you should be able to touch it. It was on you like a cheap cloak. Men were collapsing, weeping like children, vacant stares on some. Wild eyed panic on other faces. One screamed shrilly and drove his own dagger into his chest, falling to the floor, quite dead.

Grayhawk struggled to find his voice; it was as though his throat were constricted. At first barely a croak, then as he gained control of more of his own mind "Dragon Fear!" he shouted "Dragon Fear. It's not real. Shut it out of your mind." Shouting louder now. "Control your mind! Do not fear! Fear is the mind killer. Control, maintain control."

At first they glared at him as though he was the source of it all, then at each other. Glaring as in hatred, swords and daggers clenched in white knuckle fists, turning this way and that looking for an enemy to strike.

The level of intensity seemed to plateau at that point. Men sagged, leaning into the walls or on each other for support, shaking their heads trying to clear thought and regain control.

Then the roaring began, as though a giant furnace had been opened, accompanied by a rapidly increasing smell of sulfur and burning fish oil.

Down one of the sentry chutes and bursting into the chamber, there erupted, a ten-foot long gout of yellow-orange flame, catching two Knights and fully engulfing them. Turning them instantly into human torches, they never even had a chance to scream. Literally melting them into two heaps of glowing embers, in less time than it takes to realize what has happened.

Again the gout of flame shot into the room which by now was half filled, from the top down with smoke and soot. The temperature of the room was becoming unbearable. Grayhawk fell to his knees gasping and croaking, "Get down. Everyone get down on the floor." A third time the flames came and the chamber was even hotter and now spinning. Then the darkness came and nothing.

Grayhawk was pulled back from a dark, warm, comfortable place by a whoosh of cool air and the echoing sound of voices. It was like being pulled out of a dark hole back into the light.

As full consciousness returned, sort of all at once, he became aware that he was face down on a stone floor. He was extremely tired. His face felt like he had a bad sunburn. There was the smell of singed hair, burnt fish oil, and sulfur. Along with the sickening sweet smell of burnt human flesh. The combination was making him want to heave up his dinner.

There was cool air coming from somewhere, and the smoke seemed to be moving and lessening. The voices were coming clearer now. Sir Owen saying "everyone stay where you are for a few minutes while the smoke clears some. The ramp door is open now and fresh air is coming in. Be patient, we will get to all of you very soon." He could hear some moaning from here and there, choking and coughing coupled with the sound of men beginning to move about, trying to get their bearings.

Grayhawk then rolled onto his back as the air cleared even more. He began to see lights as some got lanterns and candles going.

"By the All Fathers beard" he thought to himself "we have been attacked by Dragons!" Creatures supposed to be long extinct. Killed in some long ago war.

Within an hour all who could were up and moving about, though, with difficulty and slowly. It seems that a bout with Dragon Fear is akin to a bout with Death. It leaves a person weak in mind, body and soul. Breathing all that smoke and soot didn't help either. Some were burned, thankfully none badly, though none were in condition to fight or ride. Many had blank expressions, or vague questioning looks. By first light many were still wheezing and coughing. Most were covered in the black soot and a greasy, nasty smelling, extremely hard to clean mess.

Well into the noon hour, it took for Sir Owen and a handful of Knights and Sergeants to get the entire group out into the open air, cleaned up, treated for wounds and fed a meal. Grayhawk worked alongside. Helping wherever and however he could.

During the course of all of this Grayhawk and Sir Owen surveyed the site, reading the signs and talking to everyone still alive. They dug around in the rubble here and there trying to ascertain what exactly had happened here.

By late afternoon they had a consensus of opinion. One, they really were attacked by two dragons who came in from the south, broadcasting their fear before them, like beacons of light. Secondly, that three of the Sentries had been frozen by the Dragon Fear and had died at their posts, before they could jump down the escape chutes and close the steel doors behind them. Thirdly, the dragons then used their flame breath to try to kill everything in the chambers, blowing down through the sentry chutes. In one of the chambers the pressure had blown open the ramp door. This was a chamber where a third of the horses were stabled. Since Dragons love horse flesh, they had then fully ripped into that chamber and had a feast, leaving when they had gorged themselves. Four, this probably saved everyone who was still alive. When Dragons are done feasting, they return to their lair and sleep for a week or two. Five, the Dragons had been sent, specifically to their location, looking to kill everyone in this party. Which meant, of course, that the Dark Lord knows we are headed for Solace and why. So we will be attacked again as soon as he knows we survived this attack.

The attack has cost the group seven Knights, eight Sergeants, and twelve horses. Their remains were buried, at least what little could be found, in one hole in the ground with no ceremony. That would happen at another time. Ceremonies and invocations make ripples in the planes between the worlds. None could be afforded just now.

The following morning at first light, the thirty six remaining souls, mounted up and rode out towards the south east. They spent another long grueling day, short rest stops, and hard hours in the saddle. In addition to being on guard in case of further attack. None came, and after a sunrise to sunset hard day's ride, during which they had covered twice the normal daily march distance, they came at last to a camp site beside a small lake.

Camp was set up quickly in the gathering darkness. Small sheltered fires were lit. Supper was prepared. Horses and equipment were looked after. Sentry rotations were set. In which Grayhawk insisted on being included, and into a cool evening breeze through the trees, with a three quarter moon shining off of the lake, and in the extreme quiet of the deep forest all around them. They did all collapse into a long quiet and peaceful night.

The next morning after conferring for a bit, it was decided not to break camp until midday, in order to allow the cleaning of all personnel, horses, gear and clothing. And, to allow the animals a mornings rest and graze. A respite much needed by all.

Mounted and moving after the noon meal, they continued at an easy pace until an hour before sunset. Then they turned up into a thick forested area for a mile or more until they came to a rock escarpment taller than a castle wall, where there fell a water fall into a deep pool. The water was cold, clear and good tasting. Here they made camp, built fires, cooked an evening meal, relaxing, smoking a bowl of tabac and sharpening weapons. No one was talking very much.

Another restful and quiet night passed. At first light all were up and moving, packing the camp and seeing to their personal equipment.

As Grayhawk set foot to stirrup and rose into his saddle Sir Owen spoke up.

"My Brothers, loose thy swords in their sheaths. For this day I sense we will do battle."

"Aye!" said Grayhawk "I sense it too! And it will be hard fought." With that they rode out, each absorbed in his own thoughts.

Chapter Eight

Thirty six grim faced fighting men rode out of the camp at the waterfall. All could sense an aura of impending danger. As they rode, double file, they moved through the deep forest along a different track than the one they had come in on. All felt as though they were being watched by some evil thing.

In fact, they were. Many miles away to the south in Spanos, at a monastery of the Dark Lord, sat a senior Dark Priest. In a conjuring chamber next to a pedestal bowl of black liquid he was chanting and casting his evil sight to the north, searching until he detected movement in the deep forest.

Once the target was located he focused his concentration, until moving images of men on horseback appeared. Because of the thick forestation he could not get a clear picture of individuals, but he knew he had found his quarry.

He then swiveled on his stool to a small table on his left. He took up a quill, dipped it in a vial of his own blood diluted with brandy, and wrote a pair of lines in strange runic symbols. This was the official battle code of the Dark Lord, which only he and his demons and priests can read.

He then folded the square of parchment and rolled it. He motioned with his arm and a very large Raven dropped from a ceiling beam and perched on the table. Around his neck on a silver chain he wore a message tube. The priest took the tube opened it, inserted the message and closed the tube. Then looking into the Ravens eyes, he cast a mental picture of another priest at a Drulgar encampment to the north. The bird hopped onto the pedestal and then to the window ledge and out of the window.

As the Raven took flight, the priest fell, face forward onto the writing table in utter exhaustion. Scrying over a long distance takes enormous amounts of physical and mental energy. Not to mention that failure in the Dark Lord's service can be very painful at the least.

Many miles to the north and east Grayhawk and party rode as quietly as possible due east from the rock wall. The forest floor was spongy and soft, helping to muffle their passage.

Over an hour later the large Raven dropped soundlessly out of the sky and landed on a T perch in front of a rune covered animal hide tent, emitting a nauseous squawk as he landed. A priest poked his head out of the tent flap and seeing the bird with the message tube, nodded his head and said "Ah at last." Stepping out of the tent, he approached the Raven, took the tube and chain from around its neck. He opened the tube, shook out the rolled piece of parchment into his hand and opened it. He scanned the lines of runes several times to be sure that he understood the message completely. He then took a small bronze horn from his belt and blew a long flat note.

The Drulgar camp immediately exploded into frantic activity, gibbering in their guttural language as they collapsed their tents and began rolling and packing their gear. Leaving the camp fires burning, and the ground littered with cracked bones which had been sucked dry of marrow, human bones, large and small. These were the remains of their last captives, taken in raids on farms and small villages. For days after their departure the stench of this camp would keep even the wolves away.

Within half an hour they were ready for travel. Divided into two groups, one a group of one hundred or so individuals who formed the attack party, the other forty comprised the reserve force and who brought along the tents and supplies, and they also forged along the way attacking any farm or wagons that they happened upon. Even small hunting parties, when they could ambush them. They dearly love to eat man flesh. It's their favorite.

The Dark Priest conferred briefly with the Drulgar leader then the two of them moved to the head of the attack party. The leader gave a growl and the whole group, headed by their leader and a dark priest moved down the path to the east at a loping run. Drulgar can run as far as forty miles a day if they have to, and still fight when they arrive.

About fifteen miles east and a little south of the Drulgar, Grayhawk, Sir Owen and the thirty four other Knights and Sergeants were riding at a good walking pace, partly to conserve the horses strength, and so they would not blunder into an ambush.

Both parties moved in an easterly direction at a shallow, decreasing angle which would intersect eventually this day. At the present pace and course the Drulgar would be coming from the right rear quadrant. If no alarm or forewarning was given they would run in total silence up to the human party, and then attack from the rear without stopping.

Grayhawk and Sir Owen conferred while riding stirrup to stirrup. Both had experience in these types of fights. Grayhawk was presently saying

"Sir Owen, I feel a presence of evil in the wood this day."

"Aye, my lord, I feel it too!" he answered grimly. "What say you we should do?"

Grayhawk replied. "I believe they are coming from the west, and will, if they can, attack us from the rear. They will come up, as quietly as they can."

"Drulgar, my Lord?" asked Sir Owen.

"Aye, most certainly they are. They would be the only dark forces I can think of, other than Dragons, who could travel that rapidly in order to catch us. Myth has it Dragons will only fight in daylight, when they are attacked."

"I too have heard that in the tales about them. Let us hope that it is true. If Dragons were to catch us here on horseback, even in the forest, I feel we would all die!"

"True enough, so let us do this, increase the pace to a canter for the next hour or so, and then we will stop and prepare a good meal. For I believe we have several hours yet. We will let the horses graze and have some water. Then let us move on at a good pace for another hour or so, all the while looking for some hillock or other defensible high ground, or even a thicket. There we will stop and set up our defenses and let them come to us. For we shall surely be hard pressed, as you know their normal battle group is around a hundred with thirty to forty as reserves."

"A good plan, my Lord" answered Sir Owen, "and both the men and horses will be somewhat rested, if things were to go badly and we had to cut and run."

Most of the group had overheard every word of the conversation and were nodding in agreement as the word was passed to up the pace. In less than an hour they came to a wide shallow stream of clear cold water. Crossing to the other side, they stopped for a meal and to rest the horses. Their supplies were still quite good and so they ate smoked meat, cheese, trail bread, wild onions, drank strong tea and everyone had an apple.

Approximately an hour later, still not quite full midday by the sun, they doused the fires, cinched up their saddles and gear and rode out of the encampment. This time due east. For the better part of two hours they cantered through the woods, crossing streams, shallow draws and gullies, until at last they reached a very large meadow. At the south end of it the ground rose sharply upwards for a good fifty feet to the tree line. Close to an ideal place, to prepare for an attack. There was even a spring a short distance back in the trees.

"Let us make our stand here" announced Grayhawk, as he rode up the incline. "Here we will have the advantage."

"Excellent" said Sir Owen as he dismounted, looking up and down the tree line. "They must gain the top to effectively attack us, whilst we shoot arrows down on them. When they are too close for arrows we will employ lances. If they push us back into the trees then it will be swords and axes."

"And after that?" asked a young Knight.

"After that, why if there is an after that" said Grayhawk, "It will be "To horse! To horse!" and run like hell!" Everyone was laughing. They moved up into the trees, picketed the horses a good fifty paces back from the open. Sir Owen posted a detail of three Knights to guard and tend to the horses, which would remain saddled during the coming fight, in case things go badly and retreat is called for.

Grayhawk returned to the ledge above the meadow and immediately detailed six men to each end of their chosen stand area, to cut as much brush and tree limbs as possible for use as a fire barrier to prevent flanking. In each pile a high mound of kindling was prepared and a lamp full of oil was poured over it. Hopefully that would rapidly flare into the entire brush pile and make it both too large and too hot to break through.

The rest of the party set to, dragging logs out of the forest and felling some of the smaller trees in order to make a makeshift barricade across the front, at the top of the slope. An hour later the defenses, such as they were, were in place. The day had grown quite warm, and all were sweating from their efforts.

Grayhawk and Sir Owen conferred on the conduct of the battle. They decided to divide the line of defense into two. Grayhawk commanded the right side and Sir Owen the left. Everyone in the party was assigned a position.

Grayhawk then ordered that everyone, in turn, from each of the command areas, would go to the pool created by the stream and immerse themselves totally, getting their clothes under the chain mail armor wet, so as to help with cooling during the fight. Sir Owen shook his head laughing.

"I truly never would have thought of that!! But it is surely an excellent idea. From where did you learn such things?" he asked "If you don't mind my asking." Grayhawk replied, smiling.

"From time spent wandering as a mercenary. A midday battle in the dessert can be brutal. I have seen strong men literally keel over dead from the heat and exertion, men, who were born and raised in the desert. Also, if you will, Sir Owen, have every man drink as much as he can hold, then have the water skins refilled and placed along the line."Within a short time all was done that could be done. Fourteen Knights and Fourteen Sergeants stood on line across a fifty pace front. Grayhawk and Sir Owen stood their positions centered on either half, about three paces back. A six man force with bows were posted twenty paces to the rear as both a reserve to close gaps that might occur, and to shoot arrows into any enemy who broke through the line.

All stood in readiness, dripping wet, in a light breeze and warm afternoon sun. The last man on each end of the line lit a torch and stuck it into the ground, to be used to ignite the brush piles. All were quiet. Each lost in his own thoughts.

Not so the approaching Drulgar, they could now smell the men and their horses. They were loping along grunting in their guttural, not quite speech. Each no doubt counting a victory already won and dreaming of feasting on both horse and man flesh this night. After all, the Dark Priest had promised it, and all knew the Dark Priests were never wrong.

They were closing now; soon they would run up behind the humans and attack from the rear. It would be over quick, and then the roasting and toasting could begin. Good munching and crunching. They ran out of woods and into the bright sunlight, the smells were strong now. Then, right ahead the tracks of the humans through the grass angled to their right and across the meadow. Soon now they would have their prey. Across the meadow they ran in their shuffling gait, not seeing too well in the bright sun, running in a line four abreast.

Sensing the kill now, their speed increased, which distracted the Dark Priest who was running a little off to the left side of the group. He was, at the moment, trying to sense exactly how far from the human's rear they were. They were halfway across the meadow when it hit him

"Damn, they have stopped!" he thought to himself. "They are taking a break, no doubt. Well, it will be their last!"

Grayhawk had passed the word, as soon as he could see movement on the far side of the meadow, for everyone to kneel inside their makeshift barricade to make them harder to spot until the very last minute. It worked. The Drulgar ran up to within fifty paces of the barricade before it dawned on the Dark Priest that the ambushers were being ambushed!

The Dark Priest slid to a stop almost at the bottom of the incline and begun screaming in some language only he knew. The Drulgar paid him no heed and kept running. They started up the incline when the first two ranks literally sprouted arrows and went down in a jumble, causing many others to become entangled in the pile. Others began shouting war cries and went around the pile still headed for the top. Many of them also sprouted arrows and tumbled back causing others to trip, but not all.

The priest finally got himself together and began spell casting and hurling very real, melon sized fireballs up the hill. One hit a Knight in the chest and engulfed him. He was screaming in a jelly like mass of fire. At the same time a number of Drulgar had gained the top and were being engaged with swords, axes and hammers by the Knights and Sergeants of the Order.

Both of the brush piles on the ends of the barricade were now beginning to burn furiously, causing the Drulgar to concentrate on the middle. One climbed onto the top and grabbed a Sergeant by the head and pulled him over the top and into a group who began hacking him to death while he screamed. One raised a crude axe to chop and suddenly sprouted a black arrow from his eye, but another took his place. A fireball hit a Drulgar in the back engulfing him and the Knight he was fighting.

Grayhawk had come forward to the line, and it was his black arrows that were still taking toll. Sighting again, he was hit from the side, his arrow missed the mark. When at the same time, a fireball whooshed passed him. The young Knight, who had saved him, helped him up and said with a grin.

"Better watch that fellow with the fireballs, Sir. He is really quite good!"

"So I see" answered Grayhawk. Grayhawk pulled another arrow from his quiver and knocking it. "Let us see if he is armored" as he stood, drew and loosed, all in one motion The arrow flew true and hit the Dark Priest in the center of his chest and bounced off. The Priest staggered back a couple of steps and then threw three fireballs, one after another, at where the arrow had come from. All struck low in front of the barricade which was already burning in four or five places. The whole front of the area was becoming quite hot.

The Drulgar by now had lost over half of their number. The Knights lost about a third. There was close quarter fighting all up and down the line, but many more of the Drulgar were falling than humans. It was at this point that the Drulgar reserve arrived about thirty of them. Again they came charging straight at the middle of the line. They ran right up the incline to pull down the barricade using whatever they could, including their bare hands. Grabbing onto what was the now burning barricade they began to pull it apart, to force an opening that they could attack through. The Priest was hurling fireballs but he was tiring and some didn't even make the top.

Three things happened at the same time. The barricade came apart in the middle, the burning pieces flying right at the faces of the

Drulgar who were trying to pull it down; the Dark Priest, who saw this as his chance, conjured up two huge fireballs, one in each hand and threw them both at the opening. They struck on either side, too low, right in the midst of the Drulgar. As he conjured again for two more fireballs and just as they flared into being, Grayhawk stood, drew his bow, took aim and loosed. The arrow flew straight and true, taking the Dark Priest through his left eye and out the back of his head. He stiffened and fell over backwards, a flaming fireball in each hand. He was immediately engulfed in bright green and blue flame. His burning produced thick oily black smoke. The Drulgar were still fighting like mad, but their numbers were dwindling and the Knights began coming over the barricade and through the hole in the middle. With the help of Grayhawk and the archers who were in reserve, the fight only lasted another ten minutes or so.

One hundred thirty, Drulgar, one Dark Priest, five Knights and a Sergeant were dead, and more of the Knights party, were wounded seriously but not mortally. The battle had lasted less than an hour. It was just two hours past mid day. The stench of the burning minions of the Dark Lord was enough to make a strong man retch, and many did.

Back out on the meadow the few remaining Drulgar, who were guarding their baggage train, saw the demise of their fellows and ran away for parts unknown. The Dark Lord does not tolerate failure.

Grayhawk looked down at the carnage on the slope before him. Even though the wind was coming from behind he could still smell the evil and foulness from the still furiously burning Dark Priest and it made him queasy. Sir Owen came up at that point asking

"What makes them stink so?" holding a wet cloth before his nose.

"Evil" Grayhawk replied "During their training they absorb much evil into their blood, and even more is fed to them in a blood and drug concoction."

Sir Owen said "Grayhawk, we have won ourselves a short advantage here. By all rights we should have lost this fight, and they would now be preparing to feast on our flesh."

"That is the truth Sir Owen" answered Grayhawk. "We have won ourselves a little time. Their friends probably won't begin to sense something is wrong until this time tomorrow."

"Aye, my Lord, I agree. How do you think we should proceed? Our men are tired but not used up."

"Good, let us gather up our gear, tend to our wounded, bury the dead, and get ourselves mounted and away from here as rapidly as possible. Since they obviously know we have been moving east by southeast, let us head due south until full dark, camp for the night, then continue on south until midday tomorrow. Then we can turn back to the east."

"Sound thinking, my Lord" said Sir Owen. "Let us make it so. For I fear most the damned Dragons coming upon us in our camp. I fear we would have no chance of surviving such an attack.

"My thoughts exactly" answered Grayhawk. "Somehow or the other we have to discover a way, or method for killing the damned things. Since they have obviously returned to the world as the Dark Lords servants, they are probably our most dangerous enemy."

Sir Owen walked away shaking his head. "Kill a Dragon! Now there is something I would like to see."

"Me too!" thought Grayhawk to himself "Me too!" An hour and a half or so later, they were mounted and moving. Riding due south in the stream for a mile before moving back on to the floor of the forest. Four hours later at twilight they were almost twenty miles from the battle site. Finding before them a thick forested area of large tall trees they moved into them a ways, selected a campsite, and set about pitching a trail camp and preparing supper. The wounded were tended to. All were doing as well as could be expected. Now, if no serious infections occurred all would recover completely.

A quiet, if tense, night passed uneventful amongst the large trees. Whenever the breeze would stop the forest became so quiet it almost hurt the ears, causing men to turn fitfully in their sleep

Chapter Nine

They were up at first light, and had a quick meal of trail bread, with strong tea. The wounded were doing a bit better. Again the group moved due South. They were down to thirty men total now and seven of them were wounded. By pressing as hard as they could under the circumstances they had covered another twenty miles when they stopped by a clear forest stream for midday.

A good sized boar had been taken along the way, by one of the outriders who rode the animal down with a spear. Not very sporting, but it was effective. At any rate all were grateful for the meat. An enjoyable lunch of pork, pan fried, seasoned with crushed red peppers, along with trail bread and tea.

They took an extra hour at this point to allow all to bathe in the cool water, clean their personal gear, and tend to harness tack and weapons. Wounds were cleaned and dressings changed. Even the horses were unsaddled and allowed to roll in the deep grass beside the stream.

Grayhawk surveyed those around him as he sat cleaning and sharpening his blades. "These are good men" he thought "they do not talk much, but all are friends. They are very professional in their conduct. Any order is obeyed without question or rancor. They share equally, all that they have. Even when sorely wounded they do not complain. They are quick to laugh at a joke or smile at another's folly. Yet, young as they are, if left alone they all have that far off stare of soldiers who have seen too much horror."

Grayhawk was becoming gradually aware of some subtle changes in himself, as if some inner being were slowly awakening. All of his senses were becoming sharper, a little at a time. He was now able to sense the presence of evil. The Dark Priest had registered in his mind when he was half way across the meadow. He had actually felt the hate radiating from the man. That is, if he was still a man. The only clear sending had been during the fight when the Priest and Grayhawk had made eye contact across the way. A low gravelly voice in his mind had said "I have come to kill thee and I will eat thy heart!" "Well" thought Grayhawk "Fortunately for me, that plan did not work well!"

When all was ready, Sir Owen gave a hand signal and all mounted. They moved out at a walk heading east by southeast. Only now they were on a parallel track forty miles south of their old one. Again, grim faced fighting men rode away from a battle. For now victorious, but they had no time for celebrations, and with the certain knowledge, that their next battle could be their last. Even worse was the threat of Dragons! They are creatures right out of ancient lore. They were thought by everyone to be extinct. Even if this party of Knights were the only ones that they attacked. It would not be long, before the news ran through the land like wildfire in a high wind.

Far away to the south in the heavily jungled, mountainous land called Stygius, by most. Deep in his mountain grotto the Dark Lord himself stood shaking with rage, blood dripping from his clawed hands. The human slave messenger, who had brought him the news of the Drulgar defeat, at the hands of Grayhawk and the Knights, had died shrieking as the Dark Lord had literally shredded him. Now the werehounds were busy eating and lapping up the blood. All other creatures of the underworld had fled for deeper caverns and tunnels, to escape the wrath of their great and evil overlord. Whose mind, was now embroiled in a maelstrom of blood lust and evil machinations. For many millennia, since his being cast down by the All Father, his hatred for the humans had festered within. At first he had wanted to turn them to his will, and use them. Now he wanted to crush them and watch while they were tortured to death and then eaten by his own creations, like cattle.

The All Father's pets, with their "souls' and "love." They had almost become greater than all other beings. But He, the Dark Lord, had put a stop to that. The war of the heavens had almost destroyed the humans. But, he and his followers had lost the war. As a punishment, the All Father had changed him from a being of light and great beauty, to his present form of hideousness and banned him forever from the celestial presence. He had even taken away his name and dubbed him Lord of the Dark Places. "I will still have my revenge on these Human vermin. Soon now they will all be mine. I will breed them like sheep and they will feed my armies. My revenge will be complete when it is I who rule the universe .One day when I have won all the power. On that day, I will roam the surface again. Once again in the light of the sun, and the humans will die screaming."

Turning then on his heels, his great strides taking him quickly from the main hall, back down into the caverns, to his private places, where the planes meet and where no other being dares to go. He wore an aura of great power and hatred around him like a mantle. As he strode away, the lesser creatures of the dark domain began to come out of their hiding places for food and mischief

Much closer to Grayhawk's party, along the northern border between Gaula and Keltan, the Dark Priests had by now deduced that their quarry had once again evaded them. The message received down the line from the Dark Lord was not a pleasant one. Now at three different locations along the eastern part of the border there were Priests furiously burning astral energy, scrying for the Knights exact location. Thick forests and distance made their work extremely tiring. Already four different Priests had collapsed from exhaustion, one had died.

By evening of that day Grayhawk and the others had made good time and distance. Although they did not know it, they had still not been located by the Dark Priests. They were now within one full day's ride of the border and the Tuscana River which ran south from Lake Gani down to the coastal city of Tuscana. Sir Owen informed Grayhawk that they would need to travel up river to the lake in order to reach their destination. After conferring on the matter it was decided to turn further south and approach the port city form the north, coming no closer than necessary in order to obtain boats for the trip up river to the lake.

The next morning they arose to dark gray skies and drizzling rain. The rain lasted all through the day and slowed their progress somewhat. It was getting dark when they arrived at a point some five miles north of Tuscana and about a mile from the river itself. They stopped for the night in the ruins of a caravansary or traders fort, long out of use but still standing. At least they could get everyone and the horses under shelter. Large fires were laid and set ablaze. Before long everyone was warm and well fed. Clothing and gear was spread out, or hung everywhere possible to dry out. Out of the elements at least, for the rains came heavy and the winds were up, lightning and thunder crashed most of the night and did not fully abate until mid morning.

The effect of this weather on the Dark Priests and their efforts to scry was absolutely blinding. The Dark Lord was in a state of fury in which none dared approach him. Many of his subjects including Dark Priests would die screaming as a result of this failure.

Towards noon, the rain and wind died down and the lightning abated somewhat. Grayhawk dressed in his plainest brown leathers and boots. He chose one of the Sergeants who was of darker complexion than the others. They removed all of their equipment that could be identified as Templari. The two men rode out of the fort on the still soggy muddy road headed towards the river, which was only a mile or so distant. When they arrived at the banks, the river was high and muddy. They turned south and rode towards the city for another mile. They came to the start of the populated area where they immediately began to see some river folk dwellings, some docks and a few warehouses and a few flat bottom river boats and barges. Making their way on down river a ways they came to a sort of cove or backwater. At a long dock on the north side, there were three good sized riverboats, with sails and long sweeps. The kind of boat needed for going up river against the current.

"Well" said Grayhawk "I think we have found what we need. What do you think Elwin?"

"Don't know much about boats, my Lord, but they look capable" the young Sergeant replied.

"Aye, they will do" said Grayhawk. "Now let us see if we can strike a bargain."They rode up to the largest of the buildings, a sort of warehouse. It was constructed of wood and stone, double doors at one end, and a row of high windows running down either side. They were met as they rode up by two very tough looking men and a buxom red headed woman who held a spear.

"We seek to hire boats for a trip up to the lake" said Grayhawk as they reigned to stop before the river men. "Are those yon available?"

"They are!" replied the man on the left. "What need then, would a Blademaster have of riverboats to go up the river I see no cargo wagons, or pack animals? Or have you left them at the old fort?"

"I have indeed" replied Grayhawk. "It seemed to me to be easier to come and negotiate first."

"Ah, well now that is true, I suppose. My name is Olion. This is my brother Nylen and my wife Silan. Tell me of your needs Blademaster, and why this young Temple Knight goes about out of uniform? But first, come inside. Let us have a brandy, and we'll talk." motioning for them to follow him inside. The end of the building towards the river proved to be living quarters. Very nice ones in fact! A benefit no doubt, of being a shipper and trader, and probably a smuggler as well. If the truth be known.

After a glass of excellent brandy and an hour of negotiating it was agreed that for one hundred fifty gold sovereigns and three of the pack horses Olion and company would ferry the entire group to the fishing village on the north shore of Lake Gani. They would be taken on board his three boats before daylight tomorrow morning at a little used landing some six miles upriver. The price was just a little high of fair. But after inspecting the boats Grayhawk was satisfied. On the ride back to the fort they were detected by a Dark Priest scrying over his bowl, but they were deemed to be either mercenaries or bandits and they were going the wrong way.

The Dark Lord's fury over the inability of his priests to locate the party had not abated and two of their Chief Priests had been executed by Dragon Fire and the image sent to all of their order for them to contemplate.

At midnight that night Grayhawk, Sir Owen, all the Knights and Sergeants mounted their horses and rode out of the old fort over towards the river road and turned north for the hour ride to the landing. When they arrived, the boats were already there with loading ramps down. The loading and casting off took less than a quarter of an hour. Then propelled by six long sweeps to a side they started up river. Each boat was over thirty paces long and had a crew of ten.

The current was strong because of all the rain, but progress was made. With the sun in the morning came a good wind from the south, the sails were raised and the going was made easier and swifter.

"At this rate" proclaimed Olion, "I will have you at your destination by late tomorrow. But for the life of me Sir, I cannot fathom why you travel to such a remote place. There is nothing there. The village is small, slow, and dull."

Grayhawk replied, before Sir Owen could react. "We are taking a mountain vacation in Auserlia to do some hunting and fishing."

"Oh! Ho! Ho!" Olion roared, rocking back on his heels, hands on his hips, looking up towards the sky. "Are you listening to this? A Blademaster and his friends, Near to three dozen Temple Knights, are going to the mountains for some hunting and fishing. A vacation he says." All of Olion's men were now laughing. "And for sure I am the Warlord of Keltan and these, are my household cavalry. That is a good one Sir! That is a good one!" and with that he turned and still laughing headed for the stern of the boat.

Grayhawk turned to Sir Owen who was looking on with one eyebrow raised, and trying very hard not to laugh.

"I don't think he believed you My Lord."

"No I don't think he did" replied Grayhawk. "Imagine that!" All that day they made excellent progress, the wind held. At dark they turned to using the sweeps, so as not to run aground or against a deadhead under full sail. The Knights and the Sergeants both stood turns at the sweeps. So they were able to continue upriver all through the night and entered the lake before daylight. The wind was light but strong enough. Before the noon hour, they arrived at the docks of the town.

Chapter Ten

Sir Owen and two of the Knights stepped ashore on a deserted stone quay. No people were visible, but the place did not look deserted. A number of chimneys gave forth smoke, and there were all sorts of domestic animals about. In short order however, people began to appear, heartened no doubt by the Templar insignias and weapons. Within the hour all had been offloaded, while the Knights were being shown to one of the stone garrison buildings. They would spend the night here. Sir Owen accompanied by Grayhawk, Olion, his brothers and his wife to the traders Guild area. After introductions were made, and a glass of brandy served, Sir Owen and Grayhawk said their goodbyes. Along with a promise that if they ever came a-hunting this way again, they would stop in to visit Olion and company.

After the passenger departed, Olion quickly bought a mixed cargo of animal hides, flints,, woven wool blankets and clothing, shearling wool vests of the finest quality, casks of mountain berry wine, and pale ale, along with numerous other items not available to the lowlanders along the coast. Olion was extremely pleased, knowing that his profit from this trip would pay off all his debts and still leave his money box full.

He also took with him a list of goods that the local traders and shop keepers wanted. He had made many trips to the towns on the south side of Lake Gani which were in the land of Troscai. This whole north side of the lake was said to be deserted except for wild animals and evil spirits. Now he knew why, only once in a while would a small boat with trade goods come down the river. All of the things he had seen in the Trade Guild storehouses told him that there were a lot more people here than anyone realized. This was in fact a Templar Garrison but he would keep that bit of information to himself. Being a shrewd trader anyway he would have kept the secret of the place, not to mention what the Templars might do, if he brought trouble to their door.

In fact of the matter there was a full garrison, as of right now over a thousand fighting men could be mustered for defense. But from looking onshore from the lake, which was the only approach, it didn't look as though there were more than fifty. The waterfront was just that, a front. Beyond the back wall of the village, there began a series of defense walls, one uphill from another, about a hundred paces apart. Twenty feet high and massive gated. The gates were offset one from another first on the right of the wall, the next on the left, so that the road zig zagged back and forth. There were in total ten walls each about two hundred paces wide and four paces thick, solid stone cut from the mountain itself. The spaces in between the walls were fruit and vegetable gardens well protected from most weather. They were watered by small flowing streams and in direct sunlight almost eight hours a day.

Beyond the tenth wall the valley opened to half a mile wide, and a half a mile deep. Another larger garden area with fruit trees down the side walls, small aqueduct walls bringing irrigation of cold clear mountain water. As he rode through the center gate of the eleventh wall and into the real city of Solace, Grayhawk realized this is not a natural valley; this was all cut from the living rock, long, long ago when the full power of magic was still on the earth.

It was small as cities go, less than a half mile square, and it was just that, square. The streets were cobblestone and about six paces wide, they were laid out in an intersecting grid of square blocks, each was one hundred paces square with eight blocks to a side. The two center streets forming a cross were double in width, or about twelve paces wide. The four block square comprising the center was kept open as a park, with trees and fountains. The other sixty blocks were all fully built on. The buildings were a mix of styles from everywhere Grayhawk had ever been. The tallest were three stories, some square and flat topped with gardens on the roof. Others steep roofed with gables. Still others turreted and ornamented like small castles.

There were flower boxes in almost every window. The city was immaculately clean and the only smells were of flowers and cooking. "Absolutely amazing" he thought "No dark alleys, no run down tenements, no smells of sewage and animal droppings."The people were friendly, going about their business as usual. Some few stopping to stare at Grayhawk, clad in his black leathers. Even stranger, except for a few belt knives here and there, no one appeared armed.

He commented on the lack of weapons to Sir Owen, who smiled and replied "They are here my Lord, just out of site. Behind every door is an arms rack. While there might be an occasional fight here, no one would ever dare use a weapon. This city is under Templar Law. You can carry weapons of course, if you so desire, but other than a knife, hardly anyone does. Admittedly it is sometimes very uncomfortable for a soldier at first."

"Well" answered Grayhawk "Owen, I believe that is the most I have ever heard you utter at one time. You must be very fond of this place."

"I am Sir!" said Sir Owen with a huge grin. "I Am." They rode into the center of the city and around park square to the north side where they came to a large Inn. It stood some three stories tall, flat roofed, on the corner of the north road. It had double front doors in the center and double high carriage doors on the left side, the stable no doubt, and sure enough it was towards this entrance that Sir Owen steered them through the doors, and then down a slight ramp, into the stable area. Again the apparent cleanliness, it was almost unnerving. Here only the smell of fresh hay, horses and leather with the slight hint of liniment.

They dismounted as two stable boys approached and took the reins. Owen hung his sword belt over the saddle horn, keeping only his dirk. Grayhawk followed suite and soon they were up the three stairs and through the side entrance into the Inn. The place was large inside with high beamed ceilings. Everything wood including furniture was varnished with dark brown spar varnish. There was a long bar on the back wall, at least twenty large round tables with six or eight chairs each. The floor was hardwood planking that was also varnished. There were round, thick woven rugs under most of the tables, rich battle scene tapestries, on the walls between windows. Above every table a wagon wheel chandelier with six bronze, polished lamps, which suffused the place with soft yellow light. Both highlighting, and being absorbed by the dark stained wood.

The whole effect was like the main salon on the finest passenger/ trading galley ever to sail. This was combined with the smell of roasting meats, simmering stews and fresh baked breads. It all made Grayhawk feel like he really was on a "Vacation" in some exotic land. No wonder Owen was so fond of this place. It felt, well, comfortable. A feeling Grayhawk had not often known. The Inn Keeper greeted them like old friends just returned from a long journey. The serving maids were lovely and smelled like fresh bread. Owen ordered the meal saying

"Bring us some of everything you've got. We are long on the road and sorely tried! Now we would enjoy ourselves with good food and good company." Not long after, the other Knights and Sergeants began to arrive. Soon the drinking, eating, toasting boasting and tall tale telling began in earnest. Vivid descriptions were told of the battle scenes, along with sorrowful tales of lost companions.

Later in the evening when they were being shown to their rooms, Sir Owen, who by now was well into his cups, told Grayhawk "Tomorrow is a free day. Sleep as long as you will. You will be summoned, on the following day." The room on the third floor he was given was large and roomy. There was a four poster bed, a wardrobe, a dresser, a sideboard, with both water and brandy and a small loaf of bread with cheese. There was a small fire burning in the grate.

His bags had been unpacked and his weapons were lying on the bed along with a rather flimsy nightshirt. He chuckled to himself wondering if they would be shocked to know that unless in extreme cold, or camp conditions, he normally slept in the nude, with a dagger and a short sword under the pillows. Many a warrior has been killed in his bedchamber, entangled in a sleeping gown or nightshirt.

He undressed and moved about the room snuffing out the four large candles that were burning, thinking to himself, "This place is surely a wonder. The wealth exhibited here is substantial." And as he climbed into bed "The Templar are certainly not a poor monastic order of religious warriors. This valley and this city are far older than they should have been and everything here was created by magic power, obviously wielded by the Order. Just how long ago?" he wondered. "And where did "they" come from? Was this the fabled Garden of the All Father? As old as time itself?"

Sleep came upon him amidst jumbled thoughts which turned into chaotic dreams. Grayhawk awoke at first light, same as always, but this time he snuggled down inside the covers and went back to sleep. For over two hours more, until a slight knocking on his door aroused him. After donning a robe he then went to the door and opened it. There was no one there, only a breakfast cart, with far more things on it than he could possibly eat. He brought it in the room. The smells were tempting. There were even rashers of bacon, warm rolls with butter and a dark berry jam. There was hot spiced tea, and dried fruits and cheeses. He ate more than he had intended.

Grayhawk did relax on this day, as much as was possible for him. He took a long hot bath, had a great message followed by a cool bath. An hour nap, then his exercise and stretching workout, a short slow cadence sword and knife routine. He then cleaned sharpened, and oiled, or waxed all of his weapons, his bow, even the arrows and their heads. Finally, late in the afternoon he did an hour of meditation. By eventide he felt better than he had in a long, long time.

With a clear mind and a relaxed body Grayhawk ventured down into the hall of the Inn proper. There were a number of people present, eating and drinking, even a few women seated here and there. A minstrel or bard was seated on a stool by the fireplace, plucking a strange gourd shaped instrument with a long neck and strings, singing what must have been some sort of love ballad. Anyway, he couldn't quite make out what the words were.

He took a table by the south windows, looking out into the park area. They were just lighting the Street lamps. It was not quite full dark. There were still a good number of people moving about outside on the street.

Just then, the Inn Keeper himself, a very large man with a full beard and a long mustache, came up and sat a flask of wine and a pewter goblet on the table. "Try this, my Lord Grayhawk. I think you will find it enjoyable. It is from the south of Troscai. It should go really well with your meal. Sir Owen asked me to explain to you that he and the others who traveled with you are called to some duties with the Order this night, but that they will rejoin you in a day or so, after you are called to the temple. They will meet you there when the time is right."

"Ah! Well" said Grayhawk. "I was wondering. Thank you for telling me Sir. And if you don't mind telling me, just exactly where is this Temple? I haven't seen anything yet that looks like one."

"I'm sorry Sir" the big man said "I thought you knew. The Temple of Solace is another twenty miles up this valley. It is very high up. This valley was put here both to support and defend the Temple from the forces of the Dark Lord. Because of the magic laid upon it, and the direct edict of the All Father, no evil may enter here. They have been searching for it for millennia. It is hidden from both their sight and their sense.""As I understand it" he continued "Tomorrow you will be summoned up there. And there you will be given great knowledge and power for use in the Service of the Order and the All Father. That being the case, we have prepared for you a special supper to go with the wine. And later even better cognac from Gaula for after. So sit back and relax, enjoy your meal. And in case you are wondering. No it is not to be your last."

"Well!" said Grayhawk "I am most glad to hear that." With that, the serving girls appeared carrying covered dishes. First there came a roast crown rack of lamb on a bed of wild rice. The outside of the platter surrounded with early green peas and pearl onions, with butter and cracked black pepper. A side dish of a pungent, dark, mint sauce, a silver bowl of sautéed truffles, very hard to get since they grow underground and are usually found by specially trained dogs, digging for them in the forest. Fresh dark bread, butter, and a plum pudding, with a sugared crust. "Ah" thought Grayhawk "If ever a man had to have a last supper, this would be the one to ask for." He ate far too much, and drank more wine than normal, followed by several glasses of excellent cognac. When he finally got back to his room he said to himself "So this is what they mean by "as drunk as a Lord" just before he fell face down across the bed, fully clothed, and out like a snuffed candle.

Grayhawk arose an hour later than usual, but with no ill effects from the previous night. He preformed his morning stretching routine, bathed and dressed in his best leathers. He was just finishing a second cup of tea when a heavy knock came at the door. Opening the door, there stood a Knight in white with a red sash and red Templar Blood Cross on the front of his tabard. A gold chain around his neck held a pendant with an all seeing eye. He was an older fellow, this one, with both his hair and beard going white.

"Good morrow, Brother Grayhawk. I am Brother Tinian, Senior Warden of our Order. I am to be your guide and escort today."

"Well Met! Brother Tinian. I bid you good morrow." The two grasped forearms in the traditional warrior greeting. "Come in, may I offer you a cup of tea? Or should we be going?"

"We should be going, my Brother, you have a long day before you. You may go armed if you wish, but pray leave your other gear here. It will be taken care of, as you will not be returning here for some days."

"I will carry only my dagger and my person. I need naught else, let us be on our way."

"Excellent" replied Sir Tinian. "We will go by horse. The distance is some twenty miles, but we will be in no great hurry, and will stop on the way for some refreshment." The two then proceeded down the back stairs to the stable, mounted their horses which were both saddled and waiting.

Riding out of the stable entrance to the Inn, turning left and then left again onto the north road. Brother Tinian stated "This will give me time to fill you in on some of our history." Smiling broadly, he continued "there are brothers here who claim, not to my face mind you, that I have the ability to talk a stone into shedding tears, and a mountain troll into unconsciousness. Since a lot of our history, laws and rituals are learned by rote, I can understand why they might say that."

"Well!" said Grayhawk "I have had experience at learning rituals by rote, as you may know. Almost all Blademaster training is done in the dark."

"So I have heard" replied Sir Tinian, "Some fine day I would like to hear how that is accomplished."

"Done!" answered Grayhawk "Anytime you wish."

"Very well then" Sir Tinian began. "That you are now a member of the Order and far above the normal entrant rank of Apprentice. Many of the degrees of procession through the Order have been omitted or passed over. You, because of your innate magical abilities, probably inherited through your family bloodline from an ancestor who was a sorcerer or wizard. You have been selected by a higher power to become an adept, a term which in other instances or other languages means "Sorcerer or High Priest" or even "Chosen One."

"An adept of the Templar Order is imbued with powers most men will never know or even know of. How much power you will have is dependent upon your own personal abilities those you were born with. At a minimum you will be able to communicate with the "Source" a power contained within the Temple. All knowledge that is contained therein is yours for the asking. You will be able to conjure the forces of nature to your aid. To "see" if you will, inside the mind of evil. To sense or "cast" for their location in proximity to yours. You will be able to communicate by mind link with other Adepts. Your primary mission and goal is to defeat the forces and the aim of the Dark Lord. I don't think I need to tell you of your fate if taken by his forces. The last two who fell into his hands were roasted and eaten, literally.

Now then for a bit of History we fully believe that our Order was first formed over sixty millennia ago, during a time when the earth was warm and fertile. At the end of war in Heaven between forces of the Dark Lord, and the All Father. The All Father sentenced the Dark Lord whose name is "Lucifer" meaning "Beautiful Light" to be transformed into a horrid, ugly creature, and that he was given rule over the netherworld, or realm of the damned, from deep caverns within the earth. He was given the power to deceive, lie to, and tempt humans into his service by any means other than direct force or enslavement by conquest. The Order of the Temple was created to monitor these activities and to educate humans as much as possible to the purposes of the Dark Lord. And, to fight against his forces whenever and wherever possible so that the All Father would not be forced to step in and destroy utterly what which he had created and who had once been his favorite, and sat at his right hand.

At one time, before this last time of ice and cold, The Order had Lodges and Chapter Houses all over the world and over two hundred thousand Knights all reporting to the Temple here at Solace. The ice came purely from natural reasons, having to do with the earth. For many thousands of years, both this Temple and the Dark Lords, which is far, far down in the South in a land call Stygius, were covered in ice over half a mile deep. All of the City States and Societies which had existed were wiped out by the cold. Humans were reduced to wandering bands of Nomads living as hunter-gatherers. Almost all of the Dark Lords beings or peoples were destroyed.

Now that the earth has warmed again He is once more creating new evil beings such as the Drulgar and even bringing back Dragons from a clutch of eggs he had hidden in caverns. Thus far he has only been able to hatch two, but he has as many as twenty more. We must find this clutch of eggs, where ever his Priests are keeping them. Find them and destroy them, at all costs. If they are allowed to hatch and reach maturity the Dark Lord will gain control of the earth. Humans will become fodder for his foul forces, bred like sheep in holding pens and served up as roast meat for their supper.

If this should be allowed to happen, the All Father will return and destroy the earth completely."

They rode on in silence for a ways until Grayhawk finally spoke. "I understand fully what you have spoken Sir Tinian. Many things are now clear to me. I see the truth of it! Verily! Therefore then I surmise that this quest and talk of finding and destroying these eggs is going to fall upon me to accomplish."

"Yes, Brother Grayhawk. Should you choose to accept the challenge. It will become your quest. But not yours alone, you may choose such companions as you think necessary, or even an Army if you deem it needed. The "Source" has identified you as the man for the job. We will support you in any way necessary or possible."

"And why? Pray tell, was I chosen for this mission" asked Grayhawk.

"That is not known to us" answered Tinian. "The "Source" made the selection; the "Source" is linked directly with the All Father in some manner which we cannot comprehend."

"Is the "Source" then a person?" asked Grayhawk.

"No" replied Sir Tinian, "the "Source" is not of this earth. It is a force of heaven. We see it as a bright light. It has a voice that we can hear and understand. It is said that it has all of the knowledge that has ever been, or ever will be. You will see it for yourself when you are called in to the hall, in that house not made by hands." They rode on as Sir Tinian described the organization of the Order. The command and control functions, how once again they were beginning to spread over the surface of the earth, gathering information on the Dark Lord's forces. While attempting to spread the idea of justice and the rule of law to distant lands and people.

He talked of the rise of a great civilization, in the land called Aegia. How they had recovered some of the artifacts and knowledge of the time before the ice, and were learning by experiment how to use them. He spoke about the great ice still covering the most Southern Continent, and all traces of the civilization buried therein. How great glaciers had scrubbed many areas, and by their movement removed all traces of others. The Temple itself had been totally encased in ice for thousands of years and all direct contact with the "Source" had been lost. For many generations the Order survived only as a legend and passed on by saga ministers or oral history story tellers.

When the world had thawed once again, some nomadic hunter-gatherer tribes came looking for the source of an ancient legend "The Gods on the Mountains." When, at last they were finally able to get inside the Temple. The "Source" contacted them and the reeducation of man began.

After stopping for lunch at a way station about ten miles up the valley, another low stone structure with a garden on the roof, made to look like part of the landscape. They passed people working in the fields and gardens all along the way. The people were very tall, mostly fair, with blond hair, obviously a race of north-men, but different somehow. Continuing with his dialog, Sir Tinian said "The melting of the great ice packs brought about its own problems. A large part of it occurred very rapidly and the floods were terrible. Many lives and sometimes entire societies were lost. Where they once lived is either now under water, or scoured clean by the water. A sort of balance was maintained, evidenced by the fact that as some parts of the earth were inundated other parts were now free of the ice covering.

During these times the Dark Lord was deep under the earth brooding and scheming ways to gain control once the surface was stable again. It would seem that the cold doth cause him intense pain."

"Ah!" said Grayhawk "this then, is the reason that the Norda are so seldom attacked or even made aware of the Dark Lord's doings. Their being so to the far north."

"Quite so!" answered Tinion. "Though not as severe, his minions do also suffer the same affliction from the cold. And know also that one of the wards surrounding this mountain is intense cold."

Chapter Eleven

It was at this point that they topped a small rise they had been riding up. Both men stopped their horses. There for the first time, in the distance, a mile or so ahead, stood the Temple. It was a square structure with a colonnaded front. Its color was a pearlescent white, with almost a pink undertone Grayhawk marveled at the simple beauty of it. It was not ornate. Not that he could see from this distance anyway. But none the less, it was beautiful to behold. The air above it seemed to shimmer. Sort of like ice crystals in the sun. He could sense the power emanating from the building. It made him feel good.

"I perceive thou hast felt the presence of the "Source" Brother Grayhawk. It is somewhat akin to sunshine on a warm spring day. Is it not?"

"Aye" replied Grayhawk "it has that feeling and more."

"Let us then ride on my brother, for as thee have sensed the presence of the "Source" It is aware of thy presence." With that they spurred their mounts up to a cantor and soon crossed the remaining distance and reined up in front, where they were met by two young girls in white robes with gold sashes. "These two" explained Tinian "are temple acolytes. They are among the ones who keep the temple, so to speak. They make sure all is in order, see to the comfort of visiting brethren, care for all the animals and mostly see that we are all where we are supposed to be, at the appropriate time. There are twenty or so of them here at one time, both boys and girls. The "Source" communicates with them directly, so don't be alarmed if one of them suddenly turns to you and says "you must go here, or you must do thus. I have been here for over twenty years and they still manage to really startle me from time to time."

"I shall attempt to keep my composure My Lord" answered Grayhawk. As the acolytes led the horses away, Sir Tinian and Grayhawk went up the nine stairs to the porch of the temple. The entryway had no doors upon it. There were no bright lanterns or torches that could be seen yet the interior was as light as the daylight. There were no frescos, no God scenes or battle paintings, no carvings, no tapestries, no statuary.

"Beautiful but plain" thought Grayhawk. "This is exquisite white marble, and oddest of all, it appears to be one single piece. There are no seams. Is that possible?"

"Yes Brother Grayhawk, it is possible" said Tinian, as if overhearing his thoughts. "I thought the same when I first arrived here. Now you are but wondering how did I know your thoughts. I too am an adept and between us we may communicate without speech." It was at this point Grayhawk noticed Tinian's mouth was not moving. Yet he had heard when Tinian spoke.

"Can you then hear what I am thinking?" asked Grayhawk.

"Nay Brother not your innermost thoughts, I cannot. They are protected by the shields of your mind. If it were not so, it would be far too easy for one to control the mind of another. When one either frames thoughts as a question, or projects them in conversational manner they may be heard by others."

"Ah, I see. I think. It would seem then, not a good idea to talk to yourself, even silently whilst in the proximity of other adepts."

"Too true!" answered Tinian. "It can prove to be most embarrassing. Trust me on this. For I know all too well. After a bit you will be able to tell when another is within range of your thought. Further, with practice, you will have the ability to contact another over great distances, as though they were but standing in front of you." Before he could form an answer a soft bell rang, sort of a crystal tinkle, like perhaps a small hand bell a lady might have beside her bed.

"We are yet summoned into the Temple. Come let us proceed" said Sir Tinian holding out a hand as though showing the way. As they entered the portal or doorway there was a short hall of about eight paces which ended at a blank wall. There were arched doorways on either side of the hall leading into side rooms in which nothing but bare walls and floor could be seen. Yet, Tinian veered neither left nor right continuing straight towards the wall. As they approached the end of the corridor the wall seemed to disappear in a blur and there was an arched doorway some ten feet tall and about eight feet wide. It was filled by a solid metal, gleaming door with an all seeing eye over an embossed garden scene of flowers and trees. "Mithrail Silver" said Tinian's voice in his mind "a gift to the All Father from the Mountain Dwarves, it was hand made by them many, many millennia ago. They had now stopped before the door. There was no handle apparent. "You must request entry Brother Grayhawk. In your own words"

Grayhawk spoke out loud "I Grayhawk of Norda request leave to enter this temple."

The great door swung silently inward allowing a cool damp breeze to wash over them as though they were being cleansed. Beyond the door as they stepped through Grayhawk could see a wide gray marble walkway with low height walls. It was colonnaded every five paces or so, on both sides. Beyond the sides and somewhat below appeared to be, for all he could see, slowly rolling, white puffy clouds. The walkway continued straight for twenty paces and then there were three steps up. Another twenty paces of walkway and another three steps up and beyond that a third set. Three sets of three.

After they had crossed the distance, up the three sets of steps, at the end of that walkway section there was a pointed archway. It was larger than the first and beyond it appeared dark. But, as he stepped through that arch, Grayhawk realized with his whole being that he had just stepped onto the astral plane, and that he stood inside that house not made by hands. It was as though he had entered a huge temple made entirely of rose colored crystal, of a quality never seen by man. It was enormous and yet he could see the outlines of the building, if you will, and all of the rooms and chambers. At the very center was a bright pillar of pure white light.

In the heavens beyond, clearly seen through the temple walls, he could see stars, suns, planets, comets, asteroid belts, great celestial rainbows and pinwheels of every color imaginable. All of it seemed to be in motion, ever changing. "Behold" said a strong voice in his mind "Behold the workings and wonders of the Supreme Architect. Behold the creations of the All Father, the one true God."

Grayhawk stood still, turning his head slowly to take into his memory as much of the wonder as he could absorb. After a while he spoke out loud. "How far am I seeing?"

"Millennia," the voice spoke in his mind. "You see for millennia. For here, time and space are one. What you look upon has already happened, has never happened. Will surely happen or may yet come to be. But know this you are part of the whole. Your being and your soul matter. The All Father knows you personally. You are one of his warriors and he is pleased with you." Grayhawk looked down at this point, and discovered that the wondrous scene was even below the temple. The floor was made of the same crystal material.

"Come forward" said the voice. Lord Tinian had his hand on Grayhawk's right shoulder as sort of a steadying gesture. In truth it was very near to overwhelming to the senses. The two slowly stepped forward towards the pillar of light that was the "Source." They walked for some time and it became even more apparent how large the Temple actually is. Grayhawk looked back; the doorway through which they had entered looked very small indeed. "What you are seeing" said the Source is where the Astral Plane touches the Plane of the Living Souls, where on, your earth is located, with many other star systems and planets." Grayhawk felt as though he were walking through the air. The floor felt solid enough beneath his feet but his eyes and senses told him that he was in the void of space and time.

As they approached what appeared to be the center of the temple it became apparent that the Source was emanating from a round raised dais as large as a ball court, with three steps up to it. The "Source" itself was truly a pillar of moving, shimmering, white, blue and silver light, moving like a column of shooting water going from the dais off into infinity. When they arrived at the base of the dais they stopped and marveled at the beauty of it. Both calmness and benevolence radiated from it with almost palpable waves.

"Well met Grayhawk, Blademaster of Norda, Warlord of Keltan, Duke of the Southern March, and Adept of the Order of the Templari. You are truly welcome here. I am the Source. I have existed here since before time. I am a servant of the All Father whom your people call Odranna." At that moment, there occurred a sort of shifting of the light pattern in the column and then therein appeared the countenance of a bearded man. It appeared as part of the column but as though within it, larger than a man, smiling, eyes moving, then the mouth, as it spoke again. "Perhaps it would be easier for you if I wore a more recognizable form."

"Well met, my Lord" said Grayhawk "As to they form, anything you may wish is agreeable to me, for I will carry the images with me for the rest of my days. It is my Honor and Pleasure to stand before you"

"If I were a human" said the Source "This is approximately how I would look to you. "Now I will answer your questions Grayhawk," spoke the face in the pillar of light. "What do you wish to inquire about?"

"What is life?" asked Grayhawk.

"Life is the animation of a corporal being to the level of self sustainment by the Spirit of the All Father. This may or may not be accomplished with conscious thought being applied on top of instinctive survival, growth and procreation instincts. The purpose of life is to further the growth of the universe. Through trial and error species and beings are allowed to develop over millennia. Some achieve full growth potential. Some do not. Those which do not are discarded. The All Father controls the universe through the application of his law. This first one is called the Law of Natural Selection by Survival of the Fittest."

"Are we humans really made in the All Fathers image?"

"Generally speaking, Yes."

"Why are we here? I mean all humans. What is our purpose?"

"Over more time than you can conceive of, the All Father has had to battle the force of Darkness. Many of the original Beings of Light have been destroyed in these Wars. Then, there came, at last, the treachery of Lucifer and those who followed him down into the darkness. The All Father knew this was coming and decided to create new beings to aide him in his struggle. He decided on the human form, and chose this planet for the colonies. Thy folk called them the gardens of E-Dan, which was one of the names the All Father is known by. The last Celestial War was fought literally over the control of your kind and your development as corporal beings, who breathe life and posses souls."

"The purpose of your existence is to be born, to live a life, whatever sort of a life that circumstance and or fate may set in store for you. During that life you must experience all the range and depth of human emotions which you can handle. You were given each a "soul" within you in order to record all of your emotional experiences and your reactions to them. In addition, a record of your deeds in this lifespan is recorded. When your lifespan is ended, no matter how, your 'Soul' is read. If you are then judged to be worthy, your being then moves on to the next plane of existence. There you will experience another 'lifespan', though totally different, of trials and tribulations. Nine times total this will happen to your essence or being. If you do but pass all nine, you will become a 'being of light' and enter into the presence of the All Father. If thou fail any portion, you can be sent back to start it all over again. Other, worse dispositions of a being, are possible and when deemed appropriate they are used. You do not need to know what these dispositions are."

"What is magic?"

"Magic is pure and simple, the allowance, by the All Father, of the use of a small portion of his creative power by a human being and even more seldom, by select other beings or animals. It may be used for good purposes only, or it will backfire against the user. The exception to this rule is when magic is used against the force of Darkness, the Dark Lord, or any of his minions or creations. Then and only then it may be used to destroy, or as a weapon in combat. Know you this, only the All Father has the power to destroy the Dark Lord. You may defeat him, but not destroy. "Know then also, that all things are in a state of flux. No future is exact. The All Father has woven the fabric of time long ago, but the weave of fabric has many twists and turns. It is also flexible. It can be bent, or even broken in places. Because your race of beings, have been given the ability to reason and problem solve, much latitude is given to you. Both collectively and individually as people, to effect the journey forward. Where it might all end, or lead you to a place in time so far distant and warded from view as to be beyond comprehension."

"It is therefore, imperative that a being who is born with the ability for reason and complex problem solving to strive for righteousness, truth and justice, being neither false nor pompous. Each of these beings then will come to understand, that all that is required of them by the All Father is that at some point in their life, before they draw the final breath, that they, of their own free will must make the 'choice'. That is the choice between darkness and light, or good and evil. However you may care to phrase it." "A thinking being must serve one side or the other. Any, who cannot or will not make the choice, will, at death, simply cease to exist leaving no trace."

Grayhawk stood there in silence for a time, sort of far-seeing out into the swirling sights and colors of the Astral Plane. Finally, he spoke. "I do but see the truth of it My Lord, all of it. It is all complex and yet ultimately simple. How is it then, pray tell, that I can so easily grasp all of this. Yet most 'men' go their whole life time without this knowledge being made clear to them."

The 'Source' then replied the face smiling and the eyes seem to be twinkling. "Brother Grayhawk, I have not said the journey for your kind would be made easy. It is not, and will not be made so. For if it was easy and without cost, then there would be no challenge or adventure left in life. Living life is in and of itself a challenge for all thinking beings."

"Secondly, know ye that within thy head, the brain that you use every day, realize only thirty percent or so of its full capacity and potential. The remainder is closed off until such time as the All Father deems you to have progressed in evolution as a species, far enough to require the capacity to increase."

"I have but partially turned a key, so to speak, to allow you as an adept to use more of your capacity. This enables you to have and use more 'Magic' how much more, none can tell until you begin use of your powers. All of which is being given unto you to enable you to complete your assigned tasks."

Grayhawk did truly feel as though his mind had been opened further. Now he could envision possibilities that heretofore he would not have. Now, he knew that he had certain powers and abilities that were not there before. The session went on for what seemed like hours. Many subjects were broached; many questions were answered, until at last there was a long silence.

"And now" said the Source, "I must conclude this session with you. Now you are surely a full Adept. I have given unto you all that I am allowed. But, we shall meet again from time to time" again with that smile and the twinkling eyes. Then the face was gone, only the pillar of lights pulsing with power remained.

He stood there then for some time, just looking slowly around, absorbing as much of the spectacular panorama as he could. Then there came a soft cough from behind him, and he turned to find Sir Tinian standing there.

"I do apologize, Brother Grayhawk for disturbing your thoughts. But, we must be going now. You have many things to prepare for and your companions yet to choose. Plans must be carefully laid and arrangements made."

"Aye!" replied Grayhawk, "What you say is surely so. Yet I believe you to know as well as I, when the first battle cry sounds, all plans seem to fly away on gossamer wings.

Tinian smiled and shook his head in agreement. The two then turned and walked back across the transparent floor towards the door. Once through the door it closed softly behind them. They walked down the three tiered, or leveled, walkway with its tall columns on either side with dark starry sky above and rolling white clouds below. Tinian asked

"Are you versed in the legends of your homeland, Norda?"

"In most of them, I believe. Why do you ask?" questioned Grayhawk.

"I thought it might interest you to know that when the All Father is present in the Temple this pathway does glow brightly with a spectrum of color. And that it is called "Bifrost"

"Grayhawk stopped. Looking all around and shaking his head in wonder. "So then Odranna's Rainbow Bridge from Heaven to Earth is real! The myth is reality! I am most amazed."

"Aye!" said Sir Tinian, "Real enough for you to be standing on it!"

"Would that I could see it aglow, just once fore I pass from this life" said Grayhawk, still looking around.

"Who knows" said Sir Tinian with a shrug. "Perhaps it may come to pass. It has been many a millennia since he was here last. Here in 'person' that is. His presence is always amongst us."Then they passed though the front portal and back into the marble hallway of the Earth

Temple and out onto the porch. Grayhawk was looking to the left and the right, into the glare of the early morning sun.

"My word!" he commented, shielding his eyes. "It would seem that we have been talking all night."

Lord Tinian, who was taking the reins of his horse from one of the acolytes, stopped and turned to look at Grayhawk, laughing and shaking his head. "My Brother, it has been over two months since we two crossed the bridge and entered the door."

"Two months! That is not possible. Is it?" Scratch his chin. "What's this? Good Grief, I seem to have sprouted a beard!" Now the acolytes as well as Tinian were laughing. The horses were bobbing their heads as though they were also amused.

"Well" said Grayhawk, taking the reins handed to him, placing his left foot in the stirrup and stepping up into the saddle. "I have not worn a beard, since I worked in the land of Persus, where a man is not accounted a man unless he hath one. "What think you Ladies?" he said leaning down toward the two acolytes who had been holding the horses, with a huge toothy grin. "Does the beard suite me well? Or not" Both girls ran away laughing."What! Ho!" He cried as they ran away. "Is my beard so funny looking then? Tinian, what say you?"

Both men were mounted now, and turning their horses southward towards the village of Solace.

"I think perhaps my brother; it is the combination of the beard, the lion's mane hair and thy very rumpled looking clothing, which all together make you a very scraggly looking fellow indeed."

"Scraggly looking, me" said Grayhawk, laughing. "I am surely not prepared to believe such a thing."

"Then mayhap it was your odiferous state. Can you not smell yourself?" Tinian, now grinning broadly, replied.

"Yes, well, I had begun to notice a certain, "cache" permeating the area" said Grayhawk, sitting up straighter in his saddle. "But I didn't think it was me! What about you? Sir Senior Warden, you were there as well."

"Ah, yes, well. Truth be known, Sir Adept. It was your full initiation to the 'Mysteries'. I did but leave from time to time for rest and sustenance… and of course an occasional bath. After all, my brother, I have for certain already spent my times before the 'Source'. They were four in all, each more intense than the last."

"I know, I know" replied Grayhawk. "When I first entered the Temple, I had all of those questions in my head. For instance, just what does Senior Warden mean and what do you do? Now, I know that your primary mission is to see that all of the 'wards' and protections are in place so that no evil being may penetrate this place. Second, that you are in fact Governor/General of this Valley and all who are in it. That final dispensation in all matters of justice and governing here come from you. And, yet your attitudes and manners give no hint to your power or station and you move about with no escort, not even clerical staff."

"Oh that!" said Sir Tinian "Well when they need me for some urgent matter they summon me, but that is seldom. For now I will ride with you down to Solace. Tonight, at the Inn, why not have a celebration of your elevation, with a liberal application of good libation and perhaps even a little good food!"

"I concur completely my Lord. But I think first a long hot bath is in order" said Grayhawk, sniffing himself and making a face. The ride back was uneventful. They stopped at the way house only for a cup of strong cider and some cheese. Then they rode the rest of the way in conversation about Dragons and their eggs and just how the Dark Lord had managed to bring them to a state capable of hatching after so long a time. It is generally believed that Dragons are virtually immortal, highly intelligent, and some few of them are born with magical powers normally only seen in human wizards.

They arrived back at the Inn in Solace at the fifth hour past midday. Both men stabled their horses and went up the back stairs to the third floor. Sir Tinian explaining that

"The Inn here is actually where I have lived since coming to Solace twenty five years or so ago. My 'official quarters' so to speak, are here on the 3rd floor."

They parted at the landing on the third floor. Grayhawk going off down the hall in one direction, Tinian, in the other. As he walked into his room, Grayhawk noticed, everything was neat and clean. Weapons were laid out on the bed along with a bath robe and towels, slippers on the floor beside the bed. Stripping off his really smelly clothes and dropping them on the floor at the end of the bed. Thinking to himself as he donned the robe and slippers "I'll take those down later, and clean them myself." Grabbing up the towels, he was out the door and off to the baths.

Ah yes! The marvelous feel of hot water was akin to wonderful. Someone had already added soap to the bath water but he still lathered himself head to food three times before he was feeling really clean. The room contained three large tubs. Each was about eight feet across and over three feet deep. One was hot for soaping and washing. One was hot and clear for rinsing and one was cool for the final rinse. The hot ones were kept that way by baked clay chimney pipes from a basement fire pit passing through the bottom of the tub from side to side. "Absolutely ingenious idea" though Grayhawk. He loved to relax in the large tubs. After a good hour and a half in the bath, Grayhawk toweled himself dry, donned his robe and slippers and headed back up to his room. Arriving there he found the dirty clothes gone, a small pitcher of wine and some figs on the sideboard, and clean drawers, shirt and leathers laid out on the bed. "I'd really like to know who does all this" he said out loud to no one in particular. "I never see any humans up on this floor."

Pouring himself a cup of wine, and eating a few figs as he dressed, he thought to himself "I feel not tired at all, and only now, at the end of the day, do I begin to feel hunger. Strange and wonderful, are the doings and beings of this place. I even begin to wonder if Tinian is a real person or in my imagination."

"Quite Human Old Boy" Came the reply in his mind. "Seated in the Dining Hall starving, waiting for you!"

"Oh Brother!" said Grayhawk, out loud this time "Broad beaming again, was I?"

"Yes and loudly" said Tinian's voice in his head. "You really must work on your control!"

"So I see" said Grayhawk, "Or rather hear!" as he headed out of his room towards the first floor and the Dining Hall or Great Room. They then proceeded to enjoy a great meal of roast pork (wild boar actually) green onions, long green beans, hot rye bread with butter, Dark Bock beer to drink and a really rich berry cobbler with whipped heavy cream. After the meal they, along with several other Adepts, including the Innkeeper, all sat talking, smoking their pipes and drinking good brandy until well after the midnight hour.

Chapter Twelve

Next morning was the first time that Grayhawk had even given thought to the journey ahead. First he must return to Keltan to the King's City to confer with Killian and to see the Queen once again, of course. Who would go with him on the mission? How many? What weapons? What equipment? How would they travel? When to start? And yet, with all the myriad of questions before him, he was not anxious or despairing. He was in fact calm and comfortable within himself. He knew that he would begin today, in fact, to answer all of the questions.

Though quite early still, he had already packed his things, dressed, and trimmed his new beard and moustache. He then carried all of his things and weapons down to the stable. He ventured into the Inn to see about some breakfast. There, much to his surprise, not only was Sir Tinian, but also Sir Owen and all of the other Brother Knights who had accompanied him on the journey there and fought so well together as a group.

Ah, it was good to see them again. As with all men who have gone into battle together and come out the other side, there is a spirit-bond. In addition these men were all members of The Order. The greetings all round were warm and genuine.

A capitol breakfast of strong tea, scones and orange jelly called 'marmalade' imported from a long way south of Solace at the bottom of Troscai.

Finishing his breakfast, Grayhawk was leaning back in his chair enjoying a second mug of tea, as were most of the others. Looking across at Sir Owen he inquired "Well, Sir, are you prepared for the return journey to the King's city? And hopefully, this time without meeting any Dragons!"

"Most assuredly My Lord, I believe we are all anxious to return to hearth and home. How soon will we be departing?"

Sir Tinian spoke up at this point. "On this very day Sir Owen and within the hour." Everyone perked up at this point, smiling, nodding, and raising tea mugs in toast.

"However!" continued Tinian, as everyone present turned to look at him. "You will not be returning by the same route. Although believed by most to be the only way in, there is at least one other route."

"Ah Ha!" said Grayhawk. "I knew that any place as well designed as Solace would have one or more 'other' entrances or escape routes. Whither then do we go, by this route?"

"Your final destination is of course the King's City and your homes. You only are required to make a slight detour through Dwarvenholm."

"But Sir Tinian" protested Sir Owen and several others, "Dwarvenholm is but a myth. Dwarves do not really exist!"

"Oh quite the contrary my Brother" said Sir Tinian, raising his hands to quiet the protests. "Dwarves are very real, at least the ones I have met are, and all told, I believe there are about fourteen thousand of them. Further they all live in their mountain keep. It is aptly named Dwarvenholm. It is located north of here inside of a mountain, eh, several mountains actually. You will of course all experience this myth personally as you will be traveling there, in order to obtain some items Lord Grayhawk will need on a further journey, which he and certain others will be embarking upon, after returning to Keltan. But, he will explain all that to you at his convenience, at some later time. For now, my Brothers, be content to go and see a living 'myth'. So finish your breakfast at will and hold your questions for now. We will depart within the hour. I will escort you to the trailhead and see you off."

All were in excellent spirits as they prepared their mounts and saddled up for the ride north. The distance, Tinian had informed them, is about forty miles to the gate and that they should arrive there just before full dark.

This was to be quite the day for all. Most of the Brethren have never seen the Temple. Grayhawk was somewhat astonished to hear that. He had naturally assumed that every Knight at some time or the other would have occasion to visit the Temple.

Some hours later the group rode directly by the Temple at not more than fifty paces distance. It seemed that all were in reverential awe, hardly speaking to each other, craning their necks while turning in their saddles until the road dipped down again and the view was but lost.

After a bit everyone seemed to regain most of their composure and normal conversation resumed. They arrived at the north gate, just before full dark, as Tinian had forecast.

The north gate of Solace was actually a large stone wall across the mouth of a narrow gorge. This wall was as tall as two men and five full paces thick with a set of iron bound hardwood doors in the center. Each door was made of timbers over a foot thick. The iron and the wood were black with age, each having its own patina. They looked as if they had been painted or varnished many times over.

There were four walking guards on top of the wall, two on either side, and two guards at the doors. They were huge Northmen dressed in furs and armed with their famed battle axes.

"Do you know, my Brothers" spoke Tinian out loud "That I find it to be most a interesting trivial fact that both the tallest and the shortest races of beings on this world prefer to fight with the battle axe as their primary weapon, the Northmen and the Dwarves. Yet, they are in no way related and have very little contact with one another. One race is only four feet tall, the other generally over seven. Yet, their axes are very similar design. How do you suppose that came to be?"

"I had not known that, Sir Tinian" said Sir Owen. "Perhaps you will enlighten us."

"Nay Brother Owen, I cannot answer that, and I have inquired amongst both races. It would seem that they have no ideas on the subject either, but both smiled when told about the other."

As they reined up before the gates, Sir Tinian spoke again. "We will camp here for the night. There to the left in that stand of trees, there is a good spring. We are stopping here because beyond those doors is no longer Solace and no one ever goes into those mountains at night." At which point the Northmen were closing the doors and barring them high and low with heavy iron bars.

As camp was being set up torches were being lit to provide light and campfires started for preparing the evening meal. A large wagon pulled up in front of the camp and Sir Tinian had everyone come forward and receive a rather large bundle. It contained a complete shearling-fleece cold weather clothing outfit, consisting of pants, boots, vest, parka with hood, and mittens. Explaining to all about the sometimes severe cold encountered in the mountains. In addition, each man received a food pack for ten days. Each contained dried meats and sausages, trail bread of course, dried vegetables for soups, as well as meal for thickening them, plus dried fruits and tea. Water was not a problem in snow country.

Several Knights commented on the size of the food packs, to which Sir Tinian replied "You will soon enough learn that in severe cold, high in the mountains, you must eat almost twice as much, in order to maintain energy levels, especially if attacked by mountain trolls or the occasional great bear."

"Mountain Trolls, Great Bears?" came the exclamations all round. "Surely these creatures don't exist!" said a young Sergeant. "They are simply not real! Are they?"

"Ah young Sir" replied Tinian "They do most certainly exist. They are quite real and both are extremely vicious. Both hate humans. When they stand straight, both are almost twice your height. They will attack without warning. They are hard to kill. Boar spears or lances are best against them and, oh yes, the trolls travel in pairs, sometimes three. The bears are usually solitary creatures."

The talk in camp became very animated at this point. Dwarves, Dragons, Mountain Trolls, Great Bears, Drulgar, Sorcerers and who knows what else! All had heard of such things of course, beginning when they were children, but such tales were supposed to be of ancient times and places. The discussions went on for hours, while weapons were extra cleaned and oiled, and of course sharpened to a razors edge. Even Grayhawk set to preparing his own including selecting a stout boar spear. While he sat working on them, enjoying a pipe of tabac and a good hot tea sweetened with honey, Tinian came over and sat opposite of him. He filled and lit his own pipe, then leaning forward he spoke.

"Brother Grayhawk, much have you learned while here. This knowledge, will certainly serve you well, in your coming travels and adventures. You must take every opportunity now to develop skill with your powers. This first trip to Dwarvenholm will give you good excuse to practice. You should be able to detect the presence of these creatures before they can mount a surprise attack. You may even be able to read their thoughts, though jumbled, both troll and bear. It will take you and your group some three full days to reach the keep at Dwarvenholm."

"It will be bitter cold, you must maintain vigilance at all times. You will come to four different forks in the road. Stay to the left each time, even if you detect danger ahead, do not take the right fork. There are prepared caves along the way to overnight in, use them."

Grayhawk sat listening, nodding his head from time to time, smoking and working on his weapons. He was in fact absorbing every detail of what the Senior Warden was conveying to him. Only the intense look in his eyes gave away how attentive he was.

Sir Tinian was aware of this and so he continued.

"The Dwarves are aware of your coming. They are aware of your mission. They will assist but, only they may tell you what that assistance will be."

"I do not need to instruct you on what will be the cost in human misery if those Dragons are allowed to hatch and once again become an airy"

"Yes, My Lord. I understand fully what would be brought about if we should fail" said Grayhawk, tapping out his pipe. "I have been witness to their power. The thought of twenty or more of them attacking a city is not something I ever wish to see."

"With that then, my Brother and fellow Adept, I must be off. I have other matters to attend to. Have all in the group, don their winter garb before exiting the gate and be immediately on your guard. There have been attacks in the past within sight of the gateway." Both men rose and clasped forearms in the warrior style. Smiling now Tinian said "Keep yourself alive Blademaster; I look forward to our next meeting."

"As do I My Lord" answered Grayhawk.

Sir Tinian, Senior Warden of the Temple Order turned and waved a farewell to the others. Then he strode out of camp and into the darkness. Sir Owen came over to Grayhawk's small fire and sat down on a cut piece of log. "I wonder where he goes when he leaves in the dark, like that"

"Probably would be better, Brother Owen" said Grayhawk "to wonder how he goes!"

"Gads!" said Owen. "I had not thought about that!"

"Yes" said Grayhawk. "He does posses tremendous powers, yet he does not show them openly."

"It is said" remarked Owen, while lighting his pipe with an ember from the fire, "That Sir Tinian is the greatest wizard the Order has ever known."

"I believe it." answered Grayhawk "I believe it!" The night passed without incident. Grayhawk slept soundly awaking just before daylight, as did most of the others. They breakfasted on the last of the prepared food brought in the wagon, black bread with butter and honey, roast stag and lentil soup.

"Eat as much as you can hold" Grayhawk said to everyone. "You will surely need the energy this day." Being young men and soldiers everyone readily complied. Within the hour all were fed. The camp was struck, all supplies loaded on the packhorses, their winter gear donned, looking somewhat like big brown bears with spears. They mounted and rode double file to the gate.

The big Northmen were there again, and moved to open the doors to the North Mountains of the land of Auserlia. A place said to be inhabited only by monsters. Now they knew what was meant by 'monsters'. The Northmen banged the flat of their axes once against their own chests in salute, which Grayhawk and the others returned by raising their spears. As they rode past, one of the big men with a broad toothy grin said "Eine Gute Riese, Vielspas!"

"What did he say?" asked Owen. Smiling, Grayhawk replied

"He said 'A good journey. Have fun."

Chapter Thirteen

With that, they were through the gate and the brutal cold hit like a hammer, as they passed through the ward shield. The sun was out, but the cold was unbelievable. Grayhawk drew his first deep breath almost as a gasp. It burned like fire. As soon as he could Grayhawk pulled up the face flap of his parka and said to the other riders behind him "hoods on, face flaps up and breath through your nose."

Putting on his mittens he could hear the word being relayed down the line. He could hear others coughing and swearing. Owens voice came muffled from behind his face flap

"Ye Gods, I have never felt cold as intense as this before!"

"I have" replied Grayhawk "both in my home land and in other mountains such as these," gesturing with his arms. "When it is clear like this it is the coldest. This will kill a man left exposed in a matter of half an hour and we are not used to it." So once again, thirty six men of Keltan rode into an uncertain future, warriors all, even the youngest. They had become comfortable as a group, and that made them stronger.

At midday they stopped for noon to prepare a meal and rest their mounts. The fires were quickly going but they did not seem to be putting out any heat. Snow had to be melted in cook pots for both man and animals. Tea had to be drunk quickly or it would freeze in the mug. Pots of thick stew and trail bread were quickly consumed. The animals were given an extra ration of grain. Grayhawk had everyone smear soot from the fire mixed with a little oil under their eyes to help with the glare from the white snow. Fortunately they were riding a lot amongst the gray rock formations and not across snowfields.

The miles and the day seemed to go on forever. They were at twilight when then came around a turn in a narrow gorge. There ahead lay a small alcove or pocket in the rock face perhaps four or five paces deep in size and at the rear was a wooden stockade built across the mouth of a large cave. The inside was big enough to hold a party twice their size, horses and all. There were great stacks of fire wood and tied bales of animal feed. There were crude wooden racks and shelves holding piles of thick woolen blankets and food supplies.

Large fires were quickly lit and within a few minutes the atmosphere, though a little smoky, was bearable. First order of business was making hot strong tea with honey for every man. Stripping the gear off the horses, rubbing them down, giving them all the feed they could eat and fresh water. In short order, men were shedding their winter gear as they warmed up. Some had close to frost bite on toes, hands and faces, but none were serious. A large meal was prepared and they ate as though they hadn't seen food for days. Much talk followed then about surviving in the cold and what precautions to take.

Every one of the men appeared to be dog tired and after a heavy meal extremely droopy eyed. The cave was very warm and comfortable now. The horses were already asleep. Grayhawk said "I will take first watch at the door, everyone else go to sleep. No guards outside tonight. It is too cold and anything that would attack us has to break in that heavy door." There were not many protests and within a quarter of an hour snoring could be heard coming from some piles of blankets.

Grayhawk sat cross legged on the floor in front of the door. There was a slit about an inch high and a foot across through which he could see most of the clearing. He eased himself down into a meditative state focusing his mind on his untried Adept powers. He began slowly at first to cast out his awareness, searching for anything he could find. First to the clearing in front of the door, then down the trail the way they had came. Becoming aware of the animals in the area, not many life signs did he find, small animals in hibernation sleeping away the winter. Then casting wider out, some distance away, two valleys over, he located a pack of wolves, the big ones of the mountains, a hunting pack on the move down the valley away from here. It was a little disconcerting, to find no sign at all of anything dangerous, especially up the trail where they were headed. He went back over the area ahead again. This time he focused as hard as he could. A trace of something in several different places was all he could come up with.

Drawing further on his powers he sought answers and things became clearer almost at once. Mountain Trolls and Great Bears, both are natural creatures in their own habitat. He could sense no evil in either because there is none. They might be mean as hell, but they are not from hell. Therefore, they leave no evil taint. Then he realized why he could not detect them. In this severe cold they are probably all taking shelter in caves too! Since they were not close by and could not be detected there probably was little danger of an attack this night.

Grayhawk then allowed himself, for the first time since coming out of the Temple, to concentrate on his own personal powers. Looking for his potential as a wizard to understand and cast spells. How would one set about casting a spell? Someone had told him once that the greatest wizard in the world would be the one who could think of what he wanted to do, point his finger and simply say 'make it so!' The power would come straight from his mind not from memorizing some archaic mumbo- jumbo dialog that had to be spoken before a spell would work. "Excellent!" said a soft voice in his mind. "Now you are learning Blademaster."

He then realized that the average wizard or sorcerer had to have the words in order to focus his power and then concentrate it to make it work. The words were an amplifier. Now he thought 'Am I able to do things without the words?"

Standing and sliding back the lock bar on the door he opened it just wide enough to let himself out. He stepped out into the bright moonlit clearing in the intense stillness and deep cold. He walked down the clearing a ways looking for something to test his theory on. Spying a rock some distance away, half covered in snow, about the size of a man's head. Focusing his power, pointing his finger at it, he said 'move'. The rock shook some but stayed in place. 'Not enough power', he thought. Trying again, this time turning his back, he focused his power and his energy. Spinning around, stabbing his finger forward and literally screamed in his mind "MOVE!!" The stone shot away from him with tremendous force, struck a larger rock some fifty feet away with a loud CRACK, ricocheted up into the air and quickly went out of sight in the night sky. "Eh! A little too much force on that try" he said to himself, "but I believe with practice I might master this use of powers. The key of course will be, knowing when to use it, as well as how."

He then slipped back inside the door, closing it behind him. Standing there for a bit, he allowed the warmth of the cave to envelope him. He resumed his sitting position before the door, again looking out through the slit, this time with a better grasp of the use of the power as an adept. All through the long night Grayhawk sat in meditation, deep thought processes opening further doors in his subconscious, allowing knowledge and understanding to combine and become part of his conscious thought. Finally, just after daylight he came back to present tense reality, awakening fully rested as though from a long nights sleep.

He rose to his feet fully refreshed and set about waking the others. Sir Owen thought it was his turn to watch until he noticed day light coming through the cracks of the door. "My Lord!" he exclaimed, "I have slept through my watch."

"Calm thy self" replied Grayhawk. "I kept watch this night, so that I might meditate unto myself. I am fully refreshed. All of you had some much needed beauty rest. But looking around I see that it did not do much to improve upon your 'beauty'." All were awake now rested and in good humor. In short order a meal was being prepared of good strong hot tea with honey and a hearty porridge of oats and dried fruit.

An hour later they were packed, horses saddled, the cave cleaned, fires were out and all donned their winter gear. Everyone led their mounts out into the bright morning sun and bitter cold, again smearing soot under their eyes and down the top of their nose. Taking heavy boar spears in hand they mounted as one, some horses bucking and crow hopping a little in protest. Within minutes they were moving up the trail again at a good pace. Through the morning they kept a good pace, stopping every hour to get down and walk for ten minutes. This was done in order to keep circulation good in the legs; riding too long in the cold sometimes makes it so that a man cannot stand up when he dismounts. He can feel neither his legs nor his rear end.

At the noon hour they came upon a copse of trees on a good sized open shelf with the sun shining directly on to it and out of the wind. Grayhawk had an uneasy feeling but it was important to rest and eat to handle the rest of the day. As a precaution he had Sir Owen post a guard on all four sides.

Moving quickly the group set about the business of noon camp. Fires were started, pots full of snow put on to melt, the horses stripped, rubbed down and given grain. Here in the sun, out of the wind, it was still cold but much more bearable. Most of the men had removed their parkas. The smell of dried meat and vegetable stew was almost pleasant.

At that moment, Grayhawk had his first experience of sensing another beings presence. Jumbled thoughts of hunger, anger, fear, attack, kill, eat, man thing, all coming in a rush, and all coming from his rear as Grayhawk, started to shout a warning to everyone. Across the camp to the east where the hill sloped down there came bursting into view, as it came over the top. The largest reddish brown bear, anyone had ever seen came roaring and challenging. It landed on all fours and then stood erect, wagging its huge head from side to side. In the stillness the roar was deafening. Everyone just froze for a second at the awe of this thing, with its great front paws spread wide, each bearing claws that must be eight or ten inches long, the thing was awesome.

Now the horses joined in the fray, screaming, bucking, and kicking with their hind legs, rearing and trying to bolt, seemingly all at the same time. Absolute pandemonium erupted in the camp. Men were hollering, running to retrieve their spears from where they had left them, falling over each other in the process. The bear now standing fully erect must have been at least fifteen feet tall. 'Good Lord' thought Grayhawk 'how will we ever kill one such as this!?' The bear now dropped back down on all fours and came charging forward roaring, huge muscles apparent even under the long fur of its coat. One could even hear the clicking of its long claws on the rocks as it moved.

"Directly in the bears path stood the one guard on that side, the shortest and probably the youngest Sergeant in the group. He was a seventeen year old named Guillome. The boar spear in his hands looked to be way too large for him. Many men including Grayhawk were running to his aide, but the bear was almost upon him. Suddenly the bear stopped only a few feet in front of the boy, roaring, shaking its whole body like shedding water, and stomping up and down on one front paw and then the other. Its great mouth was open wide and he was swinging his head from side to side. The bear took a great breath and sort of coiled to launch forward.

Guillome, moving faster than should have been possible, stepped forward towards the bear. Bringing his spear up to shoulder height, with both hands on the shaft, he drove it point first down the bears throat, about four feet of it in fact. The bear immediately exploded in rage, ripping the spear out of the youngster's hands as it threw its great head to the left. At the same time its right front paw swept out and took the lad just above the knee and the great head swung back to the right with the boar spear sticking out of its mouth. The shaft of the spear struck young Guillome, on the side of the head with a resounding 'crack'. The combination of the high-low blows sending him spinning in the air like a cart wheel to land in a crumpled heap.

Tearing at the spear now with its paws the bear was trying to get the shaft back out of its mouth. Still roaring, now through bloody foam, its dying rage was total. Even its eyes had gone blood red. Within a few seconds another spear was thrown into the side of its chest, then another and another. Its movements were slower now. Then two more spears and the great beast stopped moving. It was lying on its side and it drew its last breath. Guillome was still alive but unconscious. He had a great gash in his upper left leg despite the fact that he was wearing his shearling pants, the thickness of which had probably saved his leg.

It took a bit to get the camp back to normal, to round up the horses and sort out the gear and supplies. In a while everyone was well fed. Guillome's leg was sewn up and his head bandaged. All present had praise for the young man both for his courage and his coolness. Many men would have run, and the bear would have torn them to pieces. No one knows why but the great bears hate humans.

Two travois, or drag pole harnesses, were made, one for Guillome and one for his trophy. A short time later they were back on the trail.

The afternoon proved to be uneventful, though Grayhawk did sense two mountain trolls off in the distance and not a threat.

This day they arrived at the cave campsite a good hour before dark. Not long after full dark the group was feasting on roast bear meat and passing around the bag full of bear claws and teeth. The front canines were over 4 inches long.

Guillome regained consciousness during the evening and much to everyone's relief he was still himself, some had fear brain damage from so hard a blow to the head.

He could not bring himself to ear the bear meat saying that he felt like he knew the creature too well.

Again, the second night over much protest from Owen and the others, Grayhawk took the watch. Sitting before a very similar door in a very similar cave, he began meditating, exploring within his mind both the possibilities and the realities. Once again he did venture outside to try his powers, moving rocks, causing fallen logs to ignite and then extinguish, casting out his sense looking for further dangers in their path. They had been extremely lucky this day. If that bear had gotten in among them, many would have died. Of course now young Guillome would be forever known as 'Bear Killer'.

Grayhawk had allowed himself once again to go into deep mediation. When he felt immediate need to come out of it was in the last hours before dawn. All of the sudden the cave was very warm and the silence around him was deafening. His first thought was that they were under some sort of attack. Not so, his logic and training told him. He stood to his feet, drew his sword and opened the door. He stepped out into a white wall of falling snow, big flakes falling silently, already over an inch on the ground. In addition the temperature had risen considerably. Sensing movement behind him, he turned to find Sir Owen and several others coming out of the door to look around in wonderment.

"Where, pray tell, did this come from?" asked Owen, shaking his head. "Oh this is just what we need, blinding, heavy snow."

"Agreed" said Grayhawk "and I had no sense of it coming."

"Well at least it has warmed up some" said another. "That deep cold is defiantly not to my liking!" Others were nodding in agreement.

They returned inside the cave then and on this day of the journey at first light the rode out into a heavy snow. Young Guillome, the 'Bear Killer', was complaining loudly about having to ride on a travois. They traveled at a good pace in almost complete silence, their sounds muffled by the heavy snow. When they stopped for a meal it had snowed almost a foot deep. By the time they found the next cave, which they nearly missed in the limited visibility of the evening, close to two feet of new snow was on the ground. If it continued at the present rate they might not be able to go on.

To make matters worse Guillome came down with a fever and his leg began to swell and fester. In their scant medical kit they found some herbs to help with the infection and made him a broth containing the herbs and some poppy oil potion to help him sleep. Just before midnight the snow finally stopped. Looking out the door of their shelter Grayhawk could see nothing but fog or mist. Casting his senses out, this time he detected the presence of Trolls, a group of a half dozen or so. They were a hunting party from a larger clan. He couldn't tell if they were directly on the path ahead, but if not, they were close. They were huddled down for the night. They were cold, irritable and hungry. What was worse was that they knew a party of humans was coming and they intended to find and attack them.

Grayhawk finally slept for a few hours. He awoke before daylight as one of the guards was adding more wood to the fire. "Sorry to have woken you My Lord" said Sir Gustav, one of the oldest of the group.

"Not at all, my friend" replied Grayhawk. "I am quite refreshed and ready for another day here in winter wonderland!"

"Oh definitely" said Sir Gustav smiling.

"How is our 'Bear Killer' faring?" asked Grayhawk, nodding at the blanket covered figure on the other side of the fire.

"He sleeps, but fitfully" replied Sir Gustav. "The medicines are helping but not strong enough I fear to overcome the infection from the bear's claw. We had best reach Dwarvenholm today and hope they have some competent healers. Or, at the very least our young friend could lose his leg."

"Agreed" said Grayhawk. "It is the fourth day and we should be there before dark."

Grayhawk then set about putting large pots of water on to boil, getting out the supplies for breakfast and tea. He worked smoothly and quietly. By the door Sir Gustav and Sir Gilead stood watching. "Just you look, at this picture!" Gustav said nodding at Grayhawk.

"Eh?" said Sir Gilead. "The Warlord of Keltan, an Adept of the Order and a Blademaster to boot, and he is making breakfast for the troops. A wonder to behold, is it not?"

"Aye" replied Gilead "That it is. This one will do, aye, this one will do."

When the breakfast was over and the camp was struck all were ready and mounted. Grayhawk held up a hand and said "Men, your attention for a moment please. I have sensed the presence of a band of Trolls somewhere in the area. I cannot yet tell precisely where. There are about 7 of them. What is worse is that somehow or the other, they are aware of us and our coming. So no doubt they will try to lay an ambush for us. Let us hope that I can detect their location in time. So this day, be especially alert all the time. They say that the Trolls are twice the size of a man and ten times as strong."

"Well so was that bear whose carcass is on a travois just yon. Our young friend there on the other travois proved sure enough that a boar spear is match for any size critter." All were smiling and nodding at that. Many "Here Here's could be heard.

"So then, if each of you" continued Grayhawk "will please keep spears handy and your eyes open, so that if we are attacked, we can acquit ourselves well. Today let us travel with the pack horses and the travois in the middle of the formation and two of our strongest fellows at the rear."

They then moved out up the trail, two abreast, thirty five stalwart warriors and one wounded. The horses kept plowing through fetlock deep snow. Except for the occasional snort of a horse or cough of a man the snow deadened the sound of their movement quite well.

Within an hour on the trail they came to a rock gorge between two tall mountains. Here the road split or forked. One road going to the right and down into the gorge, the other, to the left, and along the wall of the gorge. The walls towered high on either side, less than a hundred paces wide. The road was a good ten paces wide with only about a foot of new fallen snow on it.

At least the Trolls have not been this way. Grayhawk could sense their presence even stronger now but the rock walls prevented an exact location from being determined. All he could tell was that they were within a mile of here. Looking up at the towering slopes above, all glistening white, the tops were not visible because of clouds. Grayhawk motioned for all to dismount and lead their horses. A spooked horse here could easily pitch a man over the edge, and like the tops of these two mountains the bottom of the gorge could not be seen either.

"Look up" he said to everyone. "Do you see those high slopes covered with snow? If they start to come loose, an avalanche it is called, that snow will entomb us all at the bottom of this gorge, probably forever. So, let us move along the road as quietly and quickly as we can and pray that the Trolls aren't lurking in here somewhere." It was now a very somber looking group, trudging through the snow looking up, then down, and staying as close to the wall as possible. For over an hour they traveled until at last they were out of the gorge and at a second fork in the road. The right fork went down to the east and was wider and the left went up towards a pass between two lesser peaks.

As directed by Tinian, Grayhawk signaled for all to mount and they rode to the left. His 'sensing' of the area told him the Trolls were now ahead of them and they were hunting for the group of humans. The chance to attack a party the size of this one was more than the Trolls could pass up. He caught some crazy mixed thoughts now and again "Much man flesh, many horses. Horse only good boiled! Make attack, find humans. Kill all. Eat good, no more cold and hungry."

The snow on the ground was thinner here and so they walked the horses at a bit faster pace. To the top of the pass took an hour. The road on the other side was wider and wound downward until it disappeared into the mist of a long valley. Just over the top of the pass they came upon a rock ledge, wide and flat, fifty paces wide and two hundred paces long. The only way they could be attacked was from the road.

"We will stop here for noon" said Grayhawk to Sir Owen "a bit of rest and a good meal before riding down into the mist of that valley yon." "I agree totally My Lord. From here it looks cold and wet."Everyone else felt the same and it seemed like a long time had passed since breakfast this morn, there was firewood on one of the packhorses so it only took a bit to get the meal going. While it was cold, gray and overcast, there was no wind blowing. That made the stop on this open rock ledge much more enjoyable.

Sir Owen posted six men with spears towards the road, the only way onto the shelf. Looking at Grayhawk with a sheepish grin, Owen said "That damned bear from Hell scared two years growth off me!" Chuckling, Grayhawk answered

"You and I both, my Brother" Frying up some bear meat for lunch was excellent along with trail bread and a little dried fruit. Even given the amount of the bear's flesh they have already eaten there was still well over four hundred pounds remaining on the travois, frozen along with the huge hide.

While the food was being prepared, Grayhawk took some time to walk out to the edge of the rock shelf and 'cast out with his senses' since he didn't know what else to call it.

He found the Trolls moving up a narrow gorge somewhere up ahead trying to get up to the road and set up an ambush. Their leader was having some trouble controlling them. They all knew that they were in Dwarf territory and Dwarves are known to hunt Trolls sometimes just for sport. Trolls also hate Dwarves.

Mostly the Trolls were hungry, cold and tired. For five days now they have been on the trail, a hunting party, and the rest of the clan was waiting, expecting them to return with 'much pot meat', many bones to crack for the marrow. Man flesh was best, but any meat would do, even Dwarf. Fortunately for them, Trolls can go for as long as a month without eating, or until they kill one of their own.

As they prepared to mount again after the meal stop Grayhawk raised his hand for everyone's attention. "My Brothers, the trolls are ahead of us, there are six of them, they are a meat hunting party and we are that meat. I don't quite know how they know we are coming but they do. I can sense them, even some of their thoughts, ugly my friends, very ugly. It would appear that to them we are nothing but stew meat.

We will avoid them if we can but if we must clash with them use boar spears and go for the belly or the throat. These are their two most vulnerable areas. Show them no mercy for they will surely show you none!"

All equipment was checked. Everything that could be, made double secure, sharpness of spear points checked and double checked, swords loosened in the scabbards. Everything was in as good a state of readiness as could be. They rode off of the ledge turning left and headed down into a valley thick with mist or fog. They were riding towards certain danger. This group of fellows was always eager to face danger or battle, thought Grayhawk, not one of them is showing undo fear or nervousness. He smiled to himself, in their own right they are a dangerous bunch.

A quarter of a mile or so down the road they descended into the fog. Not quite as thick as it looked from above but a person could see only twenty paces or so in any direction. It was much colder in the fog. In short order there was a frozen rime on every beard or mustache in the group. The horse's breath looked like steam.

All sound was muffled in this gray world of intense stillness. This was an absolutely perfect place for an ambush. Casting again, Grayhawk sensed the Trolls were nearer and seemed to be towards the front, though at what distance he could not determine. Less than a mile, he thought. 'Lord how I wish I had the experience with this sense power to be more concise'. He knew full well that a vague warning is far better than no warning at all.

Chapter Fourteen

They moved forward at a walk, spears lowered, Grayhawk had the lead. Sir Owen had rear guard. No one was talking. Only the muffled clop of the horse's feet could be heard. Eyes were scanning left and right for some telltale sign of the enemy.

They had traveled almost a full mile before Grayhawk sensed them really strong and close. He gave the hand signal to dismount and form a phalanx or wedge forward. With Grayhawk taking the point position, he was followed two, followed by four, who were followed by eight. Sir Owen did the same to the rear, minus one warrior left to guard the wounded Guillome who had a high fever and was sedated.

Because of alternating either rock face, drop off or thick brush, Grayhawk felt strongly that the attack would come from the front. He had heard somewhere or the other that Trolls prefer to fight with heavy long clubs. Only rarely would they fight using a spear. They did not possess the dexterity to use either a bow or a sword. They were nine or ten feet tall and some weighted as much as a horse.

Now their thoughts and positions were becoming much clearer. 'Smell man flesh! Supper comes Kill, crush! SMASH BONES! ATTACK NOW! KILL ALL! EAT GOOD! HORSES TOO! MUCH, GOOD MEAT' First they could hear only low grunting, sort of like pigs rooting. Then they could feel the stomping footsteps as they approached, shuffling faster now.

Then, they were there, six great hulking shapes in the fog, ambling forward as a group. When the Trolls sighted the men they began howling their war cries, sounding sort of like a cow in pain, bellowing and raising their clubs high.

They came on in a rush, thinking to sweep the roadway clear of these humans. Grayhawk ran forward towards the one directly in front of him. His spear held low, raising it at the last moment as practiced, to come at the creature's belly, but as he brought it up he drove it into the ugly brute's groin. Roaring in pain the Troll swiped with his club hitting Grayhawk on his left shoulder, knocking him down.

The sounds of battle and pain closed around him now. As one of the beasts tried to stomp on his head, he rolled further to his right in a ball and came to his feet. Fully behind the red veil of the bezerker now, both his sword and short sword drawn. There before him another of the brutes was roaring his defiance. Grayhawk was now in his realm, a Blademaster of Norda in full combat.

Another of the Knights ran in front of him to engage the Troll only to have his spear knocked to the ground and the Troll's club struck him on the head in a full power, downward stroke. Grayhawk clearly heard the man's skull being crushed. The man fell dead and the Troll stomped on him, while coming forward to get at Grayhawk. Moving forward, Grayhawk spun, blades going around like two scythes, the great sword took off a hand and half of the forearm. The short sword came around and drove twelve inches of cold steel into the Troll just below the left breast. The Troll stopped, stunned at the sight of his arm stump pumping blood. Grayhawk did not stop, spinning until he was behind the brute; he drove his great sword upward point first into the base of the skull, protruding a foot out of the front of the Trolls mouth. Turning the blade a quarter turn to the left he ripped it out and to the right, half severing the Trolls head, which then fell face forward dead.

As Grayhawk recovered his faculties and started to move towards the middle of the fray, where he could still hear roaring and shouting, there was a great roar of rage and pain followed by the sound of a heavy body hitting the ground.

Just that quick, the fight was over. The toll, however, was heavy. Five good men had died in taking the six brutes down. Three others were wounded and Grayhawk's left arm was now just hanging there numb.

Like every commander before him, who had come out of the far side of a battle, "It could have been worse!" he told himself. The fog seemed to really close in on them then, it was wet, cold and dismal. A couple of the men stumbled around, dazed no doubt by blows from a four foot long heavy wooden club. Grayhawk couldn't tell yet if his arm was broken or not but he still could not move it.

All of the Trolls had been killed. Some of them took six or eight thrusts from spears before going down. Now looking at them lying in odd positions in pools of blood, one could see how truly ugly they were. Their skin was gray/green color, their heads were huge with almost human faces and they were almost totally bald. They had a few sporadic tufts of wiry looking black hair and gray eyes. Their hands only have three fingers and a thumb and their feet only four toes.

The fight had lasted only a quarter of an hour, but it took more than two hours to tend to the wounded and to wrap in blankets, the bodies of the five men killed. They were placed across their saddles, as there was no place here suitable for burying them. There was not much in the way of grieving for these lost friends, not outwardly any way. All warriors understand that, in battle, men will fall. That is the way of it. The loss is felt by all.

Sir Owen tapped a small cask of brandy and gave everyone a good half cup. Most drank in silence just happy to be alive. They were still in awe over the power and ferocity of the Mountain Troll which until today none of them had ever seen, and really did not believe they existed.

As they rode on this time, the number of fighting men still capable was reduced to 25. Half the number they had left the academy with three months prior.

Grayhawk's arm was beginning to ache and throb, 'not broken though' he thought. That could have been a crippling blow and a one armed Blademaster was a short lived one. The brandy definitely helped, and he had rigged a sling to help support the arm. Now he had to mount his horse from the right side, which was certainly better than to have someone help him into the saddle.

The road at least was flat and fairly smooth as it continued to angle downward through the mist. Within the hour the road began to switchback as it went lower, with sharp turns at the end of each leg.

Though it was late afternoon they broke out torches because of the darkness.

Finally after no less than fifteen steep courses with a complete one hundred eighty degree turn at the end of each, they came out on to a flat road. Grayhawk could not tell for sure as they were in dark gray mist but he thought they were now moving west.

After what he gauged to be approximately a mile the mist grew a little lighter, which turned out to be, a short distance later, a torch lit bridge over a roaring whitewater mountain river. There, not seventy five paces beyond the bridge, the road ended at a set of high carved doors which looked as though they had been cut from the rock itself.

The doors were carved in panels of intricate patterns, in which each one looked like a drawn maze with a square in the center containing chiseled runes. "Runes of the old Nordic language or I am very much mistaken" Grayhawk said to no one in particular. "Aye" said Sir Owen coming up beside him that is indeed what they are. I studied them as a child in Danfinia." "As did I in Norda" replied Grayhawk. "But these I cannot read. They make no sense."

As they came to the end of the bridge the doors, with a great shaking and rumbling, began to open inward. Inside the doors, through the widening crack could be seen a huge vaulted, torch lit tunnel. As the doors spread further open they could see that they were powered by eight short, stout, bearded Dwarves on each side, dressed in thick soled stubby boots, leather breeches and tunics with wide leather belts. Each carried a dirk on his belt and a serious looking double bit war axe on his back. Each of them had a bushy full head of shoulder length hair and full beards with drooping mustaches. The hair color ran from bright carrot red to deepest auburn to dark chestnut.

As the doors opened wider, arrayed in a military rank and file formation, what must have been at least a thousand more Dwarves came in to view. They were all dressed similarly to the party at the door except they all had weapons to hand; mostly axes, but a few swords and short lances could be seen. They were standing twenty across and the ranks seemed to go back forever.

The group that had opened the doors now did an about face and their axes came to hand in one fluid motion.

Grayhawk and party were all across the bridge now and reined to a halt. He raised his right hand, palm outward to show he came in peace. He then gave the word for everyone to dismount. When they had done so and placed their spears on the ground Grayhawk and Sir Owen took five paces forward. They stopped and once again raised hands, palm outward to show that they were empty.

A group of three Dwarves stepped out from the front rank and took five paces forward their weapons held at the ready. The Dwarf in the middle was wearing what had to be Mithrail silver chain mail and a gold coronet around his head of long pale blond hair.

"A prince of the royal blood, no doubt" said Grayhawk quietly to Owen.

"Aye, so it would seem." He replied.

As the prince came to a stop Grayhawk and Owen both bowed to a forty five degree angle, proper for a prince. The Prince spoke then in a surprisingly loud and gruff voice, rolling his r's.

"Who comes here? State your names and your purpose. If your faces or your hearts are false, you will be killed."

"We are Knights and Sergeants of the Templar Order. I am Grayhawk an Adept, Warlord of Keltan, and Blademaster of Norda. This is Sir Owen of Dan, Commander of Knights. We traveled from Solace by order of Sir Tinian, Senior Warden of the Temple. We come to ask conference with the Dwarven King and the hospitality of Dwarvenholm. We have twice been attacked on our way here. First, by a great bear, and then again this very morn by a party of six mountain Trolls. We have slain these enemies but have sustained losses and injury among our party. Our faces are true. Our hearts are true. We come to thy door in peace.

At this point the Dwarf on either side of the prince seemed to be quietly advising him.

Nodding his head he said aloud,

"I have been informed that you are who you say you are. The Templar are friends and are always welcome among us." "I am Drinach, my father is King O'Dinald. Our healers will care for your wounded. Do you wish to have your dead cremated so their ashes may go back with you to their home?" Grayhawk looked at Owen, who responded,

"Aye, Highness that would be most kind of you."

"Lord Grayhawk, you spoke of an attack by Trolls. And that it was this very morn? Can you tell me about, where, this took place."

"Certainly, your Highness, it was near the top of this road, where the mist is the thickest" replied Grayhawk.

"Excellent" said the Prince. "I will send a party up immediately."

"May I ask you why?" said Grayhawk. "Do you go to dispose of the carcasses?"

"Oh no" said the Prince. "We will skin them out, when boiled and properly tanned, Troll hide makes excellent boots. We have few other sources of leather. A fitting end for them, don't you think?"

"Absolutely Said Sir Owen, "I like it!"

Once the official welcome had been given the warriors all relaxed a bit. Grayhawk and his party were escorted into the tunnel. While they were speaking with the Prince, Grayhawk and Owen were taking in all of the sights and sounds.

Looking up, Grayhawk noticed what must have been at least a hundred 'murder holes', small openings in the ceilings and wall through which an archer can rain death on any intruder. Across the very front of the cavern or tunnel just outside the great doors was a row of small spouts with a perforated cap on each of them. These are ports to pour flammable oil on the enemy as part of the defense of the entry port.

The Dwarven healers came out of a side door in the tunnel. They were dressed in gray robes, carrying large bags with should straps, typical of healers everywhere. In short order the wounded were taken to the hospital. The bodies of the deceased were laid onto litters covered with blankets and given a blessing by a Dwarf in a long dark blue robe who had an all Seeing Eye medallion around his neck on a silver chain. Then they too were removed through a side door.

The bulk of the Dwarven fighters who had been assembled were also disbursed through some of the many side doors not previously visible.

"Leave your horses and your long weapons here, they will be cared for' announced the Prince. "Carry weapons you will comfortable with, but I assure you there will not be need of them. Nor your heavy winter clothes, in Dwarvenholm they are not needed."

"My folk will take care of all, and as for your dead, they will lie in repose tonight. You will be shown where the chamber is. Tomorrow morning we will hold funeral services and light the pyres. Their ashes will be placed in silver urns for you to return to their families." Sir Owen and the others looked extremely relieved to hear this.

The entry hall or tunnel was now almost empty only a few dwarves remained. All were headed for one of the many side doors on either side of the tunnel. As the Prince led them into one of the doors Grayhawk thought he would have to duck down or walk stooped over. To his surprise and delight the tunnel they were now in was five feet or so wide and a good seven feet tall. The air was fresh and cool. Light was provided by both torches and a soft blue/green glow. Grayhawk knew from his training in caves that it was coming from phosphorus.

They traveled thusly for what must have been a mile or more, many turns, stair step up, then stair steps down. They were walking rapidly, mostly in silence except for the occasional scruff or scrape of someone or something on the wall.

Then the air became decidedly warmer. Grayhawk's new senses were assailed by myriads of layered smells of wood smoke, cooking, beer, leather, steel, coal smoke from forges, rope, varnish, and many, many 'people'. Not too many paces later they emerged into a giant arched roofed cavern. The points of light coming from torches, fires, forge furnaces, lanterns were in the thousands. As near as could be reckoned by any of the stunned human warriors, who stood there in awe, this cavern was a thousand feet tall, a thousand feet wide and over a mile long.

What's more, quite contrary to legend and popular belief, Dwarves do have women and they don't have beards. They do have children. There were numbers of women and children moving about the open spaces and peering out windows cut into the solid rock walls. The windows went up at least six levels on both sides of the chamber. "The living quarters no doubt," thought Grayhawk.

The ceiling of the cavern sparkled like stars in the heavens and added to the feeling of vastness about the place, and to its wonder and beauty. They had all stopped and were slowly looking around with utter amazement on every face. None even realized they had stopped.

"Well Blademaster!" said the Prince, hands on his hips and a great toothy grin. "What say you to our humble abode? How does it compare to where you trained?"

"There can be absolutely no comparison here" replied Grayhawk. "I did but spend two years in a deep, dark, dank hole in the mountain. This is truly a beautiful sight to behold. Your people have done wonders to be sure. I commend you."

"I thank you on behalf of the Dwarven folk" said the Prince. "What you see here took a thousand years to create. It was basically finished that long ago as well. We will still be improving it a thousand years from now."

One of the Knights spoke up "Are you saying Highness, that there have been Dwarf folk dwelling in here for over two thousand years now?"

"Nay Sir Knight" answered the Prince, "My folk have been working on this chamber for that long. They have been living and working inside these mountains for longer than you would believe. There are other older chambers such as this which are no longer inhabitable, though this is the largest."Now Lord Grayhawk, my people will show you and your men to quarters where you may clean up and rest a bit. Perhaps some good beer will help."

"Beer?" echoed several in the group.

"Ah!" said the Prince "You fellows have never tasted Dwarf Brew? A treat I assure you. I will have some brought to you. Go and rest and refresh. I must make report to my father the King. He will probably receive you officially and welcome you with a feast. It has been a while since we have had guests. He will want news of the outside world. You will be informed if any of your wounded is critical. Otherwise they will be cared for."

With that the Prince strode towards the middle of the chamber. Another stout dwarf who had the reddest hair anyone had ever seen, stepped forward and raised his hand and said

"Greetings Templars, I am Wojan, Leader of a Hundred. I bid thee 'warriors welcome' (a traditional old templar greeting). Follow me my brothers and I will show you to your quarters," holding out an arm to show the way. They all followed to the right and across the chamber diagonally to the opposite wall, through a doorway, down a short hall and up two flights of stairs, all cut into solid gray rock. At the top landing another door opened into a long dormitory with beds, wash stands, and wardrobe cabinets, enough for at least 50 or more. "Make yourselves at home here. This is traditionally a Templar Lodging. The entrance to the bath and the latrine is at the far end. Sleep any where you like. You need carry only a knife for eating here."

Chapter Fifteen

The whole experience of being underground, especially surround by solid rock was a little eerie for everyone except Grayhawk, who was quite comfortable with it. The hall they were in was brighter lit than the outer areas. There was a candle lantern above the head of each bed and on the two long tables down the center there were several more. The ceiling was arched and at least ten feet high at the center. So that the effect of the room was warmth with yellow light from all the candles and open space. You could just barely feel the air moving against your face. It helped greatly with the closed in nervousness a lot of the brothers were feeling.

A few minutes later a troop of Dwarves began bringing in all of their saddle bags and the supplies from the pack horses, depositing them in the middle of the floor. A fellow with wavy chestnut brown hair, who appeared to the leader, said "We did not know how much of your baggage you might need so we brought it all along!"

"Many thanks Master Dwarf" said Sir Owen. "I know I need some clean clothes."

"We noticed!" said the Dwarf with his hands on his hips and a huge grin. "You lot smell like bears and trolls. Well, have a good bath and we'll all hear your tales over a good meal and beer!"

"Here here!" said most of the knights in unison. (As you know, dwarves are renowned in myth for their love of beer.) With that the dwarves left and everyone began to sort out the bags, each and selecting a bed. Grayhawk chose one about halfway down on the left side, Sir Owen taking the one across from him on the right. Soon weapons were clanking and boots clunking on the floor.

The Brothers were all going through their packs for clean small clothes, razors and other personal items. One of the young Knights, Sir Tomas, shouted from the door to the bath "Brothers, come and see this. You will not believe your eyes. It is surely a wonder to behold." All quickly gathered up their things and hurried down to the doorway, through the door and down one flight of stairs and into a steam filled room some fifteen or so paces by about thirty paces. The room was lit by oil lamps on each wall. There in the floor, cut right into solid rock, was a pool of hot water, crystal clear, about four feet deep, easily discernable as there were four lines of soft green, glowing phosphorus running lengthwise on the bottom of the pool. Somehow or other it was imbedded into the solid rock bottom.

The pool was two thirds the width and two thirds the length of the room. There were low benches along either side with folded, thick drying cloths lying stacked three or four high on top. There also were some cakes of a substance called 'siefe' by the Dwarves. It was a soft soap made from animal fat, cooked with lye and lilac flowers. Unlike the hard, harsh, stuff they were used to.

Well it smells good, makes bubbles on the water and really does help get one clean. However, Dwarves for sure don't bathe very often, and they never smell like lilacs!

Within minutes everyone was naked and jumping into the water. No false modesty here! It was fantastic. The water was just warm enough to be really comfortable. The siefe was a new but pleasant experience. Grayhawk even washed his hair with it. Soon all the others followed suit.

After half an hour of this enjoyment, everyone's hands started to get really wrinkled and it was decidedly time to end the bath. Soon everyone was dry, warm, and clean and dressed in boots, leggings and tabard style tunics coming half way to their knees and emblazoned with a Templar emblem on the left breast. Grayhawk was dressed similarly only his clothing was all leather. All had broad leather belts about their waists with a sheath dagger on the right.

A short time later there returned, Wojan 'Leader of a Hundred'.

As good a way as any to identify ones rank, thought Grayhawk. "For soothe!" said Wojan "smells like a field of flowers in here!" Grinning again "I see you Barbarians have found the bathing pool and the siefe."

"Aye" said Sir Owen "and we like it too!"

"Just don't bathe too often Brothers. It will be hard to impress an enemy when you smell like a love bower." Everyone was laughing at that. A mug of good Dwarven dark beer, and a warm bath had taken their minds off of the events of the journey. Suddenly it came to Grayhawk 'just as it was intended to do. Very smart and very good of the Dwarves' he thought to himself.

Looking into Wojan's eyes he said "Master Dwarf, we thank you for both the kindness, and the hospitality."

"Aye!" came a voice from the rear "And the beer's good too!" Everyone was laughing again. Wojan replied,

"Oh that's only day beer. We don't serve the really good stuff until supper!"

"Do you mean to tell us, Master Dwarf that you have a better brew?"

"Aye!" said Wojan "That we do. But first must come the presentation of you lot to the King. After that, supper, and then begins the serious drinking."

"0-ho!" said Owen. "Pray do lead on good sir. Did you hear?" He said looking around, "Serious drinking! That is what the fellow said, serious drinking" more laughter this time with applause.

"Very well then" replied Wojan "Challenge accepted, but first follow me to the King's Hall. Business must come first my brothers, business first." Taking Lord Grayhawk by the arm, followed by Sir Owen coming along next. Wojan announced "My Brothers it is Dwarfish Custom for the leaders to come first, followed by the eldest of the warriors on down to the youngest. As in battle the elder warriors are allowed to fight first. They know more about fighting. The youngest learn from watching them, and if all the elders are slain the youngest still survive to carry on the clan.

It took a few minutes to sort out the ages and dates of birth among those in the same year. Soon they were all tramping single file, down the stairs and out into the main hall. They continued in a line heading towards the right and the far end of the hall where it appeared as though the light was much brighter.

They moved out into the center of the hall, and began passing between rows of shops and stalls on either side of them. All of them lit from within by yellow glowing candle lamps. There was no dwarf present in any of them. They passed knife makers, axe makers, boot makers, clock makers, pot makers, jewelers, tailors, furriers, and every sort of artist and craftsman trade you can imagine weaving looms, and other such things.

Small shops they were, most perhaps eight foot by ten foot. A few were twice that size. There was no one in them. All of their wares were still in the open and on display.

"Where is everyone?" asked Grayhawk of Wojan.

"They have all gathered in the Kronehalle" he replied, "We haven't had visitors in a long time, so everyone wants to see and hear the proceedings. They want to hear what news you bring of the outer world."

They tramped on down the center aisle, heading towards the north end of the chamber which now appeared to be aglow with light. Now they could hear the low buzz of lots of people talking. When finally they came to the end of the shop area they found themselves at the top of an amphitheater. It was bowl shaped with at least fifty rows of benches all filled with dwarves. There was a long flight of stairs heading downward from where they were at the top of the bowl to a flat half circle of open space at the bottom. All talking ceased as the appeared at the top of the stairs. Wojan held up his hand for all to halt. Now all could see the dais that ran across the back of the amphitheater like a stage. Thereon were the King and Queen's thrones of dark polished wood that appeared to be rather ornately and heavily carved.

On either side of the thrones were two rows of chairs with arms, also of dark carved wood. Most spectacular was the back drop behind the thrones and the source of the glowing white/blue light. There were crystals of every hue and color, some over twelve feet tall, magnificent, beautiful beyond belief. The light seemed to twinkle and flash all throughout the display which must have been fifty feet or more wide. The light did not distract or hurt the eyes.

Wojan was grinning like a crocodile. "Impressive, wouldn't you say?"

"Absolutely" replied Grayhawk. Sir Owen and most of the others just stood there blinking. Not completely overshadowed by the crystal display were the King and Queen of Dwarvenholm, 0'Drinain and Giselle. He was, attired in his gold and silver armor, battle axe across his lap, and her in a silver dress with a gold bodice. Both were pale blonde, with shoulder length hair, looking very much like twin siblings from here. 'Cousins' came, the unbidden thought into Grayhawk's mind. This is acceptable here when no other clan can be reached to furnish a princess. The prince was seated on his father's right. With a nod from his father he arose and stepped to the front of the dais, carrying a long silver staff which he banged the end of down onto the floor three times, each ringing like a bell in the vaulted chamber.

"Who comes here?" he demanded in a loud voice, rolling his r's. Wojan stepped forward and answered

"Majesties and Brethren of Dwarvenholm, I present to you this day an Adept, Brother Knight of the Templar Order, Grayhawk, a Blademaster of Norda and Warlord of Keltan, Brother Knight Commander Owen of Dan and these fine brother warrior knights who accompany them. They have arrived direct from Solace."

"What do they seek from the Dwarven folk?" the Prince's voice rang out loud in the hall.

"They do but seek our aide on a mission against the Dark Lord in his domain" Wojan answered.

"And what exactly is this mission against the Dark Lord, Brother Wojan?"

"They are directed by the 'Source' to go into the domain of the Dark Lord in order to slay the Dragons he has awakened and to destroy their egg clutch, My Prince" answered Wojan.

There arose at this point a general alarm among the Dwarven folk. Loud cries of alarm could be heard, such as "Dragons? What Dragons? All know there are no more Dragons! The Dark Lord has Dragons! When? How? Are we in danger of an attack from them? How many?!!!"

The king, though still seated, raised his hands in a motion of silence. The Prince banged his staff three more times on the floor. "Order, my people, we will have order here. All questions will be answered in due course." The Prince spoke even louder than before and at that the crowd seemed calmed and returned to their seats.

The King arose from his throne at this point. He said "Let these honored visitors be received in due and proper form. In keeping with the customs of our folk, a feast is declared in their honor. Time enough for talk of Dragons and Dark Lords on the morrow! Come forward Brother Knights of the Temple. Introduce thyself to the Dwarven folk here assembled and be welcome."

Grayhawk stepped forward to the first step down. He introduced himself to polite applause from the Dwarven folk and continued on down the central stairs to the bottom floor in front of the King's dais. He was followed in turn by Sir Owen and then every member of their party according to their age, beginning with Sir Walter the eldest and ending with Sir Godfrey the youngest. Once they were all down the stairs the King and his entire party stood. The Prince announced the formal reception over and invited all to attend the feast in honor of their guests.

Wojan motioned for Grayhawk and the others to follow, and exited to the right side of the King's dais through an arched door, down a long hall and then down further on a wide staircase into another great hall. It was lit by oil lamps and glow crystals. This hall was again a large and open, airy room, two large open firepits in the center, attended by numerous dwarves in white linen aprons. They were turning and basting what appeared to be, four great Auroch bulls mounted on spits. On either side of the fire pits were row after row of long low tables along the wall with x leg stands holding beer kegs between them.

On either side of the hail across from the fire pits were large arched portals, two to a side, through which were even more dwarves with white aprons who were carrying large trays and steaming platters on their shoulders, obviously coming out from the kitchens. At either end of the hail were great staircases coming down from an upper level. They were, at a guess, fifty feet wide and the Dwarven folk were moving down them and spreading out among the tables grabbing mugs and forming lines at the beer kegs.

The smells coming from the roasting bulls and the other foods were wonderful. Grayhawk looked up and saw that there were great smoke vents cut into the ceiling. The room was warm and inviting. The sounds of laughter and enjoyment were beginning to increase as the hall filled.

The King and his party arrived as Grayhawk and the Knights were on the main floor moving toward the center. The Royal Party dispersed and moved among the tables with everyone else. The King and the Prince both took trays and platters from the cooks who were bringing them out of the kitchen. They went about setting them on various tables, laughing and joking with all around them.

Grayhawk smiled as he took all of it in, thinking to himself, "if all the Kings of the world would but conduct themselves so, the world would be a far better place." As they approached the area of the firepits, the roasting bulls could now be seen for how truly large they were. In addition they could see that other animals, deer, pig, and stag were also on spits.

Wojan stopped them with a raised hand. "My Brothers, you are among friends here. Sit where ever you can find a seat. Eat, drink, and enjoy this feast in your honor. Never fear if you drink too much. Someone will show you to your quarters. Grayhawk, you and Sir Owen are bid to come and sit with the King. He would talk with you."

As the others disappeared among the Dwarves they found themselves a seat and a beer mug. Wojan guided Grayhawk and Sir Owen through the throng to one of the tables along the side wall. It was a round one with about ten dwarf sized chairs and two larger ones. The King was already seated and waived to them "come join me. We've even found a couple of chairs big enough to accommodate you two."

"We thank thee for the hospitality and the comforts of Dwarvenholm" said Grayhawk as they walked up to the table. The King arose and gripped forearms first with Grayhawk and then with Sir Owen.

"The formal thank you is noted Grayhawk but here in the Prosit Halle we are very informal. Here we relax and anyone can talk to the King or the Prince or any other without ceremony. In here I'm called O'Drinain and sometimes even worse things. In here if you have a grudge against another you can start a fist fight or even a food fight, but no weapon may be drawn in anger. No matter what! The penalty is death!"

"Ye Gods!" exclaimed Sir Owen as they took their seats at the table.

"That rule will certainly keep me peaceful." "Aye" said Grayhawk "I fully agree and I know for sure that I will not start a food fight either. There must be at least five thousand souls in this hall. Can you imagine all of them throwing their food at each other?"

"It is surely a sight to behold" said the Prince as he joined them at the table. "I have seen it. It takes days to scrub the place clean afterwards. This is the King's table and even it is not safe."

"Aye" said the King, laughing. The only real benefit to sitting here with me is that you don't have to stand in line for food or beer. They will serve it to us here." And, sure enough, at that point other dwarves began setting down, mugs and beer, while others brought steaming platters of piled high sliced meats and other dishes which turned out to be various kinds of mushrooms in gravies and sauces. This along with good hard, dark bread slices.

Their plates were heavy, dark green obsidian glass, with streaks of what appeared to be real gold. Everyone, of course, had his or her own personal eating knife of six or eight inches length. This of course made getting food from the platters to your own plate, at a table often, most interesting. Fortunately they made it through the meal without any serious injury. Grayhawk and Owen were finished eating long before the Dwarves even began to slow down. They were absolutely amazed at the prodigious amount of food and beer these folk could consume at one sitting. The food was delicious. The beer was excellent, a dark nutty flavored brew with a thick foam head. It was almost cold and went down easy.

Long into the 'night' the feasting and drinking went on. Grayhawk lost all track of time. Many folk came to the table to ask questions, or just to talk. Some came to air gripes to their King, others to find out about the outside world. Of course everyone wanted to know about the dragons. A few talked of the old legends among their folk of the Dark Lord and his minions. Even drinking moderately, at some point Grayhawk found the world got fuzzy. He found himself being led through cool ventilated tunnels, which were defiantly a relief, and finally being shown to his bed by Dwarves who were obviously drunker than he was. Most of the other Knights had already returned. Some looked like they were dead. Others were snoring vociferously. The last thing Grayhawk remembered was someone hollering at someone named Ralph. 'Not one of ours' he thought.

Chapter Sixteen

Grayhawk awoke after what he thought must have been an extended sleep. Looking around the room he could see none of the others were awake yet. As he was not one who suffers from 'morning after' or alcohol hangover, he took a quick dip in the bathing pool and then into his morning sword drill routine. He was at it for over an hour before any of the others began to stir. As Grayhawk finished one of his routines, he noticed Wojan the Dwarf Knight standing in the room by the door.

"Greetings Blademaster!" he said quietly.

"Greetings Sir Wojan" he replied. "Have I kept you waiting for long?"

"Nay my Lord, a few moments only" "You move well indeed Blademaster" said Wojan. "I do not envy your enemies."

"My thanks Brother Wojan" he replied. "Have you news for me or did you come to see if we survived the night?"

"Both" said Wojan with a big smile. "There are wagers on the condition of you and the others. All though" he said holding up a small hand "The Dwarves are impressed with the drinking abilities of the Temple Knights. Most of the time Men do not stand up well to our beer."

"It is potent indeed my brother" said Grayhawk smiling. "Most of them are still out as you can readily see" gesturing in sweeping motion with his arm. "What news do you bring?"

"Only that, the King would speak with you and Sir Owen. At your convenience of course, he awaits you in his morning chamber."

"Do I yet live?" there came forth a muffled gruff voice from the covers of Sir Owens bed. "I heard voices and then my name and I wondered if it were the boatman calling me to cross over. But, the pressure on my head tells me I do yet live."

"That you do Owen of Dan" said Grayhawk, grinning. "So stir thyself from repose as we are summoned into the presence of the King"

"At your convenience of course!" said Wojan, also grinning.

"Which translated of course, means immediately" said Sir Owen, sitting up on the side of his bunk looking like a refugee from a bad drunk.

"Of course" replied Wojan. "He is the King after all. But, I think he will make allowances this morn. I will return for you in half an hour.

"Thank you Brother Wojan. We will be ready when you return." Said Grayhawk as Wojan departed chuckling and Owen wrapped himself in a blanket like a hooded monk and walked down toward the bath talking to himself. Grayhawk stripped and jumped in also, washing away the sweat from his workout.

Half an hour later they walked out into the hallway fully dressed and combed. Wojan met them in the stairway.

"Ah, looking much better I see" he said grinning.

"Well" said Owen "I'm glad one of us can see, I think I am blind. Oh no, wait, whew! My eyes were closed." This time they crossed straight across the Halle to the doorway where stood two Dwarves in armor, with Battle Axes to hand. As they entered the doorway between the guards Wojan explained

"The guards are there to let everyone know that this meeting is an official "State Business" affair and no one can interrupt."

"Makes sense" said Owen "everything around here is pretty informal. It's a good way to mark the difference." This time they mounted a long flight of steep stairs with a small landing at the top, and an ornately carved wooden door shaped like a shield. This chamber used to be the clan war room, but, explained Wojan

"We haven't had a war in so long it is now just called the Morning, or Audience Chamber." They entered through the door into a fully wood paneled and wooden floored chamber, about one hundred feet long by forty feet wide. Down the middle ran a long wooden table, itself some sixty feet long and ten feet wide. On top of it were a proliferation of scrolls, maps, huge leather bound books and an oil lamp every five feet or so. There were ink wells with writing quills standing up in silver vases.

The table could have easily seated fifty or more Dwarves, and at least that many chairs were pulled back from the table, and lining the walls on both sides. Half a dozen or so chairs on the far side were pulled up to the table and occupied by Clarks, all female and all busily working with quill and ink on various parchments, scrolls and books. The King, O'Drinain, and his son Prince Drinach stood at the far right end of the table. O'Drinain looked up as they entered and waved them over.

"Come in, Come in. I hope you are in good health and spirits this morn" said the King smiling.

"We are well Majesty" replied Grayhawk "Just moving a trifle slow this morn."

"As are we all" said the Prince, rubbing his temple.

"Well then" said the King "Let us refresh ourselves before we get to the business at hand." With that he picked up a small bell from the table and rang it several times. At this point a section of the wall paneling on the back wall clicked open and swung outward revealing a passageway. Through the opening several more females pushed out three small serving carts on wheels. The first had two large steaming pots of tea, mugs and pots of honey. The second had breads, rolls, butter, sliced meats and cheeses, and mustard. The third had pastries, filled fruit pies and other delicacies, Grayhawk and Owen did not recognize.

There was also a smaller round table at the end of the room, to where they all adjourned to in order to breakfast. Grayhawk had just begun to feel really hungry and this was a welcome treat. Everyone else probably felt the same because for a period of time there was very little talking. Finally there came a sort of general sigh of relief from all present. They had eaten everything from the carts and most were on their second mug of honey laced, strong dark tea. Everyone sat back in his chair feeling much better.

As soon as the servers had cleared the table and left another big pot of tea on it, they quickly departed through the 'secret' panel. As the panel closed behind the last of them the King said

"If you would all be so kind as to pull your chairs close to the table, we can begin the business at hand."

As they did so the King reached inside his robe and brought forth what looked to be a golden egg. When he sat it down on the table in front of Grayhawk it could be seen that it was an egg shaped golden ball about 4 inches tall, the bottom or larger end was flattened so that it would not fall over and that it appeared to be hinged in the middle.

"This is for you Adept Grayhawk" said King O'Drinain. We dwarves have held it for you since before you were born, by order of the 'Source'.

"What exactly is it?" asked Grayhawk, picking it up and turning it to and fro to look at the intricate and delicate engraving which covered the surface.

"Open it" said the King "and see for yourself." Holding it in his left hand, Grayhawk grasped the top half of the egg with his right hand and folded it back. From within came a bright blue, yet cool, light, which faded in a couple of seconds. There within was revealed a gold ring with a large blue egg shaped stone as center piece with a white diamond on either side. All of the rings surfaces were engraved with runes so tiny you could just make them out.

"A Ring, for me?" asked Grayhawk, looking puzzled.

"Aye" relied the King. "It is the ring of a chosen Adept. It has the power to amplify your magic, to enable you to scry over great distances, to read men's minds, to cloud men's thinking and vision. You may even speak with the dead. All of its powers are not known to us, for it was not created on this world. You must wear it on the middle finger of your left hand. But not all the time or it will begin to cloud your mind, like a mild potion for sleep." Grayhawk lifted the ring from the egg with his right hand. He sat the egg back on the table and then slid the ring onto his left middle finger. It fit perfectly and felt warm. The stone was like looking into deep blue water. Something clicked in his mind and he physically felt the connection to the rings power take hold in his mind. Everyone present just sat, looking at him, waiting for some reaction or sign. He nodded slowly, looking at each of them in turn.

"I can feel its power in my mind" he said. "I have no idea yet what all I might be able to do. It will no doubt take some time to come to grips with."

"Well and good then" said the King. "The egg goes with it. Keep it in there when you are not wearing it. Oh! And don't wear it when sleeping unless you are in danger of attack. Otherwise you will not sleep well." Now he continued, on to other matters.

"First, we the Dwarvenfolk wish to assist in your upcoming mission. I have counseled with my son and the elders of the clan. It has been decided that Prince Drinach will lead a group of twenty five of our best warrior/stonecutters. At present the only one here who knows exactly what quest you are embarking on is I, per request of Sir Tinian. I agree that it is best if not everyone in the world know and subsequently be talking about it."

"I agree" said Grayhawk, nodding his head.

"Good" continued the King. "I will send Sir Wojan here" pointing at him "as second to my son. So that if you have no objection, my son will accompany you to Keltan in order to establish formal diplomatic relations between us, for the first time in over a thousand years. We would like to have trade with an outside nation again. Would we be welcomed? Do you suppose?"

"Oh, absolutely Majesty" replied Grayhawk. "After they recover from the shock of finding that Dwarves actually do exist." Everyone chuckled at that.

"Very well, then. My son will select two, to accompany him as retainers; they will go along with you Grayhawk, as my personal envoy. Sir Wojan will take charge of the other twenty three and proceed south to the city of Tuscana, where according to Sir Tinian; they will meet up with a Buscan pirate you all know named Olion. He says he has 'obtained' the finest ship ever built. Together they will sail around Gaula and Spanos to Keltan, Then up the river to the King's City. Sir Tinian informs me that this will give you, right about six weeks from today to return home, gather the group you wish to accompany you, and be prepared to embark on a voyage all the way back around to Aegia and then as far up the Nahilia river as you can. Or by another longer route if you so choose."

"Yes Majesty, and that's when the real fun part will begin" replied Grayhawk, leaning back in his chair. "This journey will be one of the most dangerous ever made by anyone. The Dark Lord's servants and priests will be constantly searching for us. They will be looking to destroy everyone involved. While they also do not know the exact nature of the mission they know from the portents and prophecies that a major event is coming. They know that it will be directed against them. So they will do everything in their power to stop us. Traveling by ship as much as possible will make it harder for them to find us."

"Only one other aid for your quest have I to give you" said King O'Drinain "but it could well be the most important." With that he walked over to the front wall of the chamber and opened a panel of the woodwork. He disappeared into the opening only to reemerge a few seconds later with three large leather bags, tube shaped, which were about three and a half feet long. They were made of very stiff leather, ebony black with shoulder straps and a round leather cap on one end. They clanked a little as he moved indicating something of metal was inside. 'Too short for swords' thought Grayhawk. His interest was now peaked. Something to aid us he thought, they must certainly contain weapons of some kind.

The King brought the bags over to the table and leaned them upright against the side of the table. Picking up one of the bags and sliding off the end cap, he tilted the bag onto the table bottom end up. As he did so there slid into view and out onto the table twenty five of the deadliest looking arrows anyone had ever seen. They were all metal, with shiny, nasty looking, barbed, 4 inch, three blade heads on a thirty two inch satin silver metal shaft, with three shiny four inch long, metal fletching or feathers on the rear.

"These" said the King "are the last seventy five Dragon Bane arrows known to exist in the world. They are tipped with enchanted Mithrail silver heads and fletched with the same material. The shafts are a very light weight metal which only a few Dwarves know how to produce." Everyone had picked up one of the arrows and they all were examining them.

"Look how sharp they are" exclaimed Owen as he shaved a patch on his forearm.

"Only a strong archer with a strong bow can use them" said the King. "They will only penetrate the scales and armor on the chest and underbelly of a dragon. They will not work on the heavy armor on their backs. Choose only the strongest and best archers, Grayhawk; train them well, for surely your very lives will depend upon these arrows."

"I bid you take them, use them as you will, recover them if you can and return as many as possible to us for future use."

"We will make every effort to do just that Your Majesty" said Grayhawk. "I do not know how to thank you properly for I was indeed in some want of a solution or a weapon which would be effective against Dragon kind. For, I know that we will surely encounter them on this journey." Grayhawk stood facing the diminutive King his blond head barely reaching Grayhawk's chest, but they clasped forearms in traditional warrior style. Grayhawk noted that the King's forearm was as thick and muscular as his own.

"Well and done then" said the Dwarven King. "There is but one other task I would lay upon your shoulders Lord Grayhawk. And that is this, if any way possible, bring my son back alive!"

"I hope to bring us all back alive your Majesty" replied Grayhawk. "If it is the All Fathers will."

"Good, then we will leave it in his hands and help where we can. Now it has come to be the time for you and yours to depart from Dwarvenholm and begin your journey to face destiny. I will pray for your success and look forward to the next time when we can all drink beer and laugh together even unto telling great shining war stories of what was."

"Lord Grayhawk we bid you farewell. And thee also, Sir Owen and Sir Wojan." With that the King embraced his son. "Come back to us Son!" he said.

"I will Father" replied the Prince. The King turned and strode from the room and down the stairs to the great hall.

Prince Drinach looked a little misty around the eyes. Wiping them he said sheepishly "I've never been away before. I've never even been much outside of this mountain."

"Well my young friend" said Sir Owen "you really are in for some surprises."

Sir Wojan spoke up. "Then let us be off, Blademaster, your folk are already moving through a tunnel which will bring you all out of the mountains in a small valley which lead down into eastern Keltan. All of your wounded men are up and walking, including the 'Bear Killer'. When we asked about the hide and flesh, of the bear he said

'You keep it! I never want to see it again'. So the King will have the hide in his library as a rug."

"Excellent!" replied Grayhawk "Let us gather our things and be off."

"Already taken care of" said Sir Wojan. "Prince Drinach knows the way you must go. I will take my leave of you now. If all goes well, I will see you in six weeks." They each exchanged arm clasps, and said see you soon.

The Prince said "Follow me" and headed down the stairs and out into the great hall. Moving at an angle to the right they crossed the hall and went behind the row of shops. About halfway down the line a Dwarf held open a stone slab of a door and they moved into a dimly lit passage way that seemed to stretch a long way. The group of them walked for what must have been three hours, through other stone doorways and down other long passage ways. No more oil lamps were present here, only glowing crystals set in the ceiling every so often. Eventually they came upon an alcove in the wall and here they found food and water.

After an hour of rest they were up and moving again. This time there were long staircases, both up and down, more long straight passages, one of which ended at a stone door. This led to another passage and then an alcove with bed platforms cut into the walls.

They slept for what Grayhawk felt must have been about six hours. They prepared a good meal of bread, sausages with cheese and hot tea. Then they were moving again.

After moving through two more break periods they at last came to a larger chamber, fifty feet or so across, with a small double door in the far side. The door frame and lintel was extensively carved in ancient runic symbols. The Prince went over to the door, placed a hand on each of the double doors, spoke some Dwarfish words, none of which the other could understand, and the doors swung outwards.

Chapter Seventeen

The cool mountain air rushed in, and all could see through the doorway, a dark night sky with millions of stars. Grayhawk was first through the door and out into the night air. The feeling of the dome of the night sky was one of immenseness and for the second time in his life Grayhawk felt very small. The ledge he was standing on was overlooking a moonlit mountain valley falling down and away from him for a long distance. The ledge ran down and to his left to a small clearing or meadow and there he could see a camp with tents and lanterns, people and horses. Fires were burning and the smells of food were carried on the night air.

A couple of deep breaths and he looked around to the others. Sir Owen was looking out at the valley with a big smile, but Prince Drinach was down on his knees with one hand on the wall of rock for support. He looked up at Grayhawk and with a weak smile he said "I wasn't prepared for how big it is out here." Grayhawk gave him his hand and helped him to his feet. "Wait until you are on the ocean Your Highness. It gets even bigger." People from the camp were now moving up towards them. The Prince waved his hand and said a word. With that the portal doors closed behind them.

"Well!" said the Prince "I said I wanted to have an adventure!"

Several of the brother knights were coming up from the camp below in the clearing. But Grayhawk and the others, though tired, started down the trail on their own. It was good to see everyone again, especially Guillome who had been sorely wounded in the fight with the bear. "Bear killer Guillome" as he was now called was moving surprisingly well. The side of his face and head were nasty purple and yellow in color as the swelling went down and the bruising began to heal. In fact, all those who had been under the care of the Dwarven healers were doing remarkably well and all spoke very highly of the care they had been given. You could tell by his eyes that this made the young Prince very proud.

All of their gear and their horses had been here waiting for them when their guides led them out of the mountain. They were the two elder Dwarf warriors who had been, chosen to accompany the Prince as his retainers. They had all emerged from the mountain about midday and subsequently had set up camp to await Grayhawk and the others.

It was only just now full dark. Supper was cooking and the camp fires were a definite welcome after being inside the mountain. The air was fresh and cool. Sir Owen made the statement that he had not known before that rock has a smell of its own. The Dwarves all laughed and asked him "which kind did he smell? Was it Granite, basalt, or limestone? Each smells different, you know." Owen laughed and shook his head.

"Hey! I thought I had done well just to determine there is a smell."

The Prince had informed Grayhawk that there was very little chance of their being attacked by anyone or anything at this location. So, the evening was one of relaxation and camaraderie. After a good supper of stew, black bread, cheese and tea, all present sat back to enjoy good brandy and a bowl of tabac. A minimum guard was set before all retired for the night. Grayhawk slept better than he had for a long time. He awoke at first light. As Sir Owen was also awake moved into an open area and engaged in sword drill routines and then mock combat for over an hour. Prince Drinach and his two warriors sat and watched intensely during the whole time.

Two hours later the camp was packed and they moved out down the trail. Prince Drinach and company were riding chestnut brown ponies with flowing blond manes and tails.

"It is said that Dwarves hate horses" said Sir Owen riding next to the Prince. "Yet you ride very well."

"Well, Sir Owen" replied the Prince "These are not horses, they are ponies. And it's not that we hate horses, they are just too big for us to ride and it takes a lot of Dwarves to eat one."

"EAT ONE!" said Sir Owen looking truly shocked. "How in the world could you eat a horse?"

"Oh" said the Prince "We generally like them roasted on a spit, but baked is good too!" Sir Owen looked a little sick and both his mount and Grayhawk's craned their necks around to give the Prince a decidedly evil look. Grayhawk had the distinct impression that the ponies were laughing. The Prince just sat up straight in his saddle and looked smug.

It took until midday the following day to come out at the end of the valley. As they climbed a gentle slope of grass up to a saddle between two low hills they came upon a stone marker about four feet tall. One side read KELTAN and the other AUSERLIA Faces lit up and there was some good hearted cheering for a few minutes and a lot of bantering about what they were going to do first. The Prince spurred his pony up beside Grayhawk's horse. "Looks like these fellows are glad to be back at home. Well, I mean at least in their home land."

"Aye" said Grayhawk with a smile "It has only just occurred to me that we have been gone for over three months. Closer to four by the time we get back to the King's City. The real hard part of course is the fact that we have lost a full third of our original company. So many good men are dead." The comment seemed to sober everyone and the whole group fell silent. Grayhawk was sorry that he had ever voiced it out loud. All rode in silence for some minutes. But then as though inevitable, someone made a comment about gloom and doom. A few minutes later the whole group was talking again about the good things they have been missing from home.

The Prince and his two companions just shook their heads in amazement at how much talk there was about women. It seems that Dwarves would never carry on so. Sir Owen observed that

'Then perhaps they should start', which caused the Dwarves to look at each other with raised eyebrows. The first days ride in Keltan was peaceful; if a little cool, with a fairly stiff breeze. That night they found good shelter in an up-thrust rock formation that blocked the wind effectively.

All day long and on into the evening, as they cooked their supper meal and set up camp, Grayhawk was having feelings of impending danger to the group, and some sort of a sense of an evil presence. At about the fourth hour after darkness, some two hours before midnight, Grayhawk wrapped in his traveling cape, Adept ring on his finger, and fully armed. Informing Sir Owen of his intent did move some little distance from camp to the top of a thirty foot tall rock with a flat top. On top he found a fairly large area of approximately twenty by forty feet, oval shaped and very flat. It seemed as if it had been leveled by man for some purpose or the other.

The wind from today had died down considerably though it remained wet and cold. 'There will be a frost this night' thought Grayhawk to himself as he went to one end of the oval where he could face back to the east towards Solace and where he could watch the only easy access up to the top. Sitting down, in a cross leg position, and tucking his cape around himself like a tent, putting up the hood, of course with both swords quick to hand. He set about calming his mind and thought patterns to begin casting with his senses, in order to determine the source of unease that he was feeling.

He didn't think that the group was in danger of an attack but he had to be sure. His first casting was a general sweep of three hundred sixty degrees of the local area where they were camped.

He then began searching both slowly and carefully, in increasing outward spirals, for a total distance of five miles. He could detect nothing more dangerous than a pair of mating wolves who were engrossed in their romantic antics. Just as he was finishing with this he became aware of at least four separate bands of scrying energy coming from the southwest. He could tell that the sorcerers doing the scrying were very tired and that they had located nothing.

'They seek us still' he thought. 'We dropped from their vision weeks ago and they still seek to locate us. I should send them a nasty surprise using their own energy beams. But if I do they will then have the general vicinity we are in. He kept his own energy levels very low so as not to attract their attention and soon their beams became narrower and weaker, until finally they stopped. 'For the night!' though Grayhawk 'they will be at it again at first light, no doubt.' Still he could sense evil. Some vile taint was on the wind. It was as yet unrecognizable to him but Grayhawk did not doubt that it was emanating from part of the Dark Lord's power.

And then, all of the sudden, some ten feet in front of him, there grew into being from a small white spot in the air, a great white oval of light some ten feet tall. All around the edges, radiating outward, were rays of gold, light blue and pure white light. It was as though a star had suddenly appeared up close. Grayhawk rose to his feet leaving his weapons on the ground for he knew inside his heart that this was not an evil apparition or ghost. There stepped from within the oval of light, onto the rock, a being of great beauty, a man, or a kind of man. He, at least Grayhawk thought it was a male, was over seven feet tall, long brown wavy hair, green eyes that seemed to glow with an inner fire. He wore a long flowing pure white robe with golden lapels and a golden cuff, boots of gold that looked like the metal itself, and at the waist, a sword belt of gold with a glittering silver buckle and hung on the left a great two handed long sword in a gold and silver sheath. His left hand resting on the pommel of the sword, his right thumb hooked in to the sword belt.

"Greetings Lord Grayhawk," he said as he took a step forward out of the oval of light. "I am Michael, I come from the presence of the All Father to bring you his blessing and to impart some information" He held out his right hand and Grayhawk stepped forward and gripped forearms with him in warrior style. "Greetings Lord Michael" said Grayhawk as he felt the strength of Michael's arm. 'Not of this earth' he thought to himself. "No" said Michael, smiling, "I am not of this earth, although, long ago, my brothers and I did walk upon it. Before Lucifer's war, when your race was new. But that is a story for another time. For now I have come to tell you, the Dark Lord, as he is now referred to, has become aware that you are a threat to his plan and his quest to take possession of this planet and all who inhabit it. If he wins he will conquer, enslave and destroy utterly your race, even those who are foolish enough to believe they can serve him. He does not know yet exactly what you plan to do, and you must take every measure to ensure he does not find out. For if he knew he would hide the eggs where they would never be found.

He does not believe you will attack him in his domain, for he knows you cannot kill or destroy him personally. He would sacrifice every other being he controls to stop you.

He can be wounded. He does feel pain. He does not normally fight with weapons. He never did like to, but he will if necessary. He is half again as large as I. Though, if any man could fight him, it would be a Blademaster such as you. Know this also. To help with your mission others are coming to join your group. In addition to the Dwarves, there are twenty of Odranna's Chosen from the caverns in Norda, en route to the King's City. They will travel only at night, because of the light. They trained you, so you know their value in a fight underground. Lastly a small group from Danaan will accompany you. They are Elves and they are masters of archery and concealment."

"Elves!" said Grayhawk. "Yet another people I thought only existed in myth and legend."

Michael smiled again. "Across this universe and on the Nine Planes, Brother Grayhawk, there are thousands of species of 'people' and sentient beings. Even I cannot name all of them. Know ye also Blademaster, Dragons are sentient beings. They feel, they think, they care for their young and they will die to protect their eggs. Not all of them are evil. Remember this. It will be important to you one day.

One last thing have I to impart to you Lord Grayhawk. The evil that you sense this day, a sort of miasma on the air, which is Lucifer himself casting from within his hole in the ground. Because of the form he has been given for his body, he cannot use his powers fully. If he ever regains his true form he will be more powerful than any of us, including me. Should you come face to face, so to speak, with him call him 'Lucifer' that is his true name and the use of it causes him pain. When you are speaking of him, call him by name. To refer to him as the 'Dark Lord' only increases his power and mystique. I must depart now Lord Grayhawk. My duties take me to other places. We will meet again I am sure." Extending his arm again Grayhawk gripped it saying

"Can I have but one question of you before you go?"

"Certainly!" replied Michael. "You wish to know who I am and where I come from" again with that radiant smile."Very well then I and all of my brothers are the direct servants of the All Father. We are the first beings he created after the creation of the universe. We assist him in all things. We helped to create your kind. When he decided what you would look like and said 'Let us create man in our image' he was talking to us. We have existed for longer than you can calculate. And 'yes' Lucifer used to be one of us. He was the most beautiful of our kind, our brightest light. But he wanted to be the All Father and there was a war. He lost and those of our kind, who sided with him, were cast out into the realm of evil. Those who still exist are there still." With a sad look on his face Michael lifted his hand in a farewell wave and stepped back into the oval of light and disappeared.

Grayhawk stood there pondering all of it until the cold wind made him begin to shiver. Shaking his head as though clearing a fog, he pulled his cape closed about him, picked up his weapons and returned to the camp. Laying down on his bedroll with his cloak still wrapped around him and the hood pulled up he immediately went into a sound sleep and slept the rest of the night through without a dream He awake in the gray light of dawn. There was a distinct chill in the air. He had not gotten into his bedroll so he rose to his feet, stretched and went out of the tent into a cold thick fog, almost icy, thick and wet.

"Where did this come from?" asked Sir Walter, one of the older Knights.

"If I told you" said Grayhawk, "you would not believe it."

"Now Blademaster" said Prince Drinach, "what pray tell do you mean by that?"

Grayhawk smiled to himself. 'Thank you Michael'. Now there will be no effective scrying for our location. Even the sense of evil from Lucifer was less this morning.

All that day they rode in thick fog, relying on the built in direction sense that all Dwarves are born with and some casting by Grayhawk. All in all it seemed like riding in a dream, no real sense of distance covered and not one living thing did they see that day, neither fowl nor beast, and not even any sign of habitation or people. All knew though that this most eastern part of Keltan was yet uninhabited and frequented only by hunters and the King's Rangers who patrol the borders.

By evening the fog had cleared and the stars were out in force. They found a good camp site in a thicket of briars, canopied open areas almost like rooms, plenty of grass for the horses and ponies and a good bubbling spring for water. After the fog lifted the temperature had come up considerably, much to everyone's relief. Soon the whole campsite was hung with soaked travel cloaks and personal clothing. It seemed as though everything they possessed had soaked through.

Later, as the camp settled down around a number of small fires and ate a supper of stew, trail bread, cheese and tea, everyone seemed at least to be comfortable again. Some of the wounded were still healing, but doing well. Prince Drinach, Sir Owen and Grayhawk were at one of the fires with their sleeping gear laid out back towards the wall of the thicket. Everyone checked their weapons, mostly for rust, and then settled back for a bowl of tabac and some brandy.

"My Lord Grayhawk" said the Prince, "I cannot but think that you did have something to do with today's fog! Is that not so?"

"Nay my Prince" answered Grayhawk "It surely was not I. Though, I do believe that I know who it was." Both the Prince and Sir Owen turned to look at him at that point. Grayhawk took a drink of brandy from his mug and began: "You see, last evening when I went out from camp, up into the rocks to cast about and see if we were facing any dangers, I did have a most unusual visitor." He then proceeded to tell them of Michael and his conversation with him. When he finished telling the tale, he leaned forward for a brand from the fire and relit his pipe, then leaned back against his saddle. Sir Owen said nothing, just puffing on his pipe.

"We do know of those beings" said Prince Drinach. "In our lore there are tales of being visited by Michael, Gabriel, Uriel and others whose names I cannot recall. I never was really sure whether or not they were just myths and legends. I guess I will have to reevaluate now. It seems though, I recall Michael as being the protector and patron of the warriors. Perhaps that is why you were visited by him."

"We too" said Sir Owen "have such beings in our lore. Grayhawk, you surely know that Danfinia and Rungar share the same legends of Odranna and his sons and daughters."

"Aye" said Grayhawk "I do know that. I am here to tell you now that all of these tales, myths and legends of the Gods and their families and their servants and so on, are just different accountings of the same story. There is only the one All Father, no matter what he is called. What is more, Michael and his brothers once walked this earth. That I am sure is where all of the tall tales and legends stem from. For they were all beings whose powers and even their physical size made them seem as giants and even as gods to the humans and other races upon this planet."

"What you say certainly has credence!" replied Prince Drinach.

"Aye" said Sir Owen "It changes my mind and outlook on many levels."

"Indeed, indeed" Said Grayhawk. "I see the truth of it. I surely see the truth of it."

For some time the three of them sat there with the warmth of the crackling fire, smoking their pipes and drinking their brandies. All lost deep in thought about the scope and magnitude of it all. The night passed, starlit, quiet and peaceful. Everyone was up at first light and an hour later they were moving west through the forest at a good pace. All knew that in two days they would be back at the Academy where they had started from.

That day and the next it rained off and on. Just enough to slow travel some. Other than that, the journey was uneventful. They arrived at the Academy on the afternoon of the third day. The whole cadre and corps of the place turned out to greet them. Sir Gregory was most glad to see their return. In short order the news was dispatched by courier to the King and Court, both the glad tidings of their safe return and bringing with them a delegation of the Dwarven Clan and Crown. Of course the sad news of their losses on the journey were also conveyed and that they would rest the night here at the Academy and would arrive in the afternoon tomorrow at the King's city. Everyone was totally amazed to learn of the existence of Dwarves and to meet them face to face; well this was cause for celebration. So, a feast was hurriedly set up in the main dining hall. While it was being prepared quarters were assigned.

The Prince was given the King's room, which he promptly announced to be big enough to house about twenty Dwarves, and offered to take a smaller accommodation. Since he was visiting Royalty, he was informed by Sir Gregory that was out of the question.

The instructors and students had insisted upon taking charge of the animals and the cleaning of everyone's gear. Which left the entire group free, to adjourn to the baths for a long soak and a mug of beer. Grayhawk stayed in the hot soapy water for as long as he could stand it, then a quick dip in the cool water rinse, and up to his room for a set of clean clothes.

After a short while in his room a knock on the door and there was Sir Gregory. "Come in, come in. It's really good to see you again Sir" said Grayhawk.

"Likewise" replied Sir Gregory. "I was concerned. I have heard from Sir Tinian on the perils encountered along the way, Drulgar, Dark Priests, Dragons, A Great Bear, and Trolls. Couldn't you find any normal foes to fight?"

"Well" said Grayhawk "We did look for some. But those were all we could find."

"All of these things are going to make the Legend of Grayhawk much larger than life you know" stated Sir Gregory as he came into the room and took a seat by the window. "Which I am afraid is going to cause you some problems."

"Problems?" said Grayhawk "Don't I have sufficient problems as it is? What other problems do I have coming?"

"You will have to deal with every popinjay in the land, who will want to challenge you. They will say that your deeds are all lies and that in reality you are a coward and all that sort of thing."

"Oh, I see now" said Grayhawk "the no-names who think that they are great swordsmen. They will want to 'knock me off my high perch' so to speak'."

"Exactly" replied Sir Gregory. "How will you deal with them?"

"Well, I'm not going to spend my time answering their challenges and killing idiots in sword fights over something as vague as 'honor" said Grayhawk.

"Good" said Sir Gregory. "I mentioned it to you so that you will not be taken off guard the first time that it happens. The attack may not be what it seems." Grayhawk stopped in the middle of donning his shirt.

"Hmmm" he said. "Yes, I'll be on my guard. It's hard to believe humans can be stupid enough to fall for Lucifer's ruses and lies, much less that they actively aide him in his bid to dominate the world and totally destroy mankind. Bah! Enough of this! Let me tell you of a conversation with Michael and of the other things I have learned on this journey and to ask you to help me learn to use and control my powers better." Gregory smiled

"I will be delighted to help in any way I can and please do tell me more about Michael. I have heard of him but never seen him." For two hours over a pot of tea and several pipes Grayhawk related every detail of what had transpired while Gregory sat riveted, asking the occasional question, especial about Michael. When he at last came to the end of the narration, Gregory's eyes were misty; he smiled and said "So the eternal and immortal Knights, the Servants of the All Father, do in reality exist. They are the order from whom we are descended, long and long ago." Grayhawk thought for a moment.

"Of course," he said "I see the truth of it!"

Sir Gregory stood and stretched. "Well then let us put off further discourse for now and go down to the dining hall and enjoy a good meal. I have heard your version of all that happened but now I want to hear the Knights Tales, which of course will become the public record, with all the embellishments and exaggerations."

"Aha" said Grayhawk as they went out of his room. "I see the truth of that also! When retold, a man's deeds are always larger than he is." The dinner meal was excellent, roast boar with wild onions, green peas with carrots, black bread, butter, jam and plenty of good beer. Not quite as strong as the Dwarves brew, but even they enjoyed themselves. They listened to at least three versions of everything that had happened, each more glorious than the last. The best story of course had young Sir Guillome attacking the great bear with a pointed stick, straddling the beast like riding a horse and stabbing it to death.

Needless to say a good time was had by one and all. The celebration went on until well after midnight. As usual Grayhawk was up just after daylight. He took a hot bath and was sitting in his room enjoying some tea and cheese with sliced apples. Looking out the window he saw the arrival of several of the King's couriers. There were messages of welcome for the Dwarf Prince, and word that he would be officially received at court the following morning. A message to Grayhawk from the King welcoming him back and that the Queen Mother was very pleased that he had returned safely. That message for some reason made him nervous.

By midmorning they were packed, saddled and ready to move.

One Hundred and Fifty Knights and Cadets were to escort the visiting Prince of Dwarvenholm and the Warlord of Keltan. Grayhawk has almost forgotten that he held that title and all of the pomp and ceremony that came with it. Of course visiting Princes were always a big social occasion. He could imagine the turmoil in the Royal household, everyone trying to prepare for a state visit. 'Glad I'm not there today' he chuckled to himself.

Chapter Eighteen

The escort contingent was led by Sir Gregory himself, with the Knight Templar Standard Bearer to his right. Then came the Dwarves, Prince Drinach looking quite regal in his gold and silver armor, a helmet with white plumes was mounted behind his saddle, very striking that the ponies mane and the Prince's hair were the same pale blonde. Geldon the senior of his two retainers who held the rank equivalent to a captain, held the Dwarvenholm banner. It was a bright green field with a silver harp embroidered on it.

Grayhawk came next, Sir Owen riding to his right. He found all of this amusing. By right and position he could have 'led' the procession and somewhere or the other he had a flag, Royal Blue with a crown and crossed swords on it. Sir Gregory had been most pleased when he had asked him to take charge. They moved at a moderate pace until the middle of the afternoon. All of the villages they passed through were, of course, turned out to see a real dwarf. They were well mannered, smiling and waving.

Mid afternoon they came to a prepared rest stop, with tents erected and a good meal waiting. There were even baths for those who felt the need. There was indeed a great deal of washing and polishing of gear, everyone digging out his best clothing and boots. White Templar tabards with their red blood crosses on them were donned. Horses were groomed and fed. All of this was done without any instruction or orders being given.

Grayhawk was smiling so much at all of it, that Sir Owen asked him repeatedly what was so amusing. Sir Gregory overheard and said "Why Sir Owen, do you not know that a certain Royal Lady eagerly awaits return of our War Lord?"

"Why no, I never!" stuttered Sir Owen. "I mean, I...."

"Oh yes" laughed Sir Gregory "it is most hard to envision the Lord Grayhawk and a woman." Prince Drinach walked up at that point.

"A Royal Lady you say! Might we know whom?"

"Why none other than the Queen herself" said Sir Gregory.

"Oh my" said Drinach "Oh my" Grayhawk squinted at them with a hard look.

"It's a very good thing I regard you lot as my friends" he stated.

"Too true!" said Sir Gregory. "Nobody else could put up with you!" with that they all laughed. Although they did not notice it a lot of folks around them let their breaths out and found somewhere else to go.

When the rest hour was over and they prepared to mount Sir Gregory ordered a short brandy for everyone. "Gentlemen" he said loud enough for all to hear, "ride tall, make yourselves proud, in three short hours we will enter the King's City escorting the War Lord of Keltan from a most dangerous mission in the field and we have the distinct honor of escorting his Royal Highness, Crown Prince Drinach of Dwarvenholm. This is the first visit to our land, ever that we know of, by the Dwarves. You will not see the likes of this again in your lifetime." Everyone cheered and applauded. As they mounted Prince Drinach said

"I guess I never thought of myself as a crown prince before and I'll wager a keg of beer it will turn out to be a major pain in the backside!" Now as they rode on, the villagers became larger and closer together. Twice as they rode through a village they saw a courier in the King's livery gallop off towards the city. 'Progress reports' thought Grayhawk and just shook his head.

A bit further and they noticed off in the distance, on both sides of the them, out in the fields and by some trees, mounted, small units wearing forest green uniforms moving along keeping pace with them. "I hope those are friends" said Prince Drinach, nodding his head in their direction.

"Yes" replied Grayhawk "They are the King's Rangers, the

Bordermen. I guess he is not going to chance an attack happening this close to his capital."

"A smart fellow your young King" said Drinach.

"Yes he is indeed and a good one too! You will like him. You are quite a bit alike."

"Oh, you mean he is short, blonde and good looking like me!" laughed the Prince. Grayhawk chuckled. "Well! Two out of three, anyway" Then they emerged from the trees, turning left onto a wide, tree lined road, which ran straight for about half a mile and ended at the north gate into the city. Set in the middle of the north wall. The wall itself was some thirty feet high crenellated, with a tower every fifty feet. Not noticed until you were right up on it. The last five hundred feet of road, ran through a watery marsh right up to the city wall.

"Well" said the Prince, "I'm impressed with that. It would be damned hard to attack that wall. Dwarves would be up to their armpits in mud."

"A feature put in by the King's Grandfather. The south wall is on the river and the east and west approaches are narrow" replied Grayhawk. "Apparently the old King's enemies got right up the wall three or four times and he finally got tired of it. So he had his engineers turn the whole area into a swamp. They call it a marsh."

Outside the gate came the official military welcome. One hundred mounted, heavy cavalry lancers on each side of the road facing each other. As Sir Gregory reached the first of them, a sharp command and the troopers, all with pennant tipped lances, couched in stirrup cups, canted their lances forward at a forty five degree angle, a practiced precision move which formed an arch of triumph for the party to pass into the city through. Into the city they rode, the street were lined with throngs of cheering people, some women and girls were throwing flowers from balconies and rooftops. The smells of a city washed over them, as it was coming into evening, just an hour before full dark. The smells were of wood smoke, food cooking, tar or pitch, rope, leather and many other smells, both bad and good. Then came the wet musty smell that only a port city on great rivers can have. Grayhawk could see that the Dwarves were particularly affected by it.

On to the center of the city they rode, through curious throngs of people. At the circle in the center they turned right across the circle and then half right again onto the avenue of the Royal Palace. As they rode up to the Palace gates which were standing open and manned on either side by troops in the King's blue livery. Trumpets blared three times as they rode in to the court yard of the Palace, opened in the middle, packed with people all decked out in their best finery.

Standing on the steps up to the Palace proper was King Killian IV of Keltan, dressed in black and silver with black boots. His long Auburn hair loose and down on this shoulders. His father's greats word slung across his back, handle over his right shoulder, wearing a small gold coronet of a crown. He did not look like a man who had just turned nineteen years. To his left one step above stood the Queen Mother, also auburn haired, dressed in a long, dove gray gown with a cream colored lace bodice, she was also wearing a small gold coronet crown. Her hands were hung down by her sides, the right one trailing a long cream colored kerchief which hung all the way to the ground. 'Still the most beautiful sight I've ever seen' thought Grayhawk. Their eyes met and for long moments he could not look away. When he finally did the King, who was smiling, winked at him.

Saved at that point by the booming voice of Sir Gregory "Your Majesties, I have the privilege and honor this day to announce the return of his Lordship ,Grayhawk, War Lord of Keltan and accompanying him as an Emissary, from his father the King of Dwarvenholm, Crown Prince Drinach, of the Kingdom of Dwarvenholm. The whole place fell silent at that, King Killian and his entourage started down the steps as Grayhawk and the others dismounted and came forward. Again Sir Gregory's voice though not as booming. "Your Highness may I introduce you to their majesties Killian IV King of Keltan and Aurelia, Queen Mother."

"Well met Prince Drinach" said the King, extending his hand.

"Well met Sire" replied Drinach as the clasped forearms.

"Welcome to Keltan both as friend and Royal Emissary."

"I thank thee for that welcome Majesty" replied Drinach "On behalf of my Father and Mother." Taking the Queen Mother's hand in both of his be bowed and kissed her hand. "Your Majesty" he said with a wink "I have heard of your beauty and grace, even in Dwarvenholm."

"Oh really, your Highness" she said looking at Grayhawk. "You must tell me all about it."

"It will be my pleasure" replied Drinach. Now both of them were looking at Grayhawk with cat smiles.

The King and his mother then went through the group of travelers, thanked each Knight or Sergeant for his service. When the Queen came to young Sir Guillome his face still discolored, she touched his face and said

"Sir, you are certainly young to have killed all those bears by yourself. You are very, very brave." Guillome could not speak, now he was bright red and all he could do was stutter. The whole group was laughing at his discomfort. The King then walked up several stairs, and turned to address everyone. "Let us adjourn for now, my people and give our visitors and travelers a chance to rest, and refresh themselves. In an hour we will gather in the main hall to dine and celebrate." The crowd began to disperse at that point still very much in awe of the young Prince. The King motioned for Drinach to accompany him and started up the stairs to the front entrance of the palace proper.

While the other Knights and Cadets moved with the horses to the stable areas, Sir Owen, Sir Gregory and Grayhawk turned to ascend the stairs along with other members of the Royal household and court. Just as Grayhawk started to look around for the Queen she appeared beside him and took hold of his arm.

"Were you perhaps looking for me my Lord?" she said with a smile and a shake of her head to resettle her hair.

"Yes your Majesty. Quite frankly I was," replied Grayhawk with a big toothy grin, placing his hand over hers on his arm. They all went up into the foyer or entry hall of the palace. The King himself was showing Prince Drinach to his quarters.

"Well come along then Sir Warlord of Keltan" said the Queen. "The least I can do is escort you to your quarters." All of the sudden everyone around them had somewhere else to be and quickly. People departed in all directions.

"Most unusual" said Grayhawk, raising one eyebrow. "How, my Lady did you manage that?"

"It was very simple My Lord" she replied. "I merely told them that if they did not leave us alone I would have them all, boiled in oil."

Laughing, looking around at the empty hallway Grayhawk replied "I think they believed you!"

"I should hope so" she said with a big smile. "I am still a Queen you know."

"That you are My Lady, very much so and a really pretty one too!"

"My goodness!" said the Queen. "A Warlord, who can flirt, isn't that some kind of an oxy- moron or something?"

"Most likely" he replied. "Whatever shall I do? Shall I be a straight forward War like, very proper and reserved state official all the time?"

"You do" she answered "and I will have you boiled in oil!"

"Oh! My. That would be very unpleasant!"

"You just remember that" she said "now here we are at your chambers My Lord. You will be so kind as to open the door so that the Queen might inspect them."

"But of course your Majesty" as he opened the door and bowed very low, sweeping one hand as a gesture to enter. The Queen gathered her skirts and stepped past him as she entered. She grabbed him by the collar as she went past pulling him into the room. She kicked the door shut with her right foot. Then her arms were around his neck and he pulled her tightly up against his chest. He held her face in his hands looking into her eyes. Then their mouths found each other and the kiss lasted for a long minute, while the room seemed to slowly spin around them. When they finally broke apart the blood was pounding in his temples. She was so beautiful. The smells of her hair and her perfume were like a flower garden in summer. Her eyes were very shiny and her breath was warm on his face. "Oh by the way!" she said, lifting her head back to look up at him. "Did I not tell you, that I am in love with you?"

"No my Lady you did not tell me."

"Well" she said pulling his head down for another kiss "I am in love with you." They stood embraced for long minutes. Alternately kissing and expressing their love for each other until she finally said "Enough, this is making me crazy to have you. Either take me to your bed, or take me to the great hall for supper!"

"Oh indeed" said Grayhawk "and wouldn't that just be a scandal if we didn't show up for the feast."

"My Lord" she replied, "I was thinking of your reputation not mine!" Laughing and arm in arm they went out of his quarters and down the hall towards the feasting, which they could hear had already begun. Through a smaller passage they entered the hail right behind the Kings chair. The King noticing their entrance rose to greet his mother and Grayhawk as did every other person in the hail. "Well don't stop eating because of us" she said, "We're hungry too." Everyone was applauding and cheering. The King held the chair for his mother and then handed Grayhawk a small leather bag.

"I knew you didn't have time to do it, and I thought you might perhaps, be in need of this." Grayhawk, who had just stepped past the Queen on her left and was about to sit down in a chair being held for him by a page. He stopped looking puzzled at the little bag, opened the top of it and tipped it up over his left palm and out fell a gold ring. It was a band, set all the way round with pink opal inlays. The King tapped his mother on the left should and she turned to see the ring lying in Grayhawk's hand.

"Oh!" she said, putting her hand in front of her mouth.

"Aurelia I" Grayhawk started to say but that was all that came out. She picked up the ring, slipped it on her left ring finger, stood up, put her arms around his neck, looked into his eyes and said

"Of course I will" and kissed him, hard, At this point the King was banging his sword hilt on the table.

"My Lords and Ladies, if you please quiet down, I have an announcement. It would seem that my mother the Queen and Lord Grayhawk have become engaged to be married."

Pandemonium erupted in the hall. Lords and Knights were banging sword and dagger hilts on the tables. Ladies were applauding and everyone seemed to be shouting at the top of their voice. The Queen was holding up her ring on her hand for all to see. Now the trumpets were blaring, drums had appeared from somewhere and were adding to the noise. The King came over and put his arms around their shoulders. Standing between them, grinning like a crocodile, the King leaned over and said in Grayhawk's ear.

"Stuck like a bug in a rug! Eh! Old Fellow" Grayhawk just stood there speechless. The Queen was radiant, beaming with tears in her eyes. Finally someone pressed a mug of brandy in his hand. Grayhawk took a good swig of it and some of his consciousness of his surroundings came back. Then there came a blue light in his mind's eye and he could hear the voice of the Source

"Congratulations Blademaster. You have done well" and the light faded.

Grayhawk looked at the King who still grinning, winked at him and took as step back and pushed the two of them together. She had her arms around his neck and she still had tears in her eyes.

"You called me Aurelia" she said "You said my name," then she kissed him again and the whole room went crazy. The congratulations and the partying went on until well after midnight. Everyone including the King wanted to know when. The Queen just smiled and told them all. We will announce that sometime tomorrow. Grayhawk just looked at them and said

"What she said." Somewhere later in the midst of all the toasting, dancing and singing, Aurelia took his hand and looked at him.

"What made you give me the ring tonight?" He smiled and said

"Oh the opportunity seemed to be at hand! Sort of presented itself, so to speak. But I didn't seem to get the chance to actually ask you to marry me!"

"Well" she said "the matter seems to be settled anyway. But if you really need to ask, do it later when we are in bed."

"Your Majesty!" he said looking quite shocked. "You don't mean?"

"That is exactly what I mean My Lord. Have you any objections?"

"Why! No As a matter of fact I don't" he replied. No one knows where the two of them stayed that night except perhaps a trio of young pages who may have had something to do with it, but they aren't saying. In later years all three were to become quite notorious in the King's Secret Intelligence Corps.

The following day was slow starting after the party, but by the noon everything was in an uproar again. There were preparations to be made for a Royal wedding but no one knew when. The King would only shrug his shoulders and say

"I have no idea." The Queen was secluded in her chambers with her ladies and there seemed to be quite a party going on in there. Grayhawk was in his offices going over stacks of intelligence and scouting reports, receiving agents, spies, emissaries and Military Intelligence Officers. He was the only official of the Kingdom who was excused from attending Prince Drinach's 'Official' reception at court. It was a very formal, solemn and pomp filled affair, receiving, Dwarven Royalty after at least a thousand year period. Formal relations were reestablished, with each nation to furnish an Ambassador and a trade delegation. There were long speeches, banners and military salutes. It lasted over two hours.

At the very end Queen Aurelia was announced into the court. She was received onto the dais by the King whom she kissed on both cheeks. "Your Majesty" she said smiling, "will you be so kind as to announce that Lord Grayhawk and I wish to be married here in three days time."

The King bowed and said "It will be my very great honor, Mother." Holding her hand he turned and looked at the Seneschal, who promptly banged the end of his staff three times loudly on the floor. "My Lords and Ladies, it is my very great honor and deep pleasure to announce to you, that three days hence, at this time of the afternoon, Her Royal Majesty, My Mother, Queen Aurelia will be wed to Lord Grayhawk in solemn ceremony which will take place here in the throne room."

With that the Seneschal declared the ceremonies over and the court emptied almost immediately. There were myriads of social etiquette to be dealt with. The King was still standing there holding his mother's hand. "You realize don't you, Majesty, that the dressmakers and tailors will be in a state of revolt by the time of the wedding."

"That's quite alright your Majesty" she replied. "They will have full purses to soothe their bad attitudes."

"Too true" said the King "and what about you? Really Mother are you happy?"

"Yes Killian, I am. So much has changed in the last five months. There is so much more danger and evil. I intend to have as much happiness as I can. If the world ends before I am another year older I don't want it said of me 'well, she never really tried'."

"I agree fully Mother. Life is too short by half as it is."

Chapter Nineteen

At the same time a long way to the south, across the Mediaterre Sea, in the city of Tripos, in the land of Merkesha, the Dark Priest Rigorta sat in a small palace near the port and the docks. This area in any city is where to obtain information, to engage in one's personal pleasures and vices and, the best place to obtain sacrifices without any real notice of their disappearance.

Reclining on a divan covered with silver cushions Rigorta contemplated how to get back to Keltan, in such a way as to not be noticed by that damned witch Knight Gregory or that fool Captain Grayhawk. He was still furious that his plan to overthrow the Pentharious line had not worked. Everything had been so carefully planned and then that idiot Grayhawk had interfered. 'Well, one day I will roast him on a spit, alive!' For now though he could do nothing. When they burned down his house in the old city, they had destroyed his gateway into the city, and scrying didn't work. It was as if all of Keltan was under a protection ward. But even old Gregory wasn't strong enough to project one that size. Almost four months now, he had no word of what was happening there. 'Not much' he thought to himself, deviously. 'These humans think they have won. One day I will return there and they will die by the thousands on the, alter of the Dark Lord.'

Rigorta was determined that one day he would be High Priest to the Dark Lord and even dreamed that in reward for his service the Dark

Lord would, after his death, make him a major demon to help rule the new world when they had won. After all, his Lord had summoned him into his presence 'Evil be Praised' and had charged him personally with finding out what the new plans of the, Templar are. Something is in the offing. A constant flow of astral energies have indicated major things happening, but the damned accursed wardings, of the 'Source' block all but limited efforts at scrying. Thus far he had sent over a hundred spies, in all directions trying to find where this damned 'Solace' place is. So far none have ever returned to report. "One day!" he thought to himself "I will find it, and for that alone the Dark Lord will make me High Priest, he has promised."

Back in Keltan in the Palace, with the ceremonies ended, King Killian and his Mother, Queen Aurelia walked arm in arm. They were engaged in small talk and planning for the wedding. Not really intentionally, but never the less, they ended up at the doors to the Offices of the Warlord, smiling and nodding at the two guards stationed there.

"Shall I announce thee, Sire?" asked one of them, stepping from the right to grasp the handle of the door.

"No announcement, if you please just open the doors for us." The two guards complied and opened the double carved wooden doors, at which the King and his mother walked in. Grayhawk was immediately aware, even with his back to them, standing at the far right of the chamber, in front of a table full of parchments and scrolls.

"Ah!" he said, "unless my senses deceive me, their Royal Majesties, The King and Queen Mother of Keltan have just entered." Turning to see them both, standing there looking puzzled.

"How on earth did you know it was Mother and I?" asked the King as Aurelia came forward and embraced her now Fiancée.

"Well Sire, it really was easy. There are three things that told me it was you. First I felt the pressure in the room change as the doors opened. Second, I smelled the woman I love. Only she smells that way. Thirdly, I knew that only my King and his mother may enter here unannounced as long as my guards are still living, and I hadn't heard them dying."

"Hmpff" said the King "you make it sound so easy. I would have been lucky have guessed that the doors had opened. But, since I can tell you would rather talk to my mother than me, I shall leave you two alone and see if some of the cooks might find it in their hearts to feed their King."

"We should follow him" said Aurelia, "just to see the show when the King arrives unannounced into the kitchens."

"I'll bet that will be something indeed" replied Grayhawk. "But let's allow him his fun. I am sure we will hear the tale by tomorrow."

"I agree" she said. "Now, what shall we talk about?" They talked for over two hours about their love, the wedding, the estates in the south awarded to Grayhawk by the King. He had never seen them. She told him all about the Manor House, the grounds, the gardens, the vineyards and so on. They parted then to prepare for another large, loud dinner celebration in their honor.

Grayhawk and Aurelia took their leave of the party after a couple of hours. With the help of certain young pages, they had a food tray and a good bottle of brandy placed in the Queen's chambers. Well prepared, in advance, by the Queen's Ladies. That night was one of lovemaking bliss for the couple, in solitude and quiet, by a good fire. Unknown to them, the level of protection for their privacy and their lives was ordered by the King himself. All routes to the Queen's chambers were guarded by soldiers of the King's Guard, whose loyalty was above reproach, and by three young shadows. They were very slippery agents indeed; each carried two eight inch blade, razor sharp, double edged daggers. The three of them were but fourteen years old. They had long been friends of Prince Killian, now the King, and had been involved in many an escapade of skullduggery and night time raids upon various pantries and spirit closets.

They knew every secret passage, tunnel and escape route, every store room, armory and dungeon in the Palace and the surrounding buildings. The three were cousins from the southern border region, brought to the city as orphans, when their village had been wiped out by raiding bandits from Gaula. The Queen had taken them into the Royal household as adopted cousins and made them pages at seven years of age. She had mothered them along with her own children, had them schooled, taught to read and write, math, geography, languages, and they loved her for it, without reservation, the three- Arthur, Paden, and Geran. No one really suspected that the three young chuckle faced pages with their silly haircuts and constant antics, always in some minor trouble or the other, were actually deadly knife fighters and sort of junior grade spies for the King, by their own request.

The only odd thing that happened that night was the arrival at the north gate, just after midnight, of an emissary from the Academy. Two Templar Knights and their escorts, along with twenty very large men, on very large horses were admitted through the gate. The Guard Officer had been told to expect them within the next three nights. They were escorted to the Palace their horses were put up in the stables. The big men were caped and hooded, with great swords on their backs and each carried a bow and war quiver. They were shown down to a large store room under the stables, which had been turned into a makeshift barracks for them.

"Odranna's Chosen!" said the King to Grayhawk the next morning as the two sat to breakfast in the King's morning room, next to his chambers. They ate warm black bread, butter and honey, with strong tea. "Are they as tough as in the legends?"

"Tougher by far" replied Grayhawk. "They are huge, muscled descendants of the Ancient Northmen. I am related to some of them by blood. Several of them are my former teachers. This group is from the sorcerer clan. They are chosen as children for their magical abilities."

"So they are what, exactly?" asked the King. "War Mages? "

"Yes, although I have never seen them use magic" replied Grayhawk. "They are very quiet and reserved for the most part. Make no mistake though Sire they are all, in fact, Master Blademasters!"

"Good fellows to have with you in a fight! Eh!" said the King.

"Absolutely" said Grayhawk.

"Well then I am pleased they will be going with you. How shall I receive them? At Court?"

"Nay Sire" said Grayhawk "It would be best if you and I went this evening after dark. They sleep the daylight hours. Their needs are simple. They exist on meat, mushrooms, (any edible ones) bread, butter, nuts and berries, tea, some beer and brandy."

"So be it then" replied the King. "We will see them well supplied, and come evening, we will introduce ourselves. You know it is really a good thing for a King to have advisors and such around him."

"Why is that Majesty?" said Grayhawk.

"Well I would never be able to remember all of the things necessary to maintain, eh, what is that word?" "Do you mean, Decorum, Sire?" asked Grayhawk.

"Exactly" said the King. "I can't even remember the name of it." Grayhawk smiled.

"You are but a young man yet, not six months on the throne, and that gained only when your father was murdered by members of his own family no less, even if prompted though they were by the Dark Lord's Priest Rigorta."

"True enough my friend" replied the King "by the by what of this Rigorta monster, any news? Have we been able to locate his whereabouts?"

"Aye" said Grayhawk "some news. We believe his location to be in the city Tripos down in Merkesha. Lord Gregory has spies en route there now. He hopes to have them in place within a few weeks." "Well good enough, I suppose," said the King. "All Father knows that I would dearly love to have him here as guest of the Crown. For a few days only though" smiled the King.

All that day the entire Royal household was totally in an uproar with preparation for the Queen's wedding to Grayhawk on the following afternoon. Just before late afternoon turned to evening there came word up the river of the arrival of a Royal ship from Danfinia.

"Ah" said King Killian, when informed. "Some of my mother's family, no doubt come for the wedding. She will certainly inform us presently. Nay immediately" he said pointing at the doors to his audience chamber just as they opened and a Royal Guardsman announce.

"The Queen Mother, your Majesty!" She came, rather swept, into the room radiant and smiling. "Why, my son, are you pointing your finger at me?" she asked.

"Not at you, Your Majesty, only the door" replied the King, rising to give his Mother a hug. "I see some members of the Danfinian Court are arriving for the wedding. Shall I receive them in person, as King?"

"A nice dock side reception would be good my son, not too formal. I am going down to receive them and I would like for you and Grayhawk to be there. If you can" she said still smiling.

"Oh-Ho!" said the King bowing. "There is an Imperial, Maternal

Edict, if I ever heard one." Everyone in the room was chuckling. "I and the Royal War Lord will of course be in attendance."

"Very well, Your Majesty" said the Queen returning the bow "see that you are not late. Say, one hour then, at the Royal Dock' and with that she turned and exited the room. The King then ordered coaches, both for his Mother and her ladies, and another for the guests who were arriving and one for Himself and Grayhawk.

"This means, of course," he told everyone "that there is at least a Royal Prince arriving. So prepare accordingly." That order precipitated a myriad of actions. These included assembly of a Royal Honor Guard, Security Details with archers for some of the roof tops, extra soldiers to barricade and close some side streets, criers to ride through the city announcing the arrival, and the preparation of chambers. Signals would be sent from dock side as soon as it was known what rank, and how many were in the Party. Grayhawk just had time to change into one of the five new outfits the Queen had made on order for him, before his return from Solace. This one was dark red dyed leather breeches, vest, and black sash and black knee high boots, white puff sleeved, lace front shirt, and a matching leather jacket, a wide brim, flat crowned hat topped it all. Minus, of course the long plume, which he had removed. "Ridiculous looking feather" he said. The King was wearing similar, all in black with a gold sash and a small gold coronet crown. The big one is just too damn heavy! Both men were armed with short swords and dirks. Not too much armament for a reception.

They rode the quarter mile of cobblestone streets down to the quay. The King ribbing Grayhawk about becoming an old married Baron, growing grapes and cabbages. Since the battle in the forest and all the events that followed the two had become best friends, an unusual status for both men. Yet they were comfortable with it. They were formal when the situation required and oft, in front of strangers they acted as though they hardly knew each other. As they arrived at the quay and dismounted the couch all was in readiness. Sharp looking horse guards in their polished steel cuirass and helmets, gold sashes, shiny black boots, dark blue tunics and trousers, lances with white pennants, grounded butt first, at the parade rest position. All symbols meant to convey a peaceful reception of friends or family. Citizens were crowded in throngs behind the lines of guards and soldiers. They were excited and a little noisy but well mannered. They had not been much exposed to pomp and circumstance other than what some got to witness inside the palace from time to time. This was different, their Queen was being married. To a hero no less, and these visitors were royalty from the Kingdom of Danfinia and related.

The ship from Danfinia was close to the quay now, a trim looking craft with Dragons Head bowsprit, a row of oars down either side, a single large mast with a square sail which had been furled and lashed to the cross-spar, a row of battle shields, all were round but painted with different colors and designs. They were mounted in a line down both side rails. The ship was easily one hundred twenty feet in length, with a massive steering oar at the back. There were two low deck houses, one before and one aft of the mast. There were at least one hundred large men onboard the vessel. Most were manning the oars and the steering oar. At a sharp command from a man standing at the rear of the deck. The oars came up out of the water, silver droplets reflecting in the late day sunshine. At the same time a man in the bow hurled a weighted leather line to the quay, where it was caught by waiting dock hands. They quickly pulled over a larger rope from the vessel and began pulling it towards the quay. Another command from on board and the oars were pulled into the vessel at an upward angle until they cleared, then went straight up all at the same time and all came down like falling playing tiles, one after another and were stowed along the side rails. A rear line was heaved and the vessel was made secure to the quay.

Two big men carrying curved rams horns stepped to the side raised them to their lips and blew a long, deep wavering tone for about ten heartbeats, lowering their horns and stepped back. Two of the King's Huntsmen in green stepped forward with their horns, which look like two circles of brass pipes, raised them to their lips and blew three distinct pealing notes, each about three heartbeats in answer. One of the men on the boat stepped up to the side and said in a loud voice,

"Hail Killian, King of Keltan, we are of the Royal House of Danfinia. We come in peace to attend the wedding of Queen Aurelia."

Killian stepped forward and answered, "Hail Royal House of Danfinia. I am Killian IV, King of Keltan and bid you Royal welcome." A gang of dockworkers manhandled a large wooden ramp up to the side of the vessel and men on board made it fast. Eight large warriors dressed in leather and furs, all with long hair in the Northman style, armed with short battle axes thrust through their belts came down the ramp two abreast. At the bottom they formed two lines facing each other and stopped.

King Killian and Grayhawk had come forward and now Queen Aurelia came and stood between them, linking her arms in theirs. The King placed is other hand over his mothers on his arm.

"Be good to see some of your kin again, ah, Mother?" he asked. She was smiling, almost misty eyed.

"Yes, my son, it will be very good. I hope you will like them."

"Oh, I'm sure that I will. You still haven't said who exactly we are receiving." At that point there came a booming voice from the ship.

"Hail Keltan! Her Royal Highness, First Daughter of the King, Princess Elysia Myriam," and there appeared at the top of the gangway a vision of grace and beauty in the form of a five foot tall, slender, fair skinned girl of about sixteen years. She had enormous green eyes, an aquiline nose, if small, and full red lips. With thick wavy auburn hair which hung down to the middle of her back. Though young she had a woman's figure. She was wearing a rust colored flowing gown with a white bodice and long sleeves. Around her neck was an emerald on a gold chain that almost matched her eyes perfectly. A small gold coronet for a crown held her hair in place.

Killian just stood there, transfixed. He could see nothing but this vision. Long moments passed, his mother was smiling that knowing smile of hers, holding her sons arm. Everyone seemed to be holding their breaths, not wanting to disrupt this moment! Grayhawk smiled, and somewhere far away in his mind he heard a bell ring and the faint chuckle he had come to know as the 'Source' for whenever he caused some event to happen as planned. Finally Queen Aurelia stepped forward and the young Princess came quickly down the ramp, holding out her hands. The Queen mother took them and the two embraced warmly in some small talk no one else could hear.

King Killian still stood there motionless, hardly even blinking, obviously totally smitten by the girl. Grayhawk was trying hard not to laugh, as were most of the others present. The two women turned and came back towards the King. Grayhawk finally had to say in a low breath "Killian." The King, sort of startled, straightened his posture and said under his breath "decorum first" and stepped forward to greet their guest. The Queen spoke up. "Your Majesty may I present Princess Elysia Myriam of Danfinia."

"Welcome Cousin to Keltan. We are most pleased to have your Highness in attendance at these festivities."

"Thank you Your Majesty" she replied. "I came as soon as we received word of the wedding." The King who had now regained his composure and the twinkle in his eye, said. "And we are very glad that you did!" Now it was her turn to blush. The King began, gesturing towards Grayhawk.

"Highness, may I present." Her raised hand almost touching his chest stopped him.

"Oh this is without doubt, the Lord Grayhawk, Warlord of Keltan." She reached out her small hand and clasped forearms with him, warrior style. "Hail Blademaster!" she said.

"Hail Princess" he replied "Well met."

"Aye" she replied looking him in the eyes. "Friends?" she asked.

"Friends" he replied, the traditional greeting given to a Blademaster by another in the northern lands. Other introductions followed between both parties and the unloading of the vessel had begun. There was much activity on the quay. So the King announced

"Let us adjourn to the Palace and allow these men to finish their work." With some last minute instructions to the commander on duty about billeting and feeding the Princesses escort, they then boarded the royal coach for the trip back to the Palace. The Princess, along with the two ladies who accompanied her, went with the Queen in her coach. As they sat down in the carriage, Killian said with a great huge grin "Did you see her? Grayhawk, did you see her?" Is she not the most beautiful thing on this earth?"

"Well" said Grayhawk "I had noticed that you were somewhat taken with the lady."

"Somewhat?" he replied. "Somewhat?" Then he started laughing "You knew! Didn't you? You knew!"

"No one told me anything" said Grayhawk. "But the instant she appeared on that ramp I think everyone in the Kingdom was aware of her effect on you."

"So that is what magic is!" said Killian leaning back in his seat. Meanwhile, a little ways ahead of them, in the Queens coach, the women were all talking and laughing. The Princess was still bright red and big eyed.

"Oh Aurelia" she said "You didn't tell me he was that good looking. I didn't say anything stupid did I? Do you think he liked me! Did I look alright?" The more she talked the more the others laughed. By the time they arrived in the courtyard of the palace, and were dismounted, all had tears in their eyes and their sides hurt. Seeing them, the King inquired

"What on earth? Is something wrong Mother?" This invoked further gales of laughter and tears. The women, about a dozen in their group now, ran up the stairs and into the Palace. The King looked at Grayhawk puzzled.

"I take it, my Lord, that this is some part of the official woman's ritual?" Grayhawk, nodded sagely.

"Aye Sire, I believe that it is. I have seen similar behavior in the past when women are preparing for a wedding or such."

"I believe My Lord that this calls for a brandy. Wouldn't you agree?"

"Oh, Aye sire most definitely."

Dinner that evening was an all male affair. It seemed as though every woman in the Kingdom had secluded themselves in the wing of the Palace where the Queen's apartments were.

Chapter Twenty

Lord Gregory arrived from the Academy with a contingent of Cadets not long after dark. King Killian, Sir Gregory and Grayhawk adjourned to the War Lords Offices, along with several of the King's advisors. There the discussions went on until midnight, everything from Dragons and the dark Lord, to the nuptials on the morrow.

Sir Gregory, in his other function as Chaplain to the Royal family would be performing the wedding ceremony. The King could of course officiate, but he vowed bodily harm to anyone who suggested it. The men folk retired for the evening at midnight, but in the 'women's wing' the lights burned bright until three in the morning.

Just after daylight, Grayhawk who was awake, though still lying in bed thinking about Aurelia, heard footsteps running down the hall. This cannot bode well? He thought as he jumped out of bed and began dressing. An urgent knock on the door followed.

"Enter!" he said aloud as he sat to pull on his boots. The door opened and the Captain of the Royal Guard entered.

"Forgive me My Lord, but I thought you should know first."

"Take a breath Captain" Grayhawk said "What should I know?"

"My Lord another ship has appeared in the harbor, a war ship. How it got there without being seen, I do know."

"What is it doing?" asked Grayhawk as he went to the window, opened it and looked out.

"Nothing My Lord" answered the Captain, "just sitting there."

Sure enough, almost half a mile away, past the Royal docks, sitting in the middle of the harbor was another Dragon boat. Though smaller than the Princesses boat, this one was darker in color, even the sail was black.

"Inform the King!" said Grayhawk reaching for his weapons. "Assemble a company of Guardsmen, mounted, in the courtyard as fast as you can."

"I've already taken the precaution of doing that My Lord. They will be ready when you arrive."

"Very good Captain, thank you. Inform his Majesty and ask if he could please meet with me in the courtyard."

"Aye Sir" said the captain, saluting as he turned and ran down the hall. Grayhawk now dressed and armed, grabbed a hat and ran down the hall himself, his two guards following without a word. He arrived down the front steps of the Palace into the courtyard, where a company of twenty Royal Archers were mounted up, bows strung, and war quivers of fifty arrows each on their backs, short swords and dirks. His own horse was there, looking squinty eyed and mean as sin. "I feel the same old boy" said Grayhawk. Taking a minute, while waiting for the King to arrive Grayhawk drank some watered wine and ate some bread offered by a young Page, after first seeing that all the soldiers were also given some.

The King came sprinting down the stairs a few minutes later. "Well, what say you My Lord, friend or foe?"

"I'm hoping friend Sire, since they have done nothing since they arrived sometime in the night."

"Good grief, I hope so" replied the King. "If we have a fight on my Mother's wedding day none of us will ever hear the end of it."

Laughing as he mounted. "Well Sire, we would most certainly not want that."

"You think I am joking Grayhawk but I'm not. You've never seen her mad, I have."

"Very well Majesty. If you give us leave, we will go and see what these folks want and try not to start a fight."

"Oh, of course you have my leave. Go, go and see. I'll watch from the Parapet to see if I need to wake the entire Palace." Grayhawk saluted and turned his horse towards the gates which were now opening. He rode out followed by the archers, riding two abreast, each carrying his bow and two steel tipped arrows in his left hand. It was full daylight now as they rode through the city and down to the quay, horses hooves clattering on the cobblestones in the early morning light. Some few of the citizens were looking out of their windows and doors to see what the racket was all about.

As they approached the dock, the ship could be seen clearer now, dark gray in color about two thirds the size of the Danfinian vessel. It was narrower in the beam, shark like and probably very fast. A golden eye was painted on the bow. Grayhawk called his group to a halt. They dismounted as one, and formed a line behind him, each rider walking his horse up to the line. Grayhawk could see a number of figures standing on the vessels deck, but they were still a good bowshot out into the harbor.

The ship from Danfinia had been moved to the far left of the dock, so the area in front of Grayhawk, going out to the dark vessel was open. Grayhawk walked forward to the edge of the dock, his archers moving up to about five paces behind him and were standing at the ready. Everything then was still for a few minutes. Then two additional figures appeared on deck of the dark ship. Then there came a hail

"Greetings, Grayhawk, War Lord of Keltan."

"And Greetings to you!" replied Grayhawk. "May I have the honor of knowing whom I am addressing?"

"Of course My Lord" was the reply. "I am Allanfair of Danaan, this is my sister Aileoren. We have been asked by Lord Tinian to assist you in certain matters. May we approach?"

"Please do" replied Grayhawk. The ship literally began moving sideways towards the dock. 'Hmm' thought Grayhawk to himself 'some powerful magic at work here.' He could sense the vibrations but they were somehow subdued or restrained. As the ship, drew closer to the dock. Grayhawk motioned to the archers to move forward and take the lines so the vessel could be secured. There were a dozen or so people on deck. All were caped and hooded in some silvery shimmering material. He could sense that there were some magical properties in their clothing, their weapons, but mostly the vessel itself. He could see them clearly now, tall and slender, almond eyes and olive skin. As the boat touched the quay two of them stepped to the rail and on to the shore.

"Well met, Sir! Both a Blademaster and an adept, now that! Is quite a combination, I am Allanfair, this is my sister Aileoren. We are the Tuatha de Danaan, or your folk would refer to us as elves or the Fairfolk."

"By the All Father's beard" said Grayhawk. "Dragons, Dwarves and now Elves" grinning and shaking his head, "Are all the myths of my childhood to come true?"

"It would certainly appear to be so" answered Lady Aileoren, smiling broadly as she removed her hood. Grayhawk's eyes widened as he beheld the sight her. She was just about the most beautiful female he had ever seen. "But understand also that you Sir are one of our childhood myths, A Blademaster of Norda, the fiercest warriors on the planet, covered in blood and glory many times over. Bowing to no King, taking women as he will, riding great Norda Warhorses through the land, undefeated in war or personal combat."

Grayhawk was laughing now. "So that is why the ladies are all afraid of me! I have often wondered."

"Indeed" said Allanfair. "I very much wanted to be a Blademaster as a youth." Removing his hood, he was also a good looking fellow and his hair was white, not pale blonde, not Mithrail blonde, his hair was white, as were his eyebrows. His eyes were deep blue. Just as remarkable, his sister's hair was bronze colored and metallic looking, down to her waist, as was her brother's but hers was loose, straight and silky looking, his was in a ponytail with a gold band. They were both his height and they looked straight at you when talking. That's when he noticed that the ladies eyes were the most jade green he had ever seen.

Grayhawk then dispatched a rider to inform the King of their new guests, a party of fourteen elves from the Isle of Danaan, have arrived for a visit. Introductions were then made all around to the other members of the group. All were beautiful people, and their ears were only slightly pointed. Allanfair turned from looking at the city folk who were beginning to gather and gawk and point. Grayhawk had already positioned the guardsmen who came with him, to cordon off the dock area so the people were kept at a polite distance.

"Lord Grayhawk, I do perceive a good deal of tension in the air. Have we arrived at a bad time?" "Nay my Lord" said Grayhawk "In fact at an excellent time. You see is the wedding feast of the Queen Mother. She is to be married again this afternoon." "Well that is excellent. Aileoren do you hear! A wedding, The Queen Mother is to be wed this day. We have never seen a Royal wedding of your race."

"Indeed" said his sister. "Who may I ask is she being married to?"

"I have that honor" replied Grayhawk grinning.

"Ah, now I know where I felt the tension from" said Allanfair. "My heartfelt Congratulations My Lord."

"And mine as well" said Aileoren. Grayhawk exchanged grips with the two as well as with all the other elves who offered their congratulations. As this was going on, riders could be heard coming through the city and presently the King trotted into view on a fine spotted gray. Behind him was a company of the Royal Guard. He brought his horse to a halt, dismounted and came forward, removing his glove and extending his hand.

"Halloo" he said with a huge grin. "So elves really do exist! Well met and welcome to Keltan." The Elves all staged a courtly bow. "Oh please" said Killian "we're not that formal here and besides, I am young enough that it embarrasses me to have people bow to me. I am Killian the fourth, King of Keltan. I bid you welcome." He then exchanged grips with every one of the elves. When he came to Lady Aileoren, he stopped, looked at her for a moment and with a wink said "My Goodness My Lady, you are truly beautiful! And armed too! I'll wager that your suitors are polite indeed!" She had been smiling, now she was laughing heartily, as were all the elves.

Carriages were summoned. The Elves and all their baggage were transferred in short order up to the castle. Word ran ahead of them like wildfire. Elves, real live elves were coming. Most of the town's people were turned out now along the route. Virtually all residents and guests of the King's Palace were in the courtyard as they arrived, except for the Queen, the Princess and some of their ladies. Aurelia could not be seen in public before the wedding. Soon Elves were talking to Dwarves and Men and vice-versa. Lord Gregory intoned that

"It would be a day, long remembered by all sides and he hoped that it would mark the beginning of strong alliances." Soon after, the Lady

Aileoren and her two female companions, who were also very beautiful Elf women, were whisked away by some of the Queen's Ladies to the forbidden female zone of the Palace. Not to be entered on this day by any male on penalty of excommunication from the human race. After an hour of letting everyone get to know everyone else, the King invited Lord Allanfair, Prince Drinach, Lord Gregory, Sir Owen and White bear, the chief of Odranna's Chosen, to breakfast with him in his morning room. White bear, a huge man, battle scared, with chestnut brown hair streaked with gray, and light gray eyes, came bareheaded. Being bareheaded above ground was a sign of respect to the King.

King Killian was aware of this and as soon as they entered the palace he said

"Clan Chief White bear, please don thy hood and be comfortable." White bear responded while putting on a loose woven hood of black material which cut the light significantly but he could still see through it

"My thanks Your Majesty the light is intense and hard to bear." Once in the morning chamber, pages served them a breakfast meal of oat and honey porridge, sausages, several kinds of cheese, dark and light brown bread, strawberry preserves, some fruit tarts and a bowl of nuts, with hot tea and cider. For a time not much was said as the group of different 'men' consumed a good meal and tried to relax. After the meal was done, as pipes and tabac were passed around, the remains of the meal were cleared away. King Killian whispered something to a young page that nodded and said

"It will be as you wish Sire." Soon all pages withdrew and the doors were closed. Killian and Grayhawk closed the shutters on the two windows and Grayhawk removed the pouch from his vest pocket containing his Adept ring. Sir Gregory had already put on his. And Grayhawk was not surprised to see White Bear slip one on his finger.

"Three Adepts in one room!" said Lord Allanfair, "Surely the Dark Lord himself could not interfere!" Prince Drinach's eyes were big. Sir Owen, smiling, said nothing. The King was intently looking at the rings; each in turn was starting to glow with a faint blue aura about them. Sir Gregory spoke up,

"Please, everyone carry on with your smoking and relaxing, while we insure that we cannot be spied upon nor even over heard. It will take only a minute or so. Grayhawk, you are senior, we will follow your lead."

Grayhawk realized, having made the link, he was in contact with his ring. "When did I become senior he wondered to himself." Pushing out with his mind only slightly, he could sense Gregory who was familiar, and White bear who was not. He connected with both of them and their power was greatly magnified. Using their combined power he formed a great blue bubble of power over the entire city then strengthened it three times.

"Now, that is done" he said "let's see if they can penetrate that."

"I think not!" said the voice they all recognized as the Source. "Well done Blademaster. You are truly safely warded now." The others in the room had not heard those words although the elf probably was aware of what was happening.

Far away in the city of Tripos in the land of Merkesha in a dark palace within the city, a scream of rage and frustration was heard. The Dark Priest Rigorta, in a full fit of rage, is now vowing revenge against the entire world. He can sense some sort of gathering, something of importance, and then was cut off just as his vision was about to clear.

Leaning back in his chair Grayhawk said "We are now warded, within and without. No one may eavesdrop on what is to be said here." An hour later Grayhawk had related every event as it had happened, starting with the attack in the woods and ending with the arrival back here at the King's city. Lord Gregory took over then and started with

"My Lords, Your Majesty. We are now faced with grave circumstances and condition with which we must deal. Lucifer has found a cache of Dragon eggs. We believe there are twenty of them in all. They were hidden back in antiquity, probably by the Dragons themselves, to prevent the extinction of their race. How Lucifer found them we do not know but he has them, and what is far worse he knows how to hatch them. He has thus far, successfully hatched two. We think they are both females. That leaves at least eighteen more. At least one of those is bound to be a male. If Lucifer manages to hatch a male and binds him over to his service, the resulting mating would produce enough Dragons to rule the world in only a few years time."

"However" continued Grayhawk "there is apparently a problem with getting the eggs to reanimate and hatch after so long in hiding. It requires some sort of Dragon magic that is long gone from this earth. How he got the first two to hatch is not known. But the baseline here for all of our races is that we must go and find these eggs. We must destroy them all, and the two Dragons already hatched. And if that is not bad enough for you, then consider this. The eggs are now being kept inside the Dark Lords mountain complex down in Stygius."

"I have heard it said in ancient tales" spoke Prince Drinach "that Dragon eggs are harder than stone. How exactly does one destroy them?"

"According to ancient records there are two ways only" began Sir Gregory "they can be frozen solid for two weeks at least and then they can be shattered by a powerful blow from a metal hammer."

"And the other way?" inquired Sir Owen. Gregory answered

"By a hardened steel and Mithrail silver dagger with a triple edged, triangle shaped blade of elfish design and make. It must be hammered in at the small end of the egg so that it splits into three sections."

"Do you mean perhaps" said Lord Allanfair "a blade like this one?" as he pulled out a dagger from his belt sheath. It had a round, black and gold handle, a triangle hilt and a ten inch blade. Just as described by Sir Gregory. "My sister and I both have one, handed down forever through our family. Now I know why. And of course why we were contacted by Sir Tinian and directed to come and meet with all of you. He did say there would be a perilous journey involved."

King Killian asked "Sir Tinian contacted you? How? Exactly! I thought he was in Solace."

"Well" said Allanfair, "My sister and I were having a noon meal at her house, when all of the sudden he was there at the end of the table. He addressed us both by name and said 'You don't know me, but I know you. My name is Tinian. I am Senior Warden of the Temple Knights. I am appearing to you now by astral projection.' He went on to say that the time had come for the Elves to once again become involved in the struggle for control of the earth. We talked some about the past and about the future. Once we had agreed to do whatever we can, he showed us an image of Lord Grayhawk and said we were to come to Keltan to the King's city to meet with all of you. We are to help plan a campaign involving a perilous journey, to accomplish a very dangerous and important mission. Since, well quite frankly, Elves are easily challenged, here we are!"

"Very good Lord Allanfair, and glad we are to have you with us" said Grayhawk. "Now I believe that we have been given the means to destroy both the Dragons and their eggs. Lord Tinian has caused the appropriate groups of folk to gather up for the job. Minus one and that is the group who bring the ship we will use for the journey. One that is both large enough and fast enough to transport us all. The ship is on the way from Troscai, I believe, with Captain Olion and a crew of Buscan pirates from the south of Spanos. Along with a contingent of Dwarves on board sent by King O'Drinain. All things being equal, Captain Olion should arrive here in approximately four weeks. So, in addition to my wedding, we have that long to plan and obtain such supplies as we will need for the journey."

The group discussed plans and ideas for another half an hour or so, and then adjourned so that everyone could prepare for the wedding. Already the smells of roasting meat and pastries could be detected, even on the top floor of the Palace. All over the city as well, in the Inns and Taverns as well as the vendors along the streets and in the market place, the mood of the people was one of great happiness. The Queen was dearly loved and Grayhawk was thought of as a great hero. Of course the whole city was buzzing about the latest arrivals. Elves, can you imagine that! And the presence of a group of Odranna's Chosen from Norda, even though they only come out at night. All in the city knew they were there, and then, add a contingent of Dwarves and a Princess from Danfinia. Well, it certainly made for high times!

The wedding was scheduled for the third hour after noon or midday. Grayhawk and King Killian were pretty much left to themselves all through the middle of the day so they talked about everything. About 1 hour past midday, they went to Grayhawk's 'offices', as they were called, and had some watered wine, cheese and fruit.

Later they both parted for their separate chambers, to prepare and dress for the nuptials. Grayhawk bathed, shaved himself, all but the mustache. The Queen said she liked it. Now he stood with only a drying cloth wrapped around his middle, looking into a highly polished metal oval that served as a mirror. 'Well Grayhawk, Son of the Pietre Clan of Norda' he thought to himself "you have come a long way from those mountains and valleys where you played as a child. A hard headed boy who hated bullies and was forever fighting with one or more of them.' As a boy they had called him, 'Hard Son' and all knew that he would become a Blademaster. Now looking at his nearly clear reflection in the metal, there stood a man nearly thirty eight years old, six feet tall, heavily muscled, mustached, with many scars, but he had the hairy chest of a 'real man' as he had been told when he was a boy. The tattoo of the Rose and Dagger was known all over as that of a Blademaster. There was no better mark of honor than that. He had dark wavy hair down to his shoulders and deep green eyes, an almost square jaw. He was a little darker in complexion than most of his countrymen.

He then dressed in the black and silver suit of clothes that the Queen had made for him. Over the knee, soft black leather boots with the golden stub type spurs, which his rank as an Adept and his title as Baron both entitled him. Soft black trousers that tucked into the tops of his boots, with silver thread embroidery up the sides of the legs, all the way to the top of the waist. A dove gray puffed sleeve shirt with banded collar and tiny barrel and loop closures half way down the front, with a six inch wide, sixty inch long sash of a very soft gray material that had Mithrail silver thread woven all through it. The trousers were held up by a two inch wide black leather belt, but the sash covered it. The ends of the sash hung on the left side down to just above the knee. Last there was a square bottom leather vest with two patch pockets. The upper left breast of the vest was embossed with what was now his personal sigil and coat of arms, crossed swords with a crown beneath and a flaring hawk, talons extended, above signifying his position and protection of the crown. Embossed right into the leather then embroidered over, the swords and crown in gold, the hawk was dark gray and it even had green eyes. Grayhawk loved it. 'You look pretty good all cleaned up!' he thought to himself, 'for an uncouth barbarian' as he shoved his dirk through the sash on the left and his dagger on the right, plus an eight inch boot knife. 'Overkill?' he thought. "Hmpff, you let someone interrupt this ceremony and I'll teach them the true meaning of overkill!' He had already had the pages place his great sword and short sword in the throne area, within easy reach.

At half past the second hour he left his chambers for the brisk walk through the halls to the throne room, escorted of course by four Royal Guardsmen. It would seem that the King was taking no chances this day either. There were guards everywhere and just about every other one was either a Border Ranger with a bow or a Heavy Cavalry Trooper with Short Lance and Saber. Meanwhile over in the Queen's wing, all was in readiness. The Queen was dressed in her pale lavender and cream colored, flowing gown, with a low waist and long bodice, long sleeves with cream lace flows at the wrists and the throat. She wore cream colored leather shoes with almost pointed toes and heals about two inches high. Her hair was full, waved and loose down her back. Her formal Queen Mothers crown with the jewels sparkling was radiantly beautiful. Her eyes were wet and shiny with tears both of joy and sadness and her cheeks were flushed. Every time she shed a tear most of the other women did too. Unbeknownst to any outside of their group, all of the women, including the Queen, hidden in a pocket, through a special fold in their skirts, carried an eight inch dagger, just in case.

Grayhawk entered the throne room through the King's entrance at the rear. The King was already there standing in the middle of the room with his hands on his hips wearing a big smile.

"Well, just you look at this!" he said gesturing all around. "I never knew this old musty hall could look this good." There were flowers everywhere, garlands, wreaths, long looping chains of flowers. The upper windows of the hall, the small oval ones were open, and there were birds flying in and out. The floors, the furniture, the brass candle lamps, had all been polished to perfection. Even the marble columns looked like they had been waxed and the whole place smelled faintly of fruit and flowers.

Many of the guests were arriving and gasping in awe, both at the throne room and at their King and War Lord, who were dressed almost identical, except that the King's vest was trimmed in gold and the emblem was a crown with a straight up and down sword behind. At that point Prince Drinach and Lord Allanfair came into the hall. Both of them dressed in black with silver trim sashes, though both of their outfits were all of leather.

"Obviously," began Allanfair "my sister has been about decorating. I see her hand here."

"Ah" said the King "and just as obvious, my Mother has been at dressing the Men folk. Do you think I'll ever be old enough that my Mother will stop picking my clothes?"

"Oh certainly Sire" said Allanfair grinning "But on that day your wife will take over the duty. They were all laughing. Lord Gregory and Sir Owen entered through a side door. Grayhawk and the others redoubled their laughing.

"What pray tell is so funny?" asked Lord Gregory as he and Sir Owen walked up in their black outfits with silver sashes. Now they were all pointing at each other and laughing. And thus was born the formal black attire of the Knights Templar with sash and emblazon of office on the left breast. The other guests and nobles gathered, all thought they looked very sharp in there black uniforms with silver sashes.

Actually, three women had schemed and thought together to come up with the slightly different design for all of those represented. The only real surprise to anyone was when the members of Odranna's Chosen arrived, a few minutes later wearing long black robes with silver sashes and black hood and the All Seeing Eye on their left breast.

It was now approaching the third hour past midday. The last arriving guests were finding their places. King Killian would be acting as father of the bride as Aurelia's closest living male relative.

The throne chairs had been removed from the dais and replace with an alter draped in gold and white with the All Seeing Eye on the front. On the altar were two holly leaf crowns, two small silver and gold goblets and two gold rings. Suspended above the, alter on a silver chain was a six inch square candle lantern with red panes, it was lit, and it represented the presence of the All Father at these proceedings. Lord Gregory then came from behind the altar and stood in front, facing the assembled. Grayhawk and Sir Owen came from the right side, on the floor and went up to the center of the bottom step. They faced the assembled, Grayhawk the groom and Sir Owen as his best man.

The room fell silent and Lord Gregory intoned in a deep voice "Hail and Hail to all the Keltani and to all Nordan. Be it know then to all here in assembled, we are come together this day to mark the union of a man and a woman as husband and wife. Behold! The bride approaches" and the doors to the throne room opened. First there came the Queen's own daughters, Killian's two younger sisters. Then there entered Queen Aurelia with her son, who was wearing his crown. Behind them came Princess Elysia flanked by two of her ladies. Behind her came Lady Ailereon flanked by two of her ladies, then in groups of three came all of Aurelia's Ladies in Waiting. The crowd was silent and absolutely open mouthed at all of the beauty contained in that group.

Down the center aisle they all stepped slowly and stately, Grayhawk stood watching the two Princesses of Keltan in the lead. Sylvania was thirteen years old, and her sister Lori Anna twelve years. 'They are beautiful young girls' he thought to himself, 'Now they are to be my step daughters and I have hardly ever even spoken to them.' He smiled at them as they approached and they smiled back. As the procession halted at the bottom step, the two Princesses started to turn and move back to stand with the others present. On impulse Grayhawk stepped between them and took their hands and motioning, bid them to go up the steps on their mother's left, saying in a low voice

"We are to be family now. Your places are here by your Mother." They didn't even look at their mother or older brother. They turned around and went half way up the steps. Aurelia's eyes were tear filled, and Killian was grinning broadly. Lord Gregory's baritone rang out again

"Who then will give this woman to be married?"

"I will" said Killian.

"By what right?" asked Lord Gregory

"By the right, that I am her closest, male, blood relative."

"Is there any man present who can contest this marriage? If so you must speak now or forever lose the right." The room was silent.

"Come then, before the, altar if you wish to be joined" intoned Lord Gregory. Grayhawk stepped forward and Killian took his Mother's right hand from his arm and placed it in Grayhawk's left. Holding hands then they mounted the half dozen steps to be before the Altar and in front of Lord Gregory. Aurelia's daughters came up on her left side and Sir Owen came up on Grayhawk's right. Still holding hands the couple knelt and as they did so, Grayhawk noticed the tip of his great sword handle, just sticking out from under the altar cover. He smiled to himself and Aurelia squeezed his hand.

Gregory stood before them. "Is this an act of your own free will Aurelia of Keltan?"

"It is" she replied.

"Is this an act of your own free will Grayhawk of Norda?"

"It is" he replied. Lord Gregory then picked up the two crowns of Holly leaves, and placed one on each of their heads. "By the binding of the ancient rites" Gregory said. "By the binding of the Sacred Oaks, By the acceptance of All Father" he then picked up the Holly crowns and ceremoniously swapped them three times back and forth on their heads. Then he removed the crowns and placed them back upon the altar, Picking up the two gold rings from the cushion, he handed one to each of them. "Now as token of marriage, exchange you two, rings of gold." Grayhawk first put one on her left ring finger next to the one he had already given her. Aurelia then put one on his left ring finger.

Lord Gregory now picked up the two goblets of wine, gave one to each of them and said "Grayhawk repeat after me, I pledge thee Aurelia my troth and fidelity." Grayhawk repeated it and then drank half of the wine in his goblet. "Aurelia repeat after me, I pledge thee Grayhawk my troth and fidelity" she repeated and drank half the wine in her goblet.

"This having been done" Lord Gregory intoned "comes now the first test of trust. Each of you take the others goblet and drain it." They exchanged cups and each drank the other half of the wine. Lord Gregory raised his arms and intoned loudly "This union is joined; the pact is sealed by token and oath. The All Father's light now shines upon this couple. Woe! Be -it unto him, who would break this pact." Somewhere in the distance a single, clear bell, rang once. The room erupted into applause and cheers. Aurelia was in Grayhawk's arms and kissing him. There was much applause and loud cheering. The two of them stood at the top step of the dais, arms around each other's waist, waving and smiling. After a moment or two Grayhawk noticed the young Page at his left side, holding his swords. Taking them in his left hand, he smiled at Paden and thought to himself 'I wonder if we will ever see a time when a man doesn't have to have weapons handy at his own wedding.

"Well" said Lord Gregory from behind them "Go down and let the people see you. The parties can't start until you do." They laughed and started down the steps to the main floor. With the Queen's daughters following behind them, then the King with Princess Alysia on his right arm, and looking very smug. Next, was Sir Owen with the Lady Ailereon. They all trooped out of the throne room, down the hall and out to steps to the courtyard. At least several thousand people were waiting. There in the midst of loud cheering and applause. Grayhawk and Aurelia stepped into a flower bedecked open chariot for the traditional parade through the city.

It was a bright and sunny day. The people were out in full force to see the newly wedded couple. Even with a cavalry escort the going was slow. Finally the better part of two hours later they returned to the Palace. The festivities began immediately on their return and ran way in to the wee hours of the mornings. At an hour before midnight the newly wedded couple did manage to slip away for their traditional first night in the north tower. They actually stayed for three nights before they came back into public view. In their absence the King had allowed the celebrating to go on for two whole days before calling an end to it. A real good time was had by one and all.

But, after taking three days off, even with a new wife and family, Grayhawk knew all too well that time was short before they must depart. The stakes that were risked in this mission were far greater than the lives of the people involved. Failure might well mean the very end of the era of mankind on this planet.

Chapter Twenty One

Early, the morning of the fourth day all of the principals involved arrived in the King's morning chamber to discuss the details. They had little more than three weeks left to prepare, before the arrival of their ship. It was decided that when the ship arrived they would board and set sail the same day, if possible.

It was decided that the 'Company' as it came to be known would consist of a twenty man contingent of Knights Templar, Twenty Dwarf fighters, Twelve Elf fighters, Twenty of Odranna's Chosen and probably twenty or so of Olion's pirate crew. In addition there was Grayhawk, Prince Drinach, Lord Allanfair, Lady Ailereon, Sir Owen and Clan Chief White Bear. There were 98 souls all told. A goodly force and about the maximum number they could take aboard one ship with all of their equipment and supplies. Even if completely successful, the journey could take up to a year or longer to complete.

Meanwhile, In the Merkeshan City of Tripos, far to the south. The Dark Priests efforts to penetrate Keltan, either with a spy, or scry into the doings within the King's City of Keltan were now at a fevered pitch. Rigorta had been able to obtain some information from the spy network of the Spanos bandit chiefs. He had one of their chiefs spy leader, kidnapped and brought to Tripos by ship. Rigorta had personally tortured the man for three days to make sure that he had every detail of the man's knowledge. He had given the man, still living, to the Demon Lord Barnok for a future favor. Summoning Barnok had been a very dangerous move on his part. Demon Lords do not like to be summoned.

Barnok would have attacked Rigorta straight away, but when he saw the large, plump, effeminate Spanoan spy being offered to him it was most agreeable. Barnok did not intend to honor the agreement anyway. The fat human would roast up really well and the next time Rigorta summoned him, the Dark Priest would find himself on the spit. It was a most pleasing vision indeed.

Rigorta chuckled to himself knowing exactly what the Demon Lord was planning. Chuckling because he knew exactly how to trap a demon, even a Lord, and make him serve for a very long time. He had learned from his torture session on the Spanoan that Grayhawk had returned from Solace bringing with him a Dwarf Prince and some kind of strange or special weapon to use against the Dragons. He knew that Grayhawk was about to marry Aurelia, the Queen Mother. He knew that they were making plans for a great journey or mission. What he didn't know was exactly what the mission entailed or where it was going.

That damned city was closed off tight. They had so far caught every spy he had sent. The scryers were unable to penetrate the shields. The worst of it all is the Dark Lord refused to give him use of the Dragons to attack the city. Someday, thought Rigorta to himself, when I am the Dark High Priest I will know all. The Lord will confide in me. Smiling as he watched two new captives, who were drugged and bound, being off loaded from a cart in the courtyard below his window. Ah, he thought, a good sacrifice tonight.

In the King's City the Duke of the Southern Reach, Baron Grayhawk, was preparing to take his new bride on a visit to his holdings, was it a Dukedom?- A Barony? -A big farm? Well he had never seen it anyway. It was a two day journey almost due south. It would be a honeymoon for the Warlord and the Queen Mother. Everyone was excited and all wanted to go along. It was decided that Grayhawk's , two new daughters, Lord Allanfair, Lady Ailereon and two of her ladies, along with 2 of the Queen's ladies in waiting, four of the Elf warriors and a company of the King's heavy cavalry would go. Some one hundred thirteen souls all told. They would bring two coaches for the ladies and three additional coaches would be used instead of supply wagons. The coaches have larger wheels and are much faster on the road. A fortuitous decision as it turned out. The entourage departed an hour after daylight on a clear and sunny, warm day. They stopped for a long two hour mid day, a picnic if you will, in a grassy meadow beside a pond. The birds were singing and fish jumping. Even the most grizzled old cavalrymen enjoyed it.

A long afternoon drive through the mottled shade of a thick forest brought them at dark to a large inn with a caravan yard and barns. The inn had been prepared ahead of time, for their arrival. There were stag and boar roasting over pit fires, pheasant and partridge, lentils, wild mushrooms in sauce, several kinds of breads, fresh butter, cider and beer, fruit pastries for desert and of course, brandy and tabac.

Grayhawk had ordered the feast large enough to include all of the soldiers of the escort which made him very popular indeed. The eating and drinking lasted until an hour before midnight. Everyone stuffed themselves. Even so, at daylight next morn everyone was up. Within two hours, allowing the ladies extra time to prepare for the days travel and the men to have an extra cup of tea and a smoke, they were ready. They departed the inn at a good walk. After everyone, including the soldiers, gave a coin or two to the inn keeper and his family as a gratuity for the fine feast and the hospitality.

It was another beautiful, cloudless day for traveling. All were in good humor and spirit. Just before the noon hour they came upon a white stone monolith marker about twice the height of a man. Queen Aurelia called for a halt and when Grayhawk rode up to her coach she gestured with her right hand at the marker. "Well my Lord, you are now on your own land. This is the boundary of the southern reach. From here all the way to the border is your domain as a Duke of the Realm."

"Does that mean, my Lady, that now I must be a pain in the backside like all the other Dukes I've met?"

"Why not at all, my Lord" she replied. "You are also the Warlord of Keltan. You can be an ever so much bigger pain!" Grayhawk grinned broadly at this.

"Excellent!" he said laughing and all laughed with him. The noon break this day was shorter than the day before. Everyone was anxious to arrive at the ducal holdings and see the manor house and properties.

They road at a canter for an hour, then slowed to a walk and at mid afternoon they took a break to stretch and rest the horses for a bit. All in all, it was a seemingly enjoyable outing on a warm, sunny day. Mounting up and moving on after the break they covered an additional five miles or so. They came to a long winding, slightly uphill curve in the road. It was about a mile long and curved to the left; there was hardwood forest on either side of the road. A rider came forward from where the coaches were with a message from the Queen. The Manor house could be seen from the top of the hill it said. Grayhawk and Lord Allanfair moved to a trot, to go ahead and see the view.

As they reached the top a few minutes later they immediately reined in their horses to a stop. There before them was a valley stretched from east to west, perhaps two miles in length and over a half mile wide to the south. A little to the left down in the middle of the valley was the Ducal seat. It was burnt to the ground. Dirty gray smoke was billowing out and away from them to the south. At least a dozen other buildings and farm houses across the valley were smoking ruins. Here and there a few trees also burned or smoldered. Grayhawk had seen this many times in his soldiering days. A major raid had been conducted here, looting and killing. Now the smells came wafting over the crest of the hill. The raid had probably happened earlier in the morning. Now his senses kicked in. He cast for Dragons but found none. He did find lots of Drulgar presence. They had pulled back into the trees on the other side of the valley. They were waiting no doubt for the whole party, with Grayhawk to come charging down into the valley trying to save what they could. There was nothing left to save. He could detect no human life left down there.

"A trap my Lord" said Allanfair. "We must pull back now!" he said as he was turning his horse around.

"Aye, that it is" replied Grayhawk. "Let us get the others turned around as fast as possible. They will be coming for us. No doubt they know we are here." Grayhawk jerked his horse around and the two thundered back down the road towards the rest of the party. Grayhawk and Allanfair both drew their swords to alert the others of trouble. A quarter of a mile they galloped back. When they arrived Grayhawk reined up before the Queen's coach.

"The entire valley is destroyed My Lady" he said. "Everything is burnt. I can detect no life remaining. We must turn around and depart here with all haste. We will be pursued. We have a good start on them!" Turning in his saddle to the Captain of the Calvary and the two grizzled Sergeants of their escort he said "Get these coaches turned. We will run for the Inn. There we have a chance to defend ourselves. Out here we have small chance of surviving."

"Are they bandits from Spanos my Lord?" asked the Captain. "They will surely be mounted and will soon catch up to us."

"Nay Captain, not bandits, they are Drulgar, the Dark Lords spawn, smaller than men but tough and mean. They are not mounted but they can run forty miles and still fight when they get there. They carry only their weapons. Their support follows behind them. When they come upon their quarry they do not stop but run directly into battle. Know you this; their favorite food is roast human." This statement brought gasps from the women. While he was talking the drivers were getting the coaches turned around and headed back north on the road. There was no confusion. All was done in an orderly fashion. The Cavalry company was lined up on the opposite side of the road with sabers drawn, blades up, against their right shoulder. It was a formidable force, one with one hundred Cavalry men on war steeds. "Lord Allanfair" said Grayhawk "If we had not the women to protect I think we would stay and fight these vermin from Hell."

"I agree" replied Allanfair "unless they are numbered into the thousands I believe we could counter attack and prevail.'

"My Lord" said the young captain named Johannes "my company would be honored to stay behind and cover your withdrawal."

"I know you would Captain" said Grayhawk grinning, "but that is not a choice I am willing to make. Aurelia is Queen Mother of all Keltan, with her there are two Princesses of the Realm, an Elf Princess and a Prince of the Danaan. Their safety must be our chief concern. But, let me assure you young sir you will get to fight. I believe I can guarantee that! Now, all that being said, let us make haste back up this road. I do not believe that they can come upon us before we reach the Inn. Just in case, have ten of the troopers ride as rear guard. Have ten more, your best riders, ride ahead to alert the people at the Inn and to begin preparing the place for a fight."

"Aye Sir" replied the Captain and wheeled his horse away toward his company. In short order the couches were all turned about. The ten man rear guard was posted and a ten man patrol led by one of the Sergeants thundered off up the road to the Inn to make things ready there.

The four Elf warriors stationed themselves and their mounts between the two coaches with the women folk in them. Lady Ailereon had moved up to the Queen's coach with her sword and bow. The Queen Mother herself an excellent shot with a bow, had hers uncased and strung. The young Princesses were each given a short sword and a dagger, as were the Ladies in Waiting. The other Elf Ladies being battle trained, had both sword and bow. The rest of the Cavalry Company were drawn up in two lines, one down either side of the coaches. The entire group was now moving forward at a trot. Grayhawk smiled grimly.

"Well, at least we look like a military unit."

"How many will we be facing once they catch up with us?" asked Allanfair

"I could sense five separate groups" replied Grayhawk. Each of them is probably a company of one hundred thirty or so. So, there are probably six hundred fifty, plus at least five Dark Priests."

"How long do you think it will be before they catch us?" asked Allanfair?

"Well My Lord, I don't think they will come upon us until at least an hour or two after we reach the Inn compound" replied Grayhawk. The two of them were riding off to the right side of the road towards the rear of the group.

"I believe, Lord Grayhawk" said Allanfair "that the Queen is looking around for you. It might be advisable to talk with her a bit."

"Too true, my friend" answered Grayhawk. The two of them spurred their horses forward and quickly caught up to the Queen's coach. Riding up on the right side of the coach he handed his horses reins to Allanfair and stepped into the coach with the Ladies. The Queen was seated between her daughters facing forward and Ailereon was seated opposite facing the rear. "My Ladies" he said as he seated himself next to Ailereon and facing his new wife and daughters. He felt very proud of them just now. The two young girls were sitting with a sheathed short sword across their laps. They and their mother looked apprehensive but not scared. "This is our situation" he began. "We were supposed to ride into a trap. They wanted us to think that the valley had been raided by bandits from Spanos and, that they were gone as is usual after a raid. Because I have the ability to sense certain things I knew right away that there were, uh, other people waiting in hiding. So now we must make a mad dash for the Inn where we stayed last night. It is a place that can be defended against attack. We will arrive back there before they do and we will be waiting for them when they come. I am sorry my Ladies. We were supposed to be going to our new home."

"It was totally destroyed then?" asked Aurelia.

"Down to the ground" said Grayhawk "everything else in the valley as well. No time for that now, My Ladies. Houses can be rebuilt. For now we must all be strong and defeat this enemy." He took each of the girl's faces in his hands and kissed them on the forehead. Then, kissing Aurelia he said "Some honeymoon my love!" She had tears in her eyes. With a smile and a nod to Lady Ailereon he stepped out of the coach and back into the saddle. Moving back towards the rear of the column the two men rode in silence for a time.

While it had taken the better part of eight hours to make the trip out, they only needed three and a half to make the return. It was just full dark when they rode into the caravan yard at the Inn. Dismounting everyone and unloading all the supplies, personal gear and weapons took only ten minutes or so. The whole place was a beehive of activity. The squad sent to warn the Inn had arrived back over an hour before them. Riders were dispatched to all the local farms and wood cutters to come in with their families and whatever they could bring. People were arriving on horseback, on foot and by the wagon load. Just as Grayhawk was trying to determine how many people a squadron of the King's Border Rangers rode in. There were twenty five of them. They were on their way to relieve a garrison on the south border. They are well known for their strengths, ferocity, and skill as archers. When they fight dismounted they carry small round shields called bucklers on their non sword arm and fight with straight, heavy blade thrusting swords. They also use a short hunting spear.

Their Captain was a man well over six and a half feet tall named

Galadran, he reported to Grayhawk. "Greetings My Lord, what would you have my men and I do?"

"Well met, Captain, if under bad circumstances, we are most glad to have you with us. Please to have half of your men at each of the two main gates. The gates will be the key to defending this place. They must be held."

"We will hold them My Lord!" answered Galadran. Galadran moved to position his men at the gates. One of the Cavalry sergeants, Samel by name, returned with a count of the civilians now present in the compound.

"My Lord there are three hundred twenty civilians present, one hundred five men, many of whom are veterans, forty five teenage boys and one hundred seventy women and children. Almost all of the men came with boar spears, some also have swords. A few have axes. So it went for the next hour, organizing his forces, some two hundred thirty five fighting men. The teenage boys were organized into a fire brigade, filling everything possible with water and soaking blankets. The Queen was asked to take charge of the women and children. She had already taken over the Inn and hot food was being served to all.

The Inn itself was in fact an old frontier fort. The walls around it were ten feet high and inside there is a cat-walk going all the way around, four feet wide, about three feet from the top. It was still well maintained, a great credit to the innkeeper, Thomas and his family. The walls were manned now with one hundred fifty men, seventy five cavalry and seventy five civilians. Every other man was a soldier with a bow, a short lance, saber and dirk. The civilians were each armed with a boar spear or an axe. Half of them also had swords. Some few also had bows. A fifty man reserve force was placed in the middle of the compound. The Elves with their swords and bows were asked to defend the Inn itself.

Almost two hours after their arrival and ensuing mass chaos, there now fell an almost total silence over the place. Everything has been done that can be done. The main gates were now closed, double braced and barricaded. All that remained was to light the torches along the top of the walls. Every twenty feet there was a wrought iron torch holder built into the top of the wall. Six foot long tar-pitch torches called siege lights are used. They will burn for about three hours with bright yellow light.

Word came from the south wall that fires could be seen now about three miles out. Farm houses were being sacked and burned no doubt. "Do not light the torches until they are about to attack" Grayhawk ordered.

"My Lord, I will go to the wall and watch. My Elf vision will allow me to see them when they are coming" said Allanfair. Another half an hour passed with still no contact. Grayhawk took out his Adepts ring and cast outward with his sense. He could immediately feel the presence of the Dark Priests as they could feel him. They tried battering down his sensing, even with the eight of them combined, they could not. When they gave up trying and Grayhawk could 'see' clearer he discovered that he had been wrong about their numbers. There were in fact eight companies of Drulgar which meant there were over a thousand of them coming. They were now moving around either side of the Inn in order to surround it. They would attack from all sides. Half an hour later their circle was complete and word came from Lord Allanfair that they were some two hundred yards out from the wall and moving slowly forward.

Grayhawk cast out again, and found that five of the Dark Priests and over five hundred Drulgar were in the south. So their main attack was going to be from that side. Grayhawk ordered twenty of the reserve forces up on to the south wall to strengthen their numbers. He then sent word to Allanfair to have the defenders on the wall crouch down so that their numbers could not be counted by the enemy. He ordered the torches lit when the Drulgar were less than one hundred yards out. Word was given also to the other sections of the wall to do the same when the south wall does. The two old, scarred up, retired soldiers in charge of the reserve forces didn't have to be told what to do, they knew. As a last resort, there were about sixty armed women protecting their children inside the Inn.

Grayhawk looked once more around the compound to see if he had forgotten anything. Finding nothing amiss he ran to the south wall and climbed up to the cat-walk. He went down the line, touching each man on the shoulder or clasping hands saying to each "Odranna be with you." Everyone was crouching, waiting for the signal to rise.

Coming back to the middle where Lord Allanfair was. Squatting beside him, Grayhawk asked

"What is the story of your name, My Lord? Allanfair does not sound like an Elf name. Or am I mistaken?"

"No, you are quite right My Lord. My name in Elf is actually Allain Tal Druida Monde which in your language is Allen of the House of the Druid's Moon."

"You mean the full moon of October called by some the witch's moon?" asked Grayhawk.

"Yes, quite so" answered Allanfair. "The twelve main houses or clans of the Elves are each named for one of the moons of the year. But if you like you can just call me Allen."

"Excellent" said Grayhawk "and you can just call me Hawk. All of this thee and thou and My Lord makes me feel as though we should be delicately sipping tea with milk and have our little fingers up in the air!" Allen was laughing and agreed.

"Alright then, Hawk it is." At that point Allanfair rose up and peered over the wall. Raising his eyebrows he said "It would appear as though we are about to have a fight!" Looking up himself, Grayhawk could see dark shapes moving out at about eighty yards, lots of them.

"Everyone stay down until I give the signal, pass it along." The word went down the line. "Light torches" Grayhawk said, pointing at the ones being held by men on either side of him. Another man opened a candle lantern he had been holding and touched the flame to the end of the torch. Both immediately flared up with bright yellow flame. The man holding each torch stood up and inserted the end into a metal holder on the wall. The torch holders were constructed so that the torch leaned outward from the wall at about a forty five degree angle to put most of the light outside the wall. As the first two went into place others flared into life all along the walls. The light was bright enough the enemy who had closed to within forty yards or so could clearly be seen. Ugly vermin they were. Grayhawk realized then that only he and the Border Rangers and some of the old veterans had ever seen a Drulgar before. As for the others, if they survive the night they will certainly never forget the sight.

Grayhawk had his bow and a full quiver of fifty arrows. Pulling one out, he knocked it and saw that everyone else with a bow was doing the same. Looking at the men on either side of him, who were waiting his command, he said "Let's do it!" He stood up, aimed and let fly. Everyone else did the same. All along the front line the Drulgar were dropping. As he aimed to loose his second shot a tremendous roar of rage went up amongst the enemy and they surged forward at a dead run. Their return fire of black arrows was coming over the wall now. Men were beginning to fall. This was a most uncommon tactic for the Drulgar to walk in to a battle. They usually just ran right up to the target and started to fight. As they reached the bottom of the wall archers were forced to lean out in order to fire down on them. Some archers were then speared from below falling over the wall to certain death. "Swords and spears" yelled Grayhawk as loud as he could. He tossed his bow and quiver down to the ground behind him. Drawing his swords he moved forward to the wall. He was just in time for a Drulgar with cooking pot for a helmet to pop up in front of him as though he were spring loaded. Grayhawk stabbed forward with his short sword in his left hand taking him through the throat.

Now the noise level of war cries, screaming, shouting and metal to metal clanging had become intense. Grayhawk could sense hard fighting all along the line. The Drulgar were squatting in two man teams at the base of the wall, facing each other holding a short piece of log or tree limb between them. As their friends ran forward and stepped onto the log they heaved upward trying to literally throw them over the wall.

Most were being cut down as they cleared the top, but some few were making it. So far they were being dropped by arrows from the Elves at the Inn proper. Just then the first fireball from a Dark Priest came arching over the wall to land in an open area. It was followed by two more and then they were coming five at a time. The fire brigade boys were scrambling to deal with all of them. The battle had reached a fevered pitch now. The smell of blood and human waste mixed with that of the Drulgar and smoke was filling the caravan yard. Fires were beginning to break our here and there inside the compound. The fireballs were still coming in over the front on the south wall but because they were conjured fire they only burned for about half a minute and then dissipated. Now more of the Drulgar were making it to the top of the wall. The hand to hand combat was becoming intense. Lots of

Drulgar were dying but so were men. Even though heavily engaged in the fighting, Grayhawk knew he had already lost a quarter of his men.

As he took off one Drulgar's head with his great sword and back stabbed one behind him with the short sword, he became aware of a bright yellow and orange glow from outside the wall in the area of the main gate. Ah, so that is where the other three Dark Priests are. They are concentrating their fire balls on the gate, trying to burn through it. Two more came over the wall at the same time, right in front of him, almost knocking him off the cat-walk. The one on the right he took with his great sword, under his chin and out the top of his head, blocking a downward swipe at his head from the one on the left. Again, he almost fell backward off the cat-walk. The weight of the dead one on the right was trying to wrench his sword from his hand. The one on the left was trying furiously to hack through his guard when he had a surprised look on his face as six inches of Allen's sword came protruding through the front of his chest.

"You are welcome!" yelled Allen as he moved away to engage another enemy. Grayhawk was laughing now; the blood lust was taking hold. He started down the cat-walk towards the gate when he noticed that now the yellow orange glow could be seen through the smoke on the inside of the gate. "They are breaking through!" he yelled and jumped to the ground. As he moved towards the gate he heard the flat sound of the Dark Priests horns and suddenly there were no more Drulgar coming over the wall. Turning he yelled to Allen, who was still on the wall.

"Every other man to the gate, they are breaking through!" Allen nodded and waved as he started down the line conveying the order. Men were jumping down now and heading for the gate. The entire gate seemed to be on fire. Through the fire could be seen many dark shapes. The Rangers were firing arrows through the fire as fast as they could. The fire roared loudly. Grayhawk had grabbed up his bow and quiver when he jumped from the wall. Now standing right in the middle in front of the gate, he stabbed both of his swords into the ground, took up his bow and started firing through the fire at the moving shapes. Others were arriving now, forming a semi circle around the gate area. Those who had bows were shooting arrow after arrow into the gateway.

Now there were at least fifty men arrayed before the gateway. The fire lost its intensity and then the bulk of it died out. The gateway itself was about twenty foot wide, thirty foot deep bed of coals giving off intense heat. A solid mass of Drulgar could now be seen on the other side, clambering over a large mound of dead ones. They came surging forward, pushing forward from the sheer numbers of the ones behind. As Grayhawk and the others continued to shoot arrows into the mass there was no stopping it. The Drulgar who either hesitated or were hit by arrows went down screaming into the bed of coals as the others came over the top of them. The smoke became thick black and oily. The smell of it was overpowering. It clogged the nose and throat and burned the eyes.

The Drulgar broke through the smoke; they were half blinded and choked. The first were cut down but there were too many to stop. As they broke free of the gate tunnel the humans surged forward to meet them. An awful battle scene was unfolding in thick nasty black smoke. Hundreds of Drulgar were pushing and shoving to get out of the furnace conditions inside that tunnel, being pushed by mental commands of their own Dark Priests. The number of men was now almost a hundred, spread out across the yard. Arrows from the Elves were hissing through the ranks, each taking down a Drulgar. Once again the noise level was unbelievable, as the two sides engaged the clang of steel on steel. Battle cry after battle cry was met with shriek and howl from the Drulgar. Again the coppery smell of blood mingled with the foul smoke. The air was full of the sounds of men and foul beast dying, hacking, slashing, chopping and stabbing at each other. Grayhawk was now behind the red veil, no longer a warlord or leader. Now he was a Blademaster plying his trade with all the skill and efficiency he could muster, whirling movements of deadly blades that left dead and dying foes at every turn.

The Dark Priests had now called in all of their forces from around the Inn compound. Forcing this gate was their way to victory over the defenders. Inside were women, children, food, drink and plunder. Most of all inside was Grayhawk and his bitch Queen to be taken alive with as many of the Elves as possible. They were to be taken to Stygius, before the Dark Lord himself, to be tortured to death, and then eaten. Now that the Drulgar had stopped attacking the walls all of the men were coming down into the yard to join in the battle on the ground. Many men have now fallen but nowhere near as many as the Drulgar have lost.

Grayhawk was oblivious to all of this. He was far gone into the berserker battle fury. As were numerous other border rangers, cavalrymen, veterans, all Northmen or at least descended from them. Their combined rage and fury with the rest of the humans and Elves behind them had cut down so many of the enemy that they were now pushing them back into the gore that was inside of the gate tunnel, stepping on and fighting over the bodies of dozens of Drulgar, smoldering and stinking beneath their feet. Then they were through the gate, and out the other side. The air was cleaner, but the Drulgar weren't running. They were attempting to regroup, and, to bring up some small groups of reinforcements from their rear. The Dark Priests were still using fireballs but they were killing more of their own than humans.

Within a few minutes five of the Dark Priests were down, riddled with arrows from the Elves up on the wall. Another took a boar spear through the middle. There was now, less than a hundred Drulgar left standing. Grayhawk came out of the rage slowly. He was slightly disoriented as to his location and the area was dark. Then the fighting all but ceased. The two remaining Dark Priests each blew a long flat note on their little silver horns and fled southward into the darkness, followed closely by every Drulgar who could follow.

New torches flared to life on top of the walls. This fight had lasted for over four hours. The light now revealed huge numbers of dead Drulgar, their bodies and weapons were everywhere. The smoke and the stink were still billowing out of the gate tunnel. Forty something men had pushed through the tunnel, actually only losing a few in the process. Now they made their way back into the compound through a small side door. Inside, the pall of stinking smoke had almost dissipated. The women had all come out of the Inn and were busy turning the stables into a hospital. For there were many wounded.

Chapter Twenty Two

Grayhawk stood in the center of the compound amongst the burn marks and the dead from both sides. 'We must surely be standing in the Grace of Odranna this day' he thought as he looked around surveying the carnage. By rights we should have lost this battle.

He just stood there, alone, still holding a sword in each had. He was dog tired, soaked with sweat and covered in blood and gore from head to foot. He felt no remorse for the killing he had done. They were not people, the Drulgar; they are a contrived race of evil beings. Human and serpent merged. Grayhawk had always thought that they looked like big rodents of some sort. They serve only the Dark Lord.

Then the Queen and Allen were both there in front of him. The front of Aurelia's dress was blood stained as were her hands and arms. She saw the look of alarm on his face.

"Not mine Grayhawk" she said in a tired voice "from all the wounded, only from the wounded." Allen spoke

"Are you now, back with us Hawk?"

"What? Oh, yes I am fine. I am just really tired" he answered.

"Well, I know what will make you feel better" said Allen. "Come over here to the water duct. Let us get some of that grime washed off of you. I know it sure made me feel better." An aqua duct piped water in to a tank from an uphill spring, half a mile away. The pipe was on a swivel and Allen pulled it over the top of Grayhawk's head. The water almost knocked him down and it took his breath away at the same time. It was cold, and then it felt good. It brought him slamming back to reality, reviving both his spirit and his body. He stood there for some minutes and, with the help of a long handled brush, while still fully clothed, he managed to get most of the grime and gore off.

When he stepped out of the water stream Allen handed him a cup half full of Brandy. He downed it in three drinks. It hit bottom like a fireball and immediately began to warm his innards and his soul. It took a few minutes of wringing and shaking like a dog to get the water out of his clothes. Then Aurelia was in his arms. She was shaking very hard. Allen poured her a Brandy from his flask.

"Majesty I believe you need this" he replied.

"Yes, thank you Allen" she said taking a large drink of the Brandy. "You know, I thought I had seen war and fighting before. When I was a girl my father's army fought against the border bandits. My mother and I watched from the city wall." She was still holding on to Grayhawk and shaking, though not as hard. "This is not war. This is horror. It's base Evil and horror!"

"Yea, verily" said Allen. "This is not war over national pride, or some King's vanity, or even to put down bandits. This is a fight for the survival of all living beings on this world. Worse still it has only just begun or at least this phase of it. This war will determine the very survival of our races. We must stop the Dark Lord"

"Lucifer" interrupted Grayhawk.

"What?" asked Allen.

"I said, his name is Lucifer" Grayhawk replied. "He was once Odranna's favorite, until he turned on Odranna like a rabid dog."

"Well" replied Allen "whatever his name might be, we must stop him."

"That we must" said Grayhawk "though it will not be either quick, nor easy." All nodded in agreement.

"I must return to the wounded" said Aurelia "for now their needs are the greatest." The next few hours were spent cleaning the compound and putting out some few remaining smoldering areas, dragging the dead Drulgar and Dark Priests to a place outside the walls. On the morrow they would be burned. Their weapons were gathered and stacked up; they would be melted down and used to forge other weapons, farm implements and the like. Cook fires were started and a meal was prepared. All minor wounds and burns were attended to and all were fed.

It was now only a couple of hours until daylight. The compound had settled down to a quiet hum. After posting guards on the walls most everyone was settling down to rest or sleep, pretty much in any place they could find. Grayhawk had donned dry clothing and though he was as tired as he had ever been before, he was not sleepy. He sat on a small keg before a small fire, in the middle of the yard. Watching as the activity died down all around him. Even the hospital area was quieter now. Some few more of the wounded had died. The efforts and skilled hands of the healers, and all those helping had saved many lives this night. As he sat, he cast out with his mind as much as his tired state would allow. He could detect no presence that threatened, only the vague sense of the rapidly retreating remains of the Drulgar force. Thanks to the All Father for that. He did not believe that the Inn could withstand another attack.

He poured himself another Brandy from a small stone jug which someone had brought him with his meal. Looking around he saw that all was in order. These were all disciplined people, even the farmers and woodsmen with capable leaders among them. This was one of those times when everything possible was being done and the commander was, out of deference, given some quiet time.

Grayhawk awoke with a start. He was lying on a pallet of straw and blankets with a folded blanket for a pillow. Aurelia had been there. He could smell her perfume. It was a bright gray, high overcast day. Already it was several hours past sun up. His boots and tunic had been removed and his weapons were close to hand on his left side. 'By Odranna's Beard!' he thought. 'I don't even remember being put into bed and now everyone else is up and about, while I remain sleeping like some lout!' Quickly he donned his boots and tunic, gathered his weapons to him. While he was looking around, seeing the work and other activities, going on in the compound. All things seemed to be well in hand, making him feel even guiltier.

Allanfair waved and called to him from across the compound "Hawk! Come have something to eat." Grayhawk waved back.

"Coming, I could definitely use some food this morning!" Making his way across the compound to where the food serving line had been set up. Standing in line with soldiers and civilians, he waited his turn to be served up hot oats with maple syrup, fresh bread with butter and a mug of good strong tea with honey. Thus went the entire day, all present were engrossed in the caring for the wounded, burning or burying the dead on the human side, and totally burning every vestige of the Drulgar. Except for weapons and any valuable items such as jewelry and monies, they had stolen from their unfortunate victims. Everything would be put to good use repairing and restoring.

The repairing of the walls and gates of the compound went smoothly, mostly due to abundance of wood available in the area. By the evening meal all were wearing from a long hard day of labor, but most everything had been done. Even unto crews going out to some of the closer farms burnt by the Drulgar and starting the rebuilding process. Of course with all the gained knowledge of this experience, things were made stronger, harder and more easily defended.

It was not likely that the Drulgar would be returning any time soon, but if they should, they would find a much better prepared and determined populace waiting for them.

This battle had not been without cost, though much less than it probably should have been. Over twenty of the local citizens had been either killed or maimed. Another 1sixteen had been caught outside the wall and were butchered and eaten by the Drulgar and their dark priests. These, along with eight of the Border Rangers, two of the elves and fourteen of the Cavalry detail. Sixty dead all told and forty two were wounded, an expensive blood bill.

The Drulgar had not fared so well, over six hundred fifty of their number along with eight dark priests were killed. That is better than ten to one odds.

Late in the evening Grayhawk walked the battlefield, alone except for the sentries. Casting out, he was looking for any presence of evil in the vicinity, and none could be found. He sensed only the fading evil residue still left on the battle ground. Coming down to the center of the compound, where by the fire, were seated Allanfair, Captain Galadran of the Border Rangers and Thomas the Innkeeper, drinking tea laced with brandy and smoking pipefuls of tabac.

"Gentlemen!" he greeted them as he approached. "Please, rest yourselves." He gestured for them to remain seated as they would have all stood in his presence. Taking a mug of tea and brandy and taking a seat on a log before the fire.

"What then do you sense out there, My Lord?" said Capt Galadran.

"Nothing at all, Captain. Not for a long distance."

"Good news indeed" said Thomas.

"Aye," agreed Allanfair. "As you can see, except for the sentries, only we four are still awake."

"They are well deserving of their rest" said Galadran. "These folk have fought well, a victory to be proud of!"

"AYE!" they all agreed.

"Even though" said Thomas "Myself included, they still do not know the why of it."

"A good question is it not?" Allanfair said, gesturing with his pipe to Grayhawk. "What say you to that, my Lord?"

Looking into the fire for a moment as though pondering the matter, Grayhawk looked at them and answered. "Gentlemen, a few days ago, these people would have argued the existence of Elves. At which Allanfair arched an eyebrow and both Galadran and Thomas both nodded in agreement. "And if you had told them they were about to be attacked by creatures from the underworld, they would have questioned your sanity. Only now, afterwards, do they acknowledge the very real existence of both."

"What I have a little trouble understanding" said Allanfair. "Is this, my people have no problem knowing that humans exist! And though we had never seen them before, at least not in a long time, we know that the creatures of the underworld exist. Why do humans not know these things?"

"Ah" said Grayhawk "That is because of a thing called "human nature." Put quite simply means, if you cannot see it, smell it, touch it or taste it, it does not exist. This has given the Dark Lord his greatest advantage against man. Man has been convinced over time, that He, Lucifer, does not exist and that he is only a myth and cannot harm them."

"Why would he want to do that?" ask Galadran.

"Because" said Allanfair, "He learned long, long ago that once mankind knows of your existence, and that you are his enemy, he will find a way to fight you! He will stand against you at every turn. Lucifer does not want to wipe out the human race; he wants to own it for his personal pleasure, like so many goats or sheep."

"His hatred for us stems from a war with the All Father long, long ago. It was started because Lucifer, who was at that time one of the All Father's chosen, came to believe that the All Father had chosen Man over him as favored in the Universe. Lucifer rebelled against the All Father. A great and long war was waged. Lucifer lost, was cast down, and has ever since schemed for the destruction of man. Unfortunately that includes Elves, Dwarves and any other free thinking species or being" explained Grayhawk.

"You mean" said Thomas, rather big eyed "There are other types of people, uh beings, out there that we do not know about?"

"Yes Thomas, there are" said Allanfair smiling "More than you can imagine."

"And at that, Gentlemen" said Grayhawk, rising to his feet, "I believe I shall allow myself the luxury of sleep. Tomorrow we head back to the King's City."

"Then are we not going to go down and check the damage to your holdings, my Lord Grayhawk?" asked Allanfair.

"No. I care too much for the safety of our party, especially the Ladies, to endanger them at all, or should I say "any further" than I already have. I failed to cast for an evil presence and they almost caught us in their snare. Well! Lesson learned on my part!" The others were nodding in agreement.

"We have all done well to survive this" said Captain Galadran. "Well indeed." A peaceful night, quiet and serene, except for the nightmares many would carry with them for the rest of their lives. It seems as though everyone woke at about the same time this morning, just as the sky began to lighten. By the time the sun was up most everyone had eaten and the "Queen's Party" as they were to be hereafter know in these parts, was packed up, dressed and fully armed. It was as though no one wanted to take any chances. Even the two young Princesses refused to give up their short swords and daggers, preferring instead to belt their daggers and wear their short swords over their right shoulder in modified Ranger fashion.

Grayhawk was very proud of them, but their mother the Queen

was more than a little skeptical. "My Lord Grayhawk" she said when she first saw him. "Royal Princesses should not go about armed like soldiers"

"My dear Aurelia" answered Grayhawk with a smile, "I am not going to try and take the weapons from those two! Besides, I notice that you are wearing the same, and raising his hand to halt her protest "My love, before this is through, every child may have to become a warrior, if we are to survive!"

Half an hour later they rode out of the stockade, now known as Queen Aurelia's Stand, headed north at a good pace. Grayhawk had left Captain Galadran's Border Rangers with instructions to remain at the Inn until another company could be sent out from the King's City to reinforce them. They rode at a steady pace throughout the morning, with only half an hour for the noon stop. Grayhawk expected they would arrive approximately two hours before dark. He had sent riders on ahead early in the day to announce their return. Even before the attack he had been unable to cast for a mental link with anyone. He knew the Dark Priests were blocking and at the same time trying to intercept any information they could about the attack at the Inn. Midway into the afternoon, a scout galloped in from the North with the word the King and an "entire army" is coming very fast down the road. Grayhawk called for a halt, in an open area to let the ladies rest and prepare themselves for the arrival of the King.

Half an hour later the outriders, a group of about twenty five Knights arrived, they spoke with Grayhawk briefly and then continued on south, to scout for any sign of a following enemy force. Half an hour after that King Killian IV came into view at a canter followed by at least a thousand Knights, Cavalry and Archers in full combat gear.

Having already assembled his small force by the side of the road, Grayhawk, Queen Aurelia, Allanfair, Lady Ailereon and the Cavalry Officers stood in front. The King reined his horse in and leapt from the saddle all in one motion. He tightly hugged his Mother. "Here now!" said the King "this is not time for formality! I am here to see that my family is safe!" Releasing his mother and looking around he said "Wait where, are my two lovely sisters? Ah good! Here they are" as they came from behind, running up to be grabbed up in a hug. "And they are armed too! I know I must hear this tale!" "My Lords, Grayhawk and Allanfair" He said, while grasping each by the shoulders, "and of course, My Lady Ailereon," grabbing her in a bear hug, very much to her surprise. It is so good to see you all, and all of your company who have returned with you!" Gesturing, his arms spread wide to all of the assembled soldiers.

The King ordered camp to be established in the forested area where they had stopped. For if the whole force turned around and headed back for the city, they would not arrive until almost midnight. That would throw the entire city into turmoil.

"Besides" he said to his younger sisters, "It gives us a chance to camp out together. We've never done that before!" Two troops of cavalry were sent on to the Inn or 'Queen Aurelia's Stand'. The King absolutely loved that his mother was now a local hero. The cavalry would ride on into the southern reaches area, to survey the damages wrought by the Drulgar and the Dark Priests. They were to determine if there were any survivors amongst the populace and to report on logistical needs to begin the rebuilding. To include building a large garrison fort, in order to house a regiment of cavalry. The King also ordered four additional Border Ranger units assigned to watch and patrol the border.

As they all sat at dinner that night, around a large bonfire, the overall situation was discussed. The King expressed his anger and dismay that the Kingdom had been invaded and assured Duke Grayhawk that his manor house would be rebuilt, even better than it had been before, and all his holdings restored. Grayhawk said

"Thank you Sire for that, but it is difficult to lament the loss of that which I have never seen! I am just thankful indeed that we were able to escape their ambush plans and to survive the attack on the Inn. We were more than just a little lucky in that."

"Agreed" said Killian "All of you, and I mean all, are to be commended for your conduct and your valor on this, which turned out to be a military mission rather than a social one! I salute you all!" he said, standing and raising his Brandy glass. "Further decorations and such will follow when we return to the city. Oh, before I forget, by my mother's request, Captain Johannis" said the King, nodding at the young officer.

"Sire!" he replied, jumping to his feet.

"Henceforth and hereafter" said the King. "You and your troop of Cavalry shall be known as 'Queen Aurelia's Guard', permanently assigned to her household and under her command. You are promoted to Senior Guard Captain. Do you accept Sir?"

"I accept Sire" replied the captain. "It is a great honor you bestow upon us" with a deep bow to the King and to the Queen Mother. Everyone was applauding. Surrounded by a thousand cavalry and archers, the group passed a good evening of food and comradeship. By Midnight everyone but the sentries had retired. The following morning dawned cloudless and warm. The smell of the forest, cook fires, breakfast sausages, horses and myriads of other scents all mingled to form a very pleasant atmosphere. Most everyone slept in until well after daylight and it was not until midmorning that they were ready for travel back to the city. By mid afternoon the lead elements were entering the city gates. Within an hour all elements of the force had returned and were standing down.

Sir Gregory and the two senior warrior monks of the Odranna's Chosen were waiting on the steps to the palace along with many other officials of the court to welcome them back.

Prince Drinach of the Dwarves, it was announced by Lord Gregory, had taken command of the Kitchen and was over-seeing preparations for a great feast. When asked what the occasion was, he thought for a moment stoking his beard and then replied

"It is Thursday!" Everyone stood blinking for a second and then the King said laughing

"And so it is!!"

That works for me" said Grayhawk "let us eat!!" Prince Drinach had received them into the dining room wearing an apron and grinning broadly.

"I was so glad to hear that you lot did not get yourselves killed that I just had to cook!"

And the meal was something. Roast Auroch, roast stag, roast pork, rabbits in brown gravy, wild rice, truffles in wine sauce, hot black bread with buttered raisins and currants in brandy and honey sauce, cooked greens with turnips, mince meat pie and wild berry tarts, and of course plenty of beer, and sweet white wine for the ladies. The hall was raucous and roaring. Everyone stuffed themselves. The food was wonderful. Prince Drinach received at least four offers of marriage.

Even the Royal Princesses were allowed to stay until almost midnight. Though they had left their short swords, both still wore their daggers at their side. When asked, the King replied "Well, I am not going to try and take them away from those two young warriors." Looking their way, he also did notice that each of the young ladies had a page standing no more than three feet behind their chairs were Paden, and Geran. "Now that" thought Killian "is most interesting!" But then Princess Elysia, seated on his left touched his arm with a question and he promptly forgot all else. He was completely lost in the depth of her eyes, and her smile. The feasting lasted until daylight for those hearty enough to stand it. Most of the Royal Party had left by midnight.

Grayhawk and the Queen adjourned to her chambers where they made love all night. The King and Princess Elysia to the library along with two of her ladies and the King's young page Artur, where they talked until after daylight.

Prince Drinach and Sir Owen had disappeared, somewhere into the palace with a pair of very prominent young ladies, whose names shall remain a mystery.

Chapter Twenty Three

Though it was unspoken, everyone knew that this was to be the last feasting and partying together they would do, for probably a long time. Then next day was a very quiet one throughout the Palace. Everyone just took the day off.

The following morning it was back to business as usual. Many meetings and discussions took place. Grayhawk and Allanfair briefed the King on the fight at the Inn and the fact that dragons had been involved in the attack on the Ducal Hall.

"That is twice they have struck within my realm" said Killian. "It is probably only a matter of time until they attack here at the city. How can we prepare for that? Do you really believe they can even be killed? If so, how would that be done?" Grayhawk replied,

"They can indeed be killed, Sire. Although not an easy task, but none the less, it can be done. However, since they are directly controlled by Lucifer himself, I think he will hold them mostly in check until he is sure of what we are doing. He realizes that we are a threat to his plans if not actually to him personally."

"Aye" said Allanfair, "He will only let them be used in a limited role until he can find a way to hatch the others. When he has done that I believe he will unleash them all to attack the world." The following week was taken up with planning for the expedition. Grayhawk and Sir Owen finalized their selection of the twenty Knights who were to accompany them. Sir Gregory arrived with a contingent of fifty of his senior cadets to bolster the cities defenses.

A large caravan of builders, carpenters, stone masons and other trades along with their tools, their families and everything they could load onto a wagon, pack horse or cart escorted by one hundred fifty cavalry and archers departed for the Southern Reach Ducal Estates. Though sent by the King, everyone knew and understood they were under the Queen Mother's orders. The entire valley was to be restored and rebuilt, better than it had been before. What an ungodly sight their caravan was, absolute mayhem, over two hundred civilians and their goods. As they finally cleared the city gates, the Captain in charge reported to the King.

"Sire we have departed! Pray for us. What would normally be a day and a half journey will take us almost a week!"

"I envy you not, good Captain!" said the King, shaking his head. "At best, you have a wearisome task." The Officer saluted again and was off, bounding down the castle steps to his waiting mount. Grayhawk who had been standing off to one side, arms folded, with one hand raised to his chin. Something had been tugging at his senses all morning. Finally he had cast with his other sense and discovered what it was. The ship, it was still two days out, but it was at last going to arrive.

While far to the south in the city Tripos, in the land of Merkesha, the Dark Priest Rigorta was fuming in an ever darkening black rage. His effort to penetrate the area around the King's City, in Keltan were still to no avail. Every avenue of approach seemed to be blocked as though some unseen power were interfering at every turn. He understood the arcane powers of the Templar very well, usually finding it not quite as strong as the Dark magic. This was different, stranger, unyielding, yet subtle. He had summoned at least three different Demons and all had been unable to garner anything useful. He knew something major was being planned, a strike against himself no doubt. But he also did not think they knew his whereabouts. He had now made so many sacrifices that the city officials were getting suspicious. He would have to stop, for now.

The Dark Lord would not release the Dragons for any further raids until they had better information the activities and location of Grayhawk and the Elves, and whatever other group of morons are allied with them. "Perhaps" he thought to himself, "He would take the few weeks to make his image among the locals a bit more 'charitable', a citizen of the community, someone they could trust." Laughing loudly, he went to his evening meal. His mood was quite improved, even 'charitable'.

In the King's City, steady, serious, subdued preparations and meetings were being held in preparation for the coming 'Holy Mission', for lack of a better description. Detailed lists of men and materials were prepared and gone over, changes were made, things deleted, things added. Then they were gone over again, everyone involved wanted all things in order. But time did pass, evening came, a good supper meal, followed by tabac and brandy, along with much discussion of the journey and of all the places it would take them. This subject of fighting Dragons and Lucifer as conversation was for the most part avoided.

The next morning Grayhawk went down to the cellar area where Odranna's Chosen were billeted. He had not until now had the time to give other than official and perfunctory greetings to the warrior priests, some of whom had been his instructors. He found them in a large vaulted store room, which had been emptied for them to use as a weapons practice area. All activity stopped as he entered, until he was recognized and found to be alone. It is forbidden for any other than the chosen to look upon their training or practice at arms. Several of the elder Brethren raised hands, or nodded in greeting. Now that Grayhawk was recognized as an Adept of the Templar Order, he was considered an equal by all of the Chosen, even their leader. White Bear, approached and extended his arm in greeting, the two grasped each other's forearms in the Lion's paw grip.

"Greetings Grayhawk, long has it been since your last presence among us on the weapons ground. Now you return among us as Warlord of a mighty Kingdom and an Adept of the Templar. Did you envision such things when you left the caverns?" Smiling now, Grayhawk shook his head.

"Nay, Chief White Bear, I had not an inkling of what lay ahead."

"Truly, Odranna has smiled upon you" White Bear responded. "Thou art chosen."

"I have no suitable reply" said Grayhawk, bowing his head.

"None is required" said the Chief. "I only stated that, which is true. Come then" he said, with a hand on Grayhawk's shoulder, "Be amongst us again. You know it not, but there are four here who are cousins by blood to you. They were toddling babes when you last saw them." For an entire long day was Grayhawk together again with Norda folk, at weapons play, eating, speaking his native tongue, learning of his family, the passing of his mother and father, the state of the Clan from which he came. It was truly dark outside when he came up from the cellars and emerged into the cool evening air. He was feeling better about life in general than he had in a very long time.

A feast was being held in the Royal Hall, but Grayhawk spent this evening alone with his new family in the Queen's apartments. Quiet time, Aurelia called it. At about three in the morning Grayhawk was awakened and informed that a black warship was approaching up the river.

"No alarm" he told the Guard Captain, "this is the ship we have been expecting." As the ship was still several hours away from the quay, Grayhawk went back to bed to a very awake and smiling Aurelia. At about the eighth hour Grayhawk and the King, along with a squad of the Royal Guard rode down to the quay and up to the black ship. It was a large, long, sleek looking war galley with furled blood red sails, at least ninety paces long with that many war shields to a side. Though capable of using oars, this was a sailing vessel. She put forth an aura of strength and speed. She was also not new, but well seasoned, a veteran of many campaigns.

"Well" said the King, "I do not know about you, but I am impressed."

"Aye Majesty" replied Grayhawk. "This is some ship." Just then there appeared on the stern, or quarter deck, a half dozen men and women, dressed in the most garish and loud array of garments of every color and style, sporting all manner of swords and knives. Also there, was Wojan, leader of a hundred and the Twenty three dwarves of his contingent, and even they were sporting some colorful clothing.

"Hail Grayhawk" shouted Olion the most garish dressed of all, as he leapt to the rail on the side of the ship. "Have I brought you a ship, or what!?"

"Hail Olion!" shouted Grayhawk in return. "Is this boat the

one you are talking about? Or is this an over grown river barge!" A collective groan went up for the group on deck now numbering about fifty persons.

"By the beards of all of the Gods" shouted Olion, "A Northman who knows nothing of ships!" All were laughing and cheering now. Grayhawk raised his hands for quiet.

"Seriously, my Friends, I welcome you to the Kingdom of Keltan. I hope that your voyage was a pleasant one. I take great pleasure in presenting you all, scallywags and pirates that you are, to his Royal Majesty Killian IV, King and Ruler of Keltan." All were silent now and bowing, sweeping off feathered hats.

"I never met a King before" said Olion, "Or ever seen one!" as he leapt down from the ship to the quay, bowing again.

"Nor have I ever met, or seen a pirate before Master Olion" said King Killian as he threw over a leg and slid from his horse to the ground. "Shall we call it 'well met'" said the King extending his hand. Taking the King's hand in both of his Olion replied,

"Your Majesty, if you are willing to clasp hands with the likes of me, and call it 'well met' I will follow you to the gates of hell!"

"Well, while I believe that may well be the destination you are headed for" said the King "This time I will ask that you go with Lord Grayhawk. While I alas, must remain here, to rule this land. But, come, Master Olion. I have heard much about you. Set your watch or whatever it is that Pirate Captains do, and let us all go up to the Royal Hall and refresh ourselves." This was met with great enthusiasm, and whilst waiting for transport Olion's wife Sylan and his brother Nylan were presented to the King.

By afternoon wagons from the castle began arriving at the docks, loaded with very normal looking bales, barrels, boxes and bundles which were very promptly slung aboard in cargo nets and then stowed away by members of the ship's crew. There were no guards posted, so the scene on the docks was that of a normal sailing vessel taking on a cargo. When the crew who were ashore, were queried by townsfolk as to their destination all replied they were stopping in Spanos, then Gaula, and finally returning to Tuscana in northern Troscai, hopefully with their holds full of trade goods, which would be sold at a great profit! To any who might be watching or taking note, all appeared to be normal. But those who were watching and taking note, had already observed that these were no ordinary seamen and that they were heavily armed. However they did fail to take notice of the three young teenage boys, Pages on a day off from the castle, enjoying a day in town.

Artur, Paden and Geran, were young and innocent looking, often engaging in boisterous and sometimes rough horse play, constantly in search of sweets and treats. In fact they are already well trained observers who can communicate with each other through sign language and gestures. Blonde, redhead and brunette, all were skilled forgers, expert horsemen and of course weapons trained with knife and bow. And, as a number of agents of the Dark Lord have discovered the hard way, they are all three especially good with their long, double edged blade, called a Page's Dirk, and regarded as purely ceremonial. In most cases that is true. Most pages routinely forget to wear theirs. Only once had the weapons master pulled and inspected the three of theirs, fire blackened and razor sharp, made of a different quality steel from the standard ceremonial model. He had raised an eyebrow, looked the three of them up and down and said "I shall be watching you young gentlemen!"

So should have the two agents posing as idlers, hanging around the dock area. Though no one missed them, nor saw the surprised last look on their faces. The two bodies would become fish food. The three young pages, off on another adventure, running through the streets, laughing and joking, pushing and shoving one another. Many were the details accomplished this day by all parties involved in preparation for departure. Last minute things remembered for creature comfort and personal wants.

The actual planning for the mission itself was very simple and straight forward. The "Company" as it was being called now, knew approximately where they had to go. Preferably without being detected, caught or killed. Upon arrival they were to locate and destroy a large clutch of Dragon's eggs being held by the Dark Lord, Lucifer himself. They were to kill two full grown Dragons (fire breathing) and in the confusion of the aftermath, escape and evade while making their way back home. Very simple and straight forward right! Only in song and saga!

The dinner that night was somewhat subdued for a formal occasion. No great rousing toasts to the glory and success of the mission. Most people in the Royal Court did not even know the nature of the quest, though everyone knew that something big was afoot. Current speculation was that it was a retaliatory raid into Spanos in response to the attack on the Ducal Hall in the southern reaches. Grayhawk and Aurelia spent most of the night talking and making love, as did many others of the Company. The next morning broke grey, wet and raining. Most took advantage of that and slept in.

The day crept along at a snail's pace. The only thing increasing was the tempo of the rain, or so it seemed. By dark the rain was steady, and the entire city had boarded up tight. Grayhawk met with the King and the principle others involved with the Company in the King's library for a final Brandy and to say farewell. Blademaster, Elf, Dwarf, Knight, Monk and Pirate all raised their glasses in salute to the King. Killian raised his glass in return.

"I have no great stirring speech to bore you with" he said "only this, I fully expect all of you to return. I fully believe you will all be successful, and I really wish I were going with you. May the All Father ride with you and protect you!" After a round of hugs and goodbyes to those staying behind Grayhawk and the others took leave of the King bidding Aurelia to remain with her son. Each member of the Company went silently through the castle to collect personal belongings and gear. Then, going just as quietly, they went out of several different doors being held open by select members of the Royal Guard. Singly, and in pairs and threes by different routes ,all of the Company members made their way silently through alleys, and down wet streets to the dock area and there up one of the three gang planks onto the ship. There they were met by some of the crew already on board and shown to where they would berth.

All members made it on board without incident or accident. The dock area then sat in total silence except for the rain. Later, in silence and darkness Odranna's Chosen boarded almost ghost like. Once they were on board the gang planks were silently run in and secured. Some three hours later, at two hours past midnight, four crewmen moving through the rain let slip the fore and aft mooring lines and using long poles pushed the ship away from the dock and into the current. The tide from the sea having crested turned, and with that, the normal current of the river did take hold of the vessel and it slid away into the night without a sound. They went unnoticed by the watch on any one of a dozen other vessels in port.

Chapter Twenty Four

By the time the sun broke over the horizon behind them, they had unfurled the sails and were feeling the first rolling swells of the bay. The rain was gone, the morning was brisk and the ship was straining at the rigging, gaining speed with each passing minute. Captain Olion then came to Grayhawk.

"Have you any instructions? What course do we follow My Lord?"

"We sail for the gulf of Libiasan, with a stop along the way to take care of that beast Rigorda" said Grayhawk. "Olion you are Captain of this ship. I know naught of ships and sailing. You take us where we need to go. I and all the others shall follow your lead and command. So what say you Captain as far as instructions"? Olion stood with his thumbs hooked in his broad belt.

"Well now! Those are words to hearten the boldest of Sea Dogs. My men and I are perfectly capable of sailing this particular ship to the end of the earth and back. But, we are not a large crew. Therefore I propose to make sailors out of all of you, just in case of any problems we might encounter on a voyage such as this. Are you willing, able, and not afraid to work? Hard work it will be, mark my words."

"Well then" said Grayhawk, "I shall be first to step forward. What would you have me do?" All of the others also volunteered their services. Grayhawk was to train as helmsman, Prince Allanfair as navigator/Helmsman. Prince Drinach and his dwarves took over all ships carpenter duties, and repair of lines, sails and rigging. Sir Owen became the understudy to the first mate. White Bear and his brothers, who preferred to remain below during the daylight, would completely take over the night watch after a few nights of training.

Princess Ailereon and Sylan, the Captain's wife, along with the two Elf ladies accompanying the Princess took over the cooking as well as ships surgeon duties, as there was no proper ship's surgeon on board. And of course Prince Drinach agreed to help with meals, especially since he had never prepared seafood before. He said that a Dwarf Prince should be able to cook anything which was edible. For three days straight, they sailed due west from the coast, both for training and to throw off any who might be scrying or otherwise looking for them. Twice Captain Olion had the ship put hard about one hundred eighty degrees and sail for two hours back in the direction they came from. He did this once the first day and again on the third just to see if any ships were following in their wake.

No sail was sighted and it was good experience for all the new sailors. Half an hour after the midnight watch was posted on the third night, the maneuver was repeated for the third time, except this time instead of turning back to the west at the end of two hours, the ship turned due south. Now the journey was truly underway. A day after turning south the weather turned sour. For five days running they tacked back and forth against strong headwinds and line after line of white squalls, accompanied by heavy swells. Only ten days out of port and all ready the entire crew is fast becoming seasoned sailors. The ships morale was very good. The extra hands made everyone's job bearable. White Bear's group of the Chosen were proven to be excellent sailors handling the vessel in the dark and during storms as though they had been doing it all of their lives. Olion and all of his crew were absolutely in awe of their proficiency. Olion stated on more than one occasion

"There is no way you will convince me these fellows live their lives in a cave up in the Northlands! These fellows know how to sail a ship! How is that Grayhawk?" he said turning to look at Grayhawk who was taking a watch at the helm. "And how is it that you feel the ships mood through the wheel, like one who has been doing this for years?"

"Olion, my friend, it is like this. Once, long, long eons ago the Norda were a great seafaring people, warrior/sailors traveling unknown seas and coasts in our Dragon boats in search of wealth and glory as Raiders from the Sea. I guess the ancient tribal memory remains with us to this day."

"I have heard of this" replied Olion "but I would not have believed it could be so strong."

"Nor I" said Grayhawk "but it is there." Their eleventh day at sea the sky cleared and the wind came around from the northwest. With the sea settling into a gentle rolling swell of six feet or so, running in the same direction, the speed of the ship through the water as much as doubled. When asked by Prince Drinach if he were going to hold defensive drills to repel borders or such, Captain Olion replied

"My Prince, with this lot on board I feel sorry for any group of fools who attack this ship." At which Drinach grinned.

"Me too!" he replied, "Me too!" while fingering the edge of his axe. On their sixteenth day at sea they turned due east and sailed for a day and a half back towards the continent. They made land fall at the north end of the largest of the Moroc Island chain. They sailed into the pass between the large island and the four smaller ones that make up the group. They came to an anchorage in a protected bay which has been a haven for pirate ships and traders for many a year. There is a watch tower, if you can call it that, at the head of the bay, but it has not been manned in recent history. Ships and crews may stay as long as they like, and no questions are ever asked. They dropped anchor, half a mile from shore and a mile from the tower. This area is hot and the town stinks. Even though they had arrived late in the day, just before sunset, it was still uncomfortably warm. Tarps were rigged, both overhead to shade the decks and to act as air funnels at the hatchways. All the ports and windows in the aft castle were open. It was dark before the ship was fully secured and a meal was served. Afterwards Grayhawk had everyone assembled on deck. Brandy and water was served to all who wanted it. Most everyone had a pipe lit in short order. The breeze was cooler now. First, Captain Olion spoke.

"For any who might wonder why we are so far from the docks at yon 'town'. Just wet your finger and feel the breeze on it. I have been here before and believe me, the closer you get, the less breeze there is and the more stink. Tomorrow will be hot, but out here where we are, we will be much better off." Grayhawk then rose from where he had been sitting, pipe in hand. He addressed the assembled.

"This is the first time as a group we are together in a place where I can speak freely about our mission. But first, let me tell you why we have stopped here. We are in the Moroc Islands about three day's coastal sailing from the City of Tripos in the land of Merkesha. We have come to know that one of the Dark Lords chief priests has moved there from the King's City. His name is Rigorta. He is responsible for all of the attacks of the Dark Forces against us, even the attack of the Dragons and the murder of the King and his sons. Many things have transpired in order for us to be at this point in time and at this place. We have had help and guidance from the All Father but we are the ones assembled to do this task."

"First of all, now that we know who this demon-lover Rigorta is, and now that we know where he is, I will lead a group of the Chosen to destroy him. We will hire a small craft to take us to Tripos. We will eliminate this monster and any of his helpers we can find. Because of his command of the powers of Darkness, it must be the Chosen who do this. We will leave tomorrow evening and we should be back in seven or eight days. Once this task has been fully completed, I will explain in detail the plan for the main task ahead."

Night time here in the anchorage, though still very warm, was comfortable, with an almost constant breeze. Certainly comforting to all on board were the Chosen, who were up all night guarding against any raids by the local thug populace who, recognizing a warship with a strong crew did remain clear of the vessel. The next morning Olion, his brother and a boat crew put in to the docks to buy fresh provisions, fruits and other ships stores needed by every vessel. While there Olion made contact with a smuggler and Captain of a smaller coastal type ship and arranged to hire the ship and its crew for the voyage to Tripos and back.

Just after dark that evening an odd looking craft, about sixty feet in length, with a high bow and low amidships, powered by one large triangular or "lateen" sail and sweeps came alongside and was made fast to the larger ship. The Captain and his first mate came on board for a conference in the main salon. His ship, he explained, was a 'Dhaula', a type well known in these waters to be very fast and seaworthy. Captain

Dellasso was from Sardos and had been sailing these waters for many years both as smuggler and trader. He was a large dark and swarthy man, looking very much the 'Sea Dog' in his knee boots, baggy silk trousers of dark red with a red vest over a yellow lace up shirt. His hair swept back in a ponytail, he was carrying a wide blade cutlass with two long dirks in his belt. The first mate was very dark brown, mustached man almost as tall as his captain. He had a shaved head. He dressed in knee boots, dark green baggy trousers and a dark green vest with no shirt. His name was Ibandi and he was from Noranda on down the southern coast. He was armed the same as his captain.

Over Brandy and pipes of tabac, in the main salon, they agreed that for the sum of one hundred gold coins, the Captain and his crew would transport Grayhawk, White Bear and six other of the Chosen, to Tripos, anchor at the river and wait one day and one night. Then sail back here. Captain Dellasso said

"Normally I would want to know what the purpose of the trip is, but seeing that there are at least eight Blademasters going, all from Norda, I believe this is something to do with a blood feud. I want no knowledge of this thing. I will take you where you want to go. I will wait as agreed. If you do not return by the appointed time, I will sail to Maltasa for a cargo, and deny all knowledge of you. Ibandi, what say you?" Ibandi raising one eyebrow said

"I agree. Whatever they came from the top of the world to do it is best we do not know. I do not envy whoever the go to visit."

"Well then" said Grayhawk "if we have a contract let us waste no time. We shove off immediately. We will return in not more than eight days." Brief goodbyes and handclasps were exchanged. Ten men went down the ladder, and on to the Dhaula, and without further ado the lines were cast off. The Mainsail was raised and they sailed into the night for the inside passage around the islands. The wind was brisk from the south in the main channel passage and the Dhaula proved to be very fast indeed. No other vessels were sighted, so they sailed straight north into the Mediaterre Sea for a day. They made a turn to the east for a day and finally turning back to the southwest so that they would be seen by the Triposean patrol boats and coast watchers to be approaching from the Northeast in the general direction of Troscai. They were spotted, by two separate patrol craft, but the Captain ran up a current trader vessel signal pennant and both times the Triposean vessels veered off to continue their normal patrols looking for pirates and smugglers.

Late in the afternoon of the fourth day they sailed into the river delta and several miles up the river, passing the city proper which looked very bright white in the late day sun. On the opposite side or west bank were the large merchant enclaves, each was a separate armed camp unto itself, although the docks and wharves are public. Anyone can dock a vessel, pay a fee to the local Calphan's customs police and then negotiate individually with the merchants to sell cargo, or to obtain a cargo bound for somewhere else. The Calphan or ruler of Tripos only cares that the taxes and fees are paid for goods coming and going. Aside from that, on the west side of the river, the merchants can do anything they want, and they do.

Three of the merchants are servants of the Dark Lord and they are the ones keeping the Dark Priest Rigorta supplied with people to sacrifice. Usually they are hapless sailors, both male and female, who are taken in the alleys in the wharf district, or drugged in some tavern, then clubbed when they leave. They are never even reported missing. Over fifty in number since Rigorta arrived in Tripos, plus several of the citizens of Tripos itself. Certain captives are taken for 'special' ceremonies these are usually fair to look upon, and from the best families. They are reported as missing, and searches are made, but to no avail.

The night patrol strength has been increased; the wealthy are hiring body guards. Not even the cutpurse and burglars guild has any idea who is responsible. Since, no bodies have ever been found. The current belief in the street is that a gang of slavers are responsible. Rigorta is so sympathetic that he has offered a purse of twenty gold pieces for information. The only one, who has come forth so far, wound up lunch for a demon.

Past the city and the Merchant Docks, the river to the south widens into a lake, half a mile wide and twice that in length. It is called the Refuge; many vessels in this part of the world call it home. It is far enough up the river from the sea that the great storms hardly bother it. Even now there are over a hundred vessels anchored up and down the length of the Refuge. Many of them are Dhaula so when they drop anchor in the middle of an area full of the same type ship, they just blend right in.

The first mate, Ibandi, and three crewmen take the ships boat which will hold six, maybe eight, and head for the city docks. There they will buy a long boat, one capable of holding twelve men. So they won't have to make two trips to get everyone ashore. Ibandi and his little crew return in under five hours rowing an almost new looking longboat complete with oars, a step down mast and sail, with the ships boat in tow.

"Hey Ibandi! Well done!" called out Captain Dellasso as they come along side. "Was this a lucky find or did you steal it from the quay?"

"Neither" he yells back. "I merely went directly to where they tie up the boats seized for non-payment of port fees, paid the fellow in charge a jug of Brandy from Troscai, a captured pirate's dirk, and two gold coins."

"Like I said" says Dellasso "you stole it!" and everyone is laughing.

The boat is well made; the type carried on large merchant ships, twenty four feet long, six sets of oars and it will seat twelve, plus a coxswain or steersman. It is very seaworthy and it also has a step-down mast with a good sail. It is very fast in the wind.

"We'll have to bring this one along with us when we are finished" says the Captain. "It will tow very nicely."

"My thoughts exactly" says Ibandi as he climbed aboard the ship. "And I know a couple of places where we can put it to good use."

The rest of the evening is spent as local custom calls for. Each new arrival anchors and rests their crew for the first night so that the following day can be a long, full one of trading, selling, buying and deal making. Only after all business has been concluded, and hopefully arrangements for a new cargo have been made, then are the crewmen allowed to draw against their pay and go ashore to sample the delights of the open and tolerant city of Tripos.

Dellasso does have some trading goods on board, so mid morning, the following day, the Captain and three crewmen take the ships boat and row to the customs house to pay the fee of four silver coins to cover both the moorage and trading. Then they row to the west side to the merchants docks.

Once there the Captain does some dickering with one of the more honest traders. After an hour or so he comes away with a fair profit for the goods he has on board, having brought some samples with him for show. Then he turns right around and haggles for a half cargo load of flour, oil, dried fruits and nuts, wine and brandies which he knows will fetch a good price back at the island, where such things are always in demand. The three crewmen row back to the ship. In order to bring the vessel back to the traders dock to unload and load. Captain Dellasso and the trader have coffee and brandy. Coffee being the preferred delicacy in this part of the world, very strong, cut with a brown sugar and then spiced with orange brandy. In an hour the ship is brought back to the dock to be off loaded and the new cargo loaded. While all of the 'extra' members on board spend a very hot and uncomfortable two hours in the forecastle and aft compartments, out of sight. By all outward appearances this is a normal trading vessel and crew. Once they are back at the mooring sight in the lake all the hatches are reopened and everyone then can move around a bit.

Chapter Twenty Five

Now that legitimate trader status has been established for Captain Dellasso and crew, their leaving with the tide on the morrow, before dawn, will of itself cause no alarm. The tide will begin to turn at about three hours after midnight and will last about one and a half hours before full low tide.

In the late afternoon Dellasso sent four of his crew ashore in the ships boat for an evening on the town, so as to arouse no suspicion. They will tie up at one of the guarded city docks. For a small fee the guards will see that the boat is not stolen. They tell them that they will return a couple of hours before midnight as do almost all of the other crews ashore for the evening. This night there are many crews and boats moving across the refuge and the river. The night will be moonless and dark, so each boat has a lantern and each vessel in the moorage has two stern lights showing.

At dusk, the First Mate, Ibandi returns in the longboat. He and two other crewmen have been on a scouting mission into the city, supposedly looking for the best pipe and tabac merchants. They found and purchased a hundred weight of fine smoking tabac and a good number of pipes, both clay and black briar. Ibandi is laughing as their small cargo is unloaded onto the larger vessel.

"I thought we might have some difficulty finding this 'Lord Rigorda' without arousing anyone's suspicion but the very first shop we went to sold me a sheepskin map of the city and spent ten minutes pointing out all of the tabac shops and how to get to them. Especially Jakov the pipe maker who's shop is just down the second largest street from 'Lord Rigorda's Villa', here he indicated on the map, he says" pointing and laughing.

"So we went to pay Jakov a visit, and passed right by the Villa. It covers half of a block, with small streets on both sides and an alley in the back. The walls are solid, as high as two men and at least two feet thick. The largest entry is in the alley, a double solid wood door, big enough for a wagon to pass through. The front door is wide enough and tall enough for a man on horseback to pass. Both of the side doors are small, servants and tradesman's entrances. There are no guard towers at the corners and no firing slits in the walls. A place built for a wealthy man's privacy no doubt. Only the main street is lit at night by a torch sconce at each end of the front wall, and one on the left of the front door. The side streets and the alley are dark. According to the locals that part of the city is pretty well locked up tight at night and the streets are deserted except for the city guard patrols every hour."

"I see by your report Mr. Ibandi, that you have been a soldier somewhere before" says Grayhawk.

"Several times, My Lord" replies Ibandi "here and there, and I have heard of you before."

"Excellent information" says Grayhawk, "with this map and your report, we have already solved most of our problems." White Bear, who normally says very little about anything then spoke.

"Indeed, Mr. Ibandi we are very grateful for your report." As he began speaking, Captain Dellasso and the rest of the crew gathered round as well as the other six of the Chosen.

"Know this then" he continued, "I am White Bear Sigurdson, I am a Band Leader and an Adept of Odranna's Chosen known as the Blademasters, My brothers and I, Including Brother Grayhawk come from the far north, we are on a mission to destroy evil wherever and however we can. In this city there lives a Dark Priest, a very powerful one, named Rigorda. He is a disciple of Lucifer, the Dark Lord. Rigorda was born a human but he is no longer one. The very core of his soul is corrupt. He is the embodiment of pure evil. He must be destroyed and that is what we are here to do. This must be accomplished before we may continue on with a more important mission. Should we fail here this night, I do not believe this will happen, but if it should, run from this place as fast as you can. Sail as far away as you can and deny you ever heard of any of us. For once the eight of us depart this vessel in the long boat; there can be no turning back for us. However, if at that time, you should choose to leave, no one would cast blame upon you or your name." He paused and looked around at the Captain, First Mate and Crew. The Captain spoke.

"We thank you for being honest with us. Certainly we have wondered just what your purpose here was. But we have contracted with you and taken your gold. We will finish the contract." Ibandi and the other crew members all nodded in agreement.

"So let it be done then" said White Bear. "We will depart a half hour before midnight, taking half an hour to row ashore. We should return before two and half hours after midnight, then half an hour back to the ship. Captain Dellasso has informed me that the tide turns at three hours after midnight. If the ship is ready for immediate departure, we should be able to ride the flow of the tide down river to the sea before dawn. As there will probably be a number of other vessels also departing then, with Odranna's help we will slip away unnoticed."

As the brothers of the Chosen and Grayhawk prepared themselves, it was decided that Mr. Ibandi and one other crewman named Kalih would accompany them on the longboat to stand guard while the others went ashore.

"I should have thought of that" said Grayhawk, "very bad indeed if we were to return from this nights work to find we had no boat." They boarded the longboat very quietly and pulled away from the ship showing no lights. The oarlocks were muffled with pieces of wet sheepskin. Everyone on board was wrapped in dark cloaks and no one spoke. The trip to shore took only twenty minutes. Leaving the boat at a small private dock on the lakeshore, Grayhawk, White Bear and the six brothers of the Chosen split into four groups of two, with each taking a different route, made their way northward in to the city proper. There were still people moving about the streets at this hour, usually in pairs or small groups. All in the city went armed, so Grayhawk and the others did not look out of place.

The night was beginning to cool and Grayhawk was glad of his fighting leathers and cape. They moved silently and as swiftly as they could, remaining in the shadows as much as possible, watching out for the city guard patrols. They never saw any. It was not quite half a mile to the alley south of Rigorda's Villa that they had picked as a meeting point. Four were already there when they arrived, and the remaining two showed about five minutes later. The alley where they have gathered is extremely dark, only their acute night vision allows them to function in places where most people could not. White Bear instructed the other brothers to scout the two side streets, and the alley around the Villa for an egress point, and to listen for guards or movement from the within. All of the party is armed with swords, all carry grappling hooks covered with leather to lessen the noise, and attached to twenty five foot lengths of braided leather rope which are pitch coated. Four of the brothers have recurve bows, made from Auroch horn and wood, and a quiver of thirty inch heavy hunting arrows with a three inch hammered steel, broadleaf point. These arrows will penetrate armor at fifty yards and will take down a man or an animal at two hundred yards.

Grayhawk and White Bear watched the front of the Villa from within the shadows of a side street. There is no street traffic. Nothing is moving except the sputtering shadows from the torches at both ends of the front Villa wall. The torch at the front gate in the middle burns clear and bright with no smoke, no doubt it is magically enhanced. Grayhawk and White Bear both sense the aura of evil that exudes from the Villa like a pulsating power source. Both men have Adept rings in leather pouches inside their clothing. If either of them were brought out into the open air, the Dark Priest would know instantly that they were close by. They could sense that Rigorda was wearing his dark powers ring and that he was in the Villa somewhere in a lower chamber. As of yet he was still unaware of their presence. That was about to change. Grayhawk smiled to himself. This was an ancient blood feud between the Norda and the sons of darkness, going back to the beginning of the time of man.

The Norda and all of the other northern races of man were almost driven to extinction many eons ago, during a time called the age of science. Because Lucifer, during one of his many attempts to conquer, brought about a cataclysmic period of war and natural disaster so severe that it changed the face of the planet, totally destroying many civilizations and all their combined knowledge.

The others returned from scouting the walls. The side streets were both dark and dead silent. There was no noise from within the walls, no movement. The alleyway entrance behind the Villa had the same sort of bright torch mounted beside the gate as the one in the front. Low voices and some movement could be heard at the rear gate and the smell of a charcoal fire.

"The two side walls would seem our best approach" said White Bear. "We should separate in two teams of four, I should think. Grayhawk, you and three others take the East wall, and I and the other three will take the west. Two men armed with bows, and two armed with swords. Once over the walls, if it is not obviously a slave or a prisoner, then it dies! Be not misled by the fact that it bears no arms. This is a Dark Priests enclave. All who live within are evil. The Villa itself is the center of the compound. Once on the ground, Grayhawk you and your group head for the front entrance, which is probably guarded. Whilst I, with the others will head for the rear, at this hour, most of the staff and guards are probably gathered there. This all needs to be done swift, silent and deadly, so that Grayhawk can get as close as possible to Rigorda, before we are discovered. Even without casting I can sense Rigorda is in a lower chamber performing some dark ritual." "Aye, I sense it too" said Grayhawk. "So let us move now, while they are otherwise occupied."

While White Bear's team had only to cross the main street in front of the compound to be in place at the west wall, Grayhawk and his team had to go through the alley and jog a block over to the east. Then they had to come up to the main street and cross it to be at the eastern wall. They had agreed upon a count of three hundred to allow both groups to launch their attacks at the same time. All were in place by the stated time.

One of the brothers loosed his coil of rope and hook. He twirled the hook twice with his right hand and let fly. The hook went over the top of the wall and landed with a soft thud. A couple of sharp pulls on the rope to insure it was secure. He then took the rope in both hands, placed one foot on the wall and walked up the wall, in a well practiced manner. When he reached the top and stood, he then stuck out his right hand and another hook was thrown to him. He deftly caught it, stepped a couple of paces to his right, stooped down and secured the hook on the inside lip of the wall. Now the other two brothers with bows slung on their backs grabbed the ropes and went up the wall and disappeared over the top.

Grayhawk now took hold of the left rope and likewise went up the wall. As he pulled himself onto the top he heard the dull twang of a bow followed by an oomph sound, and then the dull thud of something falling to the ground. Drawing his great sword and crouching, he could not see the others, but there was a dark form on the ground about ten meters towards the Villa itself. It was a square three story house with a half round balcony at the third level on this side. Directly below him was a shed roof slanting down away from the wall at a slight angle, going out about fifteen feet. The roof of the shed was about three feet down from the top of the wall. Having learned in his youth the folly of jumping down onto the middle of a shed roof, he stepped down the wall to his right until he came to the edge of the shed. He lowered himself down onto the roof and then dropped to the ground beside the shed, where the other three were waiting for him. Taking a knee, sword in hand, the four were spread out across the space between two sheds. They were looking inward towards the east end of the house, across about fifty feet of gravel path and flower beds. The smell of the flowers and dirt was very strong. The only thing out of place was the body of a large dark man lying on his back with an arrow sticking out of the center of his chest. 'Roving sentry' thought Grayhawk to himself. Then as if on cue the four Blademasters rose and trotted across the open to the darkness at the wall of the house. No entry door on this end, and so far thanks to the All Father, no guard dogs or peacocks to give the alarm. Rigorda must be very confident of his guards.

There are four large windows on the ground floor each about six feet up, evenly spaced across the end of the building. No doubt all spell-warded against intruders, and dark as doom. It was the same on the second floor. There was light coming from a third floor balcony, small lanterns on either side of the doors which, could be seen as open. Crouching low and peeking around the corner to the front of the Villa, Grayhawk could see two more large dark skinned guards in black pantaloons bloused into calf high boots with gold sashes and black vests. Both were holding the large curved sword which is favored in this part of the world. They were standing in the middle of a half circle area of paving stones in front of the main entrance. They were covered in a pool of yellow light coming from the two large wall lanterns, one on either side of the front door, which was in a recess and could not be seen from this angle. The whole courtyard was deathly quiet, not even the two guard's conversation could be heard. 'More warding' thought Grayhawk. Though out from the wall, the two guards were standing side by side facing toward the front gate. It would be impossible to get both at once with arrows from this angle.

Grayhawk spoke softly to the others "I will move out from the house to the gravel path and walk around the corner towards the guards. They will hear me and see movement. Hopefully they will turn enough for you to get a good shot." The two archers nodded in agreement and moved to the corner of the house, the third brother just behind them. Grayhawk stepped straight out from the end of the building to the gravel path, then onto the path, and walked with deliberate heavy steps as though he were the roving sentry returning. He turned on the path towards the center front. He was hoping that at the distance of fifty feet or so, in the dark the others would not immediately see the ruse, and it worked. Both turned at the sound of footsteps on gravel as the look of alarm appeared on their faces and they began to bring up their swords. Both suddenly sprouted arrows in the center of their chests and fell to the ground backwards. The noise of their falling was muted by the warding.

As no other alarms sounded, apparently it was the gates and entrances to the house were where the wards were grounded, not the grounds themselves. 'No doubt' thought Grayhawk "they will trigger when we open a door or a window." As well, he noted, upon approaching the two now dead guards, they are human, so probably no mind link to their overlords, good, or, there exists also the possibility of a trap, but so far nothing to indicate that. Now they were directly under the two lamps, at the portico or front entrance to the Villa, inside the high archway at about six feet were two large, heavy iron bound doors, each about eight foot tall. The right one appeared to be open a few inches.

It was almost too inviting. Grayhawk looked at the others and shrugged his shoulders. "Sense anything?" he asked. Each of the others shook their head, no. "Oh well" exclaimed Grayhawk as he grabbed the long vertical, ornate door handle and pulled. The door swung outward with only slight sound of the metal hinges. Bringing his sword to the ready he stepped through the door into the lantern lit central hallway or foyer, a round room with a round table in the center. There was a large vase of flowers on the table, but the smell of death and decay was strong. At that instant a gong, or deep note bell began to sound to the rear of the house.

"I believe White Bear has opened the ball!' said Grayhawk as double doors to the left of the room banged open, and at least a dozen armed men poured into the room. Yelling in a language he did not understand but from their swords and knives their meaning was clear enough. The first one took an arrow through his mouth and into the forehead of the shorter man behind him. The two went down in a heap, slowing the rush behind them. Another took an arrow center chest and went down as well. The surging group had split left and right to come around their dying companions, yelling and screaming even louder now. Grayhawk was on the right, and drawing his dirk with his left hand. He moved around the table in the center to engage those who broke that way to attack. The first died with a sword thrust through his throat and a look of total surprise. While pulling back on his sword Grayhawk parried a swipe from a curved sword on his left with his dirk, and felt the metal to metal impact all the way up his arm. Ramming the man with his shoulder and knocking him backwards onto the table, reversing his grip on the dirk to a stabbing hold. As the fellow rolled up onto the table he tried for a two legged kick. Grayhawk stabbed to his left and down driving a good six inches of the blade into the inner right thigh of the man with a resulting shriek.

The noise level in the room, steel on steel, men hollering and cries of pain, furniture being knocked over and broken, men scuffling and grunting, was now quite loud. The four Blademasters not saying a word, they all were engaging the enemy with deadly efficiency. Now a large dark man with absolute hate and rage on his face came from Grayhawk's right. His curved sword already swinging from overhead in a downward, head splitting stroke, bringing his sword are up Grayhawk caught the fellows blade just in front of the pommel of his own sword. The blow was strong enough it still managed to come down and cut through the fabric of Grayhawk's cloak and cut him on the upper shoulder a bit. Sensing victory the big fellow grabbed his sword with both hands and brought it back up overhead, grinning with his eyes glaring hatred. Throwing his right arm again to block the stroke, Grayhawk reversed the dirk in his hand again, spinning to hi right, whipping his left arm around, as his right went up to block the stroke. He drove the horizontal blade of the dirk a full twelve inches under the man's arm and through his right lung into the heart. The shock registered immediately on the man's face. With his sword still held overhead he began to fall to his left.

Grayhawk jerked his dirk free, and spun back to his left to engage the next opponent, but there were none there. All the guards were down, dead or dying and the silence returned to the room, more or less. Fighting could be heard coming from the rear of the Villa. But Grayhawk had another task to perform. Find and kill Rigorda and there was not time to waste. The two archers sheathed their swords and retrieved their bows from where they had dropped them at the beginning of the fight in the round room. Moving to the rear of the room they opened the door to find themselves in an east-west hallway of polished wood floors and paneling with a number of side tables and chairs in both directions. There were four small lanterns giving off soft yellow light, two on either end of the hall with at least six doorways in each direction." Where to now?" asked one of the Brothers.

"We must find the way into the cellar. That is where he will be. Probably at this moment, summoning demons to help him. We must find him quickly," said Grayhawk. "Split up and check these doors." They checked them all, and each opened into a room, except the one directly across from where they entered the hall. It opened into a short hallway going towards the rear of the house. Now the house was quiet, no fighting could be heard. Moving into the short hall, Grayhawk was about to open a door when he felt the almost solid shielding ward, like an invisible force across the door.

Standing in front of the door, taking a moment to center his focus, he summoned all of his casting power and focused it upon the door. He simply said "Break!" while casting out with all his might. The shield ward shattered like heavy glass breaking on stone and was gone.

Grayhawk pushed down on the handle and with sword at the ready eased the door open. The foul charnel house smell was intense, as the door opened. He could see down a stone staircase, there were torches in sconces, on either side at the bottom. The air now coming up the stairs was smoky, hot and foul smelling.

Descending slowly, expecting to be at attacked at any moment. This level was used as a storage room it was open with pillars in rows. There were boxes, barrels and crates, old furniture, the normal clutter of a Villa that has been around for a very long time. Down a cleared aisle running toward the east there were more torches, two midway, and two more at the end, about fifty feet or so. Beyond that there was a dark opening in the wall. Moving cautiously through this area to the end he found another stone staircase going down further. This one was longer, going deeper and narrower than the first, it was also lit by two torches at the bottom. The stench was even stronger now, coming from below.

Again descending slowly, expecting immanent attack, the air becoming warmer and then wet, damp almost steamy. The walls and steps were wet. At the bottom the water was over and inch deep. The passageway at the bottom still opened toward the east, wide enough for two men, with an arched roof. The air was permeated with an overwhelming putrid smell, beyond rotting flesh, Evil and death. About fifteen paces or so down the passage was a bronze colored door. A single lantern hung from the ceiling in front of it, giving off a dull red light which flickered and gave the door the appearance of being covered in wet blood.

Neither Grayhawk nor his companions were making a sound. Now they moved down the passage hugging against either side. As they approached to within a few feet of the door the faint sound of screaming could be heard rising and falling from within. Some poor soul was being tormented. Grayhawk stepped to the door and grasped the sliding bolt handle, while the two archers brought their bows up to the ready, arrows nocked Grayhawk slid the bold back and pushed in on the door, which opened without a sound. The chamber within was even hotter and now came the smell of blood, urine and feces all mixed with fear, stale body odors, the strong smell of sulphur and acid, almost enough to stop a man's breathing. The scene was bathed in orange-yellow light with flashes of intense blue. The room was large, forty feet square, or so, with a high ceiling hidden by a bank of gray to black smoke. There were sputtering torches in holders on the side walls, a large pit in the center of the floor with blue and purple flames coming from it. Suspended over it was a naked, bloodied, dark haired female human with burn marks and cuts on her torso and legs, her blood dripped down into the flames. Writhing and screaming her wrists pierced by a hook, she was hanging by a chain from the ceiling, with her head back.

In front of the girl was a figure in red and black robes with his back to the door holding a glowing, hot tipped iron in his right hand and a long thin blade knife in the left one. On his left side stood a waist high tri-legged brazier full of glowing coals with a number of torture instruments stuck down into the coals. Four other robed figures stood, two on either side of the pit, watching and chanting in a deep, resonating tone, almost like growling. So totally entranced were they, that they did not notice that Grayhawk and the others had entered the room. The blue and purple flames took on a red tint and began to become brighter. Rigorda touched the iron to the girl's thigh, evoking a shriek of pain. A round black portal began to open in the flames. Rigorda flicked the knife with his left hand, slicing the girl on her side. Another shriek and more blood ran down over hip and thigh then dripped off into the flames.

The two bowmen, one on either side of Grayhawk, loosed their arrows at the same time. Both of the closest hooded figures on either side of the pit sprouted arrows from the sides of their heads then fell sideways into the figure next to them. The chanting suddenly stopped, Rigorda froze, both hands in the air. The flames from the pit turned so dark red they were almost black. The girl was shrieking hysterically and violently convulsing. From the pit there came a howl of rage, so loud it hurt the ears. Rigorda spun to his left, throwing the hot iron like a knife. It burned the bottom of Grayhawk's left ear as it went by.

"Kill them!!" Rigorda was screaming, his eyes bulging and his face dark in a grinning rage; all of his teeth were exposed. The bows twanged again and two more robed acolytes went down, one screaming. From behind the pit area came at least a dozen more who had been hidden by the darkness and their black cloaks. Around either side they came howling in blood fury. Rigorda now drew a black, short sword from within his robes. Still holding the long blade knife in his left hand, his face contorted.

"Youuu!" he screamed in a gurgling growl and launching himself straight at Grayhawk. "Now you are mine!!"

"I think not!" answered Grayhawk as he parried both the sword and knife, with his own sword and dirk. The loud ringing of steel on steel almost drowned out by the fighting and yelling going on around them. The attack carried Rigorda past Grayhawk. Rigorda's momentum propelled him on into the now close fighting mass of Odranna's Chosen and the evil acolytes. Grayhawk ran to the right side of the pit. The portal was still partially opened under the girl and a long thick, black shiny bifurcated tongue was licking the blood on the girl's legs and thighs. The girl was now either unconscious or dead, just hanging limp with her head back. There is only one slim chance for the girl Grayhawk thought. The chain ran through a steel hoop affixed to the ceiling, the other end hooked to a ring on the floor in back of the pit. Running around and grabbing the chain loose, he backed up a couple of steps. He let loose of the chain and as the girl's body began to fall he ran to the edge of the pit and leaped, grabbing the girl with his left arm, as his right slashed downward. His sword severed the beast's tongue. Landing heavily and rolling on the front side of the pit, the girl landed in a still heap. He had knocked over the brazier, sending hot coals skidding across the floor under the feet of the fighters.

As he was getting to his feet, he saw Rigorda again coming at him. While at the same time behind him, howling in pain and rage, something big was trying to come through the now collapsing portal to the underworld. Rigorda now growling like a beast himself, was on him, sword and knife trying to slash and stab, slash and parry, metal ringing on metal. Then Rigorda over extended his sword arm. Grayhawk's sword flashed, severing the wrist. Rigorda shrieked in pain as his sword and hand rolled into the pit. Still Rigorda came on, his eyes glazed over and that evil rictus grin. Grayhawk ducked under a swipe of the long knife, driving his dirk deep into Rigorda's rib cage. Jerking the blade free and spinning behind him. Grayhawk then stepped back and kicked Rigorda in the small of his back, propelling him over the edge of the pit and straight into the huge bloody, tooth filled maw of some ugly creature from Hell. Rigorda was emitting a high pitched squeal when the jaws closed and the creature fell back through the portal, which then winked out of existence.

The pit was an empty square hole in the floor, about ten feet deep, black and burnt, but no fire or heat remained. All of the acolytes were down, some sixteen total, all human, all Dark Priests in training. With Rigorda now gone, a serious blow had been dealt to the Dark Lords plans, at least in this one area. The girl had also died, but at least she was not taken to the underworld in the belly of a beast. Rigorda's hand and sword were recovered from the pit; it more resembled a claw than a hand.

White Bear and his group came into the chamber. All told they had killed over thirty acolytes and other servants. White Bear ordered that the pit should be half filled with wood, boxes, crates, smashed furniture, broken up wooden doors and anything else they could burn. Then two kegs of oil for lamps, and two kegs of brandy found in the first cellar, were poured in. All the dead bodies were brought down and dumped on top, except for the girl and Rigorda's hand. Then, carpets, rugs and tapestries were rolled, tied and laid end to end from the pit, through the cellar, up the stairs and almost to the front door. These were then heavily soaked with lamp oil mixed with olive oil and brandy. Several small kegs of oil were opened and turned over in the main hall of the house. The inside of the whole Villa was mainly wood and paneling, it was going to be a grand fire. The body of the dead girl was laid out on the front lawn on blue velvet drapes torn from the Villa. Rigorda's hand, still gripping the black sword was also left behind.

All of the raiding party except Grayhawk then exited by the front gate. He stood at the open front door of the Villa for the span of ten full minutes, both to allow the others a good start for the boat, and to contemplate what had happened here. At least no other innocents would die in this place. Smiling at that thought, he tossed the small lantern he was holding into the foyer of the villa. As he stepped out, closing the heavy door behind him, flickering flame shadows were already dancing on the front windows.

Moving swiftly over the front path, and out the front gate of the estate, he closed it behind him and hearing the lock fall into place. He broke into a trot heading out of town, down to the lake shore. Within ten minutes he arrived at the longboat where the others were waiting. As he pushed the boat out from the shore and scrambled aboard, he noted that no fire could yet be seen from the town. Hoping that nothing had happened to put the fire out, he sat looking back as the others rowed out toward the middle of the lake and the ship. All the others were intently watching also. A few minutes later as they pulled a long side of the ship, the sky over the town began to show a bright, pale yellow. Soon, as the anchor was brought up, and the bow came around with the current, flames could be seen, yellow and blue with other colors in them.

As they passed by the city docks, small groups of people could be seen, here and there watching the fire grow. By the time they were half a mile past the city, the flames looked to be a hundred feet tall, going straight up into the air and extremely bright. Everyone was up on deck, though no one spoke, pipes were lit and brandy flasks were passed around, and although it was near dawn, the stars did seem to be especially bright in the sky. By mid morning they were clear of the river mouth and sailing due north at a good speed, through dark blue waters. They continued until nightfall, having sighted no other vessels during the day, now sure of no pursuit, they turned back to the southwest, toward the Moroc Isles.

Their course this time took them to the west of the Moroc Island's northern tip. Then they turned south. Sailing against the wind and having to tack the ship back and forth cost a full day in time. They sighted only one other sail. It was close inshore to the island, sailing north, with the wind. In three days they were entering the sound at the north end of the big Island. Timing their arrival for after full dark in the bay, at two hours after midnight, Grayhawk and the Chosen who accompanied him climbed back aboard the main ship. Taking leave of, and bidding farewell to, Captain Dellasso, Mr. Ibandi and their crew.

The tale of the raid was well recounted in true Nordic Saga style to all on board, who assembled mid ship. Since not one soul was lost amongst the raiders, and all wounds were minor, it was a well received celebration complete with acted out fight scenes and descriptions of the fire as seen from afar.

The tide turned before dawn and the black ship sailed out of the bay, turned westward without sound or commotion. Only Dellasso and Ibandi, standing on the aft deck of their ship noted their departure. "Any idea where they are headed?" asked Dellasso. "None what so ever!" answered Ibandi. "But where ever it is, that bunch goes either to start a war, or perhaps to finish one!" "Count on it Mr. Ibandi, count on it." replied Captain Dellasso, Grinning broadly while shaking his head.

Chapter Twenty Six

Due west they sailed until well out of sight of the islands, then turning their course once more to the south. On what was perhaps a mission of no return for any on board. All of whom understood that by now the Dark Lord knew what had befallen his minions in the city of Tripos. Though none on board knew firsthand just how great Lucifer's rage was, but woe unto those of his creatures unfortunate enough to be within his grasp. Many died. Horribly indeed!

The earth shook and volcano's erupted in the land of Stygius. Three days later the two black Dragons attacked Tripos in the middle of the night. Half of the city was destroyed along with at least a dozen ships on the lake. Not having seen or experienced true Dragon fear, or Dragon fire in human memory (the beasts were widely thought to be only a dark legend). The effect on the people of Tripos was profound. As ships went out from the port, the tales were carried far and wide. Dragons have returned to the earth! Have the end times arrived? Terror and confusion were rampant. Will the Dark Lord surface and rule the earth? Oblivious to any of this, the Company, in their swift black ship, sailed south with a fair wind and calm seas. Good progress was logged each day in the ships book. Four full days on this course took them past the lands of Chadia, Noranda and Suranda where they turned due east and headed towards the Bay of Libiasan and the delta of the Mamba River.

Even before entering the delta, the smell of jungle permeated the air. The water turned from Azure blue to mud brown and the ship slowed as it began to sail against the river current. Sailing is difficult because the winds swirl and change direction often. Look outs must be posted to watch for rip tide effects over the sand bars. They passed the rotting hulks of several ships that had run hopelessly aground and had to be abandoned. The last few miles up the delta are a little easier. The flow of the channel from the river is wide and much easier to see and navigate. On the high ground north of the river sits the city of Nigossa. It is a trading port for goods coming down river, such as rose wood, ebony wood, diamonds and other jewels, animal pelts, some gold and silver, jungle bird feathers and all things exotic including many herbs and poisons.

Taken back upriver are more mundane things such as tabac, brandy, flour, cooking oil, knives and weapons of all sorts. Surprisingly A half dozen or more ships a month call on Nigossa in the land of Libias, some coming from as far away as Gaula or Persus. Whatever cargo they bring, it will be welcome and will fetch a good price, even slaves. Who will disappear into the interior, never to be seen alive again.

Here, below the city, the river is over half a mile wide. Arriving after dark, they are towed, against the current, by a hired tow-galley of forty oars, to a cove on the south shore. They are now about half a mile above the city, where they anchor, and are immediately surrounded by small merchant boats known as "Bum-boats." Taking care to observe the local amenities and customs, the crew does some lively bartering for fresh fruit, fish, wine and oil, tabac and other items any normal crew would. This is to avoid suspicion. Within half an hour the boats have all wandered off and now the ship will not be a mystery to the locals.

Stretching to the south from Nigossa are grassy plains, then the Sulumbasa mountain range, and finally the coast. To the east, about three days travel begins the jungle proper. It starts as scrub on the plain and after another days travel becoming thick, hot, stinking triple canopy jungle. This is home to huge leopards, panthers, and snakes that either kill a man with their bite or crush him inside their coils and then swallow him whole, not to mention spiders, centipedes, scorpions, leeches and mosquitoes, of all sizes. All in all, it is not a very nice place.

After the second day, no one on the river was paying attention to the sleek black ship anymore, even though, the crew were obviously pirates. At midnight the third night the 'Raiding Company' as they had come to refer to themselves, slipped ashore on a dark, moonless riverbank and made their way south through the grasslands on an ancient hard packed trail. The 'Company' consisted of Grayhawk as leader, Lord Allanfair as second, Sir Owen and twenty Temple Knights, Prince Drinach and twenty five Dwarf warriors, ten Elf warriors, two Elf Ladies, Clan Chief White Bear and twenty of Odranna's Chosen, Lady Ailereon, Eighty three souls in all. All dedicated to handing a major defeat to the Dark Lord's plans.

Captain Olion, his wife and crew of twenty, will take the ship, with a full cargo from Nigossa, sail back north and then east into the Mediaterre Sea, calling at a number of port cities and trading as a legitimate cargo carrier, for a period of several months to a year. Somewhere along the way Grayhawk will contact them, to bring the ship into Ptolymius in Aegia and pick up the 'Company' or the survivors and then complete the journey back to the King's City in Keltan. Or, in the worst case scenario, if no contact is made, within one and one half years time. Olion and company are to carry on with life, because there will have been, no survivors. It was a somber parting from the ship as they all had become great friends. All understood the seriousness and gravity of the mission, and that the chance of their success was an unknown factor.

After traveling south through the night, at dawn they turned east and traveled through the tall grass at a good pace until mid-morning. Here they came upon a common feature in the grasslands, a depression or natural bowl feature with a spring, some scrub and stumpy trees, cattails, and quite a few birds. Here they rested until late afternoon. When the shadows began to lengthen, they stirred themselves, packed up their kit and moved off again to the east through the tall grass. What seemed to be an endless ocean of grass ranging from knee high to well over the heads of the tallest Northman of the group. There were actually, four or five kinds of grasses, one that was a kind of wheat, and another, the tallest, which had serrated edges and would actually cut a person's skin. Two days of this and they reached the area where it changes from grasslands to scrub and trees. This same day, Captain

Olion and crew sailed the black ship out of the Mamba river estuary and into Libiasan Bay with a full cargo of exotic woods, spices, chests of exotic bird feathers, even furniture and clothing.

The 'Company' halted for the day, earlier than usual because the growth had begun to thicken. They all began to feel an air of evil, a sense of the darkness about the place, not something one could clearly identify. Though a number of local horses had been procured for a 'trading' venture, they could not be taken into the jungle, but they had transported the heavy pack boards, supplies and weapons for the group.

In the morning the horses were turned loose and seemed even more than eager to head back to the west. Half the day was spent putting together the supply packs, having to modify them to fit the stature of the carrier. Everyone except Lady Eilorian and four of her Elf warriors was fitted with a heavy pack. Lady Eilorian would be head scout. Her Elves served as rangers in their home land, and all were deadly with bows, swords and knives. They carried enough supplies for eight weeks of steady travel, hopefully supplemented by hunting along the way, and foraging for anything possible.

So after a short mid-day break, they all hefted up their packs. Then, with Lady Ailorian and her ranger-elves leading the way, the Company moved out, covering several more miles within a couple of hours. First the brush became really thick, then it became wet, and then it got hot. By late afternoon they had covered about five miles and were in triple canopy jungle. The ground either squished or crunched. It seemed as though everything had thorns. Sometimes they took turns having to hack their way through vine entangled undergrowth as tall as a man. Every hundred paces there was a stream or small river to cross, or so it seemed. The streams were clear, cold and fast running, the water from them was drinkable. The rivers were slow moving brown or green water which stank like rotting vegetation. At one crossing they saw a huge snake moving down the river, with a head as large as a hunting hound and at least twenty feet long.

They saw quite a number of other snakes, but they had all moved away from the trail as fast as they could. At one place where there were plantain fruit trees they saw a bright green spider as big as a serving platter, attack and kill a bright red and yellow bird of the same size.

Somber faced indeed, were all of these folks from the northlands. Just before dark, about ten miles into this mess, they came to a clear stream that split in two with a gray stone outcropping in the middle, almost flat on top. The height of it was about eight feet above the underbrush but still under two canopies of cover, a good place to camp, as they found out when they reached the top. They found that it had been used before, but not in some time, judging from the remains of old fires.

They also found out that darkness in the jungle happens quickly, one minute there is light, and the next there is not!

Soon the camp was set up, fires were burning in previously dug fire pits, and a meal was prepared. Everyone used the stream to clean themselves and their gear. All were very tired but glad to be on the final trek. Guards were posted and the others relaxed, smoked pipes and talked. All but the guards were asleep at an early hour, lying about in the open; packs were being used for pillows. By two hours past midnight all had come to know just how cold the jungle at night can be. Big and small alike were digging in their gear for something warm to cover with. None had ever experienced a swing in temperature of that many degrees before.

Though still quite cool at daylight the next morning, by an hour later the onset of the day's heat could begin to be felt. At midmorning it rained for half an hour. "Ah, relief" thought everyone. Half an hour after the rain stopped it had gotten even hotter. Then everyone realized it was not mist they were making their way through, it was steam. There was absolutely no breeze or movement of air. It was as dark as dusk. The jungle was absolutely awash in sound, many species of birds, even howling monkeys, insects that click, buzz and whiz. Everyone's clothing was soaked with sweat. Their eyes were gritty, red, swollen and burning. Breathing was difficult, most were raspy or coughing.

Everyone was doubly on edge because often there would be snorting, coughing or roars from what they believed to be big cats of the jungle, though thus far none had been seen.

The evening of the third day, after crossing brown water rivers at least four times, or maybe the same river looping back and forth, they found out about leeches. It seemed that everyone had a few, some had many, and some were in very private places, and had to be removed with a heated knife blade. By the end of the fourth day everything metal had began to rust, silver jewelry turned black and all leather had some green verdigris growing on it. An early halt was called just to deal with all of this.

There were no existing maps of this area, and no one in the party knew exactly where they were heading or any idea of just how far the Dark Lords Mountains were. So they just continued to struggle through the dense jungle, heading north east as much as possible. By the end of the tenth day, all figured they had covered about one hundred twenty miles. The problem was that no one knew if they had already traveled a fourth, or a tenth of the total. They were all becoming acclimated to the jungle, learning how to survive and travel through it.

One very large, black panther, weighing about two hundred pounds lost its life by mistaking a dwarf warrior for its supper. They had eaten the panther meat and the Dwarf fellow had a new black cape. An irritable Dwarf with a battle axe is not likely to be anything's supper!

On the twelfth day they came out of the jungle on to a plateau covered with palmetto scrub and grass. It was a good twenty miles across with a number of small lakes on it and some small palm and fruit trees growing around them. The Elf scouts killed a huge boar hog of about six hundred pounds, so the 'Company' took a break for two days to eat, relax and dry everything out, clean all of the weapons and mend one's own gear. Then it was across the plateau and back down into the jungle again. The only other living thing, they have seen have been animals. They have seen evidence of old camps on the plateau, sometimes they saw strange marks on a tree or rock. Not even a footprint.

Though the jungle itself is oppressive and has a vague feeling of evil it did not feel as though they were being watched, very strange considering the territory they were headed into. As for the 'Company' itself they had now been together long enough, both at sea and trekking through the jungle, that everyone was well acquainted and lifelong friendships had been formed.

After twenty one days everyone in the 'Company' was becoming a truly hardened 'trekker'. They began staying up a little later in the evening. Sword and axe practice began again. At twenty five days the bows came out and there was archery practice before dark, and even into the twilight it began in earnest. All of the elves and Odranna's Chosen had bows. Each archer had a bundle of seventy five arrows, which meant that counting Grayhawk, there were thirty three archers and between them they possessed over two thousand four hundred war arrows, and a few hunting and practice arrows, not to mention the three bundles of 'special' arrows to be used against the Dragons.

Their hunting and foraging skills improved dramatically and they began to eat more and better. So that by the time they had been in the bush for a full thirty days they had covered over four hundred miles, all on foot, through some of the toughest terrain on the planet.

That day they came to a large river, because of their heavy packs and gear, they had to construct four long rafts. They crossed the river at first light the next morning without incident. Once across they discovered they had entered a new territory. Even the foliage was darker in color. Flowers were larger brightly colored, often shiny with loud perfume smells, almost overpowering. Some of them were. Now they encountered more snakes, larger ones, and lizards, spiders great and small. They even had to cross and army of ants, each over an inch long, the trail of them was over three feet wide and had to be carefully leapt across. There were literally millions of them. Grayhawk was convinced that the ant scouts had followed the party for almost a mile.

By midmorning on the thirty fifth day, they had entered into a truly dark and evil realm. The ground was squishy black ooze that stank like death. All the cover was thicker. No patches of sky shone through. They moved in perpetual gloom. The air was thick with smells and steamy wet. Everything was larger, trees, brush, vines, flowers, insects, snakes, scorpions, and spiders. Everyone moved now with drawn sword or axe. Many close calls were had before a near disaster. A huge snake, some forty feet long, reared up out of a thick place and struck downward at a Dwarf. It was lightning fast, but the Dwarf was wearing a horned helmet. There was a loud 'clang' as the beast struck. The Dwarf went down and the other Dwarves attacked with axes and made quick work of the snake. The fellow who was attached was knocked unconscious for a bit and suffered from fang wounds on both shoulders. Fortunately the snake was not poisonous.

That evening the party dined on roast white snake meat. All agreed that it had excellent flavor and texture. Master Red Tuck, the fellow who had been attacked stated that in the future someone else would have to be the bait, as he had had his turn. A good laugh, but all were aware that disaster and or death could come at any time to any member of the 'Company'.

Grayhawk told them he believed, that when they had crossed the river, they had crossed into Stygius, the land of the Dark Lord. Land of the Legends of Evil, called the Blighted Land, amongst other things. Some people actually believe the Dark Lord is only a legend. There are still others who hold religious ceremonies in his name with a lot of role playing, costumes and alcohol. They have no idea of what they mock, nor do they realize what will happen to them if Lucifer ever discovers their debauchery in his name.

That evening for the first time since Keltan, Grayhawk could feel growing warmth from his Adept's Ring which he kept concealed in a secret pocket in his tunic. After informing Allanfair and White Bear, and with drawn swords, he moved off in to the jungle alone. Within only a couple hundred feet he was out of sight and sound from the camp. Finding a small clearing he put on his ring and sat on a fallen tree in the faint blue glow from the ring.

There then appeared from nowhere a white spot of light hanging in the air which grew into a ten foot tall oval of light, radiating gold, light blue and pure white. Grayhawk was expecting Lord Michael of the All Father's Host. The one who stepped through was a different being entirely, he had the same height and build, but with dark auburn hair, curly, shoulder length, with hazel eyes. The robe was forest green, with a wide brown belt, gold buckle, brown boots that looked like polished wood. In his left hand he held a long throwing spear or javelin.

"Greetings, Lord Grayhawk. I am Hubertus. I come from the presence of the All Father to bring you his Blessing and to inform you that by Rule, from here forward to either success or failure in that which you attempt on this journey. We may neither interfere nor assist in any way. Though verily, we would fair do so, if allowed. What you and your companions do is of the utmost importance. In a few days you will come out of this jungle and into the blighted lands. You are in danger from Lucifer's forces as soon as the jungle begins to thin. So be on your guard from here forward. When you come out into the open, continue to travel to your northeast. When you can see the black mountains, head for the center, on the west side. Once there, the largest volcano in the center is where you will find what you seek. There are a number of ways into the complex. The closer you come to the eggs, the brighter your ring will glow. If you succeed, and do manage to get out; then head north to the Lake of the Gods. I bid thee farewell, Lord Grayhawk, I must leave you now. I am needed elsewhere." Bowing slightly he faced about, stepped back into the oval and disappeared.

Grayhawk sat meditating for a while, in the soft blue glow coming from his ring. He understood fully the magnitude and seriousness of the task before them, and the very real possibility of none of them surviving it.

On the thirty eighth day of travel the jungle began to thin out somewhat. The next afternoon they came upon a cool clear pond of a good size. The decision was made to halt here at noon to allow everyone to clean clothes and equipment, and get some much needed sunshine. All were glad to get the muck and stench of the jungle off of themselves and their gear.

The scouts brought in a couple of large elk like animals with curious corkscrew horns, along with half a dozen large foul, never seen before. The cooking began mid afternoon and all feasted well. Smoke fires were lit after dark and a large part of the meat was sliced and hung on racks to smoke. Though the smoke was thick, the night was dark and it probably could not be seen from very far away.

Came then, their fortieth day of travel, total distance estimated at five hundred miles, give or take. Just at noon they came to the edge of the vegetation and brush. Before them, lay several miles of wheat and grass lands which had an occasional clump of brush scattered over it, with green areas indicating the presence of water. Beyond the sea of grass, the land appeared to turn black, and off in the distance to the north east the horizon was even blacker.

After supper, Grayhawk again addressed the Company as a whole. "Elves, Dwarves and Men, there's a strange brew for you!" he began. This brought a good laugh and nodding heads. "Well, as you can plainly see before you, we have arrived at the blighted lands, home of the Dark Lord and his minions. As far as we know, we have come this far undetected, of course I suspect we have had some help along the way. Now we stand on the edge of a great peril. Now, we are on our own. Our ultimate success or failure rests entirely upon our shoulders. We may be attacked at any time from this moment forward by Dragons, Drulgar, or Sobeklu or who knows what else. We must be prepared to fight at all times. All through the coming days and nights we must be vigilant or we will surely die. There can be no turning back now, we have come too far. We are committed."

That very same evening Lucifer's Priests held a meeting in the main hall of the Dark Lords fortress. They had just been instructed by their master to find where in the world Grayhawk and his companions had disappeared to. And what they were planning on doing next. No further excuses would be tolerated. The human Dark Priests very existence as a group was dependent upon success. Lucifer made it abundantly clear that he had personal plans for dealing with Grayhawk and friends, when they are captured. They must be taken alive and brought before the Dark Lord himself. Or Else!

Chapter Twenty Seven

The next morning they brought out the ancient arrows from Dwarvenholm. "Dragon Bane" they are called, said to be capable of killing Dragons. Eight of the Elves, plus Allanfair, Ailereon, Grayhawk and four others, all master archers, were each given five of the arrows. The arrows were thirty three inches long, the tips were tri-bladed razor tips made from Mithrail silver, four inches long. The fletching were also metal and four inches long. The shafts were a very strong, very light metal, of a type no one had seen before. In talking about them it was concluded that they were thousands of years old, made by an unknown people. Prince Allanfair's tri-blade dagger was compared and found to be of similar construction, and also of great age.

Traveling that day they began to detect worn trails, fresh campsites and often signs that they were no longer alone in the land. Just before dark, silhouetted in dusk, on the skyline they saw a large group, probably Drulgar, moving to the south and away from the 'Company's" route. The decision was then made to switch to night time travel so that the night vision of both the Elves and Odranna's Chosen could be put to good use. So they then traveled on after dark, until about the third hour after midnight. They came upon a large undercut rock formation where they took shelter and made camp.

The evening of their forty second day, they broke camp at dusk and with both scouts and flankers out, they continued north east towards the mountains. Two times during the night they veered their course to avoid Drulgar camps. At first light they moved into a series of small caves all linked together. In early afternoon a Drulgar company passed close enough to be heard, headed south.

And so it went, traveling by night, making wide detours around enemy encampments. No fires visible, no talking or allowing weapons and equipment to clank. When they stopped on the forty sixth day, at daylight, after traveling upward all night, they were at the beginning of a long black shadowed rift running east and up into the mountains. They were headed straight toward a huge volcanic mountain thousands of feet tall and coal black with smoke coming from literally hundreds of vents or caves. The miasma or taint of evil was profound here, exuding from every rock.

"No place for the faint of heart here" said Prince Drinach, bringing chuckles from those around him.

"And what is that rotten egg smell?" asked one of the Chosen.

"It is **sulphur,** said Grayhawk"

"Sorcerers dirt" said another.

"It is nasty!" said Sir Owen, "just plain nasty!" The travel had been difficult and quite warm before, now it was hard, sweaty work and even treacherous at times. There were loose rocks, slides, and pitfalls some over fifty feet deep, sharp and jagged edges everywhere. They moved on through it, gradually going higher toward the great black mountain. The rift itself was over a mile wide at most places with occasional pools of clear water, and also some water runoffs worn into the rock.

There was a trail or path, sometimes well worn, sometimes not. Just after midnight they camp upon the first outpost, manned by Drulgar, it had a crude eight foot high wall with a gate, lit by one feeble torch. One guard was on either side of the gate, and the gate was open. This was either a well planned trap, or they really did not know that the 'Company' was approaching.

White Bear and six of the Chosen moved forward up the trail followed by the others. Just as Grayhawk got to where he could see the gate in the dim light, two bows twanged and the Drulgar guards went down. Seven of the Chosen were then through the gate like shadows, and deathly quiet for such big men. No sound or movement was heard from beyond the wall. Many long heartbeats passed before they saw

White Bear step out of the gate and wave to them. Everyone moved forward and through the gate.

"That was too easy" said White Bear to Grayhawk, as he approached. "Eight more inside the shack, they sleep forever now."

"Well then" said Grayhawk, remembering his mercenary days. "I think there should be an accidental fire here, to cover our tracks. What do you think?"

"Excellent" said White Bear.

"Agreed" chimed in Allanfair. "I know just how to arrange that, about an hour after we are gone. A torch will fall from its holder onto a straw covered floor and with a little help arranging fuel, a right merry and hot fire."

"Hmmph!" said Prince Drinach, "All this skullduggery stuff is new to me. Dwarves would just disappear into the rocks and to the Hell with them. Two of the Elves lagged behind to see to the fire and everyone else moved on. Just before daylight there was a very bright glow from back down the trail, and a bit later the two Elf Rangers caught back up with the Company. Looking back, standing with his hands on his hips Prince Drinach stated "Looks like a Drulgar outpost managed to burn itself up! What a pity."

This morning no cave our outcropping could be found for shelter. Everyone spread out, in and amongst some large rocks going up a slope. They were looking up at the black mountain now. They were close. The group rested until early afternoon before continuing on.

Again there were trails to follow, well worn, but old, in some places blocked by rock fall. The trails became steeper as the day wore on. The rocks became more splintered and jagged, changing color even, from reddish brown and gray to flat black, then to satin shiny black and finally changing from stone to obsidian, shiny as glass and the edges as sharp as razors. The dwarves went ahead of the group now, making the tail as safe as possible.

By evening they had come to the true base of the mountain. They could see for a long distance looking back, even to where the horizon turned green. They had climbed quite some distance in altitude also. Being on the west side of the mountain and up high, the daylight lasted much longer than usual. Looking up the near vertical wall, many cave and crevice openings could be seen, some with yellow brown smoke coming out of them. Prince Drinach and his Dwarves warned all that this colored smoke was poison to all who breath air. Other openings appeared to be venting steam because it dissipated soon after being emitted, and the interior of those caves were so hot it would cook a man in short order and a Dwarf even faster than that.

It seemed extremely odd to Grayhawk that they had encountered only the one outpost and no other patrols. As always there came that age old warriors foreboding that anything which was easy, was probably a trap.

Though sentries were posted, no movement could be discerned in any direction. The temperature was moderate; a good breeze was coming around the mountain from the north. The condensation from the steam vents had cooled and run downhill in a number of places then formed into deep pools of crystal clear, cold, slightly mineral tasting water.

At almost dark, Prince Drinach came hurriedly to Grayhawk and Allanfair. "Stop what you are doing! Have everyone gather everything and follow me, now!! No questions, do it!" spoken as a war leader, not the affable Prince of the Dwarves. Without hesitation, everyone began grabbing up their gear and packs. "Follow me!!" he said again and turned up in to a space between two large rocks. Everyone was trying to shoulder packs, balance other gear and draw weapons all at the same time, Dwarf, Elf and Human. They had been at this together, for a while now.

Grayhawk and White Bear hung back until all the others were out of sight. Then they too hurried into the opening. Inside was an almost enclosed trail or path heading steeply upward for a good fifty feet, then coming out under an overhang about ten feet high, with a dark cave opening at the rear. Drinach and three other Dwarves were hurriedly pushing everyone through the entrance when all of the sudden the darkness fell. The wind began to increase and a bolt of pure silver lightning struck back down where they had been. Prince Drinach was shouting now.

"Don't stop to look! No time! Get inside now!" Then there were at least six more lightning strikes, above and around the area where they were. As Grayhawk and White Bear entered the cave, the sounds, and concussion were punctuated by extremely bright flashes of almost silver light, which were increasing in tempo and volume. As the last Dwarf entered the cave, others who had been waiting for them, then rolled a large wheel of stone across the entrance immediately turning the cave pitch black and cutting the crack and boom sounds by half. Everyone just sort of stood there in the dark, listening, waiting, faint flickers of the lightning flashes, which were coming now only a second or two apart could be seen at the sides and bottom of the stone wheel over the opening.

Someone in the back of the cave managed to get a torch lit, providing some sputtering yellow light. Then began something few in the group had ever seen before. Around the stone wheel there formed a green glow, like phosphorus but in the air, from no visible source. At the same time everyone began to notice, hair on their arms, their heads and even beards began to stand out and move. The green glow spread to the entire wheel and became a little brighter. Grayhawk was standing closest to the wheel with drawn sword in hand. His sword began to glow, and then it spread up his arm covering him from head to foot in a green aura.

"Not dangerous!" said Grayhawk aloud, realizing what he was watching. "Relax my friends! This is harmless! I have seen it before, at sea, during a storm. The ancient name for it is Saint Elmo's fire, though I have no idea who Saint Elmo was, or how he made his fire." By now almost every metal object in the cave was glowing, as were most of the people. "Light your torches and fires anyway" said Grayhawk "this green light will fade as fast as it came."

And so it was, the storm outside raged until just before first light and then dissipated as fast as it had come. As well did the Saint Elmo's fire much to the relief of all. When things seemed calm outside, still they waited a few more minutes before rolling back the stone from the entrance. As the stone moved they were greeted by an inrush of damp cool morning air and the distinct smell of ozone. As they came out of the cave they noticed lightening strike marks on the rocks both above and below them. The stone was still glowing a dull red in a few places with waves of heat rising from it.

White Bear was first to speak. "My friends, if we had been caught unaware out in the open, probably not one of us would be here this morn."

"Aye" said Allanfair, "We owe our lives to Prince Drinach."

"Agreed" said Grayhawk. "Tell us good Sir, how did you know such a thing was about to happen?"

"Well Sirs" he began, "I was scouting around looking for a way up this mountain, when I came upon the path leading up here. I found the cave with the rock wheel and immediately wondered, why such a stout defense for the entrance to this cave? I was standing here underneath the overhang. Looking out I saw outcroppings of iron and obsidian. Then I remembered from my training in working stone. Beware of any formation containing both iron and obsidian! They will build a static charge during the heat of the day. That heat will begin to rise, friction will increase the static charge, and around the mountain a lighting storm will form very rapidly. It will not happen every day but often enough to be very dangerous. This mountain has been modified or magically charged in such a way so as to amplify the effect."

"That explains why we haven't run into any other beings up here" said Grayhawk. "It is truly an effective defense system. Needing only to be occasionally checked to see if there have been any unwary intruders, who would now be fried like fritters and the Drulgar would devour the remains."

"Very efficient" said Allanfair. "Quite a disgusting practice, but efficient never the less." All agreed with him on that point.

"Think you it will happen again this night?" asked White Bear, looking at Prince Drinach.

"Aye, I believe it will, but less severe this time. I think it cycles in sets of three to five days, decreasing, and then three days of clear while the static builds again."

"If Drinach has the right of it" said Grayhawk, "Then in two days will probably come a patrol, and they will be wary after finding their torched friends, of course their lamenting will be after they have made a meal of their dear departed!" This brought chuckles and nodding of heads from the entire Company. "First thing today, let us find another cave if possible, up higher, and then we will begin in earnest to locate an entrance to this mountain. Preferably one that is not well guarded" said Grayhawk. "The longer we remain undetected the better chance we have." All were nodding in agreement.

"Well Master Dwarf" said Allanfair to Prince Drinach "Think you that, yourself and your kin, can find us another hidey hole?"

"Most certainly!" he replied. "Or if not, we will make one!" All of the Dwarves were grinning and brandishing axes and hammers.

"I doubt it not!" said Allanfair, bowing. Red Wolf, one of the older Chosen spoke up.

"Grayhawk does all this bowing and siring, go on all the time amongst Lords and Princes and such?"

"Unfortunately so" replied Grayhawk, grinning and bowing, followed by Prince Drinach, and then Prince Allanfair and Princess Aurelia and the other Elves alike. Allanfair flourished his hands and said "Why, Sir Red Wolf, at court in the Elvin Kingdom such actions are called the 'Dance of State'!"

"Sir!!" replied Red Wolf, "How in the world did I acquire that title? And by Odranna's Beard Highness, the Chosen do not, dance!" Everyone was laughing now. A good tension and pressure release, after a long, green, noisy night. By mid morning the Dwarves had located another cave with a stone wheel to secure the entrance; this one was a hard four hour climb. Again it was over and around sharp jagged rock and obsidian. At one point a long spear like piece, some twenty feet or more in length broke off high above them and came down like a falling spear, barely missing several of the Chosen who were forced to hug the rock wall of the 'trail'. It went crashing and splintering down below.

The afternoon was punctuated by cracks and booms along with sound of crashing, falling rock. The afternoon sun heated the rock face. All in the party made it safely up to where the cave was, at the rear of an overhanging shelf of rock. This one had seen more recent use, judging from the faint foul smell of the place. They had at least left behind a supply of firewood.

That evening just at dark, as everyone was moving inside the cave, when Sigisfel, the youngest of the Dwarves walked out to the front of the ledge and looked down. As he did so, the first bolt of silver lighting struck him on his helm, killing him instantly. It left him a smoldering, crackling small heap. The wooden handle of his axe was burning still clutched in his right hand. Everyone froze for an instant. Several of the Dwarves still outside uttered howls of rage and rushed to where he had fallen, pouring their water skins over him to cool the fellow down. Although they all knew that he was gone.

A second and third bolt struck close by and the wind picked up. White Bear, a very large man, ran over to the body, threw his cloak over it, bent down and scooped him up as you would a child. He ran inside the cave followed by the other Dwarves. Then the wheel was rolled in front of the door.

The storm then began in earnest, though less intense than the night before, torches and fires were kindled inside the cave. The Dwarves gathered around their fallen one, the Humans and Elves formed an outer circle behind them. Now they were one less Speaking in the ancient Dwarf language Prince Drinach delivered a somber eulogy. There was not enough wood for a proper funeral pyre, so four of the Dwarves were detailed, to go out at morning to find a suitable location which can be covered with rocks as a grave. The remainder of the night was quiet inside the cave, punctuated only with the crack and boom of lightning strikes and thunder. When the cave was opened after first light it was still cloudy and gray this day. But by mid morn the sky had cleared and the day warmer as the sun cleared the top of the mountain.

By mid-day another trail up the mountain was found leading to an even higher cave, just about half way up the mountain. When they all were all inside the cave, later that afternoon, Grayhawk then called for a conference of all members of the Company. Everyone was gathered in a circle towards the front of the dimly lit cave, seated as best they could, a flask of Brandy or two was passed, and most lit pipes of tabac. When it grew silent Grayhawk stepped to the center.

"We have been extremely fortunate up until last night, my friends" he began. "Now one of our Dwarf friends has been taken from us by the very evil powers we have come here to fight. These lightening storms are not natural, though they use natural forces. They are designed to happen in seven day cycles, three nights of storms followed by four days of calm. Tomorrow, I believe, the patrols of foul folk will set out around the base of this mountain from somewhere around to the south. Moving steady around and upward, and three nights later they will be here at this cave. I believe that not too far from here is an entrance to the mountain proper and that is where they will end their patrol."

"Shall we hide in the rocks then, until they pass, and then follow them?" asked Allanfair.

"I think not" replied Grayhawk. "That entrance may be permanently manned and guarded. I believe we should find one up higher so we can approach and gain entry without being spotted. Further I think we need to find that portal and be gone from sight before they get here. They may well be suspicious of these caves having been used recently, especially after the fire at their outpost. While they are stupid, they are also cunning."The meeting only lasted half an hour or so. Then everyone began preparing for the night.

A feeling of uneasiness came over everyone in the cave a few minutes later. Sir Owen of the Templar was the first to recognize it for what it was "Dragonfear!!" he said drawing his sword and turning toward the entrance. The fear was now palpable and felt by all.

"The stone" yelled Allanfair, who was close to the portal. All who could do so moved to the stone and rolled it to cover the entrance. The fear affected everyone, Elves, Dwarves and Humans. Some were holding their heads, eyes bugged out, taking great breaths of air. Others were down on their knees, heads pressed to the floor, some vomited. The urge to scream was powerful. They all felt the metallic taste in the mouth, the heart pumping, the hair standing on the back of the neck. Grayhawk, Sir Owen and a few of the others knew exactly what it was. A Dragon, maybe two were close by and broadcasting their fear, in the hopes of driving anything living in the area into screaming, mindless flight, running surely to their death.

There was then, close by, the sound of heavy wing beats, more than one set. They could hear loud, long, high pitched shrieks, but there was no fire. The Dragons had not found them. Yet! It seemed to go on forever, without any lessening. A number of the Elves were down, semi conscious; several of the Dwarves had passed out as well as several of the Humans. No one was immune. Grayhawk wanted desperately to roll back the stone and fight the monsters. His fear had turned to rage, as had most of the Chosen of Odranna. They stood frozen in place, swords drawn, and no enemy in sight. It was horrible to all.

Then the lightning strikes began outside. A couple of war shrieks were heard from the Dragons and it was over, just like that. The fear turned off. Many of the party fell to their knees in relief. No one moved or spoke for a long couple of minutes. White Bear spoke first, clearing his throat and looking around in the dim light.

"I would not have believed such a thing possible! For the first time in my life I have felt the fear of cowards. How is this done?"

"Mind casting" replied Allanfair. "Only Dragons are capable of it, no one has ever known how." Drinach spoke up,

"I have felt it, and I still cannot believe it happened. No wonder they were so feared in the old sagas." "What say you Grayhawk?"

"For Sir Owen, myself and some of the other Templar this is the second time we have felt it, only this time no one died. I think they did not locate us, for that stone door would not have stopped them. I hope at least they were only on a scouting patrol." The lightning strikes were at about half the number as the first storm. It was several long hours before anyone was able to sleep and even then it was fitful and disturbed. They did not open the cave at first light but waited for an hour to see if the Dragons would return, and to the relief of all they did not. While waiting it was discussed and decided that if possible the patrols would locate the entrance used by the foul folk, and then look higher up the rock face for a suitable entrance for the Company to get inside without being found out.

Three patrols of three Dwarves each left immediately. One went north, one up the rock face, and one south since the trail wound around that way.

The patrol to the north returned first saying that after two or three miles it became so rough and jagged that they could not pass. The patrol to the south came back just before mid day. They had followed the trail around until it came to a well guarded and heavy metal door entrance to the mountain.

A short while later the a fist sized rock hit not far to their right and bounced on down the mountain, clacking loudly each time it hit. Looking up, they saw, a good five or six hundred feet above them, the Dwarves who had gone up on patrol. They were leaning out, in order to be seen, and motioning with their arms for everyone to come up to where they were. So, gathering up their gear, packs and weapons they started up the side of the mountain.

An hour or so later everyone was on the rock ledge with the patrol, a ledge which could not be seen from below. The Dwarves, it would seem, have located a way in, up even higher than they were now. They were already at a dizzying altitude. They could look back down from where they had started up the mountain. So after a brief break the Company began to climb up the mountain side again. The Dwarves in the lead, Elves next, followed by the Templar Knights, and then Odranna's Chosen. For the next five hours they all struggled and sweated, sometimes having to move sideways using cracks and crevices in the rocks for hand and toe holds. Each was carrying a heavy pack on their back. A fall from here would be fatal. All were keenly aware of this fact, but climbed on anyway. There was no other choice.

At last, Grayhawk, who was climbing in last position, began to notice less and less people still visible ahead of him on the rock face. When suddenly pulling up for another hand hold, he was looking into a jagged, dark hole in to the mountain. He could feel the flow of warm, slightly burnt smelling air coming from within. The last brother in line turned and offered him a hand up. He could sense and hear several others ahead moving into the cave, which was dry, but not tall enough for any save a Dwarf to stand upright. After the light from the entrance faded they moved in total darkness for a ways. The passage seemed to be sloping uphill and curving around to the left. Soon they began to see the dull greenish, and sometimes yellow glow of the phosphorus lichens growing on the cave walls. They rested for an hour, and while doing so it came again, the fear of the Dragon. This time it seemed to come from far off and faded fast.

"I wish we knew" said Grayhawk, to no one in particular, "whether the Dragons make routine patrols or do they have knowledge of our presence."

"More important" said Allanfair, "Does Lucifer, know of our presence?"

"I think not" said Drinach. "If he did we would surely be dead by now.'

"Or even worse." said Princess Ailereon who rarely spoke about anything. The air was constantly moving, steady and slow as though being pumped. It was warm and slightly damp. Eventually they came to a taller and wider area in which there were growing all sorts of different fungi and mushrooms, most of which were edible. The bright colored ones were all deadly poison and the light brown ones with a blue ring were powerful dream buttons or so they were called, and they were hungry, it being near to meal time. They boiled some of the button ones in a broth of jerked meat and had a fairly enjoyable meal, relaxing, scattered about the wide chamber. They smoked and talked in low tones; saw to the condition of weapons, packs and supplies. They posted two guards at either entrance. They all slept the long sleep of the weary.

Chapter Twenty Eight

When Grayhawk awoke, it was because he was hungry, and something smelled good. His internal clock told him that he had slept for over twelve hours. Looking around the chamber and sensing no alarm, he then noticed several small cook fires were going and a few of the party were already up and around. The smell was that of both roasting and frying mushrooms along with pots of tea. So everyone ate well after a good night's rest. Since they were in perpetual darkness or near to it, their time was measured by sleep and travel periods. The Templar and the Elves had some difficulty with this at first, but Odranna's Chosen and the Dwarves were not fazed at all. Only White Bear and Grayhawk, were aware that time had slowed for them. They both noticed, by the growth of their beards and the fact that they had both experienced this phenomenon before, though for very different reasons.

So at the end of one of their travel periods, Grayhawk called a council meeting, telling all that they were caught in a subtle trap that they must either break free from the cycle or stay in here forever. Further, that they had already been here inside of this mountain for over three months. All were sorely distressed at the news and the "what shall we do" arguments went on for an hour. When it finally settled down to a mild roar, Grayhawk raised his hands for silence. "Rest now my friends and sleep. I will work on the problem through the ethereal, but I have to be very careful not to gain Lucifer's attention or we are all doomed. Later when most were sleeping, Grayhawk sat in the middle of the floor of a long wide chamber, eerily lit by green yellow phosphorous, vague shadows of his companions around him in the gloom, Prince Allanfair, and White Bear were seated cross legged on the ground facing him.

Grayhawk's Adept ring was very warm inside its pouch. He knew that to even expose it to the air here would instantly alert Lucifer and his minions. So he began by relaxing completely, clearing his mind of all conscious thought. A few minutes of orientation of his location within the mountain, and he began to vaguely sense the layout of the mountains interior. Most of the upper levels were traps and ruses, some still containing hapless wretches who had come looking for fame or treasure. These beings were now totally mad creatures, screaming out their existence alone in the dark. There are a goodly number of these pitiful beings, and some were hundreds of years old. The mid levels were home to the garrisons of both Drulgar and the lizard men, or more properly called Sobeklu, they were the end product of mating humans with crocodiles. There were large chambers used as holding pens for food stock, both human and animal. There were forges and furnaces, weapon making facilities, blacksmiths and many other stalls and shops along with pens where were kept the large, vicious, sharp toothed, pointed hoof, meat eating war steeds called Vulceras. They are creatures straight from Hell.

Encountering no barriers or shields Grayhawk let his sight go out further, down to another level, which on the outside would have been ground level. Here the passages were wider and lighter. Here live the demons who serve Lucifer personally. Here also were pens of humans from all over the world, every race, color and creed; these were servants and sex toys for the demons until they tired of them. Then they were roasted like fine game animals and served up for feasts or parties. Their living quarters were full of beautiful and rare furnishings, carpets, drapes, tapestries, statuary and other treasures, some older than anyone could remember. There were marble floors inlaid with gold, silver and opal, and of course at least ten, high ranking demons in residence.

Below this there were four levels of sartorial, palatial splendor, pools and entire gardens of fruits, nuts and exotic plants and orchids, including a black one, one whiff of it will put a man in a coma for a hundred years. Some ten thousand people could easily live on these four levels. Under this area however, the tunnels were mostly melted black basalt rock. No easy task, to melt basalt. For miles around a central shaft the walkways spiraled down passing many openings to other chambers along the way. The shaft itself was a good hundred feet across and the bottom could not be seen. The shaft opened into a dome of solid shiny green obsidian and quartz, precious and semi precious stones were present everywhere the eye looked. Off to one side there stood a gold engraved throne three times the size of one for a man. In front of the throne there was a white marble table about forty feet long with six chairs on either side and one at the far end.

There were thirteen total, one for each of the Chief Demons of Hell. None of whom were in attendance at the moment, but there on the throne sat a being of huge stature, heavily muscled with skin like polished dark red antique leather, yellow eyes with slit cat's pupils, slender hands, long fingers with nails like a big cat's claws, and they were dark yellow. No horns were upon his brow, just oily jet black, ringlet, curled hair, his was a truly handsome face, with an aquiline nose. Both upper and lower canine teeth were the size of a lions. Once he had been the Chosen of Odranna. The All-Father's favorite. He was called the Prince of Light. But that had not been enough for him; he wanted all of the power for himself.

He sat brooding now, as usual and he had the vague feeling of being watched. He had not felt that in a long, long time. He slammed out his senses all at once intent on trapping some prying sorcerer, yet he ran into only emptiness on the ethereal. Grayhawk had sensed the power surge and escaped, literally in the nick of time, drawing back into his mind and slamming the shields. Just in the instant that all of that happened, Grayhawk caught a glimpse of an ornate room. The room had many niches in one wall and each had a dark object in it. Each was like a melon about two feet long. That room was located off of the main hallway on the bottom level, before the shaft area.

He knew that he dare not attempt to cast again. Lucifer's mind traps were very potent and no one had ever escaped from one. In the trap, a person's life force is drained out sort of like a spider taking juices from its prey. The only difference is Lucifer takes a long time to suck you dry. Grayhawk explained his visions to everyone and all that he had 'seen' at various places along their route. There are escape portals, along the walls. They appear as very faint fluctuations in the phosphorescent glow, and are really easy to miss.

After briefing the entire Company on the situation and especially on the fact that once they were through an escape portal, they would then be visible and real to any one of Lucifer's creatures. Or, that if they moved too fast as a group and used any sort of magic, Lucifer would know in an instant of their presence and their intent. With Grayhawk in the lead, they actually did, only have to move a short distance, and there, sure enough was a difference in the pattern of the wall. Grayhawk was amazed to find all he had to do was step through it, all the while hoping that he did not set off all sorts of alarms, or death traps, but nothing happened. Soon all of them had stepped through and they found themselves standing in a very, very old carved tunnel. The tool and chisel marks were still visible. The light was less; the air was damp and fetid smelling, like old death.

"In here" said Allanfair 'we are open prey for anything that finds us, and I suspect that there are things in here we would all like to think do not exist!"

"True enough" said Grayhawk "but the really ugly stuff is far down below where we are heading." They moved with Dwarves leading, followed by Odranna's Chosen, the Templar with the Elves bringing up the up the rear. The Company took the direction with the downhill slope and moved out at slow by steady pace. The passage curved at a slight angle around to the right. It was absolutely amazing how quiet the dwarves could move.

"Short ghosts!" said Drinach with a big toothy grin, twisting the ends of his mustache.

For two and a half days they moved, ate, slept in almost total darkness and a strange wet, dripping silence. White Bear finally broke a long silent period with

"Do they not call this water torture in some parts of the world?"

"Aye! That it is" answered Grayhawk "and now I believe in its effectiveness." They were beginning to think that maybe they were in another illusion, when the Dwarves in front signaled a halt. Grayhawk and the leaders all went forward to check on the situation. A hundred paces further, the air seemed a little fresher and less wet, plus the corridor itself was a little wider and higher. The Dwarf scouts had returned and reported that the corridor ended a few hundred paces on, at a blank white marble wall, closed off a long time ago. Grayhawk and the others moved forward with everyone else following until they came to the wall. Because it was white marble the whole tunnel seemed to be much brighter.

Drinach and his four senior Stone Chiefs, as they were called, examined the wall and the whole area for some time, conferring now and again in the dwarf tongue. At last they came to Grayhawk and the others.

"Well blade master" said Drinach "It would seem that we have arrived at the Dark Lords Palace. This you see here before you is the back side of a polished marble wall, set into place by both magic and the hand of man. We believe it was sealed over a thousand years ago. There is an access door, there at the far left side." he said pointing, "It is a small door, but even the largest of our party can squeeze through it. It has not been opened since it was put in place. We do not know where it goes."

"I have seen it in my castings" said Grayhawk, "beyond that wall lies almost a square mile maze of fantastic beauty and craftsmanship, myriads of ancient treasures and furnishings, gold, silver, jewels, exotic weapons, and things of horror. There are many, many, chambers and rooms There is no counting the numbers of souls who have perished there. For that palace is Lucifer's playground, the place of the Soul Festival. It is where arch demons arrange orgies of blood and horror, for the amusement and pleasure of their master.

"So!" said Allanfair, leaning on his bow with his right foot up on his left knee. "I suppose if we get caught in there, we will not be treated well!!" Everyone was quietly chuckling, some with their hand over their mouth to keep from laughing out loud.

"One thing I must tell you all, concerning Evil and Darkness as it applies to you and I" said White Bear, raising his hand for silence and stepping to the middle "Be ye Elf, Dwarf or Man, know this, you all have a soul. Even if Lucifer himself should take you, and threaten you with eternal damnation, he cannot take your soul by force. He can lie to you. He can trick you. He can make a deal with you. He can offer you all the pleasures of the flesh that you can dream up. Or offer all the wealth that there is, but you can refuse him. All he can do then is to cause your death. No matter how horrible your death is. That part of you which live on, after death. Your Soul shall remain with the All Father, forever."

"All of that being so" said Prince Drinach, "Then the All Father will not mind if we kill all of them, and live to drink beer and tell tall tales of this?"

"Not at all Master Dwarf" replied White Bear, grinning, "Not at all!"

"Oh Good, then let's get at them! What say you Grayhawk?"

"In a short time, Good Prince" said Grayhawk, "First we must make some plans." By casting his senses out at a very low level Grayhawk had gathered a general impression of the layout inside the Palace, basically a square, almost exactly 1 mile to a side. They were presently located at the east wall, at about the halfway point. The chamber containing the Dragon Eggs was directly across from them on the west wall. Unfortunately, there were no passages through the middle, the very middle was one huge hall, with only one entrance from the south and of course, one in the floor where the Dark Lord himself could enter from his domain below. There were occasional patrols of several Sobeklu, the dark red skinned, half human, half crocodile beings. Like the one that had attacked Grayhawk during the fight in the Castle Throne room. That now seemed like a life time ago. Like the Drulgar, Sobeklu are Lucifer's creatures, cunning and ferocious, but not real bright. Avoiding these patrols with such a large party was a problem, coupled with not knowing what sort of alarms, traps or snares they might encounter. Grayhawk, White Bear and Allanfair all sensed that the palace was, at this time, fairly empty. They could not sense any groups of anything moving about. Of course that fact, in and of itself might bode of an ambush.

It was agreed that the Elves were the best suited for scouting in this place. They would go first and find empty chambers, or rooms the rest of the Company could then move to. One jump at a time, and perhaps not be discovered until they reached their goal. The door in the marble wall was pulled inward by the Dwarves, slowly looking for hidden traps, none were found. The doorway was three foot wide and five foot tall. As soon as it was clean, the Elves moved through like shadows with bows, even the Lady Ailorian, and then turned to their left or the north, vanishing up the corridor.

The corridor they were in was faintly lit, and lined with polished white marble walls and ceiling. The floor tiles were burgundy red and gold, very fancy. The walls were about twelve foot apart and twelve foot tall. There were no statues or furnishings of any kind, no pictures, paintings or tapestries, no obvious light source. Every so often in no distinct pattern there would be a doorway, all with bronze metal relief carved doors. As soon as the entire Company was in the corridor the Dwarves closed the door. This time they formed the rear guard with the Knights next, then the Chosen with Grayhawk and White Bear in the lead.

For about a quarter of an hour they moved in gloomy silence. Finally they came to a double doorway on their right which was open and an Elf was directing them into a side corridor with another double door at the far end. The other Elves were waiting inside. Motioning, with fingers to lips for silence, they closed the doors. Allanfair whispered "Patrol approaching!" and they stood there in silence and heard nothing, finally the Elves opened the door and said, "They have passed" and then they themselves disappeared into the half light.

"I cannot hear them" said White Bear in a whisper. "How do they move so quietly?"

"I know not" said Grayhawk. "There is still much about the Elves we do not know." "True enough" answered White Bear, "True enough."

On the next jog they rounded the corner on the north side and barely made it into a store room, full of every kind of silver object you can imagine, armor, helmets, chain mail, goblets, weapons, flatware, bowls and piles of jewelry, all gleaming like it had just been polished. Closing the door just in time as a large group of Drulgar came out of a side passage just behind them. Fortunately they turned the other way.

Halfway along the north passageway the Elves had opened several doors into treasure rooms. There, they found piles and chests of gold and jewels. In the middle of the floor in one of the chambers there was a mound or pile nearly five foot tall of the jewel stone called 'diamonds'. Some of the stones were as large as a duck egg. As well there were many emeralds, rubies, sapphires, and opals. Everyone filled their pockets and pouches with as much of the treasure as they could.

The entire complex was clean, but the smell of death was everywhere, rotting flesh, burnt flesh, urine, feces, and blood all mingled together. A smell none of the Company would ever forget. Beyond the treasure rooms on both sides of the hall were rooms with opulent furniture, great long dining tables and every torture device ever imagined. There were unlit braziers with irons, tongs, scissors, skewers, and blades all blackened and encrusted. In these chambers the smell was the strongest. No one spoke, nary a word was said. Everyone just looked around, most shaking their heads in disbelief. What horrors must take place on these obscene premises? Finally they rounded the last corner to their right, taking them into the eastern corridor, where in the egg chamber is located. Three more times in a short space they were surprised and almost discovered. Fortunately Drulgar are fairly stupid. The ones in here where somewhat different, lighter in color and a little taller, probably bred here as a servant class.

Prince Drinach came back to inform Grayhawk that the Dwarves had located another door in to the outer caves. This one also had not been used in a very long time. Their escape route, they all hoped. As they came to it, the Dwarves already had it open and confirmed its antiquity. Then they were there, at their final destination, the door to Lucifer's Dragon Egg chamber. The arch for the doorway went all the way to the ceiling of the corridor. The doors were almost as tall, solid polished steel, heavily engraved with Dragon scenes and symbols. One could feel the emanations of the protective wards and seals that had been placed on the doors.

"How then Lord Grayhawk, shall we open these doors?" asked White Bear.

"I believe we have the power in our Adept's rings. But, as soon as we take them out and put them on, Lucifer will know we are here, and all alarms in this place will sound. We will likely be attacked within minutes. This will be either a fight to the death, or escape, and unlike any we have ever fought before. If we manage to destroy the eggs, and then make it to the outer tunnels, we will surely be lucky this day. Prince Allanfair and Princess Ailorian have the ancient weapons needed to destroy the eggs. Each egg must be stood up long ways on the floor and the weapon placed point first on top, the weapon must be struck a solid blow with an iron hammer. The tri-blade weapon should then cleave each egg into three pieces, utterly destroying them. There are twenty eggs, not eighteen as thought, ten for each team. It should only take two or three minutes to do this. In order for any of us to escape this all must be done rapidly and smoothly. Is everyone prepared? Excellent! Allanfair, if you would please have your elf archers move down and cover the tunnel entrance. White Bear, if you and the Brothers would be so good as to split into two groups, and guard both approaches here in the corridor, your bows should work well in here."

"Agreed" said White Bear. "Prince Drinach if you would have your warriors take position behind the Brothers, in case of a break through. Sir Owen, if you will, take the Knights into the tunnel in case we are attacked from that way, and when we all fall back into the tunnel, your knights will then secure the rear and close the door. When we all have passed your position, you will break off and follow as rear guard."

"As you command My Lord!" answered Sir Owen. "Move now, my friends and take your positions, and May the All Father be with us all." The Company dispersed to their respective positions. Grayhawk waited a few more minutes, and then, brought out the pouch from within his clothing, taking out the gold ring with the bright blue stone. It began immediately to pulsate and emit blue light as he placed it on his right index finger; as White Bear did the same, a single deep bell toll was heard by all. Grayhawk was aware of it sounding across the Astral Plain, as he was also aware instantly, that Lucifer had also heard it and was casting to determine exactly what was happening. Grayhawk and White Bear extended both hands in front of themselves towards the polished steel doors. Gathering all of their powers together as one, both cast directly onto the door. They both, in unison commanded "OPEN!!" and the doors swung outward. The crackling and popping of seals and magical wards on the door was like a small fireworks display. No one moved until the display ended. Inside the room was dark. Again Grayhawk extended his hands, "Illuminate!!" he commanded and the room lit up in bright blue light. The interior of the room was empty, no furnishings of any kind, the back wall had two rows of open niches, one above the other and in each could be seen a dark oval object, shining like ebony.

In the distant reaches of the stronghold alarm gongs were ringing, and deep toned, flat note, bleating horns were being sounded. Everyone sprang forward at once to get into the room.

"Get it done quickly or we are surely all lost" stated Allanfair as he and his sister took out the tri-blade daggers they were carrying. They handed one to each of the two Dwarves chosen to use them. Aileron and Drinach removed the first two eggs and handed them down to the Dwarves. They quickly placed them down on the floor, small end up. Holding the egg steady with one had while the other placed the point of the dagger onto the top of the egg with the handle straight up. The other two Dwarves with hammers then stepped up and with a powerful downward swing struck the flat pommel end of each dagger, driving them downward into the egg, splitting them into three pieces. Unlike other eggs ever seen, these were solid on the inside as well. As the first two eggs split, a distant horrible long, screeching roar could be heard reverberating through the stronghold.

"Well!" said Grayhawk, looking very grim in the blue light, "The Dark Lord is awakened and he is aware of what we do. Now there literally will be Hell to pay, hurry!!" As Ailereon and Drinach passed egg after egg to the Dwarves to destroy, Allanfair noticed a smaller niche on the north end wall. Walking over and looking inside he saw a much smaller golden egg. In his head, a voice he did not recognize said very clearly in the ancient Elf tongue

"Take this egg, hide it on your person, and protect it! Bring it back with you to Keltan." Allanfair immediately complied. Picking up the egg and slipping it inside his tunic next to his skin. The egg felt warm and vaguely familiar.

The last of the eggs were destroyed and at that moment the entire place began to rumble, vibrate and shake. Cracks were now appearing, in the floor, and ceiling alike.

"Out NOW!" said Grayhawk, and all exited the room. Turning to their right and moving up the corridor towards the escape door. The first Drulgar came howling down the long corridor, joined by others coming from several of the side doors. The warrior monks of Odranna, who were expert archers all, began firing and the lead Drulgar went down. Behind them now came the taller, fiercer Sobeklu, and behind them, far back in the shadows could be seen even larger creatures,

'Demons' thought Grayhawk. 'We have surely shaken a hornet's nest this time.' Arrows were also coming from the other side, and then came the first casualty for the Company. One of the brothers went down with an arrow through his eye and out the back of his head. By the time, about two minutes later, when the last of the Company made it through the small door to the outer cavern, three dwarves and two more of the brothers had gone down to arrow and spear. The two foot thick stone door was closed, cutting off all the howling noise. It was braced with thick timbers found in the tunnel, and then large pieces of rock placed by the Dwarves, Prince Drinach announced

"That will hold for about a quarter of an hour, no more. Best we move fast."

"Agreed" said Grayhawk. "Prepare your selves, my friends, the real fight has not yet begun." They set off at a trot down the narrow corridor, with the Elves in the lead and Temple Knights bringing up the rear. They moved quickly. For over an hour they moved. The entire mountain was rumbling and shaking, the air reeked of sulphur and other things. In the distance, rumbling through the tunnels, passageways and caverns, great howling roars could be heard.

Chapter Twenty Nine

After a second full hour of running, and stumbling through dark winding tunnels, they emerged into a large high ceiling cavern, some fifty paces wide and three hundred paces or so long. It was lit by at least a hundred torches and in the yellow flickering light there was then revealed a double line of Sobeklu warriors with a huge green Demon pacing behind the line. His eyes were glowing bright yellow. Overall the demon sort of looked like an ancient lizard from before time. As soon as the Company came into the cavern the Demon bellowed a command, and the line of Sobeklu began to move forward, snarling and growling, some even foaming at the mouth. They were brandishing their weapons, swords and spears, out in front of them. The Company formed into a single line across, alternating with a Temple Knight, then a Dwarf, then a Chosen. The Elves deployed as archers.

When the Sobeklu had moved half way across the cavern floor, in and around large rocks, the Demon once again bellowed and they all charged. Their gnashing of teeth, howling and growling was loud in the cavern. The Elves climbed up onto large rocks, to let them effectively use their bows over the heads of the other warriors. Before the ranks closed in battle, over a score of the ugly creatures were down from arrows. The Company stood still, weapons drawn until the enemy literally, ran into them. Most of the Chosen were six and half feet tall, the Knights were average about five foot ten inches and the Dwarves were all less than five feet tall. So as the enemy closed they came against a wall of steel weapons. Each of the group members were renowned for their fighting skills, but the most fierce, close quarter battle fighters were the Dwarves with their hammers and axes.

Well over two hundred of the Sobeklu ran into battle, goaded by a Demon, their eyes glittering with the thoughts of their coming victory. As the two lines impacted, the noise level increased tenfold, steel on steel, the growling of the Humans and Dwarves, the hissing, shrieking and jaw clacking of the Sobeklu. The fight was close enough they could smell each other, see into their enemies eyes. This was hacking, slashing, stabbing, rage and fury. The line moved neither forward nor backward. Five minutes later, it was over. All of the Sobeklu were down. They had made a serious mistake, ignoring the Dwarves and concentrating their attack on the larger Humans. As a result they paid heavily. Many of their dead were missing a leg or part of an arm, or their head. At that point the Demon ran, shrieking in rage into a side passage of the cavern.

The Company had lost two Temple Knights, one Chosen and one Dwarf. There were a number of wounds but none serious. The rumbling and shaking continued to increase, cracks were appearing in the walls and floor and pieces of rock and some stalactites came crashing down from above. The stench of sulphur combined with a gray smoke was beginning to fill the cavern. The power emanations were also increasing, an evil miasma, more of a feeling than anything one could actually see or touch. At that moment Grayhawk, knew in his mind. The Dark Lord, Lucifer himself, was coming, seeking retribution for this invasion of his domain, and especially for the destruction of his prized Dragon eggs. Grayhawk began shouting for everyone still alive to get out of the caverns, to continue on into the labyrinth of passageways. For some reason unknown to them, all of the Company, could feel the pull of the outside, and instinctively knew which passage to take, even in near total darkness. Grayhawk watched the last of the rear guard Temple Knights pass into a tunnel entrance at the far end of the cavern. All of a sudden, his ring began to glow bright blue, the power fairly crackling in the air like static electricity. Back the way they had come from, He was coming, snarling, growling, and broadcasting evil power and fear. Then Lucifer himself broke into the open from a side passage, knocking chunks of rock from the entrance. Once he was clear of the passage, Lucifer rose to his full height of fifteen feet or so. His dark red skin and ebony curly hair down to his shoulders, both, gleaming as though they were oiled, and his large bright yellow cat eyes were glowing in the dim torchlight of the cavern. Snarling, revealing his four inch canine teeth, showing bright white against his almost black lips. His head was tilted back as though sniffing the air. In each hand he clasped a four foot long, half handle and half scythe blade sword of ancient style and origin.

Throwing his arms wide in the classic challenge stance, Lucifer roared a horrible blood curdling yowl and said in classic Keltanese,

"Well Human! Do you dare to stand against me in combat? Or will you run scampering through dark tunnels like a large rodent! In either case I will surely slay thee for thy transgressions against me and mine! Thee and thy vermin friends have done me grievous insult! Killed my servant and entered my house! Destroyed that which was mine! Long and pain filled will be thy death! Thy companions shall roast on spits while still living, and then be eaten like cattle by my minions. What say you Human vermin? Wilt thee stand?" In his mind Grayhawk heard a familiar voice (Even though you cannot kill Lucifer, you will have the power to stand against him, even to wound him. Your power this day is a match for his)

"Lucifer, old dog, I will stand against thee and thy evil!" replied Grayhawk. Drawing his swords and stepping out of the tunnel into the flickering light. The blue light formed an aura around him.

"An Adept!" cried Lucifer his eyes glowing bright yellow, and a huge grin as he strode forward towards the middle of the cavern floor. "Why it has been eons since I last slew and adept! No doubt, that fool, the Source has sent thee here to die!" Probably told thee that thy power is equal to mine! Grayhawk also began striding towards the center of the cavern. After a few steps he realized he was walking a good four feet above the floor and that his own physical size had increased by at least a quarter. All of this combined, meant he was now two thirds the size of the Dark Lord. As they came closer, Lucifer actually squatted down in a battle stance, making their respective height about even. Lucifer attacked first, wielding his two scythe-swords, stomping forward, eyes glowing brightly, grinning.

"Canst thee smell thy death, Human?" he asked I surely can!

"Not this day Lucifer!" replied Grayhawk as his sword came up, knocking the Scythe-sword aside and stabbing the Dark Lord in the upper right leg with his short sword. A roar of rage from Lucifer as the two stepped by each other and began the dance of death. Moving in a circle to the left, sword clanging on sword, real sparks flying from their weapons, and blue and gold sparks and flashes from their powers colliding. For two full minutes this went on, until Lucifer spun away to his right, going completely around in a spin move. His right arm staying high, aiming for Grayhawk's head, while the left came around low aiming for the knees. Grayhawk ducked the right sword cut, and dove to his right over the left. Rolling on his shoulder then springing to his feet and backing up, as Lucifer completed a second spin move. His blades hissing close, but still missing all together. Grayhawk stepped forward with his right foot in a classic lunge move with his great sword and felt the point skid off of Lucifer's left rib area. Again, Lucifer roared in rage and pain. He then executed a double overhand criss-cross move, one blade caught Grayhawk in a slice from right shoulder down across his right chest. This time it was Grayhawk who spun away in rage and pain. Backing towards the exit tunnel, coming up against a rock behind him, he rolled backwards and over the rock just as Lucifer's blades came down in a shower of sparks on the top of the rock. As Lucifer leapt up onto the rock, Grayhawk drove his left arm with the short sword upward. The point entering the beasts left inside thigh, eliciting a howl of pain and causing the Dark Lord to leap backwards off the rock. Fighting back and forth, each combatant taking multiple wounds, for close to an hour they fought thusly. Neither opponent was able to gain advantage over the other. Blind rage and hatred, was pitted against Bezerker fury. The clanging of their weapons was like the pealing of a large brass bell, heard on the physical plane and the Astral. As the fight maneuvered near to the exit tunnel, Grayhawk, for the first time, noticed that the Demons had begun to gather together in the center of the cavern. For now content, just to watch their master do battle.

'This will not last, you must leave' said the voice of the Source. 'When you can, break for the tunnel. I will collapse it behind you. Lucifer will have to find another way to pursue'. When he was within about ten paces of the tunnel and had just beaten off another windmill attack by the Dark Lord, Grayhawk reached out with his casting power, seized a boulder about the size of a horse and flung it with a sidearm motion at Lucifer. The massive stone stuck him solid, knocking him over backwards and it landed on top of him. Grayhawk did not hesitate but broke immediately for the tunnel. As Lucifer instantly caused the boulder to fly up off of him, and back towards the center of the cavern. It landed among the gathered Demons, killing two of them instantly, smashed into a pulp. The others, about twenty or so, broke into howling glee and laughter, which caused Lucifer to stop and look back at them. This gave Grayhawk the chance to close the distance and run full tilt into the tunnel. The ceiling of the tunnel passage immediately cracked, splintered, and came tumbling down, filling the tunnel completely from floor to ceiling and continued to collapse behind him as he ran down it. Running in the blue glow provided by his ring, for over half an hour he ran, taking left and right turns as though he knew the way by heart. The whole time he could hear rumbling and crashing coming from behind him.

At last he could sense he was coming to the end of the passage. Shortly thereafter he ran out into the daylight of darkened skies, with heavy wind and rain and lightning flashes. He came to a complete halt, in order to get his breath and his bearings straight. A lightening flash and strike off to his left, revealed a full battle in progress between the remaining seventy five or so members of the Company, engaged in up close fighting with double their number of the croc-men and Drulgar, along with a half dozen Demons. Looking to his right, about half a mile or so to the south the rocks were absolutely black and red with the two types of Lucifer's minions and they were all moving this way. His various cuts and bruises were painful but not serious, so he immediately turned north along the side of the mountain to where his friends and companions were fighting.

He ran unopposed, full tilt into the back of the fight, striking down half a dozen of the enemy before they even knew he was there. Still with the power of the source infused on his body, Grayhawk was like a large blue whirling, death demon as he continued to take down the enemy fighters. The sight of him infused the Company to fight even harder and within minutes even four of the Demons were downed by arrows, swords and axes. The remaining Sobeklu and Drulgar began to run back towards the south, while several more members of the Company were now wounded, one seriously.

"Gather yourselves, we have not much time, we must move off this mountain if we are to survive" shouted Grayhawk. "At least half a thousand more of these creatures move towards us, there" he continued, pointing to the south. Gathering up their gear and the wounded, they began to head down the trails off the mountain as fast as they could, reaching the bottom of the mountain proper in a short time. There the trail was wider and the downhill not as steep. The wind and rain helped to cool them as they moved; many were cupping their hands in the heavier showers catching rainwater to drink, and taking off helms to cool their heads, and everyone was steaming from exertion. After an hour, almost at a full run, with still no let up in the weather they at last slowed the pace to a fast walk. One of the wounded Knights died and had to be left, quickly hidden off the trail and covered with stones.

In another half an hour, Grayhawk called a halt for a brief rest. Although the rain and wind, still had not let up at all.

"This weather is not natural" said Allanfair "but is it friend or foe?"

"It is friend" said Grayhawk, "It offers us some protection, for the Dark Lord himself will not come out in it. The Demons absolutely hate daylight and rain, for both causes them pain. Obviously there are no human Dark Priests to lead the Drulgar and Sobeklu against us. And most of all, this heavy weather keeps the Dragons from finding us. Rest assured my friends we will have to fight and slay those two Dragons if we are any one of us at all, to return home from this place."

"They know then, that we have destroyed their eggs?" asked Drinach.

"Aye, they do" replied Grayhawk. "They are all from the same clutch." After a quarter hour break in the soaking rain, once again the Company was up and moving. Grayhawk had returned to his normal size, taking off his Adept's ring and putting in a pouch inside his tunic. "As long as I have it on" he told those around him, "It is a beacon for our enemies." Moving on down from Lucifer's stronghold mountain, still in heavy rain and lightning, they crossed a valley, at the bottom of which they were wading through two feet of fast running water. The Dwarves had to be assisted across, and the wounded carried. Starting up the slope of the next mountain to the north and heading around to the west side. After three more hours of travel their scouts found a cave entrance that was just large enough for the Chosen to squeeze through.

Inside the cave a passage at least fifty paces long led to an open chamber with a sand floor and a high ceiling, thirty by one hundred paces or so and surprisingly warm and dry. The place had been used recently, as there were four fire pits around the center about ten paces apart, and eerily, as though left for their use, there were stacks of firewood and piles of torches, which were immediately put to good use. With torches now lit, and fires being started, the light became much better, revealing, half a dozen alcoves along the left wall, and peering into them by torchlight they found bundles and boxes of supplies. There was food, jerked meat, rice, flour, oil, salt, sugar, tea, a good sized packet of spices, dried trail bread, hard spicy sausages, dried greens, dried fruits, salted fish and nuts, even brandy and tabac, enough supplies for the Company to last several months. There was even medicine, salves and creams for the wounded.

"Well, well" said White Bear, hands on his hips, as he watched the goods being brought out into the open. "Either we have stumbled into a smugglers lair or some power has prepared for our coming this way."

"So it would seem" replied Grayhawk as he looked around, "But I cannot fathom which. Does anyone else have an idea or a feeling about this treasure trove we have found?" All responded negative or shook their heads no.

"Whatever the deal" said Allanfair, "We have need of this. So let us put it to good use." Everyone was in agreement. As the storm continued unabated outside, the Company worked on drying out, treating the wounds of the battle and preparing a large meal. Brandy was passed around to all, and many lit pipes to have a smoke and relax a bit. The Dwarves blocked the entry with large rocks and after a meeting it was decided to remain in this cavern for a few days to rest, recuperate and allow wounds to heal before setting out again. Many wondered why Lucifer, the Dark Lord himself had not pursued them in order to destroy them all.

"It was the storm" Grayhawk explained. "Lightning and rain are the instruments of the All Father, he controls this planet. Lightning will completely destroy a Demon or any other of Lucifer's creatures and will cause Lucifer himself great pain. Cold rain is to all creatures of the dark realm the same as boiling water would be to us. Lucifer knows that he has yet another weapon. The two black Dragons. They can function and fight in the rain, but their vision is seriously affected by it. They can see in the dark as well as the light. Once they locate us, they will attack." The storm continued to howl outside for four more days, during which all of the Company came to realize that because of the time distortion inside the Dark Lords domain that they now had no real idea of how long they had been inside. All now had full beards and mustaches. All were now pale skinned again. Everything still seemed slightly out of context and to stand suddenly, often, brought dizziness. The Elves were familiar with the condition and assured everyone that it would pass in short order.

Even after the rain stopped it was decided to stay another week in the cave, since they now had adequate supplies. This decision was totally reinforced when, the next day, late in the afternoon the dread feeling of Dragonfear came over them all. The two Blacks were searching around the mountain for them, flying low to the ground, fearcasting as they went, and hoping to drive their prey out in to the open. The next day the Dragons returned at dark and the third day early in the morning. Though disconcerting, the Company was well enough insulated by solid rock that the fearcasting Dragons were no more than an annoyance. Four more days they lingered, while wounds healed, normal balance and feeling returned. All felt rested and refreshed and ready to move on. To the north they would journey, towards the Lake of the Gods. A large lake, high in a mountain range, it was said to be high enough up for the Gods to use it for bathing.

They were on the lower slope of the last mountain in this range in a cave on the west side. So they had to go down off the mountain and cross the blighted land, which on this side was only half as wide as that they had crossed on the west side. They left at midnight on the eleventh day after escaping the Dark Lord's lair. It was a bright moonlit night and everyone was fully expecting the Dragons to attack at any moment. Everyone who carried them had a Dragon-Bane arrow nocked on his bow, including Princess Ailorian who this night spoke quietly with everyone around her.

The journey had started with eighty three souls all told and now was down to 66 in number. Grayhawk wondered how many, if any, would reach Keltan and the King's City again. Though, he chuckled to himself, anyone who picks a fight with this group, had better know what they are doing, for these are now some hardened warriors. Moving steadily through the night, they were half way through the blighted lands by midday when they stopped for an hour to rest and eat. By late afternoon they reached the beginning of the green grass and a few trees and bushes, an hour before dusk they came to the forest-jungle, not the triple canopy this time, more open, larger trees. Moving on for four and half hours more, until they were well inside the forest, then did they stop and make camp. The last two Elf scouts who had hung back to observe, reported that they had seen the two Dragons flying around the mountains where they had come from.

Grayhawk and the other conferred for a good while that evening, all knowing that it was only a matter of time before the dragons finally located them and attacked. All were confident, or at least hopeful that it would not be this night, so a light guard was set, everyone spread out amongst the large trees, spacing themselves a good 5 paces apart just in case an attack did come. Most were asleep early. Some few, in small groups, smoked and talked quietly. A quiet night passed, the morning finally came, and most was up and about at first light.

"Today, my friends" said Grayhawk, so that all could hear, "Though we still face great danger. Today we begin the journey home."

Chapter Thirty

Knowing full well, the Dragons would eventually find them, and that the Drulgar commanded by Dark Priests would eventually pick up their trail. The Company set out through the forest, heading due north. There was no traveled trail, only occasional game runs. Three times they came to rolling grassy plain areas; some of the grasses were close to eight feet tall, the kind with edges that would cut skin. Mostly it was waist high wheat grass, green and heavy with seed. A number of streams, running with cool water were crossed. Game was plentiful. They made good time, traveling close to twelve hours a day. On the sixteenth day after the fight at the stronghold, they sighted mountains to the north. The following day their route began to climb. By the end of the day they were in an area of scattered rock formations and patches of forest. Where they stopped to make camp there were a number of small ponds of clear water fed by streams.

It was decided to stop for a full day in order to bathe, clean clothing and equipment. At daylight the Dwarves, who had discovered fishing since leaving their mountain home, were hauling in good sized fish from the largest pond. Everyone was delighted to have fresh fried fish for breakfast with their usual trail bread and tea. The entire day was spent washing, cleaning, mending, polishing and sharpening weapons, bow strings were replaced. The smaller ponds were used for bathing and clothes washing. It was a bright almost hot day, and all the low tree branches and bushes were being used as drying racks.

A hunting party of the Chosen brought in two good size antelope with long horns, like none they had ever seen before. A long fire pit was dug, and by late afternoon the smell of roasted meat was permeating the camp. Wild onions were gathered, flatbread was prepared, and dried fruit was soaked in brandy with wild honey. About half an hour before sundown the Company sat about on logs and rocks eating, what was to them, a veritable feast. Everyone stuffed themselves. A quiet, warm, star filled night was passed without incident of any kind. At full daylight everyone was up and breakfasting on the remnants of lasts nights feast, with tea.

Great care was taken to hide all traces of the camp. The fire pit was filled in, even as they were leaving, footprints were erased with branches of leaves. In front of them at a full day's travel distance stood a range of mountains and rock escarpments. These were hard rock, not volcanic, red, brown and gray, different colors of rock with green showing at the top of some of the escarpments indicating foliage. The route continued on uphill and the easiest travel was towards the north east and to the right side of the mountains in front of them.

Then there came the smell of water, must be the lake, or so everyone thought, by mid afternoon they came upon a deep gorge, with a river at the bottom, flowing to the south and east. The gorge was a couple of thousand feet deep at this point. The walls were vertical with no way to cross, so they continued northward along the western edge of the gorge. A while later two Elf scouts who had been watching behind them, came running in to report that the two black Dragons had been spotted, far to the south, back along the way they had come, flying low to the ground in a sweeping search pattern. Now they knew it was inevitable that the Dragons would track them and attack. Moving on up the side of the gorge, at a much faster rate now, searching for a position which they might be able to defend. Several areas were bypassed in the search, until at last, in the late afternoon, they came upon an area of large boulders, and a rock formation with a lot of narrow cracks and crevices or cross breaks, large enough for a man to pass through but not a Dragon. The tops were jagged and sharp, not a good landing area. The area behind, or to the west was an almost vertical rock face.

The attack would have to come from above or fly up the gorge and turn to their left. Either way Grayhawk hoped, they would both have to expose their soft underside to the archers with Dragon-Bane arrows. He also knew that this was to be a fight to the death.

There were seventy five of the ancient arrows, each said to be able to penetrate the underbelly scales of a Dragon.

"I certainly hope that is so," said Grayhawk to Allanfair.

"As do we all" he replied. The arrows had been divided up amongst the fifteen best archers of the group. Each received five arrows. The group included White Bear, Allanfair, and Ailorian, five of the Chosen, six Elves and Grayhawk. The Company spread out to find good firing positions in the rock formation; some were armed with bows and standard war arrows, others with spears, sword or axe. Taking up his position in the center, front, towards the river gorge, Grayhawk then ordered brandy passed around to all. No torches were lit, for they would be of more use to the Dragons than the men. It was dark now, with a crescent moon and a starlit sky. The gorge itself was pitch black, the rock faces were just holes in the night.

"They are coming" said Allanfair, "Off to Grayhawk's right" his Elven sight was far better in the dark.

"Hold your arrows until you have a shot at the underside" said Grayhawk to no one in particular. Then down the gorge could be seen two pairs of glowing golden eyes.

"Verdamte Holle Wurmen" (damned worms from hell) said White Bear from off to Grayhawk's left. Both beasts banked to their left at that point, just as though they had heard the comment. Their great mouths gaped open and two bright orange/red streams of fire came roaring out and splayed across the tops of the rock formation, great heat and stinking smoke, but no real damage to anyone. One beast banked left and one banked right, pulling up hard to keep from running headlong in to the rock face. Now they were roaring and screeching. They had found their prey. Circling outward for another run, one went down the gorge, one up. As they came around this time they blasted Dragonfear, so powerful, so close, many of the Company went to their knees. A few fell prone shaking as though they had convulsions. Grayhawk stood his ground, shaking his head, trying to clear it. The Dragons began their run, this time also emitting a blood curdling screech that made the ears hurt. Then came the fire, they were closer now, this time screams could be heard. Both Dragons roared in triumph and peeled off before the rock face, to come around again.

Not an arrow had been shot during the first two passes but on this third one, most had recovered enough to raise their bows. Grayhawk pulled his as far back as he could, thumb to his right ear, pointed the bow up, and as soon as he saw the underside of the Dragon he loosed his arrow. The fire was still bright and he could see the arrow strike in the lower abdomen area. The Dragon screeched, pulled left, and Grayhawk thought he saw two more arrows strike. The second Dragon was screeching as well. The smell of burnt flesh and scorched rock was intense, some rocks were glowing on top from the heat, and the Dragonfear was still intense. The rock walls seemed to amplify the screeching and roaring of the beasts, and trapped in the heat and smoke.

During their fourth run, as they passed over, Grayhawk could see a number of arrows had found their mark on the undersides of the beasts. But they were not slowing down. The whole area was beginning to heat up, the smoke was becoming thicker. Grayhawk knew that they had lost a number of the members of the Company, but he had no idea who. Now the Dragons changed tactics. They flew opposing looping patterns from north and south. One spraying liquid fire came at them from the north, while the other attacked from the south. On their next pass like this, they came in low, and as the first went over to the north, at least five arrows struck it in the upper chest, one penetrating its heart. The beast just crumpled and fell, striking the ground south of the rocks and rolling a number of times, then no further movement.

The other beast emitted a long screeching howl and shot straight up into the air, spinning as it rose, then stalled and fell over into a vertical dive back towards the ground, then at the last second, flaring its wings, reversing its body, with talons extended out like a hawk snatching a fish from a lake. The Dragon landed heavy, in front of the rock formation, on clear ground before the edge of the gorge, its eyes now blazing red. With its wings still flared out to full length, it roared a battle challenge, snapping its great jaws and swinging its head from side to side. Grayhawk and White Bear stepped out of the rocks at the same time, both with bows raised and arrows drawn. Both released at the same time, silver arrows streaking towards the Dragon's chest. The

Beast had swung his head to the right and was inhaling for a fire stream, even as the arrows struck him not two inches apart. The Dragon's head came around and the fire stream caught White Bear full on, virtually engulfing, and incinerating him instantly.

The Dragon fell over backwards, dead, not moving. Grayhawk doubled over from the heat, smoke and the gagging stench of White Bear's death. Then as Allanfair reached his side to help him, there was a dead silence. Some of the rock tops were still glowing. Then came a breeze and the smoke began to clear out. Dwarves, Elves and Men began to stumble out of the rocks, many had burns, some were still smoking, and some were seriously injured. Two of the Dwarves, who had been together, had the hair on their heads and most of their beards burnt off.

"Are they truly dead?" asked one of the Knights.

"Yes young sir, they are truly dead!" said Allanfair.

"If I had not been here, I would not believe it!" replied the young Knight.

"Neither would I" said Allanfair, shaking his head. Grayhawk was sitting on a boulder, still coughing and trying to wash out his stinging eyes with water from a skin. Drinach's beard was singed and he had small blisters on his face and the back of his hands. Lady Aileoren had singed hair and her face was bright red. Sir Owens face was soot blackened but he was otherwise unharmed.

"What is the toll" Grayhawk asked, to no one in particular.

"My Lord" say Allanfair, "Including White Bear, we have lost eight, two Knights, two Dwarves and four of the Chosen. A very heavy price paid this day."

"Not the way to view it, Allanfair" said Grayhawk. "This night, we, this Company of warriors, have stood against and slain two of the mightiest creatures that have ever lived."

"I agree" said Drinach. "I am totally amazed that any of us are still breathing. This is the stuff of sagas. This will be remembered and retold, long from now, when we are all long dead and buried. We will then be ancient heroes". In a while, after long minutes of total silence, Grayhawk stood and said

"My Friends! Let us gather up our dead brothers remains and create a tomb for them, here, in the middle of this place where they died."

Prince Drinach selected an area in the middle of the rock formation, and all remains that could be found, in some cases only ashes and bits and pieces of their weapons and gear, were gathered up and placed in the narrow space between two dark gray rocks. Working together, they all closed in the space with rocks on both ends. Then they slid heavy slabs over the narrow openings and the opening on the top, it was effectively sealed.

Afterward the Company moved on a little ways up the gorge, to a wooded area with a stream, which was flowing out to the wall of the gorge and running down the rock face to the river below. There they set up camp, prepared a meal and settled in for the rest of the night. Not much was said by anyone. All were thinking about the enormity of what they have done on this expedition, and with full realization that they still have to get back to their respective homes. They all knew that the Dark Lord would be seeking revenge for their transgressions against him. Even so, the night was quiet and star filled. Only a few were up at first light stoking up fires, making tea and smoking.

Before long everyone was up, a meal was prepared. Then all set about cleaning themselves and their gear. The burnt smell was on everyone and everything. They worked until the noon hour, trying to get clean. Then with everything cleaned, weapons sharpened and oiled, Gear all packed and ready to move out. Grayhawk looked around at everyone and said

"Let us go back down to the rocks now, and have a look at the Dragons in the daylight, and hope that we never see the likes of them again." Then he turned and started back to the south. Everyone followed, most not knowing what to think or feel about what they had seen and done.

The smell was less now, and sure enough, there were two dead Dragons. One was on its back with wings spread and it had nine of the Dragon-bane arrows sticking up all over its midsection, two very close together in the center of its chest. The other Dragon lay below the rock pile in a heap, one wing broken and folded backwards, and the other half covering its body. A number of the silver arrows could be seen in the underside of the body. At least five other arrows were either sticking up in the ground or just lying there as though they had been dropped. Most of the group was now gathered around the Dragon lying on its back, while the rest had moved down to look at the other one. Prince Allanfair spoke up.

"Friends, let us retrieve and gather up, all of the Bane arrows that can be found. They are far too valuable to be left behind. They should be returned to the Dwarves for safekeeping, in case they are ever needed again." Prince Drinach bowed to him and replied

"We will be honored to keep safe the arrows and I do believe that some proof of this shall be needed for our people back home. Let us take the teeth, the front claws and perhaps the hide from the underbelly and divide them to take back to our various people for show. In less than an hour the arrows had been recovered, all but two of the original seventy five were found. The teeth and front claws, up to what would be the elbow, and the underbelly hide, which was extremely tough and hard to cut, were removed. The outer hide could not be cut at all. As they finished up these tasks and prepared to move away from this place, they were gathered as a group in front of the rock pile.

Of a sudden, there appeared a bright silver oval of light next to the Dragon carcass, a good ten feet tall was this light. From it stepped a man, about seven feet tall. His clothing was dull, dark black material with silver borders and cuffs, black knee high boots, with a huge silver and black handled great sword on his back. He had long shiny black hair which hung in a braid over his left shoulder, a long black moustache and a pointed goatee. He had the bluest eyes anyone had ever seen. On his right hip, there hung from a black chain, going over his left shoulder, a black shiny huntsman's horn.

"Greetings my friends!" he spoke with a surprisingly soft voice. This time everyone present could both see and hear him. "I am Gabriel, a Servant of the All Father. I bring you his blessings, and to inform you that he is pleased with you. Do not grieve too deeply for those you have lost on this mission, for they are already in a better place." Stepping towards the Dragon carcass he continued "I have not beheld one of these creatures in more millennia than I care to admit! Ugly! I think is the best term to describe them. You have done exceedingly well my friends. Your journey, however, is not yet ended. You must still get back to your homes, and the way is perilous. My wayward brother Lucifer now has a burning hatred for you. His foul creatures do even now search for you, driven by Demons and the Human Dark

Priests. Lucifer himself has exercised his right to move his location, and is, as we speak arriving at his new stronghold. Well, it's not really "new" he has been there before, long, long ago." "And just where is this stronghold Lord Gabriel?" asked Grayhawk.

"It is on the other side of this world, Lord Grayhawk. On the continent you have only heard myths about, to this point. Close to the equator line on the far side of that continent. That is all I am allowed to tell you. Know also Lord Grayhawk that you are only the third human to ever fight Lucifer, and the only one to live through it. The other two died very hard. So do not linger here for long, my friends!" You are still in grave danger, for Lucifer's rage knows no bounds. "I must bid thee farewell now, I am needed elsewhere." And with that he stepped through the oval of light and vanished as though he were never there.

All, except Grayhawk, just stood there stunned, not moving or speaking. Grayhawk smiled. It certainly was unnerving to be in the presence of beings that you have been taught are only myth. Lady Ailorian had tears running down her face, a strange sight indeed. For several minutes it was this way, and then as if by magic everyone was talking at once. Grayhawk was smiling and shaking his head. He had not seen the Dwarves this animated before, except in a fight. Half an hour later they were moving up the west or left side of the gorge, moving towards what, in the distance ahead, looked like smoke. Though, no one could smell anything like a burning smell. Through the afternoon they moved, mostly uphill except for a few downhill dips. The conversations were long and intense, myth, religion, ancient history and many other things were discussed.

A bit before dark they came upon another spring and following it up and to the west a short distance, they found a wooded area, ideal for making a camp. Spirits were much improved this night and still debating, philosophizing and pontificating went on until late. The visit from Gabriel had wrought a definite change in the members of the Company.

The next morning they were up early and on the trail, and by mid afternoon they realized, that what they were seeing ahead, thought to be smoke was in reality water mist rising up out of the gorge. An hour later they could make out the falls at the head of the gorge, the water fell over two thousand feet, bouncing and rolling off the rock face. Far below could be seen a large basin or pool Two hours later they climbed out onto a flat plateau area. Only now, they were beside the river, not looking down on it. There was a forested area in front of them and mountain peaks off to either side. They continued on into the woods for a mile or so to get away from the noise of the falls and the mist.

A quiet night in the woods, and spirits were definitely better. One of the scouts had brought in a spotted deer of some kind. Everyone agreed that it tasted good with flat bread and wild onions. Next morning they were up and moving by the second hour of light. Late that afternoon they emerged from the woods on the shore of a huge lake, though they could see far dark mountains to the east and west, the north appeared to be nothing but water. Pulling back into the wood a ways they set up camp. This eve, the scouts brought in four very small deer like creatures, no more than forty pounds each. They too proved to be quite edible.

Long in to the evening hours they discussed what to do next. If they went east they would have to find a way across the river. If they went west there was no telling how far around it was to the north end of the lake. They had no boats to go across the lake.

"But we can make some!" said Prince Drinach. "How hard can that be?" Grayhawk replied

"Very hard my good friend, but there are some very large trees here we could use them to make dugout canoes." So it was decided, after serious discussion, that they would cut down five of the great trees in order to make five large, twelve-man, dugouts. So they might cross the lake to the north shore.

Chapter Thirty One

The next morning it began, first by sending out two pairs of scouts as hunting parties to hopefully keep the Company supplied with meat and to watch for any of the foul folk. The rest set about chopping down the five largest trees. Each dugout boat would be about 4forty feet long and five feet wide or so. It took the entire day, getting the trees cut down and removing all the limbs, bark and branches. It was late evening when they had dragged all of the trunks into position close to the shore, and placed chock blocks along each side to keep them steady and upright.

In the morning, with a crew of ten people working on each log, they began by chopping a V along the length of the logs on top and then a second, wider one to enlarge the cut. This work was continued then, working in teams of five men on each side, chopping into the center and removing wood all along the length as they went, they began hollowing them out. By the end of the day they were a third of the way down into the middle. By the end of the second day the logs were almost three fourths hollowed out. The last hour was spent beginning to remove wood from each side and to shape the bow and stern ends. On the third day by noon the insides were completely hollowed out. Then with two working on the bow and two on the stern, plus three each working to trim down the sides, by the end of the day they actually began to look like big, ugly boats. On the fourth morning they turned the boats over and began to shape the bottom into sort of a long V to provide a bit of a keel. The sides were now fairly flat from stem to stern. This was completed before noon. The afternoon was spent smoothing the surfaces. They were then turned back to an upright position, and the side rails were trimmed down in a long slight curve, higher in the front and the stern.

On the fifth day the interiors were finished. Slots were cut into the sides of the interior. Split, tree limb logs were smoothed on the flat side and then hammered into place as seats. At noon half of each boat crew set carving leaf blade shaped paddles, about four feet long and six inches wide at the blade. The boats were turned back right side up, and then using heavy stones and rubbing with both hands, they smoothed down the exterior of each boat as well as they could. About two hours before dark, they were as finished as they were going to get. One by one the boats were dragged down to the water's edge and pushed in, bow first, with six paddlers on board ,who could swim, just in case! Each proved to float well with no cant or lean. The men on board took each boat down the shoreline a short way and then turned around and came back. As the fifth boat was tested there came a great sigh of relief and a lot of back slapping and hand shaking. Once again they were pulled up on shore for the night.

Tired as everyone was though, the night seemed to drag on. Finally first light came. Everyone was up and packed in short order, having breakfasted on cold deer meat and flat bread, washed down with cold water. Down to the water they all trooped. The crews were divided up as evenly as possible. Three boats had twelve men crews and the other two had eleven each. There was some concern at first about overloading, but as the crews got on board and pushed off from the shore, all the craft proved to be stable and steady on the water.

It had already been decided to head north along the east coast, so that they could put in at noon every day and spend the nights on shore. They set out with half the crew of each boat paddling at a moderate rate, steering out in a wide loop to cross the river mouth because of its currents. By evening they had turned north where the shore line did at the southern end of the lake. They stopped for the night and made camp on shore.

On their second day they were more familiar with their strange craft and they made it a good distance up the coast, stopping early when they came upon a good sized stream. They paddled up the stream a ways before making camp. Hunters were sent out and returned before dark with two of the spotted deer. Everyone stuffed themselves on roast venison and all slept well that night, with a minimum guard posted.

The third day they remained in this camp, giving everyone a chance to work on personal gear, to bathe and rest. A number of folks had worn out their tunics, trousers, and robes. They had to make vests and pants from animal skins. Everyone was beginning to look a little threadbare, and everyone was tanned a dark brown by this point.

By the fourth day, the boats had become well broken in and the crews had become proficient paddlers, swapping every hour, they made good speed through the water, all that day and through the next.

Midmorning on the sixth day they spotted several, of what appeared to be small fishing boats out towards the center of the lake. At midday they could see the north end of the lake, and smoke from fires. An hour later they could make out a town or large village on the shore, which grew in size as they got closer, to a small city, of probably several thousand people. None amongst them had ever heard of this lake before, nor had they heard of the city. Grayhawk had them move more out towards the center of the lake and come abreast of each other, and then paddle slowly towards the town. There were many small craft pulled up onto the shore and tied to half a dozen finger piers. Grayhawk, in the center boat, moved to the bow and stood, ordering them to stop paddling, about two hundred yards off shore. It was only a minute or so before they were noticed, and the word went out like wildfire, there for a couple of minutes there was a lot of scurrying about in the town.

Standing still, in Nordic fashion, in the bow of the boat with his right hand raised palm towards shore to show peaceful intent. In short order there were more than two hundred warriors with bows, all clad in black with black head wrappings and black veils across their faces, bows in their left hand at their side. They also had swords either at their side or on their back. Still Grayhawk stood motionless hand raised. Soon there appeared in the center three men, dressed much the same only trimmed in silver. They were not carrying bows, but they were wearing swords. After a couple of minutes of watching, the one in the middle of the trio strode out onto a finger pier about thirty feet long. Coming to the end, he stopped, and then raised his right hand, palm out, his left resting on his sword pommel. Then he pointed with his right hand at the front of Grayhawk's boat. He motioned for them to come forward.

"Everyone remain still," Grayhawk said, looking back at those in his boat "All right now take us to the dock, nice and easy." As one, they dipped paddles and the boat began to move slowly towards the dock. When they were close enough he could see the man's eyes Grayhawk spoke. "We have come to thy land in peace My Lord. We ask only for hospitality and passage through"

"A Blademaster, who speaks in Keltani and comes in from the south? What am I to make of this?" asked the man.

"We have been on a mission in the name of the All Father and the King of Keltan. We wish only passage that we may return home. I Grayhawk, on my honor as Blademaster swear this to be true."

"I believe the Blademaster, for judging by the looks of all of you, you are not in shape to be invaders. I see among you folks I do not recognize. They appear to be the folk of old legends. But we can discuss this later. Come ashore, hospitality is granted you and your, um, adventurers! I believe that is a good term." And with that he lowered his veil revealing his face. He had a dark complexion, long mustache and a trimmed beard. As he did this, all of his warriors in turn lowered their veils and relaxed. Grayhawk motioned to the other boats and they also came slowly forward to the docks, one on either side of the two of the finger piers. The leader now smiling extended his hand in greeting.

"Welcome Grayhawk of Keltan. I am Ibn al Harani, Sheik of the Tuareg people."

"Well met Sheik Harani. I have heard of thy people." The Sheik replied

"I am most interested to hear thy tale, indeed. But for now let us see to the needs of thy companions and thyself. You are in no danger here, unless the monsters of the sky return."

"Do you mean the Dragons, Sheik Harani?"

"Yes, Dragons" he replied "we were attacked some months back. They came in the dark of night. Many of my people were killed, a full third of this city was burned and a number of fine horses were eaten by them. May Allah curse them forever!"

"He has surely done that Sheik" replied Grayhawk.

"How is this so my friend? Do you know of these creatures?

"Aye, said Grayhawk. They are no more" gesturing with his hand at the others who were now disembarking from the other boats "We have destroyed them. They are dead."

Al Harani stopped in his tracks. "Can this be?" he asked.

"Before the All Father, I swear it" replied Grayhawk. The Sheik stood still for a full minute searching Grayhawk's face and looking around at the other members of the Company. Then turning to his people, raising both hands in the air he informed his people of the news. Pandemonium broke out. There was relief and joy. The word went out quickly, and women and children began coming out of houses and buildings, dancing with joy, some down on their knees hands raised to praise Allah. It took long minutes to calm the scene.

Many among the Tuareg spoke Keltani, as it is a widely used trade language around the Mediaterre region. Orders were given by the Sheik, and the members of the Company were spread out to different houses all over town. The Sheik and his people were very pleased to learn of the real existence of both Elves and Dwarves. Both were formerly only considered people of legend and myth. They were further amazed to find an Elf Prince, and Princess and a Dwarf Crown Prince were amongst their visitors. The Temple Knights were known to exist but none had ever seen one.

Grayhawk, Drinach, Sir Owen and Allanfair were escorted to the Sheiks villa and Ailorian and her Ladies were taken in tow by a gaggle of laughing women. They were taken in and shown to bathing facilities with soap and clean linens, as were the rest of the group. All were provided with the dark garments warriors wear, which turned out not to be black at all, but deep indigo blue. The garments unfortunately, had to be modified for Prince Drinach and the other Dwarves.

The leaders robes were all trimmed in silver wire brocade, sword belts with silver buckles. They were shown how to wind the long cloth of the turban with the train hanging in the back and the veil piece hanging on the left side of the face. Knee high black leather boots were presented as well as daggers with curved blades, engraved with silver hilts and pommels. They had tea, with honey cakes and dates, and just at sunset all emerged into the park area of the city feeling much refreshed.

A feast was held in their honor that night, roast goat and lamb, couscous, honey cakes with dates and nuts, many types of fruit and both hot pepper and mint sauces and date wine. Half an hour in to the feast, Princess Ailorian appeared, looking very regal indeed, long flowing silvery robes, silver slippers, her waist length hair covered by a gossamer thin, pale blue scarf, a silver circlet with a large blue sapphire held it on her head. She came with a contingent of ten, Tuareg women, and the two Elf ladies who were all similarly clad. They were all seated to the right of the Sheik, in a place prepared for them. Everyone sat at a long low table on thick cushions. The meal continued while all the leaders gave short speeches to polite applause. Then the Sheik asked for the telling of the tale of the Companies adventure, from beginning to end.

Prince Drinach began the telling. After most of an hour Allanfair took over and the Sir Owen brought the tale up to the fight with the dragons. He then motioned to Grayhawk who told it from there to their arrival at the city. The questions were seemingly endless, and everything had to be translated into Tuareg for those who did not understand Keltani. It was the second hour after midnight when they finally finished. All of it duly recorded by four scribes onto paper scrolls.

Everyone slept in the following morning. At mid morning, the Sheik called for a meeting and over tea, cakes and fruit, they talked about how the Company would proceed on to the Nahilia River and then by boat north to Ptolymius, the chief city in Aegia. Grayhawk asked if they could purchase horses and supplies for the trip, along with the services of a guide. The Sheik would not hear of it. To him this was a state visit from Keltan, Dwarvenholm and Norda. The Tuareg would provide everything that was needed for their journey; all he asked in return, was that the group would remain here for four more days. Since a five day visit was considered an official state visit. The Sheik said with a smile

"And if you have no further need of those large boats you came in, I will keep them. My people will finish them, paint them, add sails and we will then have craft to patrol the entire lake and to visit with other towns on the west side."

"Of course you may have them My Lord, along with our thanks for receiving us in such a fine manner." The next four days were spent absolutely enjoying themselves, relaxing, eating, gaining back some strength and letting wounds heal and making a lot of new friends.

On the fourth day they were each given three extra sets of Tuareg garb and supplies of dried food and fruits, tea, tabac, spices, date wine, each was given a purse of silver coins and warned never to flash gold, especially along the river. Princess Ailorian was given a small chest full of jewelry and precious stones. Again they cleaned, polished and sharpened weapons, bow strings were replaced. Some even traded knives, swords, axes and other things for Tuareg weapons. Grayhawk, Drinach, Allanfair and Owen were each presented by the Sheik with excellent curved blade swords, with silver wire wrapped handles, and each had a large dark sapphire in the pommel. They were hard layered steel with razor sharp blades, beautiful and deadly.

Another feast was held that night, everyone enjoyed themselves and retired early. The next morning they were up at dawn and had a light breakfast. Gathering up their gear, they said a lot of goodbyes. They then mounted on the provided horses. With an escort of forty Tuareg warriors they set out from the city on the Lake of the Gods headed northwest through a mountain pass. Late in the second day they came to the edge of a sand desert. Only Grayhawk had ever seen one before. They camped early at a spring and pond.

Next morning at first light, they filled all the extra water skins they had brought. The Tuareg explained that there would be no water for three full days. They showed everyone how to apply the black charcoal and lanolin, oil mix to the area under the eye for the glare, and lanolin oil to the nose and lips to prevent cracking in the sun and heat. They rode across dunes for two hours, by then it was getting hot, they came to a hard deadpan salt flat. By noon the heat was intense. They stopped only long enough to eat some dried fruit and jerked meat, and some salt from the palm of their hand. The Tuareg informed them that the salt will keep you from falling off your horse from the heat. The horses were also watered and given a little grain.

By mid afternoon the heat was unbearable, and the glare from the salt pan was intense. Five people passed out and had to be given salt and water. By late afternoon all had dismounted and walked with their horses until dusk. As soon as the temperature dropped some, they watered the horses and rode until an hour after dark, finally stopping at a well used campground. It was a basin on top of a rock out cropping.

Fires were started for the evening meal, and by the time it was over, the temperature began to drop and within an hour everyone was cocooned in their sleeping robes. None could believe how cold it gets in the desert at night, colder than it was in the jungle. Up at dawn, breakfasted, packed and mounted an hour later. Heading into the sunrise, and the glare was like it was coming off polished white marble. Another day of building heat, sweat and discomfort, though this time everyone took salt and drank water. They came once again, an hour after sunset to a well used campground, prepared a good meal and settled in for another cold night.

When daylight came they could see, in the distance sand dunes. The Tuareg advised with big smiles that they would camp tonight out of the desert. All were relieved at noon when they came to the sand dunes. They could actually feel the difference in temperature. Late in the afternoon they rode out of the dunes and into the beginning of a grass and scrub area. Another two hours of steady riding brought them to an area of thorn bushes, date palms and palmetto. In the middle was a large pond fed by a clear stream. Here they stopped well before sundown and made camp. The horses were watered and rubbed down, given some grain and turned loose in a grassy meadow with Tuareg riding herd. Fires were started and a good meal was prepared at a number of campfires. The Company was spread amongst the Tuareg. A small tent was pitched for Ailorian and her two ladies. Everyone in the party had a chance to clean up. A place among the reeds at the south end of the ponds gave Ailorian and her ladies privacy to bathe. After full dark, all were afforded the chance to relax, smoke, and tell stories about their lives and adventures.

Though most were up at first light, none were in a hurry. They breakfasted on dried fruit, warm flat bread and tea. They gathered in the horses, watered them and groomed them. About two hours after sunrise, they all were mounted and moving to the east. The Tuareg sent a group of five riders on ahead. In two day time they would reach the river. The advance group would try to arrange for boats to transport the Company down the Nahilia, which actually flows to the north, odd.

That day they passed through a number of villages, all farming communities, who were all very respectful of the Tuareg. They are legendary in their prowess and skill as warriors. About two hours before sundown they rode into a large caravansary and trading post. There were two other merchant caravans already encamped within the walls. The Dwarves and Elves were very amazed when they saw camels for the first time, a strange looking beast. One of the Dwarves drew some nasty looks from the handlers when he asked if they were good to eat. But the Tuareg were all laughing.

Grayhawk and none of the rest of the Company were even remotely aware, that while crossing the desert, they had been finally located by the Dark Priests, who had been scrying in search of them for months now. Three companies of Drulgar were dispatched from Stygius in the south to intercept them and destroy all but Grayhawk, Allanfair and Ailorian. The Dark Lord very much wanted them as guests in his new stronghold on the other side of the world. Just how he had moved there from Stygius, no one knows. He can and does travel through the underworld plane, it is his domain.

As the group within the walls of the caravansary settled down for the evening, preparing meals, caring for livestock, cleaning equipment and other mundane chores, the Drulgar and their Dark Priest handlers, were at that very moment within five miles of them, moving stealthily through the brush towards their position.

Inside the walls, everyone, the Company, the Tuareg, the merchant traders and their guards were beginning to relax for the evening. The yard was very large; some two hundred fifty paces to a side, along the walls were sheds for stables, and of course a defensive walkway on top of the sheds about three and a half feet from the top of the fifteen foot wall. They had not been used in many, many years. There had not been a bandit raid in over a hundred years. Just at sundown, the three gates, east, west and south were summarily closed and locked by the keepers of the place. There were at least seven communal fires going around the yard. The night was clear with a half moon rising. It was warm and everyone was beginning to lay out sleeping mats and blankets.

The five Dark Priests with their three hundred sixty man contingent of Drulgar were still moving toward them at a slow walk. Several late arriving travelers were ambushed and killed within two miles of the walls. The Drulgar quickly stripped their bodies and their now dead horses. They split up the booty and left the dead travelers naked on the side of the road, telling each other that there would be much man-flesh for a feast later.

It was now full dark, about two hours before midnight. The half moon was up and inside the walls most were settling down for a good night's sleep. Grayhawk was about to take off his sword and other weapons when a voice in his mind said

"Warning, Blademaster! You are in grave danger! Give the alarm, now!!" So Grayhawk, as loud as he could muster, drew his sword and yelled

"ALARM! He shouted ALARM! TO ARMS!! We are being attacked! Arm yourselves!" Both the Tuareg and the Company were immediately up and moving. The merchants and their guards were moving much slower.

"Form circle!!" yelled Grayhawk, circling his great sword overhead. "Form circle!! Prepare Bows!!" In the middle of his yelling commands, there came from outside the walls a great shrieking, growling and howling chorus. That finally got the merchants moving. Then there began the pounding on the gates. All knew the gates would not hold for long. A quick look around told Grayhawk that there were maybe one hundred fifty fighters in the circle, not enough to have manned the walls. So it was now down to probably one or two attacks before one side or the other wins. He knew now, from the noise, that they were being attacked by Drulgar. Who were now being led by Dark Priests. Lucifer wants his revenge. And more! Wood was quickly added to the fires to give more light and the place became very surrealistic, dancing shadows and flickering yellow light. Arrows were nocked and bows were held at the ready. The only talking was the merchant group wanting to know what was happening. Grayhawk did not care to answer them. "In a few moments, you will surely know" he smiled grimly to himself. Looking around he saw all of the Tuareg and most of the Company had pulled up their veils to cover everything but their eyes, so Grayhawk pulled his up, tucking the end behind his left ear, everyone else followed suit.

At that moment fireballs exploded in all three of the gateways, at the same time, splintering them to pieces. Through the smoking opening came most people's worst nightmare. Drulgar! Ugly, mad dog slobbering, howling, screeching Drulgar. They had filthy long black stringy hair, large glaring red eyes, some with odd or partial armor, and some with helmets. All were armed with a rough looking wide blade, hacking sword. Some had two. Some had lances or spears and axes. They came pouring through the gates, and many began to sprout arrows from their chests or faces, fell and were trampled by those behind. Each archer was able to get three or four shots as they closed to hand to hand distance. As many as seventy five Drulgar were already down from the arrows.

With a roar and clash of steel they ran into the line of defenders, and the hacking, stabbing and slashing began in earnest. Grayhawk noted some dark clad figures go down but the line held and none of the vermin made it through. Many more of them were down now, making it necessary to step back for clear footing to fight. Grayhawk noticed that those coming at him were not pressing him as hard as the others around him. 'Ah, they have orders to take me alive.' And with that, Grayhawk, armed with his great sword and short sword, went behind the red veil, the bezerker trance over took him completely. He spun and twisted, stabbed and slashed, going through every series of moves he had ever learned. Many, was the number who fell by his weapons, stabbed or sliced. His speed and accuracy were as though he were possessed. Others around him fought in the same manner. Within fifteen minutes, the Drulgar had lost almost half of their number. Then, there came the flat bleating tones of the Dark Priests horns. The fight, suddenly, was over for the moment The Drulgar, were running for the exits to regroup.

The Tuareg had lost four of their number, a Knight, a Dwarf and an Elf had fallen on the line, and several others were wounded. The merchants had lost five of their number, with two more wounded. The Drulgar, however had lost just over one hundred fifty of their number, and one of the Dark Priests was killed by an arrow fired through the south gate opening, it was probably not even aimed at him. He just stood at the wrong place at the wrong time.

"Will they return?" asked a Tuareg.

"Oh yes" replied Allanfair. "They will be back, probably in less than half an hour." The heavy copper smell of blood was everywhere. The wounded were being helped to the center of the circle, along with the dead. Date wine, mixed with water was passed around and everyone drank deeply. The Tuareg agreed that they had never before seen such an ugly, hell spawned creature. They must surly come from the Dark Lord himself. After about twenty minutes, everyone was back in position around the line, arrows nocked and bows at the ready. Sure enough, within a few minutes the Drulgar came pouring back into the compound through the gateways again. Not as many were dropped with the bows this time because they were more spread out. This time the Dark Priests, in their black and red robes came into the compound behind the Drulgar. Again the fight was hand to hand, up close and very personal. The sound of steel ringing on steel was intense. Grayhawk was fighting three of the vermin, when he was noticed by a Dark Priest; who came rushing forward, trying to use his powers to subdue Grayhawk. As he did so, Grayhawk grabbed and pulled one of the Drulgar in front of himself. The priest's casting struck the Drulgar making him stand stock still. Grayhawk dashed around the Drulgar and within three paces, just as the priest raised his hands again, Grayhawk drove his great sword through the Priest's chest and out his back.

The Priest was a high ranking one and there was an incredulous, surprised look on his face as he died. Stepping forward again, Grayhawk kicked the fellow off his sword and narrowly missed being run through himself by the Drulgar who had been frozen by the Priest. Spinning to the left he felt the sword graze along his right side through his clothing. The stinging told him it had broken his skin. Another of the Priests on the right or east side of the circle tried to conjure a fireball. As he drew back to throw it, using both hands, Drinach saw him, reared back and threw his axe overhand, striking the priest high in the chest. He was knocked backwards still holding the fireball in his hands which exploded on hitting the ground, incinerating the priest and about fifteen of the Drulgar closest to him.

The other two priests were killed by a brother of the Chosen in close combat. At this point the company and the Tuareg had gained the upper hand all along the line. In another quarter hour the fight was over. All of the Drulgar and their five priests were dead, six more members of the Company had perished in the fight, which, all told had lasted less than two hours. The Tuareg had lost nine of their number, and the merchant party lost twelve, there were twenty seven total dead, a hard loss all the way around. They had stood, outnumbered by more than two to one, and totally destroyed a force of three hundred sixty Drulgar and four Dark Priests. Grayhawk could almost hear Lucifer's howling and screeching, and it gave him great pleasure! There were over forty with wounds in need of tending. When that was done, all of the weapons lying on the ground after the battle were gathered up, even the crudest ones, some were taken as souvenirs by the Tuareg, the rest were given to the merchants who were very pleased.

The bodies of the Drulgar and their Priests were placed on piles of wood and set afire. Eventually in the early hours everyone finally got to rest for about five hours, which was sorely needed by all. The Company was now down to fifty two remaining members.

Graves were dug for all twenty seven of the dead, on a small rise to the north about a half mile distant. Words were spoken by all who wished to. Then a somber group of the Company, the Tuareg and the merchants returned to the compound. With hardly a word, all pitched in and helped to repair the destroyed gates. Actually, doing a very good job in the process, and it took until late evening to complete. It being late in the day, they decided one and all to remain for another night. After preparing an evening meal they sat around the fire, speaking of the mission of the Company and all that had befallen them along the way, and explaining to the members of the Tuareg and merchants just exactly what the Drulgar were. How they were created. And how, because of their limited intelligence and slow thought processing, so many of their number were so handily defeated.

Next morning, at first light, everyone was up and preparing to depart. The merchant group asked if they could travel with them to the river, where there was a town and good trading. Two hours after daylight, a solemn and hard looking group of over one hundred rode out. All were riding silent, thinking about lost comrades and warrior brothers. They stopped at a spring for half an hour at noon, to eat a little, and water the horses. The temperature was much cooler than the desert here; they rode rapidly through the scrub lands. They stopped again mid afternoon for a short break. Not an hour later they were in an area of trees, date palms, and some tall grass. They began to see fields of wheat, barley, oats and corn, growing in square fields, with irrigation ditches half full of water. There were people here and there working them, men, women and children clad in tan or brown robes, some few with colored sashes around the waist and others with head wraps.

Moving on, while most of the people, who were very dark skinned, stopped working long enough to watch them pass. Half an hour later, they began to see square mud brick houses, most of which also had a canopy of cloth, on the roof, held up by poles, providing shade for the roof verandas. More women and children could be seen. There also were what appeared to be herb gardens, either beside or behind most of the homes, there were rock lined pathways, and a few scattered trees and bushes, some yards had grass growing in them and there were colorful curtains in the windows. Goats, sheep and cattle could also be seen, and some few horses. All in all, it was a very pleasant looking community.

The number of houses began to increase, and they were closer together, there were more people, more horses, cattle, and more sheep and goats. Dogs came running out, yapping at the horses causing some to shy sideways and even kick. Women with sticks were chasing after the dogs. There were geese and chickens running, flapping and squawking, with young boys and girls chasing after them. Then there began to be palm trees along the sides of the road with colorful monkeys, screeching as they ran up and down them. It all sounded like a true cacophony, especially to those who had been a long time in the outlands, but they had all seen and heard it before. Civilization it is called.

Chapter Thirty Two

They topped a rise in the land, and Assan the Tuareg leader, put up his right hand for a halt, if it had been his left hand, all Tuareg would have drawn weapons. The top of the rise was about a hundred feet or so wide, and there were no houses or trees on it. Beyond lay a bowl or valley about two miles wide and in it was the town or city of Ibissa. 'About ten thousand people' thought Grayhawk, as he looked out upon it. Beyond the city, at about a mile in front of them lay the Nahilia River, which looked to be at least half a mile wide. From this vantage point, the water looked to be dark, but it was late in the day and the sun was behind them.

The city itself was walled; at least a quarter of a mile square and the walls looked to be twenty or so feet tall. Within the walls could be seen many large buildings, some with spires or minarets. Outside the walls, the city had continued to grow, and, like most was now virtually indefensible. The road they were on ran straight down and into the city proper through a large arched gateway which could be seen from here as open. Assan, lowered his veil smiling, sweeping his arm out in front of himself said,

"Welcome my Brothers and Sisters to the 'great' city of Ibissa, a truly immoral place if ever there was one. Guard your purses and your virtue, equally well here my friends. This is a place of murder, lust, and greed. Everyone had lowered their veils, for the people here knew the Tuareg. If they were to ride in with their faces covered, they have come for blood, uncovered they are peaceful. Even so, the merchant travelers were allowed to ride on down the hill first, lest all these dark clad warriors cause a panic. So they sat for a time, while the merchants rode down the hill and into the city. They had previously agreed to state that the Tuareg were looking to hire some boats to carry some of their number down the river to buy horses.

After a while, they rode slowly, double file, down the road and turned right before coming to the Gates of the city, riding instead around to the south quarter, where there are open areas by the river, for traders to set up camp. There they found the advance group had already arranged for three good sized dowlas, to carry the Company on down river.

Goodbyes were said to the Tuareg and Assan their leader. The Tuareg took the mounts and without looking back, rode back up over the hill and out of sight. Still wearing the dark garb of the Tuareg, Grayhawk and fifty one members of the Company walked down to where the river craft were pulled into shore. There they made camp by the river and spent a peaceful night.

The next morning they split into three equal groups and boarded the boats, which were each about sixty five feet long, with a lateen sail and a crew of four. An hour after daylight they pushed off from the city of Ibissa and began the next phase of their journey home. The captain of the boat that Grayhawk was in informed him they would travel by day, pull in and camp on the shore for the nights and that the journey would take six days.

Back on the water again, even though only a wide river, was a relief, since they were moving down river with the current. For the most part everyone could relax, talk, smoke, and try their hand at fishing with hand lines, for the several types of fish in the river. Enough were caught on the three boats to provide a fresh fish evening meal. Because of where they were, and the abundance of traffic on the river, they did not much fear attack, even when camped for the evening. They were either near, or at small towns, at night they slept well under the stars on the open ground, with only a minimal guard, and boarding their vessels again at daylight. The days were long and not real hot, but, by using rigged canvas awnings for shade, coupled with the breeze off of the water, it was bearable.

By mid morning of the seventh day they were entering a broad river delta. The water became salty and brackish, and the salt marsh smells were strong on the wind. In the distance a yellow brown haze of dust and smoke signified the presence of a large city. By noon they could see it, sort of like a mirage in the shimmering heat. Not quite two hours later they entered a broad basin in the river and came to the port city of Ptolymius, the Capital of Aegia on the west side, and the Capital of Canah on the east. The basin or lake here was over two miles wide and there were literally hundreds of ships and boats, a major trading post for this part of the world. As well as being a free trade port on both sides.

Both cities are called Ptolymius. Each has a Caliphan, and though both sides are ripe with skullduggery, the total amount of money made trading, legal and illegal, both by ship and overland caravan, keeps them at peace, and very prosperous. They even share a navy of sorts, some fifty galleys all told. Manned by, combined crews from either side. Having been here before, back during his wandering mercenary days, Grayhawk was familiar with the place on both sides of the river. He preferred the Canah side as it was more tolerant and liberal about everything. The Aegians tend to be a bit more moralistic. So, he instructed the boat captain to head for the east side docks. Half an hour later he and the rest of the Company disembarked at the docks, it was a surprisingly clean and well kept area.

They city was large and mostly flat sitting on a built up area, about ten feet higher than the docks. The dock area was bustling with trade, crowded with people, animals, carts, and wagons. There were large warehouses and shops of every kind.

They were immediately approached by the harbor patrol, and asked to state their business. Grayhawk told them that he was captain of a mercenary company headed for employment in Gaula, a country known for hiring mercenary soldiers. He told them that a ship would be coming to transport them. He said they would be here for perhaps a month and needed to find a suitable place to rent quarters in the meantime. The guard leader was eyeing them suspiciously. Such a large group could mean a lot of trouble. Grayhawk and Sir Owen assured him that they were a well disciplined outfit and would cause no disturbances. After paying suitable city fees, he told them to look in the southern quarter of the city. There, they might find a private compound to rent, in which to reside.

Taking their leave, they proceeded on into the city, through well laid out streets on a grid pattern. Turning south on a main thoroughfare, after almost an hour walk they came to a less crowded area of walled compounds, shops and inn. They inquired with shop keepers and at a number of inns, if anyone knew of a place they might rent for a month or so. After another hour of inquiring, they were told of a man named Adonato, who might help them and were given directions on how to find him. They moved on for another mile, to the southern outskirts of the city, where they stopped for a meal at a large prosperous inn. While there the man Adonato came and found them. Over a cup of hot, strong, and very sweet mint tea, Grayhawk informed him of their needs and he said that he did indeed have a suitable place. It was a walled villa, formerly owned by a merchant who had died the previous year leaving a lot of debts, and now it stood empty.

With Adonato as their, guide they proceeded on through ever narrower streets, headed back towards the river basin. The place in question was only a couple of streets from the older section of the dock area. The villa compound was indeed large with high walls. It had a large house of two stories, with twelve rooms and a central kitchen. Under sheds in the back were two large bathing pools, and along the walls were lean-to sheds for stables or storage, even a smithy with a forge and good water well. After some serious haggling over the price by the month, Adonato went away with gold in his pocket and a smile on his face, leaving the keys for the front gate.

Prince Drinach immediately took over the kitchen, with half of the Dwarves to help him. Others went with two of the Chosen to look over the forge and the blacksmith facility. Princess Ailorian was given two of the upstairs rooms for herself, and her two ladies. Grayhawk and Allanfair took the room next to hers. Sir Own and Drinach would share one. There was a large cellar storage area and Odranna's Chosen opted to take it for their quarters. The others split up the remaining rooms with a number of them deciding to move into the stable sheds. A party of eight was sent to find the market area, before it was too late, in order to purchase foodstuffs, tabac, beer and brandy. By nightfall all were settled in and enjoying a supper meal of roast lamb and boiled crab. Everyone ate their fill, and then stayed up past midnight talking, smoking and enjoying themselves, very glad to be taking a pause from their journey.

After everyone else had retired, Grayhawk, Drinach and Allanfair moved up to the roof veranda, bringing with them, pipes and brandy. Under the heavy cloth canopy, they sat relaxing on cushions and talking for a couple of hours. When the other two had finally fallen asleep, Grayhawk took himself to the west end of the roof. Facing west, sitting cross legged on a cushion, he began to meditate and gather in his thoughts and powers. After a bit he took out his Adept's ring and slipped it onto his left index finger. The ring was glowing softly in blue.

Casting out with his minds voice, into the ethereal he began calling, to Olion, master of the Blackship. This he and Olion had prearranged back in Nigossa as the way to signal for Olion to come and pick up the Company for the trip back to Keltan. A good five minutes he sat thusly, mind casting into the void of night. Finally a sleepy and ghostly sounding voice came drifting in from the void.

"Grayhawk, my friend, do you still live? It has been many long months."

"It seems long" replied Grayhawk, "Where are you now?"

"We are in Nigossa, our second trip down here for trading" answered Olion.

"Where are you, my friend? Did you accomplish what you set out to do?"

"Aye, we did" replied Grayhawk "but it was very costly. Only fifty two of us will be making the voyage home."

"That is sad" said Olion. "Well Grayhawk we will sail on the morning tide. Where shall I come and collect you?"

"We are in Ptolymius, on the Canah side in the south of the city" said Grayhawk.

"I will not even ask how you came to be there" replied Olion. "But we are coming as fast as we can. It might be as long as a month for us to get there."

"Understood" said Grayhawk "we are well situated now. I will contact you again in three weeks time to see where you are."

"Well and done, my friend, until that time, take care" said Olion.

With that Grayhawk let the contact fade. They soon settled in to what
was an enjoyable daily routine. They still had a good supply of gold
coin, not to mention that everyone came out of the treasure storerooms
in Lucifer's stronghold with at least a money pouch full of precious
stones and gold, more than enough so that when they returned home
they all would be wealthy.

Grayhawk had taken emeralds and opals, beautiful colors, he had
thought to himself. Now glad that he did, he had a number of them set
in a silver necklace for Aurelia. The local silver and gold smiths were
among the best in the world. He still had enough left to purchase a
small kingdom. To keep up their appearance as mercenaries they drilled
with weapons, hand to hand, and archery for a full six hours a day.
All were now becoming really expert warriors with various weapons.
Learning as they sparred, the different styles, and techniques, each had
developed their own, along the way.

Thanks to Prince Drinach who loved to cook as well as fight, they
also ate really well. Everyone shopped the city for new clothes, boots,
cloaks and weapons, as well as things for the ladies and family at home.
In groups of not more than five, they explored the city and many of
the younger ones had some real eye opening experiences. This was an
ancient, wicked and decadent city, all manner of things were available.
For a price! Even though some members were indeed young, these were
some well traveled and battle hardened warriors. The locals all sensed
this and gave them a wide berth.

Three weeks later Grayhawk again contacted Olion on the black
ship. They were just approaching the passage between Sardos and
Maltasa. They were fighting stormy weather and headwinds, but
should arrive in a week. Grayhawk informed them all that they would
be leaving in a week's time, which was met with relief and happiness.

"So my friends" he told them "better get your shopping for presents
done. When the ship arrives we board and depart without a word, or
a warning. Be ready." They did shop and barter hard. They spent five
days scouring all over the city. Most had assembled large packs and
several bales and boxes of goods ready for the journey home.

The black ship arrived on the sixth day just after midnight. They
were guided in, by Grayhawk. The company was all prepared, and in
almost total silence they moved down to the dock area, loaded their

goods and boarded the ship. The ship did not even tie up to the dock. There was a good breeze blowing down river and the tide would turn in their favor within an hour. They pushed off from the dock, dropped the mainsail and in the dark of night, departed Ptolymius and headed out in to the Mediaterre Sea.

This time of year the sea was storming and rough, but five days later they cleared the Maltasa/Sardos passage and three days later, were sailing in clear weather on a deep blue rolling sea, making really good speed, headed for the Portugas passage. These quiet warm days running over a smooth sea were pretty much idle time for the Company and everyone's thoughts turned to those they had lost in battle. Olion and his crew heard all of the details and accounts of battles. They were totally amazed at what they were hearing and Olion and crew had tales of their own to tell as well. It seems that they also had made a lot of money.

By the time they arrived at the mouth of the passage between Spanos and Portugas the dark mood had broken and spirits were again high. Through the long passage, the weather was warm and sunny. They passed many ships from other countries and even outran a couple of Tax Patrol Galleys of Portugas, who would have wanted gold or trade goods before letting them proceed on.

Emerging from the passage and sailing into the Ocean off of Spanos, Olion calculated they would arrive back at the King's city in five days time.

"Close to a year, we have been gone" said Prince Drinach, standing on the steering deck, aft of the ship, with Olion, Grayhawk, Allanfair and Sir Owen. Olion laughed

"My friends you have been gone for over a year! Over fourteen months to be more exact!" Mostly they just stood there with blank looks. Allanfair finally spoke.

"It is obvious then that the Dark Lord has the ability to alter time, and perception. We were in his stronghold inside the mountain for a lot longer than we thought or felt."

"Hmmph!" said Drinach "So I am actually older than I thought I was!" This brought smiles to the group.

"I wonder though?" said Sir Owen "What changes have come

about since we left on this 'adventure'. Olion replied, hands on his hips, chuckling.

"In short order my friend, you will find out." Two days later they entered the Danaan Channel and rounded the "Butt of Spanos" as it was called by sailors. At morning light three days after that, they sailed in the river estuary, and just before noon the city docks were in sight. There were many boats on the river.

Chapter Thirty Three

Snow Leopard, one of the brothers of Odranna's Chosen, a middle aged man of large stature, a fierce fighter who hardly ever spoke to anyone, brought forth a curved rams horn, went forward to the bow, and raised it to his lips. It produced a really loud, low tone, a vibrating flat note for a good ten seconds. He was answered by four horns on shore with a long, deep brassy note.

And. Then, they were close enough to see the docks, as they came fully around the river bend. There were flags, pennants, bunting, and soldiers lining the dock side. There were fireworks going off, trumpets blaring and what must have been every person residing in the city, plus some more. All were yelling and waving a welcome.

At the center of all this, stood Killian IV, King of Keltan, dressed in formal red and black. He was even wearing his crown. Beside him, and to his right, stood the little red haired princess from Danfinia, 'what was her name? Ah! Elysia Miriam, very pretty.' thought Grayhawk. Then he saw her, in a dark green satin gown, her long brown hair blowing in the wind. Aurelia, the King's Mother and his wife. His heart was full. She was even more beautiful than he remembered.

To her left stood Lord Gregory, Master of the Knights Academy (amongst other things) and of course all the dignitaries of the King's court. But Grayhawk had eyes only for Aurelia, and she him. As lines were tossed and the ship pulled into the dock, even before the gangplank could be put in place, Killian was striding forward.

"Hail Grayhawk!!" he yelled with a grin. "Our Warlord has finally returned from adventuring the world over!"

"Majesty" he replied, stepping to the ships railing and jumping on to the dock. The two embraced, slapping each other on the back.

"It is good to see you again, Grayhawk, and all in one piece too!" The roaring of the crowd was so loud they had to yell to be heard.

"It is good to see you too, Majesty! You look well."

"Thank you" replied the King grinning. "Not too bad for an old married man."

"Married?! When did that happen?" Asked Grayhawk, looking over to Princess, now Queen Elysia Merriam whom, he noticed was with child. She was laughing and waving

"Six months now" yelled Killian.

"Well that is surely a surprise" replied Grayhawk. Killian had his arm around Grayhawk's shoulders.

"Well!" yelled Killian into his ear, "If that is a shock to you, just you wait until you hear the other one!"

"What other one?" Grayhawk yelled back The King gestured with his hand towards his mother, whom they were now approaching. She held out her hands and Grayhawk took them. "My Lady?" he said with a questioning look, she was laughing and there were tears rolling down her face. Stepping over to his side, sliding her arm around his waist, and there behind where she had been standing was a double pram, or baby stroller, and in it were two dark haired infants about four or five months old. A boy and a girl, they were both sitting up wide eyed at all the noise and commotion.

"Your Grace" said Aurelia, "May I present your son and daughter, Xanthar and Delannia!" Grayhawk could only stand there blinking. With his mouth open.

"Twins!?" he croaked and the crowd went wild. Aurelia was in his arms, kissing him, and somewhere out on the astral plain a bell rang twice in clear reverberating tones. A familiar voice that only he could hear, said.

'Well done Grayhawk'. A riotous welcome back was for all of the Company. Grayhawk's step daughters had grown, becoming beautiful young ladies. He hugged them both tight and they each kissed him on the cheek. He hugged his new Queen and she kissed his cheek as well. The handshaking and backslapping went on for thirty minutes in the midst of all the noise and confusion. He also noticed, moving amongst the group of dignitaries, the three young pages, Arthur, Paden and Geran, they had grown considerably in a year, and now they each had short swords slung on their backs, as well as their long daggers.

Many tearful reunions were there, as they came off the ship and some were very sad over the loss of loved ones. Grayhawk and several others got to hold their new children for the first time. The celebrations were a total surprise. Grayhawk finally asked Aurelia as they were getting into carriages for the trip up to the Palace,

"How did you know, My Lady, when we were going to arrive?"

"Lord Gregory" she replied. "Two days ago he came to the palace and informed Killian that you would arrive today."

"Oh, of course" he said.

"And just how did he know?' asked Aurelia.

"Why, he was told!" said Grayhawk grinning with a child on each knee, who were looking at him like 'Who are you?'

At the palace, the kitchens, were preparing a feast for the evening. The whole place was buzzing with activity. Grayhawk and Aurelia were escorted to what was now, the Queen Mother's Chambers. With a new Queen now in residence, the apartments and bed chambers had been rearranged. Allanfair, Drinach, and Ailereon were shown to their chambers. Sir Owen adjourned with Lord Gregory to the new Temple Knight Charter House in a separate building. Odranna's Chosen went again to the basement quarters, which had been totally renovated and permanently designated "Charter House of the Chosen."

Grayhawk and Aurelia spent some time alone, with their children in the Queen Mothers Chambers. Everyone had time to relax and bathe. New clothing had been provided for all.

At sundown the Royal Celebration Feast began with all members of the "Company" present, to include Olion, his wife and most of the crew of the Black Ship. Many speeches were made and a good time was had by one and all. Until, long past midnight. Before midnight, the King and Queen had retired for the night, and a short time later Grayhawk and Aurelia said their goodnights and retired to their chambers. They made love and talked until after first light. Grayhawk told his wife the entire story, leaving nothing out.

At dawn, Grayhawk stood at an open window, looking into the dawn. Aurelia came up behind him, putting her arms around him. "It is good indeed to be home again" he said.

"Do you think then that the Dark Lord has been defeated?" she asked.

"No My Lady, not even close. We have dealt his plans a blow, and now he has moved from that stronghold to another, on the other side of the world, on the unknown continent to the west. There he seethes in anger, and plots to destroy us all and to rule the world with evil. This is not the first time Man has stood against him, nor will it be the last. We will play his game again."

Prince Allanfair was their first visitor that day, arriving at mid morning. He had come, he said to present gifts from the Elves to the twins. To Prince Xanthar he presented two, perfectly round, dark green obsidian spheres, each about three inches in diameter.

"These are Spheres of Knowledge, they will help him to learn and understand. They should be left in his bed, so that he may become familiar with them. They are ancient, and contain much magic. They will not break even if dropped on the floor."

To Princess Delannia he presented an oblong, egg shaped sphere, it looked like solid gold with strange swirling patterns on the surface. It was about eight inches long, and four inches in diameter. "This, he stated, as he placed it beside her, in her crib, is for her alone. It must be kept near to her at all times. The purpose of the thing will be made clear to you at a later date." As he finished speaking, far across the astral plain, there rang out a single clear bell note, and a familiar voice spoke.

"Done and done." Grayhawk heard the voice and the bell note and thought to himself. Well! I wonder just what that portends for us? The Saga will continue. The end is not even in sight.

About the Author

Jacamo Peterson, a native of Galveston, Texas, served more than twenty-one years on active duty with the Army. He has also worked as a 911 dispatcher, deputy sheriff, police officer, disabled veterans employment counselor, corporate personnel manager, security manager, and Grand Canyon National Park Fire Department lieutenant.